Praise for *White*

"A beautiful and deeply researched novel . . . How does a woman protect her family, honor her heritage, and save herself? If you loved *Pachinko*, you'll love *White Mulberry*."

—Lisa See, *New York Times* bestselling author of *The Island of Sea Women* and *Lady Tan's Circle of Women*

"Easton eloquently reimagines her grandmother's past—a brave young woman caught between two worlds. A story inspired and inspirational, *White Mulberry* exposes the forgotten history of Koreans in Japan."

—Alka Joshi, internationally bestselling author of *The Henna Artist* and the Jaipur Trilogy

"A beautiful and poignant novel of a young Korean woman's coming of age amid the turbulence of colonization and World War II. The resilience and self-determination of the heroine vividly mirror the astonishing trajectory of her nation."

—Juhea Kim, author of *Beasts of a Little Land* and *City of Night Birds*

"A radiant debut not only about survival but about choosing one's own destiny. With lively details and taut suspense, Easton delivers a moving journey."

—Jimin Han, author of *The Apology*

"A tautly paced novel that has something for everyone . . . [Miyoung's] epic journey to live life on her own terms will keep you at the edge of your seat. An impressive debut."

—Marie Myung-Ok Lee, author of *The Evening Hero*

"Miyoung's story is one of endurance. When all is lost and lost again, Miyoung keeps going, keeps bolstering herself as the world crumbles around her. With beautiful detail, Easton paints a picture of strength, of a woman willing to do whatever it takes to protect her family."

—Annabelle Tometich, author of *The Mango Tree*

"Easton weaves an unforgettable tale of resistance, resilience, and redemption . . . I can't remember the last time I was so captivated by a debut work."

—A. H. Kim, author of *A Good Family* and *Relative Strangers*

"A scintillating debut. *White Mulberry* lives at the intersection of love, sacrifice, and deep secrets. With puissant prose, Easton captures the era, the struggle, and most certainly our hearts."

—Mathieu Cailler, author of *Forest for the Trees & Other Stories*

"A true page-turner . . . [Miyoung's] irrepressible spirit shines through in this richly detailed and compelling historical novel."

—Margaret Juhae Lee, author of *Starry Field: A Memoir of Lost History*

"I was rapt as I followed Miyoung on her journey from Korea to pursue the life she dreamed of in Japan, becoming Miyoko, and as she lost and then found herself. *White Mulberry* is historical fiction at its finest, a beautiful, searching epic about what it means to be home."

—Lindsay Hunter, author of *Hot Springs Drive*

"Rosa Kwon Easton's debut, *White Mulberry*, is a rich and deeply researched historical saga that spans nations, decades, religions, and wars. Miyoung's harrowing and picaresque journey from poverty in Korea to Japan, where she eventually serves the empire that colonized her home country, is gripping and impressively rendered. I can't wait to read what Easton writes next."

—Leland Cheuk, author of *No Good Very Bad Asian*

WHITE MULBERRY

WHITE MULBERRY

A Novel

ROSA KWON EASTON

LAKE UNION
PUBLISHING

This is a work of fiction. Names, characters, organizations, places, events, and incidents are either products of the author's imagination or are used fictitiously.

Published by Lake Union Publishing, Seattle

www.apub.com

ISBN-13: 9781662519697 (paperback)
ISBN-13: 9781662519703 (digital)

Cover design by Alicia Tatone
Cover image: ©naoki goffi / Shutterstock; ©enviromantic / Getty

Printed in the United States of America

For my family

Youth does not return
I am wearing white clothing
I will live humbly

—Miyoung

PART ONE

Pyongan Province, Northern Korea

1928

CHAPTER ONE

August 1928

The afternoon sun beat down on the yard, where a sole mulberry tree shaded a small house from the summer heat. Behind the glossy, veined leaves, Miyoung sat perched on her usual bough, scanning the vista of thatch-roofed farms dotting her village. She was stretching her neck, searching for some sweet berries to eat, when she spotted someone moving below. A stranger in a beige uniform and boots paced back and forth along the back wall. He stopped abruptly when he eyed her older half sister Bohbeh, who was tossing squash peels to the chickens.

Miyoung stiffened, gripping the thick, scaly bark with her fingernails. Once, she had seen some young men at the market staring at her sister like this—like she was something they wanted to own. While Bohbeh had blushed at the men's attention, Miyoung had thrust herself into their view. Born in the Year of the Dragon, she was ready to fight, even at eleven years old; she would torch this enemy with her fire breath and swat him with her mighty tail.

The stranger fanned his face with his cap. Was he a Japanese soldier, like the one she'd seen at Pyongyang Station snatching a bag of steaming chestnuts from a poor street vendor? Maybe this man was sizing up their house to rob them. Father said the Japanese had stolen his parents' farm after they took over Korea almost twenty years ago, so it was possible. She wished Father were here to confront the man, but he wouldn't be visiting for another month. His house was in the next village, a two-hour walk away, and he was busy with his first wife and Miyoung's other half siblings.

Miyoung looked around for Mother and caught sight of her coned straw hat in the garden next to the barley field, where she was picking yellow chamoe melon. Mother must have noticed the stranger too, because she looked up toward the house, straightened her back, and dusted off her hands. Then she limped toward him, dragging her bad leg like a sack of millet.

Miyoung narrowed her eyes to get a better look at the man, but she could make out only a mustache and some vague letters on his shirt. Mother's nagging voice rang in her ears, telling her to keep her eyes open wide so that they would look bigger. Even though *Mi*, the first part of her name, meant "beauty," Mother said her eyes were set too close and her skin too brown. Miyoung longed to be more like the *young* part of her name, which meant "brave."

Meanwhile, Bohbeh was fifteen and tall, with a round, pale face, which Mother said was a sign of budding beauty. Bohbeh was Miyoung's half sister from Mother's first marriage and obviously the prettier one. Miyoung didn't care how she looked; she just wanted to run and climb her favorite tree. Scrambling up the wide trunk and crawling along its sturdy limbs, she felt free and strong. Hiding behind the lush green leaves, she could escape and dream. The berries were white and sweet too, not red and tart like those of the other mulberry trees around town. The tree was different, like her.

Mother's high-pitched voice interrupted her thoughts. "Yeoboseyo. Hello. May I help you?"

The startled man pivoted around to face Mother. "I'm from the electrical company," he said in Korean.

Miyoung's breath settled at hearing her mother tongue, not the choppy Japanese she was learning at school. Still, he could have been Japanese, since Father said many of them spoke fluent Korean.

Mother stared up at the man and blotted the sweat on her face with her handkerchief. “Ah yes, Farmer Noh said you might be coming today. Do you think we might get electricity soon?”

“I don’t know,” the man said. “I just take the measurements for the cables and give them to my boss.”

Bohbeh walked out of sight toward the well, and Miyoung sighed, relieved to see her sister out of the stranger’s view.

Mother and the man continued to talk, but Miyoung no longer listened. How wonderful it would be to have electricity! Her classmate had bragged about buying candy under the glittery lights of a night market in Pyongyang, and she itched to see the spectacle for herself. She imagined curling up and reading next to a shiny lamp instead of a dim candle.

In her tree, Miyoung dreamed of a different future where she could study as much as she wanted, like the boys, and become a teacher someday. She wouldn’t have to listen to her parents all the time, do her chores, and wait around to marry like all the other girls in town did. Miyoung could be herself.

“Miyoung-*ah*!” her mother yelled, breaking her reverie. “Come home and clean the guest room.” Mother and the stranger stepped into the house.

Miyoung’s excitement about electricity vanished, and worry stirred again. They didn’t have any other guests at their boarding house, so the room must be for this man who had looked at Bohbeh in a way Miyoung didn’t trust. She searched the area below her to make sure it was clear, scrambled down the tree, and ran to warn her sister.

When the golden sky faded to pink and the chickens were gathered, Bohbeh returned home to wash up. Miyoung had cautioned Bohbeh to stay away as long as possible, hoping the stranger might leave. In the meantime, Miyoung scrubbed the guest room clean, per Mother’s orders, and helped her with dinner. Mother was banging pots and pans, louder than usual. Bohbeh joined them in the kitchen.

"We have a guest tonight," Mother announced. "He works for the electrical company and has to finish something in the morning."

Miyoung tensed, her eyes meeting Bohbeh's.

"His name is Chung-ajeossi," Mother said, referring to him as Mr. Chung.

Miyoung's shoulders relaxed a little, hearing his Korean name.

"And he'll be joining us for dinner."

Miyoung's and Bohbeh's mouths dropped open at the same time. Guests usually ate apart from the family. Maybe Mother had been expecting him, because she proceeded to cook a rare feast. Dried anchovies, fresh pollack, and white rice popped up out of nowhere. Usually, their dinner was eggs, fermented soybean soup with tofu, and whatever vegetables or fruit they could grow on their tiny plot of land.

Mother arranged the dinnerware carefully on the low lacquered table. A wooden binyeo, a hairpin, stuck through her low bun, holding it in place. Her creased, sunburned face looked like the hard, cracked soil she tended, and she seemed older than her thirty-three years. A soiled rag hung over her shoulder. Bohbeh looked especially lovely tonight because Mother had directed her to brush her hair and change into a fresh hanbok. Mother hadn't said anything to Miyoung, so she was glad to be able to stay in her day clothes.

Mr. Chung sat cross-legged on the waxy yellow ondol floor, which was peeling at the seam and worn in the middle. A chipped armoire, where Mother's bedding was packed away each morning, stood on one side of the room. An oil lamp flickered, casting shadow figures on the plain walls. Miyoung always loved this time of night, when her chores were done and she was about to fill her stomach—empty from her typical lunch of thin barley porridge. Her insides rumbled with anticipation for the night's banquet.

White rice steamed from a large bowl, and spicy pollack stew bubbled in an earthen ttukbaegi pot at the center of the low table.

Overflowing side dishes of young radish kimchi, fried tofu, and sesame spinach surrounded the main fare with pops of color. Mother had even prepared ice-cold buckwheat noodles in a tart beef broth, mul naeng-myeon, a refreshing specialty.

"Bohbeh, pour ajeossi some makgeolli," Mother said.

Sitting with her knees touching and bare feet behind her, Bohbeh carefully poured the milky rice wine into Mr. Chung's cup with both hands. She did not look at him. She cast her eyes down, as girls were supposed to do around elders, even though he seemed younger than Father.

Mr. Chung had dirt under his chipped fingernails. He wasn't wearing his stained uniform anymore, but his baji pants were torn at one knee and his jeogori sleeves frayed. He guzzled down the rice wine and smacked his lips while smiling broadly at Bohbeh. He must have been special, since Mother only served the alcoholic drink to Father when he stopped by to drop off salt, potatoes, and other basic items.

After Bohbeh filled Mr. Chung's cup a second time, her eyes met Miyoung's again. *What is so important about this man?*

"You are clever to find paid work from the Japanese in this little village," Mother said, pushing the side dishes closer to his side of the table. "Your wife must be happy."

"Jibsaram is glad I have a job. But she still thinks those bastards should pay me more." He called his wife a houseperson, the common term for a married woman.

Mother's shoulders slumped like she wasn't pleased with his answer. She busied herself ladling some stew into a separate bowl and setting it in front of the guest.

"I hate the Japanese," Mr. Chung said, chewing with his mouth open, "but if I didn't work for them, I wouldn't have any money. My younger brother was forced to go to Japan because he lost his job here. He found a good position, but now he's gone from us."

"What does he do?" Mother asked, her brows arching with interest.

"He's an electrician too."

"Is that so?" Mother hummed. "Japan is a rich country to take in so many Koreans, like your brother, and give them jobs."

"Yes, he makes good money. But he has no wife to take care of him."

Mother dropped her spoon but retrieved it quickly.

"And he changed his name to Haramoto." Mr. Chung tapped his fingers over his chest like he was touching the letters on the uniform he had worn earlier. "At least I still have my name. In Japan, some Koreans change their names because they're looked down on. I wish my brother hadn't given his up. Our ancestors are probably jumping out of their graves."

Miyoung had never met any Koreans who were using Japanese names. *I wonder what my Japanese name could be.* She wondered if having a different name changed who you were inside. Would she feel less lonely? Maybe she could act like a boy and climb her mulberry tree in pants rather than the chima skirt that got caught in the branches. Perhaps she could visit the country she'd heard so much about but barely understood. She recalled seeing a schoolbook picture of a lovely Japanese woman in a colorful kimono; she had been fascinated by the golden temple next to the woman. Would she need a Japanese name to walk among its mossy gardens or to gaze at its jeweled beauty in the reflecting pond?

Mr. Chung raised his rice bowl to his face and scraped every morsel into his mouth with his chopsticks. He passed the metal container for more. Miyoung and Bohbeh nibbled the precious white mounds Mother had dished out for them but dared not lift their bowls for seconds. Miyoung chewed slowly, savoring the last luscious bites. Mother fluffed another scoop of rice for the guest and seemed lost in thought.

After washing the dishes in the courtyard with Bohbeh, Miyoung climbed her tree again to look at the stars. Tiny lights in the sky twinkled to the tune of cicadas buzzing, lulling the village to sleep for the night. As Miyoung crawled about, the branches made a scraping sound on their thatched roof. Under the bright August moon, she could see the central courtyard of her house, with the kitchen to the left, the raised living room in the center, and the two attached bedrooms to the right. Mother slept in the living room, the guest stayed in the far room, and she and her sister shared the middle bedroom. Bohbeh's silhouette moved across the rice-paper screen door as she unfolded their blanket roll in preparation for sleep.

Miyoung spied Mr. Chung talking to Mother again at the entrance. She stilled so that they wouldn't hear her moving.

"Thank you for dinner." Mr. Chung's voice rang clear.

"You're welcome," Mother said. "Thank you for your hard work today. When do you think we'll actually get electricity?"

Mr. Chung turned his head and plucked his teeth with a toothpick. "Like I said before, I don't know. We're just taking measurements and making drawings. It's up to my boss."

His face was hidden by dark shadows. Clearing his throat, he changed the subject. "Remember how I mentioned my younger brother who lives in Japan? He has a big, beautiful house in Kyoto now and a well-paying job."

Mother shuffled a little closer. Miyoung's ears perked up too.

"He needs a Korean wife, and your daughter Bohbeh would be a perfect match. She could eat white rice every day."

Miyoung gasped, covering her mouth with her hand. Not Bohbeh. Not again. Three years ago, Mother had arranged for Bohkee, the eldest of Miyoung's two half sisters, to marry a stranger in Manchuria. Bohkee had also been fifteen. Bohbeh and Bohkee shared the first syllable of their names because they shared the same father, who had passed away. Miyoung remembered Bohkee's lips quivering when she heard the news, but Mother hadn't flinched.

Holding her breath, Miyoung now awaited Bohbeh's fate, afraid that Mother's answer might be yes. She did seem very interested in Mr. Chung and his brother. The trilling of the cicadas grew louder and louder.

"Let me . . . think about it," Mother said calmly.

Miyoung released the air from her cheeks. Surely Mother wouldn't let Bohbeh get married and move as far away as Japan, especially after what had happened to Bohkee. They hadn't heard from her since she'd left home. In Miyoung's nightmares, a woman's body floated in a river face down. Rumor spread that crossing the river into Manchuria meant never coming back. She didn't know whether Bohkee was still alive and longed to see her beaming smile again.

Please don't let Bohbeh go too. Marriage just meant separation and heartache. What if she never saw Bohbeh again either? Miyoung stared at the lines on her palm, hoping they would somehow tell her that Bohbeh would be staying. She would be all alone with no sister at home. No sister to snuggle a warm, newly laid egg into Miyoung's hands every morning. No one to pick wax out of her ears with a tiny wooden scooper on bath days. The spot next to hers on the bedroll would be cold when she closed her eyes at night.

Miyoung's chest churned with fear for Bohbeh's future, and hers.

Miyoung ate her breakfast slowly the next day, eyeing Mother to see if she would say anything about Mr. Chung's proposal. He had left the boardinghouse earlier, before the girls woke. Miyoung had decided not to tell Bohbeh what she'd overheard, hoping Mother wouldn't mention it either. Mother slurped her usual barley porridge in silence. The knots in Miyoung's stomach loosened when the meal ended without any talk of what had happened the previous night.

Later that morning, Miyoung snuck more furtive glances at Mother, who was pounding Mr. Chung's bedding in the sun with a paddle. Mother's face revealed only a hint of sweat from the pressing heat, and she wasn't looking at Bohbeh sweeping the floor, so maybe her answer was no. With relief in her step, Miyoung skipped outside to play and enjoy the Sunday off from school.

At lunch, Mother sat sidesaddle, facing Bohbeh, and raised one knee up. Miyoung's breath quickened, knowing this posture was usually a sign that Mother was about to say something big. She had sat like that when she told them they would need to help more around the house because of her bad back. She had assumed the same position when she announced that Bohkee was leaving to be married. Miyoung braced herself.

"Bohbeh-yah, remember Chung-ajeossi, our guest from last night? He said he has a younger brother in Kyoto who is also an electrician like himself."

Pulse racing, Miyoung looked at Bohbeh to see if she was paying attention. Bohbeh was chewing a hard-boiled egg soaked in soy sauce and watching a cricket jump around the room. She turned toward Mother, but her eyes still tracked the insect's hops.

"He's looking for a Korean wife, and he said you two would be a perfect match."

Bohbeh's metal chopsticks fell on the lacquered table, making a loud clattering noise.

"I've decided you're going to Kyoto to marry Mr. Chung's brother," Mother declared.

"What?" Bohbeh said, eyes bulging.

The room grew silent, and the only thing Miyoung could hear was the sound of her own pounding heart. Ever since Bohkee had left, losing someone she loved frightened her, and it was happening all over again. Miyoung's stomach clenched.

"You heard me. This is a good opportunity for you to get married," Mother said.

"But . . . I don't even know him," Bohbeh replied.

"Mr. Chung comes from a good family. He's a distant relative of Farmer Noh next door. Besides, all the eligible men are leaving to work in the cities, and soon there'll be no one left to marry."

The memory of eating Farmer Noh's delicious roasted corn now left a bitter taste in Miyoung's mouth.

"But why Japan? We don't like the Japanese," Bohbeh said.

Mother scowled, but the edges of her eyes softened. "Hush. He needs a Korean wife, and you'll have a better life there."

"Don't send me away. I don't want to go, Oh-ma-ni!" Bohbeh yelled, stressing each syllable of the word for "mother" that was used in the north.

Mother pursed her lips, and her hands stiffened on her lap like those of a stone Buddha.

Bohbeh stopped shouting. Her head hung limp, and she shuddered, as if she had given up.

"Eonni!" Miyoung wailed, calling her older sister, the one person who meant more to her than anyone in the world. Her eyes begged Bohbeh to fight back, to do something. But Mother's determined face stared back, and it was clear that Bohbeh would lose. She was no match for Mother. The last time Bohbeh had opposed Mother's orders by refusing to help a sick neighbor with housework, she'd gotten a lashing on her calf with a bamboo reed. Mother's eyes flashed even stronger today.

"It's been very tough for me to raise you girls on my own. Even if it might be harsh at first, this is the best way. One day you'll understand the old Korean proverb 'Gosaeng kkeut-e nag-i onda.'" *At the end of hardship comes happiness.*

What was hard was Mother's heart. Panic rose in Miyoung.

"No!" she screamed. She sprang up from the table with all her might, knocking a cup over in an angry burst. Mother's eyes shot open with surprise. Miyoung expected a lashing, but she didn't care. She knew she was next.

CHAPTER TWO

September 1928

The front door creaked open, and Father cleared his throat. Miyoung spilled the laundry she was washing and rushed across the courtyard to greet him. For two agonizing weeks, she had been counting on Father to forbid Bohbeh's marriage, and Mother said she would be talking to him about it at his next visit. Father liked to be addressed promptly, so she didn't want to let him down, especially not today.

Miyoung bowed deeply to Father. She crossed her hands and bent her knees, the midmorning sun warm on her back. She was lucky to be home from school for the annual Chuseok, the autumn harvest festival, so she could hear the conversation for herself and hopefully watch Father say no. Bohbeh had just left to gather mushrooms in the nearby forest. The dust from Miyoung's shuffling feet flew into his face.

"Why do you always run?" Father snapped, coughing. "Girls shouldn't do that, especially now that you're getting older. Your mother should teach you better."

"I'm sorry, Abeonim," she replied, using the respectful word for "father." Miyoung's neck burned from his sharp words. She cast her eyes on the floor and fixated on Father's rope sandals so that she would remember to keep her head down. She knew better than to talk back.

Through her lashes, Miyoung saw the split-bamboo hat on Father's head shake left to right in disapproval. She recalled Father's story of the gat, the tall horsehair hat his own father used to wear, topknot visible through the black mesh netting. He said the Japanese had made all Korean men cut off their topknots at the turn of the century, and Grandfather had been angry that this symbol of manhood had been ripped away. Miyoung felt sorry for Father, even though it hadn't happened to him directly. It must have hurt his pride too, since he talked about it so much.

Wiping her hands on her apron, Mother stepped out of the kitchen and bowed briefly to Father. She placed a stray piece of hair behind her ear and straightened a newer chima skirt. Her full lips were slightly parted, and her high cheekbones framed her large brown eyes. There was no doubt that Mother's beauty had attracted Father after Bohbeh and Bohkee's father died. Mother said she had been a widow for a few years and working for rent and food at a nearby farm when Father saw her raising two girls alone. He had arranged for her to run this boardinghouse, and Miyoung was born shortly after. She said it wasn't uncommon for men to have more than one wife, although Mother's face often flushed as she passed neighbors around town, and she didn't really have any friends.

Whatever affection her parents had shared back then seemed to have disappeared over the years. Father didn't smile or laugh when he talked to Mother. Even when Miyoung spied them alone, he rarely showed affection—not even a soft pat on the shoulder or a gentle brushing of hands. He treated her the same way he did Miyoung: with harsh words and no room for argument.

Father rarely stayed for more than a few minutes when he dropped off potatoes or some other necessity each month. Miyoung would see Father give Mother a small sack of coins whenever he stopped by. Other than that, the only money that came into the house was from the occasional guest. They ate fruits and vegetables from the garden, raised chickens, and made their own tofu.

"I trust everything is fine?" Father said. His words were abrupt, like he was in a hurry. Father always held his head high when he spoke. His traditional clothing—a white hemp top and baji cinched at the bottom—and his long, pointy beard made him appear taller and thinner than he was. Though he didn't have white hair like the village elders, Miyoung noticed that the other men would ask his opinion on how to best till the rice fields or why the cost of barley was rising. Father was stern, but he was also dignified and intelligent. Miyoung wished he would pay attention to her once in a while and take an interest in what she was doing. She couldn't figure out how to please him.

Mother avoided looking directly at Father too. Her shoulders were rounded, as usual, hunched from the constant bending motion of churning tofu on the stone press. Pushing down on her lower back with the palm of her hand, Mother straightened up.

"Would you like some makgeolli?" she said, offering him some rice wine.

"I don't have time. Is there something you wanted to talk about?"

"Yes," Mother said, a wobble in her voice. "I want to talk about Bohbeh. She's not here, but this is important." Even though Bohbeh wasn't Father's real daughter, Mother still consulted him about everything. The same thing had happened when Bohkee was sent away.

"What is it?" Father said.

Mother shifted her weight from side to side while pulling the edge of her apron with her fingers. "I want to send Bohbeh to Japan to marry a Korean electrician."

Miyoung held her breath for Father to say no.

"What?" Father's eyes narrowed. "Those greedy Japanese bastards! Bohbeh's not living with those colonizers."

Miyoung's heart sang at Father's refusal. Bohbeh was staying!

But Mother tried again. "I understand you don't want Bohbeh to live in Japan, but many of the bachelors have left the village. This man comes from a good family. She'll not have this chance again."

Father paced the dirt floor of the courtyard with his head down and hands behind his back. Mother pursed her lips. Miyoung squeezed her fingers tight, waiting for his response.

Mother took Father's long silence as an opening to continue. "We won't have to provide a dowry or pay a matchmaker to find her a husband. She'll not be a financial burden to you anymore."

Father grumbled something but seemed to be considering Mother's words. Miyoung had overheard neighbors saying that the matchmaker in town was expensive. The woman lived in one of the largest houses in the village, built on a plot of land given to her in exchange for her services. She was in high demand and wanted an equally high price for the promise of many sons. Miyoung remembered seeing a small, quick-eyed woman at the market with a large bag of change dangling from her wrist and wondered if she was the matchmaker they were talking about.

"I'm not the wealthy man I used to be," Father said, and it was true. He was a sharp businessman and had been well off until a few years ago. He had owned a huge house with a separate building for the women and children where she and her half siblings had played hiding games whenever she visited. Now the whole family lived in one small house, and most of the servants were gone. He had been forced to give up all his land to the Japanese. They took his workers too. Father had told Mother he had little choice but to work as a middleman selling vegetables and produce to the Japanese. He often announced that he had too many mouths to feed.

"So I guess that's what it will be, then," Father announced, almost with a note of relief in his voice.

Blood rushed to Miyoung's face. Fighting words crammed her throat.

"But . . . !" Miyoung shouted before she could stop herself.

Mother's scowl pierced her chest. She ignored Miyoung's outburst and bent over in Father's direction. "Thank you."

Father arched his brow and turned his gaze toward Miyoung. Heat crawled across her neck from Father's sudden attention. "What about third daughter Miyoung? She'll need to find someone to marry before long."

Miyoung bit down hard on her lip. Why had she opened her big mouth? Her nightmare was coming true. Miyoung's eyes darted to Mother for help, but her expression was blank. Mother wore silence like a cloak, so it was impossible to know what she was thinking. Maybe she was sad because Miyoung, her last daughter, might be leaving soon. Maybe she didn't care at all. But she sensed her mother might be hiding her feelings; she had once seen her weep over Bohkee's favorite soup, after all.

Miyoung had tried to talk to her about it then. "Why are you crying?"

Mother had been picking off the wiry ends of the soybean sprouts and tossing the stems into the boiling water with tears welling in her eyes. "A girl's fate is one of suffering. There's an old saying for women: 'First you must serve your father, then your husband, then your son.' Marriage has failed me. Living in this country has failed me. That's why I sent Bohkee to Manchuria—for a better future."

Mother thought that anywhere but Korea might be better. Maybe that's why she was sending Bohbeh to Japan too. But if Mother didn't think marriage was a good thing, why would she wish it on her daughters? Was marriage in a different country better? Miyoung's palms dampened as she waited for Mother's answer about her future.

"I appreciate your desire to see Miyoung engaged soon," Mother said to Father. "But I want to make sure she finishes primary school first. She's not like Bohbeh and Bohkee. Miyoung's teacher says she's smart, and thinks she will become a wonderful teacher someday."

Miyoung's face heated in shock. Mother was rarely generous with praise, so Miyoung's heart pumped with joy.

"A girl's place is at home, so an education isn't necessary," Father said.

Miyoung's hopes deflated. But as Father turned away, something fired up inside her, and hot words tumbled from her mouth.

"Father, I'm a good student! I get better grades than the boys!" She'd done it. She'd spoken up to Father for the first time. He tensed, and

Miyoung flinched at the possibility of a lashing. To her surprise, a faint smile flickered across Father's face. Maybe she had imagined it.

But Miyoung knew she'd spoken the truth. She always stayed after school and buried her head in her homework while Teacher Kim finished grading papers. Her classmates made fun of her because she skipped playing hopscotch in the morning so that she could read. Her test scores were higher than those of anyone else in the class. She enjoyed broadening her knowledge of the world. She was good at school and wanted to be like Teacher Kim, a woman who was bright and unmarried.

She searched Mother's solemn profile for help. She wanted Mother to stick up for her, just like she had wanted Bohbeh to fight to stay. Instead, Miyoung had protested loudly for Bohbeh, and had suffered large red welts on her calves from being lashed by Mother as a result. Strangely, it had emboldened her.

Miyoung readied herself to speak out against Father again, but Mother jumped in at last.

"Remember Mr. Shin?" Mother said. "Because I couldn't read, he stole my land! I don't want that to happen to Miyoung."

Mother had repeated this story many times to her daughters and to Father too, but her nose flared wider than before. "When I became a widow, the shady Shin convinced me to sign those papers putting my dead husband's land into his name, and then he sold it from under me!" She panted. "Miyoung needs to be educated so she doesn't make those kinds of mistakes. She's the only one of my girls who could do something with her schooling."

Mother's words warmed Miyoung like a bowl of sundubu jjigae, a delicious soft-tofu stew her mother liked to make. Mother was on her side after all. Since girls were expected to help at home, Miyoung had assumed that her mother thought little of her studies, but now she understood that they offered protection for her and her family. Talking about all this, however, seemed to take a toll, and Mother winced and grabbed a beam to keep her balance. A thin line of moisture beaded atop Mother's lip.

Miyoung glanced at Father, but he remained oblivious to her health. A somber shadow darkened his face as he answered.

"As far as I'm concerned, she's wasting time in school. But she can finish primary school, and then she'll marry. That's that."

Miyoung let out a deep breath, and the creases in Mother's forehead straightened. Relief washed over Miyoung—she'd have another year and a half, until she was thirteen, before she had to think about marriage again.

Father interrupted Miyoung's train of thought. "Come over next week to help prepare for the fall harvest festival. The girls are making a mess in the house, cutting this and that."

"Yes, Father," she said, pleased by the invitation. She looked forward to doing something fun and seeing her favorite half brother, Taeyoung. She wanted to celebrate her small victory today. Miyoung had spoken up to Father, and narrowly escaped marriage—for now.

CHAPTER THREE

September 1928

Counting birds on her two-hour walk to Father's house, Miyoung tried to forget about Bohbeh leaving home soon. She wiped the sweat from her brow with her jeogori sleeve and squatted against the beige stone wall outside Father's front door. Scents of sugar and sesame drifted from her bag, making Miyoung's mouth water. Mother had carefully wrapped sweet rice cakes in a colorful bojagi cloth for her to bring to Father's first wife as a gift. There was only enough for each member of Father's family. Out of his six children, three had married or moved away for work, so only three were still at home. Miyoung would probably have to wait until she got home to eat, since Father's first wife rarely offered her anything.

Miyoung banged the large metal knocker on the wooden door. She straightened her braids and brushed her skirt, like she had seen Mother do, readying herself to greet Father's strict first wife, who had once spanked Miyoung for forgetting to bow to her.

A loud thud echoed from inside, and footsteps approached, making a gravelly noise across the dirt courtyard. It was the same crunching sound Miyoung's pillow had made when she banged her head against it the night Father approved of Bohbeh's marriage. The hard rectangular bolster was stuffed with buckwheat grain, so the weight of her head had made a hollow in it, just like the growing hole in her heart. Miyoung and Bohbeh had fallen asleep holding each other's hands, trying to comfort one another by imagining nice big houses in Japan and all the meat Bohbeh would eat.

When the heavy door to Father's house swung open, Miyoung's fourteen-year-old half brother, Taeyoung, popped out. Miyoung's mouth curved into a broad smile, and her sadness lifted a little. She loved climbing rocks and playing chase with him, and the glow in his eyes reassured her he cared about her too.

"Oppa!" Miyoung said, calling Taeyoung by his status as older brother.

"Come in!" Taeyoung said in a deep voice, sounding more like a man than a boy. He looked taller, too, than the last time she had visited, about a month before. She wasn't used to seeing him in glasses, which he had just started wearing not too long ago.

Miyoung stepped through the doorframe and entered the courtyard of the typical traditional house, which was much larger than her own. The square open area had multiple rooms on each side and was covered by a black tile roof with curved eaves that provided much-needed shade from the hot sun. A wide, elevated porch connected all the rooms and offered a cool place to sit and drink cold barley tea. The sliding rice-paper door to the women's quarters on the right was open, and Miyoung could see that Father's first wife and her two half sisters were bent over, cutting strips of fabric and tying them onto sticks to make streamers.

"Deulowa," Father's first wife said, scooping her hand down to signal Miyoung to come in. Her voice rang flat across the courtyard and did not sound inviting. Miyoung wasn't close to her half sisters either, even though all the siblings on her father's side shared the same generational syllable *young* in their names. Taeyoung would be her only playmate in the family once Bohbeh left home.

Miyoung stopped and bowed to Father's first wife on the spot.

"Say hello to your father first. He wants to talk to you," she said. "Taeyoung, show her in." Miyoung's sisters looked up but didn't acknowledge her. A loneliness caught in her throat; she missed Bohbeh already.

Miyoung set the sweets down on the porch, and the two crossed the courtyard to the men's quarters and Father's study. They passed the living area that was already set up for the fall Chuseok festivities. A five-panel folding screen stood behind the large wooden altar, soon to be filled with plates of delicacies that would be offered to dead ancestors. Miyoung's stomach grumbled as she thought of songpyeon, the glutinous half-moon rice cakes stuffed with sesame seeds, chestnuts, and other mouthwatering fillings steamed over a bed of pine needles. The offerings had become more modest over the years due to Father's decreased income, but they would be much tastier than the ones she had brought today. She knew she wouldn't get to relish any of the delicious fare.

Miyoung would be sent home before the Chuseok celebrations, where she would eat only some simple vegetable jeon pancakes with Mother and Bohbeh. She had never been invited to enjoy the annual feast with the rest of Father's family, and it had something to do with Mother being Father's second wife. Her heart stung at the cool reception, but she wanted to see Taeyoung.

"Dongsaeng is here. Can we come in?" Taeyoung said to Father over the thin rice-paper-paneled door, referring to Miyoung as "younger sister."

"Geulae." Father said yes in a deep, strong timbre.

The two entered his room and knelt on cushions.

"Hello, Father," Miyoung said, bowing.

Father sat cross-legged with an arm draped over each knee and a newspaper spread out on the floor. His thin beard hung below his neck. He picked up his long pipe from the lacquered table next to him and inhaled deeply.

"I've been thinking about what we talked about the other day," he said.

Miyoung straightened, hoping he had changed his mind about sending Bohbeh away.

"About your need to marry," he said instead.

Miyoung slouched with disappointment. Not again. Not without Mother to side with her this time.

"I was at the local town meeting this morning, and I happened to be talking to Farmer Yang," Father said. "He has a son who is fourteen, like your brother, and wants him to have a bride in a few years. We agreed that you and he would be a good match."

Shock gripped Miyoung's throat. She knew Farmer Yang's son, Ilsoo, from school, before he had graduated a few years ago. He was a short, scrawny boy with a pockmarked face. He had bullied and teased his classmates with his big fat mouth. She had seen him kick a boy for no reason.

"But . . . he's mean!" Miyoung burst out. "He hits people!"

Father's brows furrowed, but she wasn't sure if it was because he was angry at her for talking back or surprised about Ilsoo. His eyes closed softly before they shot open again, holding the same firm gaze. Maybe he felt sorry for her, but he wasn't going to show it.

Miyoung looked at her older brother for help. He seemed as taken aback as Miyoung about her possible groom. Taeyoung was not getting married yet, because he was going to Pyongyang for high school. He was gifted in math and had gotten a scholarship to attend a prestigious school there. He would be staying with one of Father's friends and tutoring his children in return for room and board. Miyoung wished she were a boy and getting money to go to school like her brother, not being told who she would marry.

Taeyoung opened his mouth as if to say something, then stopped.

"Ilsoo comes from a reputable family, and they have a successful farm," Father said, a ring of finality in his voice.

"But what about finishing school?" Heat singed Miyoung's cheeks.

"You can still finish primary school, but you'll marry Ilsoo after you graduate." Father lifted his bearded chin in the direction of the women's room. "It's a fortunate thing that I happened to discuss this matter with Farmer Yang this morning. There won't be a need to pay the matchmaker like I did with your two sisters over there, and this match ensures you'll marry into a good family."

Miyoung followed Father's gaze across the courtyard, picturing her half sisters with men nicer and more handsome than Ilsoo. They were fifteen and sixteen, not as beautiful as Bohbeh, and not as kind. If their future marriages were supposed to make Miyoung feel better, they didn't. But she couldn't talk to Father about this anymore. She had already pushed him one too many times.

Now that there was a face to Miyoung's future husband, anxiety pumped through her veins. When she had seen the Lee newlyweds kissing in the bushes of the village, her neck had become hot. The thought of kissing any boy, let alone Ilsoo, made her squirm. And she certainly wouldn't want babies with him. Father had a lot of children, although she couldn't imagine him being very loving to his first wife, since he wasn't warm toward Mother. She never saw Father and his first wife talking either. Father's first wife always stayed in her room and Father in his. Marriage seemed miserable.

"Go ahead and help your sisters," Father said. "That's all I wanted to say. Let your mother know."

"Yes, Father," Miyoung mumbled.

Miyoung and Taeyoung stood up partway and walked backward toward the door to show respect. After Taeyoung slid the door closed, he whispered softly, "Sorry about that."

"I don't want to marry, and I especially don't want to marry Ilsoo." She balled her hands into fists.

"I don't blame you. I wish there were something I could do . . ." Taeyoung stared down at his bare feet and wiggled his toes. "Father told me it's his responsibility to marry all of you off, so I knew he wouldn't change his mind."

Miyoung's fingers loosened slightly at hearing Father's point of view. She understood he had his own worries too. "I still think it's unfair."

"I know. You're smart. You should be going to school, not me," Taeyoung said.

"I wish I could go like you." Hope drained from her voice.

"You're a good student. You picked up the abacus faster than any girl I know."

"But Father doesn't think girls need to go to school at all. I'm lucky I even get to finish primary school."

Taeyoung looked up again with a gleam in his eyes. "There are girls' middle schools in Pyongyang too, you know. Maybe you could continue your studies there before you get married."

"Really?" The prospect of going beyond primary school hadn't occurred to her, but she started to imagine herself in Pyongyang, walking through the bustling streets after school with Taeyoung by her side. She had been to the city only once, when they'd dropped Bohkee off to make her way toward Manchuria. The streets were an exciting mess of horses, carriages, and streetcars. She wanted so badly to see the famous night market a classmate had told her about. She envisioned wandering through the stalls under the bright lights, sampling all her favorite foods, including tasty soondae, or blood sausage.

"Maybe you can visit me sometime," Taeyoung said, poking her ribs playfully. "Come on, let's go outside. I have a new hiding spot I can show you. Then you can help with the festival."

Taeyoung and Miyoung scrambled onto the boulders behind the house, and when they tired of that, they played hwatu cards. Still, a black cloud seemed to follow Miyoung all day. When one of her sisters plucked the gayageum, a twelve-string zither, the melancholy vibrations pounded her temples. When she helped her sisters and her father's first wife prepare for the festival, the cornhusk dolls she made looked like monsters.

CHAPTER FOUR

October 1928

On their last night together, Miyoung and Bohbeh huddled around a map of Asia in their bedroom. Teacher Kim had let Miyoung borrow it from school, and she was surprised that Japan was not much bigger than Korea, despite its looming presence. Resting their elbows on the thick blanket that they used as a bed, they traced the path of the train with their fingers by candlelight. Bohbeh's long journey would take her from her village, Maengjungri, to Pyongyang, then to Seoul and finally all the way down to Busan, the southernmost port of Korea.

Miyoung's finger stopped moving in the middle of the sea between Korea and Japan. The image blurred as tears pooled. A single drop plopped on the map as Miyoung saw just how far Bohbeh was going. She recalled Mother saying that Bohbeh would have to cross the Korea Strait by ship to the port city of Shimonoseki in Japan and finally take another train ride to her new home in Kyoto. It would probably take two or three long days.

"Don't worry, little one," said Bohbeh, noticing Miyoung's silence. Bohbeh took her limp hand from the map and cupped it in hers.

Miyoung's sadness lifted momentarily, and her body warmed despite the chill in the fall air. "I can't help it. I'm going to miss you."

"I'll miss you too," Bohbeh said, bringing their entwined hands to her heart. "But I can't live here forever."

Bohbeh sounded grown up all of a sudden.

"I'll probably have to leave the village to marry anyway, like Bohkee did. It's my fate, I guess."

Miyoung opened Bohbeh's hand and looked at the lines on her sister's palm. The deep grooves seemed to be crossing over one another, and her fate was no longer etched in a straight line. She compared Bohbeh's palms to hers, noticing the middle crease of her own broken in the center. Their lives had been disrupted. Or was it meant to have been this way all along?

Miyoung's hope of keeping her sister home had withered this last month as plans moved forward. Bohbeh's acceptance made her departure inevitable. Meanwhile, Miyoung refused to believe that Father would actually make her marry Ilsoo and planned to get out of it somehow, although she had no idea how.

"Mother's right. I'll probably have a better life being married in Japan." Bohbeh sighed. "Who knows? Maybe I'll love this man. I want to believe there is love out there, whatever that is."

Miyoung chewed on Bohbeh's words but decided she didn't care about love. Bohbeh always had a way of looking at the brighter side of things and accepted her fate too quickly. "I'll never love Ilsoo," Miyoung said.

Bohbeh gently stroked Miyoung's head and whispered, "It's okay. Everything's going to be okay."

The following day, Miyoung walked alongside Mother and Bohbeh to the small local train station for Bohbeh's farewell. The foliage was almost at its peak, and the leaves covered the road in a blanket of vibrant hues. Bohbeh wore her best yellow hanbok, faded from washings, and new gomushin, rubber shoes that turned up at the end like duck's bills. Mother had splurged on a fresh pair for the trip because Bohbeh's old ones were worn and small. Miyoung would wear the castoffs when she grew into them, as she did with all her sister's clothing. Bohbeh also carried a new trunk containing a white hemp hanbok, a sweater, and a heavy jacket that used to be Bohkee's. Mother had scraped together the last of her savings to buy the extravagant hard suitcase.

Miyoung clutched her sister's hand the whole way, not wanting to let her go. They walked slowly to keep up with their mother's hobbling pace. When they arrived at the station, the narrow platform area was practically empty, except for a few people gathered around the ticket booth. They spotted Mr. Chung waiting by the train. He would be traveling with Bohbeh to Kyoto to deliver the bride to his brother. He wasn't in his work uniform anymore, so Miyoung barely recognized him beyond his mustache. Bohbeh's face crumpled upon seeing him, and she froze.

"I don't want to go anymore, Ohmani," Bohbeh said to Mother with pursed lips. Bohbeh was standing between Mother and Miyoung, tugging on Mother's sleeve like a child.

"Bohbeh-yah," Mother said, shaking off her daughter's hand. "Don't make a scene. Your new husband is waiting for you in Kyoto, ready to give you a better life." Mother motioned toward the train with her chin, signaling it was time to go. Her eyes seemed to soften for a moment but then resumed their hard shape. "There's nothing for a girl here but misery and hard work. You're clever and pretty. You'll have a brighter future in Japan. Go now!"

Memories of the last sister Miyoung had dropped off at the train station flooded back. Bohkee had confronted Mother at the platform too, although it was the larger one in Pyongyang. "Don't make me go! They say no one ever returns from Manchuria!" Bohkee had shouted.

"Hush!" Mother had replied. "You must accept your elders' decisions. Your new husband is waiting across the river. The Japanese have taken our land, but there are plenty of fields to farm in Manchuria."

They never saw Bohkee again, and now Mother was repeating similar words to Bohbeh. Miyoung squeezed Bohbeh's hand hard. Her sister pressed back harder. Miyoung suspected Bohbeh might have been remembering that scene too.

Mr. Chung gestured for them to come and climbed aboard the train. They resumed walking slowly toward the open door. At the bottom step, Bohbeh released Miyoung's fingers one by one. She lifted up her chima carefully. Miyoung's chest tightened at the sight of Bohbeh leaving. As if sensing her sister's dismay, Bohbeh pulled back, turned around, and gave Miyoung a big hug.

"Be good," Bohbeh said. "I'll miss you."

Before Miyoung could return the embrace, Bohbeh let go and scrambled into the car without looking back. Miyoung lost sight of her for a second until Bohbeh appeared next to the window across from Mr. Chung, who was already reading the newspaper. Miyoung glared at his bent head, furious that he had caused all of this to happen. She wanted to go back in time and erase him from their lives.

Bohbeh stretched her arms out the open window, and Miyoung grabbed her hands, desperate for one more touch. Mother reached up too but at the last minute pulled back, her face shaded with sadness. The train whistled while it pulled away from the platform, forcing Miyoung to let go. She kept her eyes fixed on her sister, as if removing them too soon would mean she would never see her again. When the train gained speed and her sister's face finally disappeared, Miyoung let the tears fall.

CHAPTER FIVE

Fall 1928

Every one of Miyoung's pores ached for Bohbeh as she trudged alone to the one-room village schoolhouse the next day. The schoolroom buzzed with forty students of all ages clamoring for their seats. The space was cramped and stuffy, though it was a brisk fall day and the clay roof and white walls were supposed to keep the building cool. The windows, lined with hanji paper made from mulberry trees, remained slightly ajar for fresh air.

Miyoung took her seat on the wooden floor toward the back with the older students. Normally, she loved sinking her nose into her books and tapping her feet to the beat of Teacher Kim's chalk against the blackboard. But not today. She stared out the window and listened absently to the lesson. She couldn't erase Bohbeh's leaving and her own bleak future with Ilsoo.

After dropping Bohbeh off at the station the previous day, Miyoung had returned home restless and lost. She'd climbed her mulberry tree, but she'd had no desire to play spy games, make up stories, or do anything fun. She'd had no appetite either, even when she'd smelled dinner cooking below and heard Mother calling for her. Mother had made Bohbeh's favorite mung bean pancakes, but neither of them had eaten much or said anything. As the day had grown darker and colder, so had Miyoung's heart.

She had hoped school would lift her spirits, but at the end of the day, she wasn't happier and couldn't bear the thought of going home to an empty house without Bohbeh. Miyoung was the last student to leave as she dawdled at her seat, pretending to do homework. The rhythmic movement of Teacher Kim's pencil stopped, and she glanced up at Miyoung from her desk. A worried look crossed her face.

"Would you come up, please," Teacher Kim said gently.

"Yes, Seonsaengnim," Miyoung said, calling her by her title as teacher. Miyoung's nerves fluttered, as she thought she might be in trouble. She walked to her teacher's desk in hushed steps.

"This is a small village. I heard about Bohbeh leaving from my neighbor."

Teacher Kim's words struck a deep chord inside. "Yes," Miyoung whispered. "She left yesterday."

A tender smile inched up Teacher Kim's lips, showing off her beautiful straight teeth. Her eyes glinted like shiny pebbles in a stream. She was a short, thin woman sporting a bob haircut—a popular style among young women. Wearing knee-high socks and a printed cotton blouse tucked into a zippered skirt, she seemed modern. A small gold necklace that looked like a plus sign graced her neck. Miyoung had seen Teacher Kim touch it with closed eyes, sliding it from side to side, and wondered what it meant.

Teacher Kim was different in every way from Miyoung's stern former teacher, Teacher Yoo. He used to order the girls to sit in the back of the room. Now they sat by grade level, and Teacher Kim beamed with pleasure whenever Miyoung did well on a test. She never punished students either. Teacher Yoo used to make them stand in front of the classroom and hold a heavy book at arm's length. Their only crime had been something minor, such as taking out of turn a seat next to the warm coal furnace in the wintertime. Teacher Kim, on the other hand, offered her students only kindness. Miyoung recalled how her teacher had brought one of her classmates a peach to take home when the classmate's father had passed away. She seemed just the kind of person Miyoung wanted to be one day.

"I'm so sorry to hear about your sister," Teacher Kim said.

Miyoung looked away as heat rose behind her eyes.

"Remember, it's okay to feel sad."

"Thank you," Miyoung said, relief washing over her.

"By the way, I told your mother you're an excellent student. Did she tell you?"

Miyoung reddened, not used to being praised or repeating praise. She had been meaning to thank Teacher Kim for her generosity, but she was nervous speaking directly to a teacher. Her teacher's understanding spurred her today. "Thank you for saying all those nice things to my mother about me."

"I expect you to continue to study hard."

"I will try my best!" Miyoung stood up as straight as possible, an unexpected energy surging.

"If you do, I'll recommend you to middle school when you graduate in a few years."

Miyoung's heart skipped. She'd been thinking about what Taeyoung had said about the middle schools in Pyongyang. Maybe that would postpone her sentence to marry Ilsoo. She pushed Father's stern face out of her mind.

Couldn't she not get married at all? Teacher Kim was single—Miyoung had seen her go in and out of a boardinghouse in town alone. On some Saturdays, she saw her by herself at the market, buying pencils that she later gave to her students. Most other women her age were married. Maybe being a teacher and earning her own income meant that she didn't have to have a husband. And she could buy whatever she wanted without having to ask, like Mother had to do with Father when it came to extras such as new clothes. Miyoung had never seen a married female teacher, at least not in her village. Miyoung wanted to figure out how Teacher Kim could provide a living for herself without a husband.

"You would be a great teacher," Teacher Kim said, upbeat. "I notice how you help the younger students with their math and hangul without being asked. They look up to you."

A tingle crept up Miyoung's arm. Mother had been right about Teacher Kim saying she was teacher material. She loved tutoring the little ones, so having her teacher acknowledge it seemed like a dream.

"You know, I learned to be a teacher from the American missionaries at a Presbyterian church in Pyongyang. Their philosophy is that girls, as well as boys, can learn and teach."

Miyoung's eyes popped open in surprise. Christians believed in educating girls? She didn't know much about Christianity, except that her mother didn't like it. They were Buddhist. She didn't trust Western ways of thinking. Even if Mother knew that Christians pushed for girls to study, she probably wouldn't be impressed. Mother had told her that some people she knew became Christians because they thought Westerners could help them against the Japanese. Mother said it was foolish to think a foreign country would help Koreans. If Teacher Kim recommended her, Miyoung would have to find another way to convince Mother that she should go to middle school.

"Why don't you be my assistant with the younger kids? You can see if you like teaching." Teacher Kim's eyes twinkled.

Miyoung's veins pulsed with excitement. "Yes, Seonsaengnim. Thank you!"

"In the meantime, I'll pray for Bohbeh's safe journey," said Teacher Kim. "And I'll keep you in my prayers too, since I know you'll miss your sister."

"What is praying, exactly?"

"Praying is connecting directly with God. If you ask him for help, he'll make himself known. He'll take care of your worries through the power of grace," Teacher Kim said.

The only time Miyoung had ever seen anything that looked like prayers was when she went to a monastery at the top of the mountain for her aunt's funeral and the monks chanted with their eyes closed. Her mother's eyes had been closed too. Miyoung wondered if her mother had been praying to see Bohkee again. She wondered if she could pray not to be sad now that Bohbeh was gone.

"Are Christian prayers the same thing as Buddhist prayers?" Miyoung asked. She didn't really understand the difference between the two, but her mother's scorn of Christians was clear. On the way to the Buddhist funeral ceremony for her aunt, she and Mother had seen worshippers coming out of the church.

"Hmmph, I heard one of the white pastors say they don't believe in rebirth," Mother had said to a lady next to her. "Even though my sister's gone, at least she'll come back again in another life. Christians only believe your spirit goes to heaven or hell."

Teacher Kim wrapped one arm around Miyoung. "Maybe one day you can go to church with me and hear the prayers for yourself," she said.

Miyoung longed to see the village church inside. She had never been invited there before. Her friend Haewon was the church pastor's daughter and one of her only friends at school. A lump formed in her throat thinking of what her mother would say if she found out she went. Miyoung wanted to pray that she wouldn't miss her sister too much and that Bohbeh would be happy in Japan. There couldn't be anything wrong with praying for that, could there?

"Yes, I'd like that," Miyoung said.

"Until then, I can pray for you right here. You don't have to be in church. You can do it anywhere. Let me show you how."

Miyoung hesitated, seeing an image of her mother's hands rubbing the wooden Buddhist beads. Teacher Kim guided her hands gently.

"You put your palms together like this and point your fingers up toward heaven," she said. Miyoung shifted in discomfort. "Now close your eyes.

"Father, who art in heaven," Teacher Kim said, "we pray that you protect this young girl who is separated from her sister. Please make sure this girl doesn't suffer too much loneliness. Grant this girl the grace to go forward despite her breaking heart. Please reveal yourself to her, just as you have done for me. She is so young, and her whole life is before her."

Miyoung's bare feet seemed to sink into the floor as a deep calm descended. Teacher Kim's voice smoothed the bumps on her arms, and Miyoung began to believe that everything might be all right after all. Maybe prayers would help her feel less lonely now that Bohbeh was gone. She would pray to be a good student, go to middle school, and become a teacher. Maybe if she was a teacher like Teacher Kim, she could delay marriage, or not even marry at all. Suddenly there was something to strive for, the possibility of a different future from her sisters'.

Hope filled her aching heart.

CHAPTER SIX

Winter 1928

As the long winter approached, Miyoung attacked her studies like a hungry tiger. She hoarded books from the classroom and devoured them by candlelight. She bounded to school early to set up class and lingered late to help students with homework. School became a den of escape and opportunity after Bohbeh's departure, even more so than before. She wanted to earn her way to middle school.

It was also a place to avoid loneliness. Miyoung played with Haewon, who had a slanted smile and a tic that caused her right eye to twitch. Schoolmates shunned Haewon for this, but she didn't seem to care what anyone thought. Miyoung admired her confidence, and they became close friends and seesaw partners. Bundled up in padded jackets, they took turns jumping hard on one end of the wooden board and making the other fly up squealing, their breath white in the frosty air.

Walking home from school one day, Miyoung confided in Haewon that she had been praying for Bohbeh's happiness and for going to middle school.

"You know how to pray?" Haewon asked, surprised.

"Yes. Teacher Kim taught me how. I've been practicing in the chicken coop. Why?"

"Most people in this village don't believe in Christianity."

"We grew up Buddhist," said Miyoung. "So it felt strange to pray to God the first time. But now that I've done it here and there, it feels more natural. I miss my sister so much."

"Why don't you come to church with me next Sunday? My father's giving the sermon," Haewon said.

Miyoung's pulse quickened; she knew Mother would disapprove of her going. Mother had become quieter with Bohbeh gone, rising earlier than usual to meditate and preferring silence during the meals they shared each day. She massaged her feet all the time, saying they felt numb, but she refused to see the shaman for help, as she had done before. If Miyoung opened her mouth to talk about Bohbeh, Mother raised a hand to stop her. The only joy Miyoung and Mother seemed to share during this time was when they received the occasional thin letter from Bohbeh. Miyoung would read aloud to Mother: "I'm all right. I made some Korean friends. I miss you." Bohbeh never mentioned her husband, which seemed odd, but she had never been good with words.

Despite Mother's scorn of Christians, Miyoung's curiosity about church won out. Miyoung even hummed while grinding barley and collecting eggs as she waited for Sunday to arrive, something she hadn't done since seeing Bohbeh off. After finishing her chores on a chilly November morning, she met Haewon at church in secret. Miyoung had told Mother she was going to the school playground. Mother had been meditating first thing, as usual, and shooed her away. Once, when Miyoung had asked her mother what she meditated about, she had said coming back in the next life with less sorrow. Miyoung had tried copying her mother and closing her eyes, but all she thought about was missing Bohbeh and having to marry Ilsoo.

Miyoung met Haewon in front of the large wooden church in town, and they walked in together holding hands. Her friend's face was relaxed, and her tic seemed barely noticeable. After taking their shoes off at the entrance, they sat on straw cushions on the floor near the front. The church was a tall, open space with peaked windows. Candles warmed the frosty air. Tiny tendrils of smoke drifted from the burning wax, causing Miyoung's eyes to lift toward the high ceiling above.

The building purred with people talking in hushed tones, laughing and smiling. Miyoung identified the woman who sold sweet potatoes at the market seated one row ahead, and mothers were rocking back and forth with their babies on their backs. The old peddler who pushed the housewares cart was bent over in prayer. It was a very different kind of village gathering than the loud open-air ceremonies at the Buddhist temple in the mountains, where the monks chanted. It was subdued and calm, not like the outdoor festivals where local performers pounded double-sided drums and swished colorful streamers.

Someone pointed to a white woman in a large black hat sitting on a bench next to the window. Miyoung noticed the person next to her was Teacher Kim. Her heart swelled, hoping her teacher would be glad to see her at church. When Teacher Kim glanced up and spotted Miyoung, her mouth curved into a big smile. Their discovery of each other was interrupted by a man dressed in a black robe clearing his throat. *He must be Haewon's father,* Miyoung thought. He stood at the front clutching a big black book against his chest.

Pastor Nam had a deep, guttural voice that climbed and fell while he spoke. He said the Bible teaches people that we are all equal in the eyes of Jesus. "There is no longer Jew nor Greek, there is neither bond nor free, there is neither male nor female, for you are all one in Jesus Christ," he said, quoting a section of the book. He seemed to be saying everyone should look at different people in the same way. Miyoung wondered if that was why Christians brought food to the lepers living on the outskirts of town. And he said men and women were equal before Jesus. Could that mean girls and boys were too? Possibility surged through Miyoung's veins. She could beat any boy at climbing trees, and Taeyoung said she was better than him at the abacus.

Pastor Nam asked everyone to sing a hymn. Melodies soared, and people swayed as they sang along. Teacher Kim's face beamed with exertion. Everyone seemed content, and Miyoung began to feel that way too.

After finishing the sermon with a prayer, Pastor Nam made an announcement. "We have a special guest here today. She's an American missionary from the Presbyterian congregation in Pyongyang and Teacher Kim's former teacher. Please welcome Sumisu-shi," Pastor Nam said, pronouncing Mrs. Smith's name with a Korean accent.

The lady guest stood up and bowed slightly. Her youthful white face glowed, and her black lace dress puffed out like an umbrella. Miyoung had never seen a Westerner before and was taken aback by how tall she was next to Teacher Kim. A mass of curly yellow hair peeked out from under her shiny black hat. She stood out in stark contrast to the group of Korean worshippers dressed in their customary white hanboks.

"Mrs. Smith tells us there might be a special group of American missionaries coming next year to build a new Christian school here," Pastor Nam said. "She'll say a few words now, and Teacher Kim will translate."

Mrs. Smith and Teacher Kim moved to Pastor Nam's spot and stood squarely in front of Miyoung. Her skin prickled at seeing a foreigner up so close. The woman's eyes were enormous and blue like the summer sky.

"Thank you for having me here today," Mrs. Smith said, as Teacher Kim translated. The foreign words sounded strange yet beautiful to Miyoung's ears. Teacher Kim must have learned English from Mrs. Smith at the school in Pyongyang, and a newfound respect for her teacher's abilities stirred.

"We're excited about the possibility of starting a new middle and high school here modeled after the schools in Pyongyang. For all boys and girls," said Mrs. Smith.

Murmurs floated across the room, since everyone acknowledged a girl's education ended after primary school except by recommendation from a teacher. Even then, they would have to go to school in Pyongyang for a fee. Miyoung knew one girl who had done that, and she came from a rich family.

"We believe girls should receive the same education as boys," Mrs. Smith said.

Miyoung's chest pounded with hope. No wonder Teacher Kim had let her help the younger students with their schoolwork and allowed the girls to sit up front. She hadn't hesitated to tell Mother that Miyoung was a good student either. It was because she was educated in this way of thinking.

After the speech, Miyoung greeted the guest and Teacher Kim, who took both of Miyoung's hands in hers.

"It's so nice to see you," Teacher Kim said. "I'd like you to meet Mrs. Smith."

Ears heating up, Miyoung lowered her head for fear of staring too much. She knew not to look an elder in the eye for too long, especially since she was a girl.

"Annyeonghaseyo," Miyoung said, greeting the pretty stranger with a shy hello.

"Annyeonghaseyo," Mrs. Smith repeated back in perfect Korean.

Miyoung's mouth parted in surprise. "Hangugeo haseyo? Do you speak Korean?"

"Jogeum," she said, squeezing her thumb and index finger to show that she spoke a little.

They all laughed, and Teacher Kim said something to the lady in English. She then turned to Miyoung. "I told Mrs. Smith that you're a good student and want to be a teacher. If you continue to do well, I'll recommend you to this academy. Wouldn't it be wonderful if you could attend the new missionary school when it's built?" Teacher Kim beamed.

"Oh yes!" Miyoung's heart thumped against her chest in excitement. She forced the image of her mother's stern face away, as Mother would probably oppose sending her to a Christian school. In that moment, Miyoung wanted nothing more than to believe she could be a teacher and not have to marry Ilsoo after primary school.

"What did you think of church?" Teacher Kim asked.

"It was nice. The songs were pretty."

"Good. Maybe you can come again?"

"Yes, I would like to."

Teacher Kim and Mrs. Smith exchanged words she couldn't comprehend.

"I told Mrs. Smith about your sister's arranged marriage. She said you must be feeling sad with your sister gone."

Tears pooled in Miyoung's eyes.

Mrs. Smith said something to Miyoung in English.

"In America, there really aren't any arranged marriages. People marry for love," Teacher Kim translated.

Miyoung's mouth fell open. She didn't know women could have a choice in marriage. Arranged marriages were the norm, and she hadn't thought much about love between members of the opposite sex before, except when she had seen the Lee newlyweds kissing. Bohbeh had talked about love and seemed to believe in it. But no one ever mentioned it around here. The relationship between Miyoung's mother and father was anything but warm.

"People think differently in other parts of the world, don't they?" said Teacher Kim.

Miyoung's skin tingled. *Could I have a choice in whether to get married?* Maybe then she could marry someone she loved or not at all. If she went to church and prayed, maybe she wouldn't have to do things the old way anymore and marry a bully like Ilsoo. A few months ago, she couldn't have imagined going to church, let alone meeting a foreigner who favored a girl's education. Prayer ignited a feeble hope.

Miyoung decided she would ask Mother more about her thoughts on Christianity when she got home. Maybe Mother would let her go to church, or even to the academy after it was built.

This chance came the next day, when Mother was about to rub her Buddhist prayer beads.

"I met my friend Haewon's father, the pastor at the town church. He seems really nice."

Mother massaged her wooden beads together, making a clacking noise.

"Christians believe girls should be educated like boys," said Miyoung.

Mother's shoulders tensed. "Christianity is a white person's faith."

"But you told Father I'm smart and should continue my schooling. They believe in education."

"It doesn't matter. They don't believe in rebirth. Besides, they're changing our ways of doing things."

"I don't understand," Miyoung said.

"I heard that a white Christian midwife told a Korean mother she should feed her baby on a schedule, not every time he cried. What kind of custom is that?! The poor baby!"

Mother's opinion of Christians seemed deep rooted, and Miyoung knew she couldn't change her mind. The next week and every week thereafter, she secretly went to church without her mother's permission. Guilt gnawed at her, but she wanted to learn more.

One Sunday, Miyoung came out of the church and bumped into Mother, who was on her way to the market. Mother's jaw clenched, and her glare pierced Miyoung like a dagger. She grabbed Miyoung by the hair and dragged her all the way home. Mother seemed as strong as an ox pulling a wagon.

When they arrived back at the house, Mother whacked her calves with three bamboo sticks tied together into a long bar, all the while shouting, "I forbid you from going to church again!"

Miyoung winced as the welts on her calves grew. Anger replaced her pain. She was determined to pray, and she would do that behind Mother's back. As Teacher Kim had told her, she didn't need to be inside a church to ask God for help. She closed her eyes before going to bed at night and prayed that if she studied hard enough, the possibilities for her future would open wide.

CHAPTER SEVEN

March 1930

"Miyoung-*ah*!" Mother yelled one evening, calling for her to come. Over a year had passed since Bohbeh left home, and it had been one month since Miyoung graduated from primary school in February. The school year always ended during one of the coldest months of the year, and this year's frigid winter was no exception.

Miyoung hurried to Mother, her chest beating for news about her future. She was thirteen now, and still hopeful that her secret prayers had changed Mother's mind about sending her off to marry.

With her wiry hand, Mother patted the heated ondol floor, inviting Miyoung to sit. She was smiling, not scowling as usual from the chronic ache in her legs. She was constantly hunched over now and slept in late most days. Miyoung had picked up all Bohbeh's chores when she left and had in time taken over more of Mother's duties, like carrying from the community well a water crock balanced on her head.

Tonight, Mother shifted back and forth on her cushion, like she was eager to talk.

Miyoung sat down on her knees in front of Mother and held her breath. The floor warmed her legs, which were cold after sweeping snow from a sudden storm off the courtyard steps. Miyoung had grown several inches in the last year, so she could almost gaze straight into Mother's eyes. Normally, Mother would want her to read aloud while she knitted in the evenings. She would smile while listening to Miyoung recite the words she could not read herself. Miyoung had tried to teach her mother how to read, but she had resisted, saying it was too late. Instead, Mother taught her how to knit, even praising her stitches. Lately, though, Mother had been dropping the needles so much that she stopped knitting altogether. Tonight it seemed she had something else on her mind.

"I talked to Teacher Kim," Mother said. "She was very polite to me, as usual. She said that you're ready for middle school."

The words Miyoung had been waiting to hear! She squirmed with excitement.

Mother shifted her legs to sidesaddle and lifted one knee up. Miyoung's breath caught in her throat; she knew Mother was getting ready to tell her something important.

"Teacher Kim recommended you to the girls' academy in Pyongyang," Mother said, without emotion.

"That's wonderful!" Miyoung shouted.

"But I can't send you there," Mother said.

A gasp left Miyoung's lips. "Why not?"

"It's a Christian school. And it costs money."

"But . . ." The world seemed to be opening up and closing at once. "How about the new school here?" Miyoung asked, grasping at what the missionary had said.

"It won't be finished for years. It's also a Christian school."

"What does it matter?" Miyoung forgot all that she had been taught about respect for her elders.

"Hush. If you're going to go to school, a traditional Confucian education is best, not a Western one."

Miyoung's head was spinning. She had been handed the gift of a lifetime, and it had been taken back in one fell swoop.

"So I've decided you'll go to middle school in Japan, where it's free."

Miyoung's eyes doubled in size. "School in Japan?" Bohbeh was in Japan. Did this mean she could see Bohbeh again?

"When I said no to sending you to the Christian school, Teacher Kim mentioned that it doesn't cost money to attend public middle school in Japan."

Miyoung pinched her ears to make sure she was hearing this correctly. This was beyond her wildest dreams.

"I thought about Bohbeh and decided I would write to her to see if you could live with her and her husband. Here is what she said." Glowing, Mother reached inside her cardigan pocket and handed over a thin letter.

"But how . . . ?" Mother couldn't read or write, so she was surprising Miyoung at every turn.

"I didn't want to get you excited, so I asked Mrs. Lee, the clerk at the post office, if she could write Bohbeh a letter."

Miyoung's fingers shook as she caressed the note. *Please let Miyoung come to Japan. My husband approves, as long as she helps with housework. I will come get her in late July,* Bohbeh had written in her usual brief manner.

"Is this real?" Miyoung shouted, sheer happiness dancing behind her smile. First, she would get the chance to go to middle school, and second, she would see her sister again! Her prayers had been answered.

Mother grinned too, not caring this time if her crooked teeth showed. When they were eating dinner alone, Mother often told Miyoung that the only two things she wanted were to see Bohbeh again and for Miyoung to be educated so that she wouldn't be cheated like Mother had been.

"How about . . . the marriage?" Miyoung asked, afraid that mentioning it might cause all this good news to disappear.

"Father told me Ilsoo has been sent to Kyushu to work in a coal mine. His family lost their farm too, and they need their son's salary for support. He lives in a dormitory with other Korean miners, and they don't allow married men."

"Does that mean . . . I don't have to marry him?" Hope swelled in Miyoung's throat.

"His parents don't know when he's coming back. I convinced Father that you couldn't wait forever if another opportunity came up."

Miyoung crinkled her face. Ilsoo might be out of the picture, but she still had to marry? Did Mother have someone else in mind?

"When Father told me about Ilsoo being sent away and maybe having to pay the matchmaker again, I brought up Teacher Kim's recommendation that you continue schooling in Japan."

Miyoung was on the edge of her cushion. "And . . . ?"

"Father was against the idea at first. But I told him that since there's a large community of Koreans in Japan, there might be more Korean men to marry there, in case things fell through with Ilsoo."

"Oh . . . ," Miyoung said, hanging her head in disappointment.

"He agreed to pay for Bohbeh's fare back and forth, and for your fare there." Mother's voice sang, like she was pleased with herself for making all these arrangements.

Miyoung's mind whirled with the mixed news. Even though Father was still worried about getting her married, it was off for now. Miyoung was thrilled to be able to study in Japan and see Bohbeh again. "Gamsahamnida!" Thank you!

"No one will be able to take advantage of you like that scoundrel Shin did to me!" As Mother said this, she blew into her hands and rubbed them, as if she were trying to get warm. What Teacher Kim called the Siberian winds were persistent this year, whipping down the mountains and drilling into their flesh. The sun went down early too, even though it was mid-March and almost time for the tiny mulberry buds to sprout in her tree, as they did every year. Miyoung tried to put a blanket over Mother's shoulders, but Mother waved her off. "I'm fine. I want you to have the best education possible. To me, that's as important as getting married."

Mother's shivering nagged Miyoung. She had grown increasingly frail, unable to move about as quickly as before. The other day, Mother had spilled all the water Miyoung had fetched from the well while transferring it from the bucket to the urn. "That was careless of me!" Mother had said as Miyoung's brows furrowed.

She worried about Mother's deteriorating health. She wondered why Mother was sending her away if it was getting more difficult for her to do simple tasks. Usually, parents wanted their daughters to live with them until they got married so that they could help them. She didn't want to ask Mother, fearing it would change her mind. Still, sadness tugged at her for leaving Mother alone, as Mother would be all by herself with no daughter to help. The excitement of a new future, however, pulled harder. Maybe Mother could join them in Japan later if it was as nice as Miyoung imagined.

Miyoung envisioned a large school in Japan with lots of books and inspiring teachers. She learned things quickly and was sure her Japanese would get better fast, especially since she already knew basic hiragana and katakana from school. And she hadn't just sat in the classroom and studied; she had helped teach the younger students, so she was already teacher material. Maybe she would even make some new friends in Japan.

"Thank you, Mother!" Miyoung said, bowing over and over. Although she might have to marry later, she had something no other girl in her village had: a chance to carve a new path for herself.

CHAPTER EIGHT

July 1930

Miyoung leaned against her mulberry tree, waiting for Bohbeh to come home after two long years. Miyoung's legs were too long and heavy to scramble up the trunk these days, but she wanted to catch the first glimpse of her sister from her favorite spot. Sweetness tickled her nose from the juicy chamoe melon she had just cut up to share with Bohbeh again, like in old times.

Miyoung had spent her thirteenth summer looking forward to the moment when Bohbeh would return to take her to Japan. Every day, she helped Mother make tofu and take care of the chickens, but her mind often drifted into wondering what her life would be like there. Some days she would be excited, but on others she would be terrified. Now Miyoung would be able to hear all about Japan from Bohbeh herself. She could finally confirm whether she had made the right decision.

The squeals of the neighborhood children snapped her to attention. Skinny figures in tattered clothing surrounded her sister like she was the last queen of Korea.

"Eonni!" the girls cried in unison.

"Nuna!" the boys grunted.

The shuffling of their bare feet shrouded Bohbeh in a cloud of dust, and when she emerged, she smiled broadly, more beautiful than ever. Her hair was pulled back in a low bun, like a lady who had gotten married in the village last year. Bohbeh was wearing a green hanbok, not a kimono, like Miyoung had seen Japanese women wear in photos. Bohbeh doled out small bits of sweet rice cakes, one by one, to eager hands.

"Welcome home!" they chanted noisily, tugging at Bohbeh's sleeves and biting into the rare cakes.

Miyoung's heart raced at seeing her sister. She rushed toward the crowd.

Bohbeh spotted Miyoung and ran over to give her sister a big hug. Extending her arms over Miyoung's shoulders, she took a long look and shook her head.

"How big you've grown!" Bohbeh said.

Bohbeh's teeth gleamed, and her smooth face sparkled in the sunlight. She was even more stunning than Miyoung remembered. The smell of roses floated from her hair, filling in the years of empty space between them. Miyoung sucked in a huge breath, trying to take her sister in.

Mother coughed, and Bohbeh spotted her standing nearby. Her small, slight body rested against the wall of the house, shaded from the sun. Bohbeh turned and walked toward her, back already halfway bent over in a bow.

"Ohmani," Bohbeh said.

"Eoseowa," Mother replied, welcoming Bohbeh home. She tapped Bohbeh on the back stiffly. A thin smile bared Mother's teeth but not her feelings. Her face was stone gray, though Miyoung had seen her sniffling as she made Bohbeh's favorite mung bean pancakes earlier. It seemed Mother was hiding sadness behind a hard mask. Bohbeh would be leaving again in a week and taking Miyoung along too. Miyoung's heart softened as she thought of her mother being all alone, not knowing when she would see her daughters again. She nudged a little closer toward her mother and sister.

Miyoung wanted to spend time alone with Bohbeh, but news of Bohbeh's arrival spread, and various neighbors soon came by to visit. A quiet moment came later in the afternoon, when Miyoung and Bohbeh stole away to the pond where they used to bathe. She was finally able to ask about Bohbeh's life in Japan.

"How is it there, really?" Miyoung asked, lying in the grass on her stomach with her elbows bent, her face pressed closely to Bohbeh's. The broad red mulberry leaves lining the bank shaded them from the stifling heat. As little girls, they used to whisper to each other like this about the photos they had seen in the store calendar. There were beautiful women wearing elegant clothes and standing in front of temples in Japan. Miyoung had imagined Bohbeh's life turning out like the lives of these women. She wanted to hear it directly from her.

Bohbeh had been unusually quiet all day, despite the visitors. Miyoung suspected it was because she was tired from her trip and all the people who had come by to see her. Bohbeh cupped her hands over Miyoung's ear.

"Mr. Chung tricked us. His brother is not an electrician but a meter reader. And he lives in a run-down area where conditions are terrible."

Shock stabbed Miyoung. "I'm sorry," Miyoung said, for her sister as much as herself.

"His name is Haramoto, and we don't live in a big house. We live in a two-room shanty."

"Mr. Chung lied about everything?"

"His brother's not wealthy, and he's a drunk."

Angry hairs stood on Miyoung's arms. She remembered Shin, who had cheated Mother into selling the farm.

"Sometimes Haramoto drinks too much and . . ." Bohbeh's eyes darkened before resuming their usual brightness. "There are reasons Haramoto acts the way he does. His boss promoted someone who is Japanese at work, even though Haramoto has seniority. His boss said if he gave a Korean worker a better title and more money, his Japanese workers would quit."

"That's not fair."

"I know. That's just the way it is. Koreans live in the slums and have dirty jobs. They're garbage workers, restaurant dishwashers, and janitors."

"That sounds awful."

"The Japanese don't want Koreans to live near them, so they don't rent to them. And Koreans can't get good jobs, because those go to the Japanese."

Clouds moved across the bright July sun, dimming the sky. Miyoung swallowed hard, comparing the life she had imagined with what her sister was now describing. She recalled Mr. Chung's comment many years earlier that Koreans were treated like lower-class citizens in Japan, but she hadn't thought much of it. Her father's attitude toward the Japanese had surprised her too. Miyoung wanted to believe that Koreans had better jobs and happier lives there. It was one thing to escape an arranged marriage but another to run into other kinds of misery. Miyoung had only been thinking about her own life, not that of other Koreans. She wondered if getting a free education in Japan was worth the dismal life Bohbeh painted.

Bohbeh inched closer to Miyoung, as if sensing her hesitation. "Don't worry. I've gotten used to it. Even though we're poor and Haramoto drinks all the time, we live in a Korean community, and that makes it tolerable. Besides, we have electricity. I can't believe this place still doesn't have any!"

A laugh bubbled up Miyoung's throat. It would be nice to see at night.

"Your life will be different. You have school to look forward to."

Miyoung's hopes crumbled again. If the Japanese treated Koreans unfairly at work, it could certainly be the same at school. Maybe she shouldn't go. She would miss Mother. And she'd never left home before.

"It'll be okay," Bohbeh said, stroking her hair. Miyoung nudged closer as memories flashed through her mind, memories of Bohbeh saying these comforting words when she'd first left for Japan and telling

Miyoung not to worry about marrying Ilsoo. It had turned out as she'd predicted.

A hot breeze lapped the pond, and visions of old bath days with her sisters emerged. Miyoung saw Bohkee's smiling face reflected in the water. Her sister looked carefree and happy. Even though no one knew what had actually happened to her in Manchuria, maybe being away from here had freed her. Bohbeh wasn't bound by Father's or Mother's rules anymore either. Her life might not be perfect, but it was her own. Miyoung wanted to know what that felt like—to think for herself. Continuing her schooling, something she couldn't afford to do here, would help her do that. And anything seemed better than a life with someone like Ilsoo, a life leading nowhere.

The call of songbirds in the pines woke her, and her courage. Miyoung knew what she needed to do. She would go to Japan to continue her education and be with her sister again. She didn't care if life was difficult there; she would make it work. Now it was the only future she could imagine for herself.

"We can be together again!" Bohbeh said, sitting up decisively.

"Yes!" Miyoung sat up too. As long as they were together, everything would be all right.

And she was sure about one more thing: men tricked women and shouldn't be trusted.

CHAPTER NINE

August 1930

Miyoung packed her meager belongings in an old cloth bag. It paled in comparison to the stiff new trunk that Mother had given Bohbeh when she left, but there was no money for another one. Miyoung was leaving home—the only place she had ever known—in one short week. Knots gathered in her stomach.

Dropping the hanbok she was folding, Miyoung ran outside to find Mother. She was bent over in the garden, picking cucumbers. "Ohmani!" Miyoung shouted. "I don't know if I want to go anymore. What if I want to come home?" When Miyoung had gotten homesick while visiting her cousin in a nearby village last year, her mother had let her return early. Surely her mother would allow her to do the same if she wasn't happy in Japan.

The cucumber Mother was holding slipped out of her hand. She straightened herself up, letting out a moan. "It's all right, Miyoung-ah, gwaenchanh-a. You'll be fine," her mother said, massaging her forearms.

Should Miyoung believe her? Coming home from a neighboring village was a lot different from returning from Japan. And watching Mother pick vegetables, which they always did together, reminded Miyoung of how nice it had been to have her undivided attention these past few years, especially those evenings when she read to Mother or they knit together on the ondol floor. What would she do without her?

She decided to talk to Teacher Kim. She abandoned her packing and nearly ran all the way to the school, which was just ending for the day. A new group of children who had advanced to the highest grade, taking Miyoung and her classmates' former places in the pecking order, came out first. Her eyes caught sight of the wooden seesaw on the playground, and Miyoung pined for her friend Haewon, whose family had moved south to Seoul as soon as school ended, Haewon's father having taken another position at a church down there. Miyoung would miss the village church too, even though she hadn't been inside since Mother had forbidden it.

Teacher Kim was wiping the chalkboard as Miyoung entered.

"It's so nice to see you!" she said, a wide grin spreading across her face.

"Hello," Miyoung said, lowering her lashes. Miyoung hadn't seen her teacher much since she'd graduated in the spring and suddenly felt shy.

"How's everything going?" Teacher Kim asked softly.

"Okay, I guess. I'm going to Japan. I . . . I'll miss you."

"I heard from the other students. I'll miss you too!" Teacher Kim touched Miyoung's shoulder, warming her up inside.

"I'm going to miss home too." Miyoung's voice cracked.

"I know God has a plan for you in Japan. You'll be a great teacher. And remember, you're not alone. He'll always be with you." Teacher Kim's cross necklace glinted in the afternoon sun.

Miyoung closed her eyes to remember this moment. Teacher Kim had inspired her to reach for more. Without her teacher, she wouldn't be on her way to Japan. And if she hadn't been introduced to Mrs. Smith, she wouldn't even know that many people believed that girls deserved to have the same education as boys. Tears welled up over what these women had opened up for her.

"I'll be praying for you, and you know you can too. Just remember to pray when you're lonely. And find a church when you get to Japan."

"I will," Miyoung said, salt water pooling in her eyes.

Teacher Kim opened her desk drawer to fetch something. "By the way, I got this for you. I was planning to give it to you before you left." It was a beautiful cream-colored journal made of mulberry paper. Miyoung smoothed her hands over the bumpy cover, her heart bursting with gratitude. She had never owned a journal before.

"Write your thoughts down in this. And think of home."

Miyoung held the journal to her heart and said a wobbly thank-you. She forced a smile onto her face to show Teacher Kim she was brave and ready to leave. But a fear of the unknown seized Miyoung again. After she left the school, she began behaving in strange ways. She forgot to brush her hair and didn't eat much, although she was usually always hungry. She walked around the village aimlessly, trying to remember everything. The more she thought of home, the more anxious she felt.

Miyoung walked to a familiar spot in the woods and strained to hear the cicadas singing in chorus. She hoped she would hear these low humming sounds in Japan. She snuck into church again just as the bell was beginning to ring and remembered the first time she sang a hymn, the melody soothing her. Teacher Kim had said God would be in her heart too, wherever she was. She hoped there would be a church in Japan, but it was bittersweet that she would no longer have to worry about her mother finding out whether she went.

She struggled up her mulberry tree one last time, her longer legs and heavier frame preventing her from climbing to the best views of the familiar mountains and fields. She would miss the branches that seemed like extensions of her own body. From the sturdiest bough, she spotted the bright-red chili peppers lined up along the dusty dirt road. Tongue watering, she savored the memory of Mother grinding spicy pepper flakes for kimchi, longing for her cooking, even though she hadn't left yet. That was when she knew she would truly miss all these things about Mother, home, and more.

When the morning of Miyoung and Bohbeh's departure came, Mother walked them to the train station. Her limp had gotten worse, so they lumbered slowly with their belongings, leaving early to ensure extra time. There were no villagers surrounding them, as they had said their well-wishes the previous day. Father and Taeyoung had said their farewells a few days ago, when they'd stopped by to see Bohbeh.

"Have a safe journey," Father had said as he pressed a thin envelope of won into Miyoung's palm. His face was without expression, as usual, but she picked up a shaky tone in his voice. It sounded like he was sad she was leaving, but the moment passed too quickly for her to be sure.

The parting with her brother Taeyoung had been especially hard. He was home from his school in Pyongyang for summer break and looked handsome and grown-up in his black-and-white school uniform.

"Write to me, okay? I'll write to you, I promise." Taeyoung had tousled her hair playfully. He had passed her a piece of paper with his address at school scrawled on it, and she held it with both hands like a priceless gift. She made a mental note to write him as soon as she was settled in Japan. She had no desire to write to Father's first wife or her half sisters, who had said their cool goodbyes on her last visit without tenderness or tears.

Though it was a sticky, humid day, Miyoung wore her best blue hanbok and Bohbeh's worn gomushin shoes. Bohbeh had also tied her old pink daenggi to the bottom of Miyoung's single braid, the colorful ribbon swishing as Miyoung walked. Mother waited patiently by the open door of the train, her long hair secured in a low bun by a wooden hairpin. She had given Miyoung her precious jade hairpin as they got ready that morning, and Miyoung felt special as she carefully placed it in her bag. The binyeo, a smooth, delicate jade stick that was rounded at one end, had been a gift to Mother from her own mother. Now that gesture had a new meaning. Miyoung realized that Mother had given her the gift because this might be the last time she would see her.

"Oh-ma-ni!" Miyoung said, exaggerating each syllable. Suddenly she felt like a little girl tugging at her mother's chima. "I don't want to go anymore!" Tears slid down her cheeks.

Both sisters had cried similar words, and Mother had not relented. Miyoung feared the same fate.

"Go to Japan and study. Make something of yourself," Mother said, closing her eyes and taking a big breath.

Miyoung felt Bohbeh's hand squeezing hers tight. She was probably recollecting her own goodbye a few years earlier and feeling Miyoung's pain as her own all over again. Dragging her feet, she followed Bohbeh onto the train.

Bohbeh had tried to ease Miyoung's mind the previous week by assuring her that everything would be fine. She had laid out their travel plans, and it had sounded exciting then. But now that the time had truly come for her to go, Miyoung saw things differently. It would be a long, arduous journey that was probably too expensive to take round trip. She was going so far away that she wasn't even going to be in Korea anymore. She was leaving her mother, her home, and her country—maybe for good.

"Ohmani!" Miyoung called out through the open window of the train, searching for her mother's face again.

Mother's upturned features softened, showing a weakening resolve. There was a wetness to her eyes that looked like tears of regret. That moment evaporated when the whistle blew and the train started to move. Miyoung sobbed as she clung to the windowsill with both hands, watching her mother's figure fade into the distance.

She fumbled around in her cloth bag for her mother's jade hairpin, hoping it would magically bring her old life back and erase this new, uncertain one. She pressed it against her chest and closed her eyes, her shoulders trembling against Bohbeh's. She was going on a trip that had no end: a one-way journey to a foreign country with no return date.

PART TWO

Kyoto, Japan

1930

CHAPTER TEN

September 1930

A foul smell struck Miyoung's nose when she opened her eyes to the morning light. The small tatami-mat room reeked of alcohol and was cluttered with overturned bottles and trash. The stench burned her nose, the same way it had when she'd poured soju for Father at his house on the day she'd turned thirteen this past year. Even though it was her birthday, not his, she was expected to pour for him at his pleasure.

She was far from home here, and alone. Thin strips of sunshine streaked through holes in the tin roof, intersecting at odd angles. Newspaper print pasted on windows cast a dingy yellow tint. A torn shoji door opened to another room where rumpled blankets littered the floor and Bohbeh's trunk lay open. Everything was quiet except for the muffled voice of a next-door neighbor.

Memories stirred of the train screeching into Kyoto late last night and Bohbeh leading her through dark, mazelike streets. They had arrived at a run-down complex filled with families shouting in Korean. Bohbeh had said that this area behind the station was the Korean ghetto of Kyoto, where students, temporary workers, and families, all seeking jobs or better opportunities, occupied cramped wooden buildings with shared walls. When they'd come in, Bohbeh's husband, Mr. Haramoto, was already asleep.

The scent of grilled octopus wafted from the open window. It reminded her of the open-air markets back home. Was it yesterday or the day before that she had left? The familiar odor warmed her tired body, and her stomach grumbled. She wanted to go outside to see what other Korean delicacies she might find, but she decided to wait for Bohbeh so that she wouldn't have to go out alone. Instead, she opened a drawer under some teacups and found a few stale rice crackers. While making loud crunching noises, she surveyed the dirty room. This was not how she had imagined Bohbeh's house to be.

Japan was not what she had expected either. Arriving by ferry from Busan to Shimonoseki, she had been shocked at the frightening sight of uniformed men shouting in Japanese with rifles over their shoulders. The ferry passengers had whispered that the port was the launching point for all of Japan's colonies in the Pacific. Soldiers marched about as if there were a war nearby, but no enemies could be seen. The Japanese soldiers she had spied in Pyongyang seemed gentle compared with these gruff men.

The journey before the ferry ride had been a blur because Miyoung had been crying behind Bohbeh's hanbok sleeve. Her sister had held her hand but didn't talk much, letting Miyoung's tears spill freely. It wasn't until she had landed in Japan and was on the train to Kyoto that the finality of her journey loomed. The morning sun had been peeking through the window, and she was whizzing past a foreign countryside dotted with rice fields, everything she knew left behind. She was going the wrong way, in the opposite direction of home. Some part of her was being left behind too.

Just as Miyoung was thinking that she wanted to go back to Korea, the front door of the shanty slid open, and Bohbeh walked in.

"Ohayo!" Bohbeh said, greeting her for the first time in Japanese. "That's how you say hello here." Bohbeh always tried to be cheerful, even when the world seemed upside down. Miyoung admired her for her positive spirit, something she lacked just then.

"O-ha-yo!" Miyoung said, the short, staccato syllables sounding abrupt, unlike the curves and dips of her Korean tongue. Even though she had learned basic Japanese at her village school, using it in real life was not going to be easy.

"I'm so glad I took the day off work today," Bohbeh said. "I'm tired from the trip and didn't want to wash dishes all day at the restaurant. Besides, I got you enrolled at the local Japanese middle school this morning. You start next week."

Miyoung imagined herself standing in front of a classroom filled with Japanese students and being unable to speak. "But I don't know any Japanese yet! What about a Korean school here?" She had heard there were Korean-speaking schools in Japan too.

"You can't get a job if you graduate from a Korean school. And they're private, so they cost money."

"Oh," Miyoung said, her head hanging. "But how am I going to learn the language so fast?"

"Don't worry," Bohbeh said, smiling. "We have some language books here. And I heard there are a few other Korean students at the school. You can ask them for help."

The thought of meeting fellow Korean speakers relaxed Miyoung's stomach.

"Besides, the school said you'll be repeating sixth grade, so you can catch up on your Japanese. Since schools in Japan begin in April and end in March, like in Korea, you'll be in the middle of sixth grade with the younger students."

Miyoung liked that. Maybe schoolwork would be easier, then. She was small for her thirteen years, so she might fit in better.

"You must be hungry," Bohbeh said, her eyes catching the cracker crumbs on the table. "I need to get some dinner for Haramoto-san, so let's go to the market."

That afternoon, Bohbeh took Miyoung's hand and pulled her along narrow, pedestrian-only streets packed with Korean food vendors and restaurants. The wooden buildings were slapped together, and Miyoung could see lines of Korean and Japanese signs. Heaps of cabbage, mounds of red pepper flakes, and vats of creamy red gochujang paste stood for sale on the road. Almost every part of a pig hung from inside a window. Miyoung slurped a bowl of refreshing Korean mul naengmyeon that reminded her of the Pyongyang-style noodles from home, cooling her sticky skin. She chomped on blood sausages while sitting atop a rickety stool outside a restaurant, her ears growing accustomed to the mixed Korean and Japanese chatter around her. The shouts of the Korean ajummas, asking passersby to try their fried mandu and sample their dried cuttlefish, warmed her homesick heart.

City life was new to Miyoung. She didn't know that buildings made of corrugated metal could lean so much without falling. People lived in shacks that were thrown together out of scraps of tin. Trash was heaped into piles and left to rot. Laundry hung between buildings, and soiled water ran down the sides of the roads. She wanted to pinch her nose at some of the awful smells.

The people looked different too. Grandmothers wore traditional Korean hanboks, but younger people donned Western clothes. A few women dressed in kimonos, and children ran around without any clothes at all, peeing on the street. Male schoolchildren wore black uniforms; girls, pleated skirts and collared shirts.

"That reminds me," Bohbeh said. "I have a uniform for you that the school gave me."

Miyoung was relieved to learn she was going to wear the same outfit as the other girls. She didn't want to stand out as the new student.

Bohbeh pulled her into a store with a noren hanging over the door, a short navy-blue curtain with Japanese writing. She picked up premade fried chicken, pickled yellow radishes, and fish cakes. These were not typical Korean dishes and didn't look appetizing. Bohbeh stopped to buy a bottle of something that Miyoung recognized from the house earlier. "Haramoto-san likes Japanese sake, which is like Korean soju. He doesn't want to have Korean food in the house. He thinks he's Japanese!"

So Bohbeh disapproved of Haramoto's liking Japanese things. She noted that her sister was wearing a hanbok and had drunk the cold Korean noodle broth directly from the metal bowl with both hands, wiping her lips with the back of her jeogori sleeve. She still looked and acted very Korean. Strangely, she recalled that there were only Japanese crackers in the couple's room, even though the market had an abundance of Korean brands.

By the time they got back home and set dinner on the low table, the hot sun was already setting.

"Tadaima," Haramoto said in Japanese, announcing his arrival home and taking his shoes off in the narrow entryway.

Miyoung's first glimpse of Bohbeh's husband triggered memories of his older brother in Korea. Mr. Haramoto was a stocky, balding man who, like his brother, had a short mustache. His leathery face was lined with wrinkles, and Miyoung guessed he might be about Father's age.

The couple greeted each other with silence, as if they were strangers, even though they had been married for almost two years.

"This is my sister Miyoung," Bohbeh said.

Miyoung bowed shyly.

Haramoto gave a quick nod, but his mouth remained shut, though he was meeting his wife's sister for the first time. He was wearing a gray uniform that bore his Japanese name, just as his brother had said. Miyoung had observed in the market that some Koreans called each other by their Korean names, but Bohbeh called him Haramoto-san, his Japanese name. He also liked to be referred to as an electrician, though he walked around reading meters.

"Itadakimasu," Haramoto grunted as he sat at the low table to eat. He chewed his food loudly and guzzled his sake in the same manner as his brother. Bohbeh motioned for Miyoung to kneel with her behind him, ready to retrieve anything he needed.

When he asked for the evening paper, Bohbeh obediently brought it to him. When he finished, he went to the bedroom and slid the door closed. Miyoung hoped she would never get married if this was what marriage looked like. Bohbeh acted a lot like Mother did with Father—obeying everything he said.

Bohbeh exhaled and whispered to Miyoung, "Now let's eat." She reset the table with spicy chonggak radish kimchi, seasoned vermicelli noodles, fried fish battered with eggs, and a small bowl of white rice. "Let's celebrate your first meal in your new home!"

"That rice must have cost a fortune!" Miyoung said. Despite the shabby living quarters, Bohbeh welcomed her generously. "Thank you, eonni. You have been so good to me to bring me here and sign me up for school."

"In Kyoto, 'thank you' is *o-kini*."

"O-kini." Miyoung tried out the awkward sounds.

The next night, Haramoto drank a large amount of sake with his dinner, more than the previous day. As Miyoung was getting ready for bed, she heard quarreling in the next room. There was a sound like the flick of a wet towel against skin, then silence. Fear for her sister crawled through her. She remembered what her sister had said at the bathing pond in Korea: that Haramoto drank a lot because his Japanese colleagues got more promotions. Maybe Haramoto had been passed up for a better job again. Regardless, Haramoto shouldn't take it out on Bohbeh. Miyoung would make sure to be extra nice to Bohbeh the next day and run errands without complaint.

For the next week before she started school, Miyoung helped Bohbeh around the house and went to the market. She studied the tattered Korean–Japanese language book that Bohbeh had given her. She memorized a few practical phrases, such as "My name is . . ." and "Excuse me, how can I find . . . ?" Then she practiced them on Haramoto when he returned from work. He was actually nice when he wasn't drinking. While reading store signs and listening to people's conversations around town, she recalled lessons from her Japanese language class in Korea. Teacher Kim had taught her to love languages, and she resolved to improve her Japanese and do well in school to make her teacher proud.

CHAPTER ELEVEN

September 1930

Nerves banged Miyoung's chest as she got ready for her first day of school in Japan. She scrubbed her face extra clean and dressed in her two-piece uniform. The black long-sleeved shirt with a white collar was wrinkled, and the matching pleated skirt was loose, but she didn't mind. She was glad she would look like everyone else. Her pulse quickened as she imagined what her new school was like and whether she would make new friends there.

Bohbeh dropped her off at the large stone entrance gate, promising to meet her after school. Miyoung watched her sister walk away and disappear into a crowd of people before she turned around to march in with the other children. The school was a combined primary and middle school, so giggling young kids crowded in with pockmarked teenagers. Bracing herself, Miyoung held her head high, trying to look brave as she headed toward the looming two-story concrete building. This school seemed so big and cold compared with her village's one-room schoolhouse. There was a spacious lawn and some bushes below the windows. Before she even reached the double front doors, a boy of about ten bumped into her and almost knocked her over.

The pudgy kid shouted something in Japanese, pointed his finger at Miyoung, and then pinched his nose. Miyoung had no idea what he was saying, but she knew it had something to do with the way she smelled. She wanted to disappear. By then, a group of children had formed around her and started to chant. Someone tugged on her braids. Miyoung's head snapped back, her face flushing hot.

Run! she thought, but then a man interrupted them. He had a dimpled chin and kind eyes behind a pair of round glasses. "Ohno Haruki, Nomura Ichijo!" the man shouted, calling the kids by name and motioning for them to go inside. He must have been a teacher, since all the children listened. Miyoung trailed behind the crowd. Everyone took off their shoes before entering the building, as they'd done at her old school, and Miyoung followed. It seemed that the younger kids went down one hallway to the primary school and the teenagers went down another to the middle school.

The teacher led her to the front office, said something to the clerk, and left. The clerk was stamping papers and ignored her. Miyoung remembered the piece of paper Bohbeh had given her with her Korean name and some other information in Japanese. She handed the sheet to the clerk, who grabbed it with two fingers like it was dirty. Seeing *Miyoung* written on the page, she thought it looked so foreign compared with the Japanese kids' names the teacher had called out earlier. Muttering what sounded like "Yamamoto-sensei," the clerk pointed to a classroom down the hall where the younger children had gone.

Miyoung tiptoed into the class, and the same nice man she had met earlier looked up from his desk at the front of the room. He smiled and gestured to an empty seat in the back. Unlike the low desks back at her old school, the wooden desks were raised, and the students sat behind them on a bench. As Miyoung made her way between two rows, someone tripped her, and she stumbled. Laughter echoed through the classroom before Yamamoto-sensei could tap his pointer and say, "Shhh." All eyes turned toward Miyoung, and the children whispered in one another's ears. She heard the word *Chōsenjin* but didn't know what that meant. After that labeling, none of the students paid attention to her. She tried hard to concentrate on the lesson, but since it was all in Japanese, she didn't understand much.

At lunchtime, Miyoung pretended to be writing in the notebook Bohbeh had given her so that she could wait for everyone to file out of the classroom. She didn't want to face the kid who had tripped her earlier. A girl walked toward her, and Miyoung froze.

"My name is Jimin," the girl said in Korean. Miyoung softened at hearing her native tongue. This Korean girl had a friendly smile and bright eyes.

"I'm Miyoung," she replied. The tightness in her stomach loosened for the first time that day, and she suddenly had to go to the bathroom. She fidgeted from side to side.

"Are you okay?" Jimin asked.

"Sorry, but can you show me where the bathroom is?" A flush crept across Miyoung's cheeks.

Jimin grinned and led her down the hall. There was a frosted-glass door that separated the bathroom area from the rest of the school. Miyoung slipped on a pair of communal rubber slippers and shuffled to an open door. The toilet wasn't more than a hole in the ground, but she was relieved to find it.

"Come with me," Jimin said when Miyoung finished.

Jimin took her to the side of the building, where a few kids ate lunch on a grassy patch. To Miyoung's relief, they were speaking Korean with one another and eating food similar to what she had packed in her lunch: a divided box of millet, kimchi, and boiled potatoes. She was reassured when they said they had been treated the same way on their first days of school.

"The Japanese kids hate us," a Korean boy with a shaved head said. "They think all we do is eat garlic, so we stink!"

Miyoung hung her head in disappointment. It hurt to be so despised just because she was Korean.

A girl with a mole on her cheek whispered, "There's only five of us Korean kids here at the primary school."

"How do you know? There're probably others at the middle school too," the large shaved-headed boy said. The buttons on his uniform were about to pop off, and his pants were too short, like he'd just gone through a growth spurt.

"Why don't you know for sure?" Miyoung asked, puzzled.

"These Korean kids are fluent in Japanese and use Japanese names to blend in, so no one knows they're Korean. See that big, tough-looking kid over there where the middle school students hang out? I heard he's the head of a Korean gang, even though he uses a Japanese name."

She looked across the dirt field and saw a group of teenage boys huddled together. Based on what had happened to her this morning, Miyoung understood why someone might want to disguise their Korean background. Since Koreans and Japanese looked physically similar, it probably wouldn't be too difficult to pass as the other. She wondered what it would be like to pretend to be Japanese. It would likely protect her heart from pain. It would be a lot easier to get by.

Miyoung spent the rest of the afternoon trying to catch bits and pieces of this foreign tongue. Yamamoto-sensei kindly offered her a Japanese language book to take home, to add to the one Bohbeh had already given her. When Bohbeh picked her up that afternoon and they were out of sight of the school, Miyoung crumpled.

"They made fun of me for being Korean!" Miyoung said, complaining like her younger Korean classmates had. Her face burned.

"What do you mean?" Bohbeh asked. "What happened?"

Miyoung explained how her Japanese classmates had treated her. "It was awful! I don't know if it would be any different at the middle school, but something tells me no."

"Shhh, dongsaeng," Bohbeh said, calling her "little sister" and stroking her arm. "I haven't gone to school here, but I've been shoved out of line at the market when wearing my hanbok around. You get used to it. But I know it's hard."

That night, Miyoung went to bed clutching her mother's jade hairpin, crying like a little girl again. She had a nightmare in which she was running through the barley fields near her old village and getting chased by Japanese soldiers. She saw her lost sister Bohkee, but Bohkee's eyes were hollow and her hair white. A ghost. Miyoung screamed silently. When she opened her mouth, no words came out. Her voice seemed completely gone, and she couldn't speak any language.

The next few days at school were no better. The Japanese kids taunted her whenever they got a chance. When Yamamoto-sensei wasn't looking, they would push her down or knock her books out of her arms. They would hide her shoes after class. The other Korean kids were treated the same.

"Why don't you fight back?" Miyoung asked Jimin.

"It's no use. They'll just do it again."

"What about the teachers? Can't they stop the teasing?" Miyoung knew that Yamamoto-sensei would tell the kids to be quiet.

"Some teachers try, some don't," Jimin said. "Most teachers just ignore it."

Miyoung didn't see much hope for change at school. Her lips wore a permanent frown, and a sadness settled in her heart.

Miyoung decided to write to her mother about what was happening and ask to go home. Even if this meant she would have to get married someday and forgo her education, the hurt was unbearable. She knew Mother wouldn't be able to read the letter herself, so she hoped Mrs. Lee at the post office would help her. She counted the days for a response, and at the end of September, a thin, crumpled letter came back that bore their old Korean address. She and Bohbeh read it together at the table. In someone else's shaky hand, Mother had written:

> Daughter,
> I'm sorry about all the teasing at school.
> It's not fair, but just know it's not your fault.
> The opportunities are still better there than here.
> Study hard. Listen to your sister and teachers.
> Remember the proverb "After hardship comes happiness."
> Mother

Miyoung creased the letter in half, folding up her loneliness. Mother had probably never planned to let Miyoung come home, and that's why she had given her the jade hairpin. Miyoung would have to live in Japan, even though she was miserable. That silly proverb couldn't be right. She couldn't imagine being happy here.

"Eonni, what am I going to do?" Miyoung asked Bohbeh.

"I'm so sorry. How about your Korean classmates? Can you be friends with them?"

"Jimin is kind and talks to me. I guess I'll just stick with the other Korean students." At least Miyoung had them.

"Wait, I have an idea," Bohbeh said. "Why don't we give you a Japanese name?"

"A Japanese name?" Miyoung trembled with possibility. "Really? Do you have one?" She was surprised that her sister hadn't mentioned this before.

"My Japanese name is Aiko," Bohbeh said. "It means 'love child.' I gave myself the name because I still believe in love, I guess. I don't use it that much, though. I prefer my Korean name."

A small crack of hope opened. What kind of name would she have? She remembered wondering whether she would change inside if she had a Japanese name. Staying true to herself didn't matter. Maybe the kids would treat her better.

"You mean you can pick a name, just like that?"

"Yes. The Japanese don't care, because your identification card shows your real Korean name."

It was true. Bohbeh had taken her to the district office to register for an identification card that said she was Suhr Miyoung.

"Let's see. Miyoung means 'beautiful' and 'brave' in Korean, right? What about Miyoko? It means 'beautiful child' in Japanese."

That sounded nice. Miyoung wanted to be beautiful and liked. Maybe others would see her this way if she had a Japanese name like that. She could grow into the brave part of her real name later.

"Yes!" Miyoung said, excitement striking again. She savored the image of the Japanese kids calling her Miyoko and inviting her to be their friend. When she got to middle school, everyone would be used to her Japanese name.

Knowing that going back to Korea was not an option, Miyoung decided she was going to push herself harder to succeed in school. Her new name recharged her. She would dress and act as Japanese as possible. It was the only way she was going to survive.

CHAPTER TWELVE

October 1930

"Miyoko, Miyoko," Miyoung muttered to herself while walking to school. Fall leaves crunched underfoot as she repeated her new name.

Miyoung approached Yamamoto-sensei before the first bell rang, her chest thumping. "Onegaishimasu. Please call me Haramoto Miyoko from now on." The request tumbled out and couldn't be taken back.

"Hai. Haramoto Miyoko," Yamamoto-sensei said, dipping his head and smiling.

Miyoung was now Miyoko. Her Japanese teacher had accepted her request, and she was relieved and sad at the same time. But it would be worth it if her new name allowed her to have more friends and become a teacher like him someday.

At lunch, Miyoko joined her Korean friends as usual, away from the playground packed with the younger Japanese students.

"So you decided to become Japanese?" Minho said with his mouth full.

No one spoke. Miyoko hadn't expected this kind of reaction from her friends. She tried to explain. "I thought it would be easier to fit in."

"Well," said Jimin, "I think that's just giving in. You should keep your own name."

Miyoko's breath caught in her throat. She had thought Jimin would be on her side; after all, Jimin had been so welcoming and had invited her into this group.

"Yeah," Jungsoo, the boy with the shaved head, said. "They won't treat you any differently because you have a Japanese name. You're just lying to yourself and everyone else."

Blood rushed to Miyoko's face. She felt torn. Guilt gnawed at her heart, lodging itself there.

The Korean kids left after lunch without asking her to join them. She watched with longing as the girls linked their arms together, laughing.

When she got home, she wrote in her mulberry journal, thinking of Teacher Kim. She decided to write to her, and when Teacher Kim's reply letter arrived a month later, she held it tight against her chest in anticipation.

> Dear Miyoung,
> I was so happy to receive your letter! The weather is turning colder here. I trust you are keeping warm in Japan.
>
> I'm glad you have a nice Japanese teacher. Lean on him for help with your studies. You will flourish as a student, I know it.
>
> I understand why you want to use a Japanese name. It must not be easy to be teased all the time. Do what you need to do to make your life a little easier. God has a plan for you, so be patient. I pray for your safety and well-being.
>
> Your teacher

Miyoko returned to school determined. For the next few months, she became fixated on improving her Japanese and read almost every Japanese book in the school library. Japanese was difficult to learn, but the sentence structure was similar to that in Korean, and she pronounced words out loud to practice her accent. Her persistence paid off, and she was soon speaking and reading comfortably. She asked Bohbeh to buy her a cheap kimono. When she wasn't wearing her uniform to school, Miyoko wore the simple purple kimono around town. Before long, she could pass as Japanese in front of strangers.

Bohbeh's lips pressed tight every time she saw this new side of her. "It's one thing to have a Japanese name, but don't forget where you came from." She called Miyoko by her Korean name at home.

"I don't like it, but I can't tell you what to do," Bohbeh said, her voice soothing. "If I were as smart as you, I might do the same thing."

Miyoko warmed at her sister's response. For her, this was the only way to get ahead in school and become a teacher someday. She didn't want to be an outsider anymore.

Haramoto, on the other hand, took a shine to the new Miyoko. He had long given up his Korean name and seemed proud of it. Lounging in a cotton yukata after work, he downed his sake in one gulp and smacked his lips.

"Nihongo ga jouzu desu ne, Miyoko-chan!" Haramoto said. He added *chan* to her name as a term of endearment and praised her Japanese.

"Iie," Miyoko said, denying the compliment. It was customary to show humility and deference when speaking Japanese. If someone spoke highly of you, you were supposed to protest.

"Your Japanese name suits you," Haramoto said.

"Ah so desu ka?" Miyoko said, asking if it was so, showing that she was listening intently.

"Since we live in Japan, we should use Japanese names."

"So desu ne," Miyoko said, acknowledging that was true.

"Changing your name doesn't mean changing your blood." Haramoto seemed certain of that statement.

"So desu ka?" Miyoko said, wondering herself. She wasn't sure.

"You get it," Haramoto said, glowing. "It's best we adapt to Japanese ways."

Miyoko was curious what people in Korea would think of her new Japanese name. How would her old friend Haewon react? What would Mother think? Her letter, which had said that Miyoko should stay put because her life was still better in Japan than in Korea, probably meant Mother would approve. Miyoko needed to do the best she could to be like everyone else, even if belonging meant letting go of everything Korean.

Regardless of Miyoko's new name, all the Japanese students at her school still knew she was Korean and continued to bully her. Haramoto's statement was true. She couldn't stop being Korean just by changing her name.

"Miyoung thinks she's Miyoko now! Well, she still smells like a Chōsenjin," a big boy named Ryusuke said, sticking his tongue out. When a new girl, Sachiko, came to school and they became friends, Miyoko was happy. But when the other girls whispered something into Sachiko's ear, she moved from Miyoko's side to the Japanese girls' circle, giggling. The rejection stung hard.

Miyoko felt split in half. She could pretend to be Japanese on the outside, but her blood was still Korean, like Haramoto had said. She remembered wondering whether it changed who you were inside if you had a new name, but she still wasn't sure. She didn't feel whole.

The longer she acted Japanese, the more her childhood self seemed to slip away, and the more her memories of her village faded. She looked in the mirror, turning her head from side to side, and the contours of her face blurred. She was becoming Japanese in other people's eyes, but there was still something missing. A gap remained in her heart for home and Mother, for the old Miyoung perched in her mulberry tree. A shadow of her former self lurked somewhere unseen.

Miyoko asked Yamamoto-sensei if she could clean the classroom at lunch to avoid others. His eyes softened as he handed her the eraser to wipe the chalkboard, and he never said anything when she sat alone at an empty desk to eat. He was kind and made students write notes of apology to Miyoko when they called her names. Her chest filled with appreciation for her Japanese teacher, but when he stuck up for her, the other kids snickered and turned up their noses even more. She couldn't win.

Another student named Yumiko often stayed behind in Yamamoto-sensei's class at lunch too. Yumiko was quiet and got along with the other Japanese students. Miyoko was curious why she wasn't outside with them. One day, Yumiko offered Miyoko her extra rice roll wrapped in seaweed, but it had been brushed with oil—how Korean seaweed was prepared. The Japanese version was made with coarse, dry seaweed.

As they ate in silence, Yumiko pulled out a pencil and wrote her Korean name in hangul—Yuhjung. Miyoko's heart skipped a beat, and she spelled out M-i-y-o-u-n-g in hangul. A smile spread across Miyoko's face as she met Yumiko's warm gaze. They ate together at lunch almost every day, whispering in Korean. She suspected there were other students who were not really Japanese and hid their identity just to get along too.

Yumiko lived close to Miyoko in the Korean section of Kyoto, and once in a while, they would meet on the weekends to explore their neighborhood. Yumiko had been born in Japan, but her family originally came from Seoul. The girls held hands and strolled by stores with colorful vertical banners advertising everything from Japanese tempura to hand-cut Korean noodles.

One Sunday afternoon on her way back from meeting her friend, Miyoko noticed a group of people in hanboks entering a discreet wooden building and looking over their shoulders, as if someone might be following them. Before the doors closed, she caught the name Grace Church written in Korean on the wall. The Japanese worshipped at Shinto shrines with bright-red torii gates; she hadn't been to a Christian church here yet or even really seen one.

When Miyoko peeked inside, she discovered a group of people praying. One of them reminded her of Taeyoung—tall, cropped hair, glasses. She imagined her half brother in a room filled with books at his high school in Pyongyang. The last letter she had received from him was short, just letting her know that he had settled in and was enjoying school. She had written him back but was too embarrassed to tell him about her new name.

The young man at the front was discussing a Bible verse aloud in Korean. She recognized the scripture from one of Pastor Nam's sermons at home. The message was "open your eyes that you may see the wonderful things in God's law."

She was immediately transported to her old village and the tall wooden church with the peaked windows. Behind a giant tree outside, she had watched the villagers gawking through glass in their simple white hanboks. Warmth tingled her fingertips as she remembered the small, humble church and how serene she had felt when she entered its doors. Maybe God had followed her on this journey and was watching out for her here in Japan. Teacher Kim had told her to trust God, but she wasn't sure she could trust anyone anymore. She was separated from everything and almost everyone she loved. She was alone.

The man who looked like Taeyoung spoke up.

"Welcome," he said to Miyoko in a soothing Korean voice. "My name is Song Woosun. Would you like to join us?"

Gentle eyes stared out from behind wire-rimmed glasses. "Yes," Miyoko peeped, reluctant to trust another stranger.

"What's your name?"

"My name is . . ." Miyoko hesitated for a second, trying to gauge whether this young man would frown upon her dual name. She took a chance. "My name is Suhr Miyoung, but I go by Haramoto Miyoko."

Woosun's smile lingered, and he seemed unfazed by her admission. Relieved, Miyoko closed her eyes and folded her palms together. After the sermon, she asked Woosun another question.

"Why are you praying in secret?"

Woosun's face fell. "The Japanese don't like it when groups of Koreans gather, even for church. They think we're forming another March First Movement like we did in Korea in 1919. The Japanese may be keeping track of our activities."

"I see." Miyoko thought of the policemen she saw patrolling the streets not too far away. She knew from talk in the Korean enclave that many different anti-government groups had formed in Japan since the Samil Movement of 1919. During that incident, Japan had brutally repressed a peaceful protest; thousands of people perished, and villages and churches were burned.

"Besides, Japanese believe in the Shinto gods, not our God," Woosun said.

Miyoko was well aware of the allegiance they pledged to the Japanese flag at school every morning, and of the abundance of shrines everywhere.

She felt at ease in this new church with Korean-speaking people, and soon she was showing up every Sunday afternoon. She learned that the congregation consisted of mostly young Korean men who attended different Japanese universities in the area. Some of the women were their sisters. Since Miyoko was the youngest girl at thirteen, they were kind, making room for her to kneel next to them during the service. A feeling of home settled inside her chest.

After Miyoko had attended church for a few Sundays, Woosun gave her a Bible. "You can have this."

Miyoko held it gingerly with both hands. No one had ever lent her a Bible before, let alone given her one, and she remembered Haewon's father clutching his while he sermonized. When she got home, she brightened at discovering that the Bible was written in Japanese with a Korean translation. She copied scriptures in Japanese, helping her to learn the language even faster. Taking in long, even breaths, she read that God would never leave or forsake her, that his love was unfailing, and that he would always protect and guide her.

Still, questions lingered. How could God allow people to treat each other this way? How could he let her classmates harass her for being Korean? She knew she should be honest about her identity, but that would mean she'd suffer. She needed to protect herself by pretending to be Japanese, even if she wasn't being true to herself. A heaviness took root in her heart for living this lie.

CHAPTER THIRTEEN

1931–1933

As the icy winds whipped across Kyoto that first winter, Miyoko quietly studied and went to church. Huddled under the heated kotatsu table at Bohbeh's house, she learned Japanese from textbooks, novels, poetry collections, and the Bible. Haiku moved her the most because they described nature, especially this one by the nineteenth-century poet and artist Hokusai.

> I write, erase, rewrite
> Erase again, and then
> A poppy blooms.

Like the flower in the poem, Miyoko burst with determination, and she became a top student at Taiho Primary School. She moved on to the two-year middle school and earned high marks there too. She ignored the torment that she and other Korean students who assimilated endured. Miyoko was right; she was not treated better in middle school. She was shunned by the Japanese girls and the Korean girls who had decided to keep their Korean names. Her friend Yumiko, who had befriended her in sixth grade, had gone to a different middle school.

The Korean middle school boys didn't fare any better. One boy who used a Japanese alias was caught stealing from another student and suspended. Several boys who used their Korean names and cut classes were known as truants and spurned. One boy moved to a Korean school, but when he tried to come back, the school wouldn't allow the transfer.

To succeed, Miyoko knew she had to keep her anger and disappointment hidden, just like she had her true identity. Besides, that was the way of the model Japanese student—not to be seen or heard in the classroom. Although it broke her spirit, she never raised her hand in class, even if she knew the right answer. She conformed.

Outside school, the Japanese people seemed compliant too. Japan invaded Manchuria in September 1931, and the new military government portrayed it as a favorable advance to gain access to natural resources lacking in Japan, such as coal and iron. But she had seen photos of soldiers there, and the barren landscape looked bleak and uninviting. A chill soaked Miyoko's bones when she thought of Bohkee, who must be braving those harsh conditions, if she was still alive.

On a few Sundays in a row, Miyoko also saw send-offs of soldiers when she walked to church. Marching bands paraded for blocks while rows of people waved small Japanese flags. Some of the soldiers looked so young that they seemed to belong more at her school's playground than on the battlefield. Sorrow stirred that many of these earnest young men with their sleeves rolled up to fight would not make it back.

While the country celebrated Japan's aggression in Manchuria, Miyoko continued to focus on her studies. By the end of her eighth-grade year, when she had just turned sixteen, her teacher Aoki-sensei pulled her aside.

"The school is recommending you for the big school," he said, beaming. Her kind teacher had become a mentor to her. Although he was male, he treated her like one of the boys and helped her with homework when she stayed after school, as Teacher Kim had.

"That's wonderful!" Miyoko said.

"Registration is next week. You'll need your parents or guardian to sign and pay the tuition."

"Tuition? High school costs money?" Miyoko said, her brows furrowing.

Aoki-sensei paused. "Yes. Unfortunately, it's not free like middle school."

Disappointment tightened Miyoko's chest. She wanted to continue her studies but wasn't sure how she would pay tuition. All this work and her efforts were thwarted.

Writing to ask Mother for help seemed the only way out. Father would not consent to more education, especially if he had to pay for it. She hoped Father had forgotten about marrying her off too, since she hadn't heard from him. She wasn't surprised, because he had his other daughters to worry about. He would probably be amazed to see her now, to see how she had matured into a young woman. She wished they had been closer.

She had gotten her period and developed curves. She wore her hair like the Japanese girls, with two short ponytails on each side of her head. Her nose became even more defined as she got older, not flat like those of many Koreans. She was complimented by Haramoto as looking "Western" and told she had her mother to thank for massaging her nose straight as a baby.

Miyoko wrote to Mother to ask for tuition money and waited anxiously for a letter back. The message she finally received was from Taeyoung, and it came from his Pyongyang address.

February 1933

Dear Miyoung,
Mrs. Lee from the post office gave me your letter. I'm sorry to bring you this news. Father says your mother is very ill. One side of her body seems paralyzed, but there's no money for her to see a doctor. She has difficulty speaking and eating. She has been forced to give up the boardinghouse and is staying with a cousin in

> another part of town. Father visits her occasionally and is helping with her living costs.
>
> Your mother asked Father to tell you and Bohbeh the news, but I wanted to let you know myself. She didn't have the heart, or the strength, to dictate it herself. I will keep you posted.
>
> I'm sorry your mother won't be able to help you with your tuition right now. I wish I could give you my tuition money. You're such a better student than I am.
>
> Taeyoung

Miyoko's breath dangled in the cold winter air. Icicles clung to her heart. When she told Bohbeh about Mother that evening, Bohbeh's face whitened. They clung to each other and wept for a long time.

"Poor Mother. How long do you think she's been ill?" Miyoko said, sniffling and thinking back to when Mother had given her that precious jade hairpin, which she still kept tucked inside a special pouch in her room. A sudden wind rattled the window, as if answering her question. That was her parting gift.

"I think she'd known for a long time but didn't tell us," Bohbeh said, wiping wet stains from her cheeks. "Remember how she'd complain of numbness in her hands and feet, and how slowly she walked before we left?"

Bohbeh gazed out the window at the falling snow. "I always suspected there was a reason she sent all her daughters away. I think that explains why she didn't talk much. She didn't want to tell us the truth."

Now she had a sudden urge to see Mother again before it was too late.

Miyoko remembered her mother bending over to pick the chamoe melon and grabbing her side in pain. "Maybe that's why she refused to take me back when I pushed to go home at first. I want to help take care of her."

Bohbeh patted Miyoko's hand. "I know. But we can barely pay for the rent and buy food. We can't afford to go back now."

Miyoko prayed for her mother to get better. She vowed to earn enough money to visit Mother and help pay for her care. She wrote back to Taeyoung right away.

> Dear Taeyoung,
> Bohbeh and I are shocked to hear the news about Mother. I plan to go to work and earn money to help with Mother's expenses. I can't start high school until I can pay the tuition, so most of what I earn will go toward what Mother needs. Thank you for being there in my place. I trust that you are healthy, and that your studies are going well.
> Miyoung

Wetness pooled in Miyoko's eyes for Mother. Meanwhile, her dream of becoming a teacher was fading further from reach. The fire that had burned inside over pursuing an education was dwindling. She recalled Mother's encouragement—that out of all her daughters, Miyoko was capable of it. She swore to make her mother proud someday.

Being a good student was her best skill. She had never done anything except simple manual labor. She helped Bohbeh with cooking and cleaning but had never earned money doing those things. She didn't know if she would be able to find a job. But one thing she had gotten better at was acting Japanese, and maybe somehow that would help her find work.

After three years of living and studying in Japan, sixteen-year-old Miyoko decided to apply for a job at an employment agency using her

Japanese name. According to Haramoto, the Japanese got better jobs and were paid more for the same job.

"When I applied to be an electrician, my employment application was tossed into a separate pile because of my address," Haramoto said. "That's how I ended up with the lower-paying job of meter reader. They knew I had to be Korean because I said I was from Fushimi-ku. Don't make the same mistake I did."

Haramoto seemed genuinely helpful, and she had seen him being nicer to Bohbeh after their fights. Miyoko decided to take Haramoto's advice and lied about her address on her employment application. When walking around a Japanese section of the city, she had seen a girl about her age go into a Japanese-style house with a curved tile roof, and she had noted her address. The Japanese didn't rent to Koreans, so they wouldn't suspect that a person from this area was Korean. She hoped the agency wouldn't check.

In this way, Miyoko got her first job as a waitress at a large Japanese restaurant. She wanted a teaching-related job, but this was the only thing available. The boss at the restaurant gave her a bright floral kimono to wear. She was good at her work, keeping track of food orders, bowing to customers, and speaking politely to them in Japanese. She and another young Japanese waitress, Masami, often shared leftovers during their break.

"You want to have some chicken yakitori with me?" Masami said one day, after the lunch crowd had left and before the dinner crunch. The restaurant was in a busy commercial area between a bank and a stationery store. The denim noren hanging over the door welcomed Japanese workers in to enjoy typical dishes of donburi and tempura.

"Sure," Miyoko said, sitting across from her in an empty booth. She took a bite and cringed at the bold, salty taste.

"Chef Miura is too generous with the salt!" Masami laughed, looking at Miyoko's reaction.

"I agree! I need some water!" Miyoko said.

The girls became friends this way, and one afternoon, a male coworker, Nakano-san, joined. He was tall and lanky, with an easy smile. He and Masami immediately started complaining about their boss.

"I can't believe Boss is making me work an hour longer today without pay!" Nakano said.

"Yeah. He made me do that the other day too," Masami said. "But my friend's been looking for a job for months and can't find one. We should feel lucky. The economy is really bad here. But it's bad everywhere in the world, according to the news."

Miyoko stayed quiet. She would never complain about having this job or working overtime. She would be peddling items in the street if her Korean identity were known.

Nakano's tone lifted the mood. "Did you see how Boss forgot his reading glasses again? He's sure absent minded these days and can't read a thing without them!"

The three of them laughed, and Miyoko relaxed, wondering if she'd finally found some new friends.

When they were alone one day, Nakano-san asked if he could walk her home from work. She noticed how much more he'd been helping with her tables when he wasn't busy. Miyoko was flattered by the attention, and she liked his confidence. But she didn't want him to see where she lived. Plus, she hadn't talked to many men alone, except Haramoto and members of her church.

When she declined, he sat with her during breaks and persisted in talking to her.

"I'm from Hokkaido. How about you?"

"I'm . . . umm . . . originally from here. I grew up near Lake Biwa," Miyoko lied.

"What a beautiful area," he said. "I'm going to take over my father's okonomiyaki shop after I get some experience here. What about you?"

"I love those sweet and savory pancakes. I'm working to save money to go back to school. I want to be a teacher."

"Hontou?" Nakano said. "That's admirable."

They chatted like this for about a month. Miyoko liked Nakano's eagerness to learn about cooking and running a restaurant, which reminded her of her passion to be a teacher. His large brown eyes were curious and probing. She found herself spending more time with him and going to different okonomiyaki street vendors after work to taste which combination of flour and grated yam made the best batter. As for mix-ins, he liked shrimp, and she preferred cabbage, although the possibilities were endless. The spicy kick of ginger, the smoky flavor of dashi, and the creaminess of the thick brown sauce drizzled on top made the grilled pancakes delicious and fun to eat. The ice around her heart began to melt.

As Miyoko took the restaurant's trash out back one afternoon, someone called to her.

"Miyoung-ah!" a man shouted, using her Korean name.

It was her friendly Korean neighbor, who lived next to them in Fushimi-ku. He was working his trash pickup route in the neighborhood.

"Is that you? I hardly recognized you in that kimono!" he said in Korean.

Miyoko's face burned. She turned around before he could say any more, but Nakano had been standing by the door and overheard. He stared at her with his mouth open wide. Miyoko rattled with shame. They didn't exchange a word. She went about her work, trying to pretend nothing had happened. Nakano refused to look her in the eye.

In the back of her mind, Miyoko had wondered if Nakano would still be as friendly with her if he knew she was Korean. She was curious whether he would be disappointed if he found out. She hoped he would accept her, but now the answer was clear. Dating and marriages between Koreans and Japanese were taboo, although she heard they existed in secret. Those relationships were criticized by Koreans and Japanese alike.

Later that afternoon, the restaurant manager asked to see her in his office. A frown crossed his face when she entered. He motioned for her to hand over her apron.

"I can't have liars on my staff. Bring the kimono back clean tomorrow," the manager said.

"But . . ." Miyoko hung her head, her neck exposed as well as her secret. Nakano had told on her. Miyoko untied her apron and handed it over to the manager before she rushed out of the restaurant. Off to the side, she saw Nakano shaking his head at her as he cleared a table. His expression was hard and cold. Masami also turned away.

Miyoko trembled all the way home. This was exactly what had happened at school—Sachiko, who she thought was her friend, had shunned her when she learned Miyoko was Korean. Another rejection. And now she was out of a job. Humiliation heated her face. The thickness in her throat grew as she walked. She would be more careful when talking with people, especially men. She would avoid notice so that she wouldn't be caught, even if it meant she would be alone. She would build a stronger wall to protect herself.

When she told Bohbeh what had happened, Bohbeh wasn't as sympathetic as Miyoko had hoped.

"I told you so. It's one thing if you're washing dishes and not interacting with the customers. The manager knows that if patrons find out a Korean has been serving food to them, they might stop coming."

She didn't dare tell Bohbeh or anyone about Nakano-san's asking to walk her home one day and then turning her in the next. She was angry that he had made her lose her job. And furious that she had trusted him, even after she'd told herself she wouldn't trust men and relationships. She couldn't count on anyone else, especially her Korean self. Her head throbbed with guilt over her lies.

CHAPTER FOURTEEN

1933–1935

It had only been three months since she'd graduated from middle school, but pursuing her education and becoming a teacher already seemed like distant dreams. A longing twinged for that part of herself that had wanted those things, but she focused on finding work to send money back to her mother.

Miyoko applied to a different employment agency and requested to be a maid this time, hoping she wouldn't have to talk to people. She decided to ignore anyone who spoke Korean to her and act as Japanese as possible. Her stomach twisted at wearing this mask, especially when she thought of Father proudly stamping his Korean name with his official name seal. Was she dishonoring her ancestors too, with this deception? Bohbeh was proud of being Korean. Maybe if Miyoung didn't care about being Korean, it would be easier to pretend to be Japanese. She would be discreet and conceal herself from everyone, just as she had in school.

Miyoko survived her next difficult employment test—interviewing with the head maid for a Japanese baron. Miyoko met her at the agency above an udon noodle shop in downtown Kyoto. Bohbeh had offered to go with her and wait outside, but Miyoko had politely declined, fearing someone might see her with a Korean woman in a hanbok and give away her secret. The stern-looking Japanese woman with glasses and gray hair peppered Miyoko with questions.

"What was your last job?" she asked in Japanese.

"I was a maid in Tokyo," Miyoko lied. "I moved down here to live with my aunt and her family."

"How long did you work there?"

"One year," Miyoko said, her throat pulsing.

The woman ran through her list of questions, checking off each one with a flick of a pen.

Miyoko responded clearly in Japanese, without a tremor in her voice. She stretched her neck tall in her clean blue-striped kimono, the only nice one she owned. She was plain and ordinary looking, like any other Japanese woman one would see on the street. Still, her jaws clenched in her fear of being found out. The head maid looked Miyoko over, jotted down a few notes, and then stood up from the table.

"The baron is a high-ranking member of the Japanese government and entertains foreigners all the time. Foreigners can be dirty, wearing their shoes in the house, and the baron would expect it to be cleaned more thoroughly after outside visitors," the gray-haired lady said.

"Hai! Wakarimashita!" Miyoko said, indicating that, yes, she understood. Her face felt feverish from her lies.

"And you understand that the previous maid was fired for tardiness, and we will not tolerate that."

"Hai!"

"Then you're hired. You'll begin work immediately as a live-in maid at Baron Ota's house on Shimbashi Street. Your salary is room and board and a fair wage to be provided upon arrival. Please report to this address on Monday with your belongings." She handed Miyoko a piece of paper.

"This is a live-in job?" She would be apart from Bohbeh.

"Yes."

Although living separately from her sister wasn't ideal, she had a job. She should have been happy, but she wasn't. She was a liar and a phony. She wasn't going to school to become a teacher. She didn't think she could learn anything as a maid. As despair rose over having to clean bathrooms and dust furniture, she remembered something the head maid had said: her employer was a baron and entertained foreigners.

Maybe there was something to learn about the world while she was working to send money home to Mother. Memories gathered of the history books she had read in school that uncovered different worlds. Miyoko would enter this job with an open mind. But she would not risk making friends or talking to her coworkers again after what had happened with Nakano-san.

Baron Ota was a politician from an old Japanese family and a recent widower. He wore a black suit and vest with a stiff white-collared shirt and tie. His large, traditional Japanese-style house was bigger and more extravagant than any Miyoko had ever seen in her life. A beautiful central garden was the focal point of the large wooden complex. An exterior hallway connected all the rooms that faced the garden for enjoying nature or watching musical performances. Miyoko was given a small room in the maids' quarters at the back of the house. It was near the kitchen and next to a few other servants' rooms.

The baron often entertained guests, so over the next several months, Miyoko learned about traditional Japanese customs. Tea was served after every meal, and different levels of honorific phrases were used according to social status. There was a Japanese dining room with a low table and a Western one with a high table and chairs. When Miyoko attended to Western guests, she learned where to place the crystal glasses, the silverware, and the linen napkins. When she ate with the head maid and cook, she practiced eating with a fork and knife instead of chopsticks.

Miyoko was acting less and less Korean and more like someone she didn't recognize anymore as she served Japanese and foreign guests. A sadness roused when she saw how far she had strayed from being Korean. She was isolated from everything she knew and becoming withdrawn. Longing and regret were her companions now, and she wanted more for herself.

Education was her answer again. Miyoko hunted for ways to continue her learning. She noticed the driver reading books in the kitchen when he wasn't working. She asked him about it and discovered he was enrolled in correspondence school as a way to earn a high school diploma. She asked him where to request information and mailed away for books that had to do with history, literature, science, and math, as well as any other books she could get her hands on. She studied in her room after all her daytime work was finished. Learning sparked curiosity and joy after mindless hours of polishing silver, dusting, and setting the table for guests. Even if she couldn't get a high school diploma, her books were constant friends during this lonely time.

Miyoko also learned firsthand how well the Japanese lived compared with the Koreans living in Japan. She swallowed her hunger, and her pride, as she served heaping bowls of white rice and hearty servings of thinly sliced beef to Japanese and Western guests. Her country was small and weak compared with other more powerful nations that she had never known existed in the world. Japan had occupied Korea for more than twenty years and treated its Korean subjects as pawns it could control. The foreigners didn't seem to care about her country's suffering, but she was starting to.

Her curiosity about what was happening in Japan and the world beyond had been piqued too. She overheard Japanese politicians talking about the assassination of the Japanese prime minister by ultranationalists the previous year. And ever since Japan had invaded Manchuria in 1931, two years before, the government had been under Japanese military control. Japan was exerting more pressure in Korea and expanding into China too. It had renamed Manchuria Manchukuo and occupied it like it had Korea. Of course, she thought of her sister Bohkee there. Japan's greed and increasing militarism had caused irreversible disruption in so many lives, and there was no end in sight.

Living at the baron's house activated something inside Miyoko. Here, life was abundant, filled with excess food, entertainment, and wealth. Everyone seemed healthy, whereas her mother probably didn't have enough to eat and was suffering from a terrible illness. She wanted to change the injustice she saw but didn't know how.

At night, regular prayer and reading of the Bible sustained her and gave her comfort. She wrote to her mother too.

November 1933

Dear Mother,

I hope you are feeling better these days. I am working as a maid now, so I am sending some money to Taeyoung to help with your medical expenses. I trust that Father is covering your living costs and you get to eat some of your favorite persimmons in the coming winter months.

You won't believe it, but I learned a few English words and can use a fork and knife. I am learning about the world, even though I can't go to school.

I've been doing correspondence school at night too. I'm keeping up my studies like you would have wanted.

You sent all your daughters away and have no one at your side. I wish I could come visit you. I miss you.

Miyoung

One summer day the following year, the head maid announced that the baron was retiring and would no longer need Miyoko's services. She had sent most of her earnings back to Mother or spent them on books, so she didn't have money to visit her mother as she would have liked. Taeyoung sent occasional reports about Mother's health, confirming that everything was stable. Miyoko had to go back to the employment agency to find another job, and her skin prickled at the thought of lying to get work again. Maybe her deception would be disclosed this time. Maybe there wouldn't be a job for her, and she wouldn't have money to send to Mother anymore. Her desire to one day go back to school was sliding away. She didn't know what her future held, but she knew she was a good maid.

Miyoko moved back in with Bohbeh and trudged to the same employment office above the noodle shop. This time, a portly man in a brown suit greeted her.

"How can I help you?" he said slowly, looking up.

Taking a deep breath, Miyoko put on her fluent Japanese. "I'd like to get a job as a maid. Baron Ota retired, and I need to find work as soon as possible."

"Ah, yes," the man said, sitting up. "I heard about his retirement from the head maid. Are you Haramoto Miyoko?"

Miyoko's neck stiffened. Why had the head maid told the employment agency about her? Did she suspect her true identity?

"The head maid said you might be coming in and left a reference for you."

She relaxed, grateful to her supervisor.

"There are no maid jobs right now. But they do need a nurse aide at a hospital in Kyoto," the man said, holding up a document. "Since you have an excellent recommendation here, you will not need an interview this time."

A nurse aide? Miyoko didn't know anything about nursing. But she thought this job might prove more useful than being a maid. She could help people who were ill, like her mother. She remembered warming up the rubber compress with hot water for Mother's feet when they got cold in the northern Korean winters, and it had felt good to relieve her discomfort. Would it be something like that?

"I'll take it," Miyoko said quickly, before the man changed his mind.

The following week, she found herself in front of a large gray building with tall windows and the sign JAPANESE RED CROSS KYOTO DAINI HOSPITAL. She entered the simple reception area and saw a corridor with narrow windows open for air. She remembered how Teacher Kim would leave the mulberry paper–screened windows in the schoolhouse ajar, even in winter, so that germs wouldn't spread. In a large waiting area, men and women, young and old, blew into their handkerchiefs; children cried; and a man slept sitting up in a chair.

Women in crisp white uniforms and starched hats bustled by, carrying metal trays with syringes and vials of medicine. A male doctor with a stethoscope dangling around his neck bent over and talked to a pregnant woman in a wheelchair. Miyoko had never been inside a hospital before, and it seemed filled with purpose. She was determined to make something of it.

Miyoko quickly learned how to change bandages and bedpans. She practiced tying tourniquets around patients' arms so that the nurses could draw blood samples. She brought patients food on rolling carts and even spoon-fed the thin miso soup to some of the sickest and most elderly patients. Joy stirred when Miyoko offered a mashed apple to an old woman and her cold hands warmed as her blood sugar rose.

Every day there was a new challenge to stretch Miyoko's mind. Helping people get better was satisfying, even though it wasn't teaching. She studied after work when she wasn't too tired, but sometimes her eyes grew heavy after doing a few math problems in her correspondence workbook, and she'd have to wake herself up. Miyoko began fantasizing about a new future for herself as a nurse.

Living with Bohbeh and Haramoto again, she was able to save more money after helping with rent and expenses. Thanks to her Japanese language skills, Miyoko earned far more than Bohbeh did washing dishes at a Korean restaurant. Plus, she was thrifty and kept a meticulous ledger of her savings.

Miyoko sent most of her earnings home to Mother every three months or so, along with a letter. Sometimes Taeyoung would send a short thank-you note back, reporting that Mother's condition was the same, and other times there would be silence. When there was no news from home, Miyoko took on more shifts and worked overtime to save up emergency cash in case Mother needed a special procedure or extra medicine. She saw families unable to pay for needed care, and it broke her heart. She vowed to work harder so that her mother could receive the care she needed, regardless of cost.

When assisting patients with everyday tasks, such as changing a woman's sanitary napkin or tilting someone's head back so that they could swallow medicine, she felt like she was helping Mother too. The distance between them closed in those moments that, in some ways, made up for the vast longing to see her. She practiced for the day she could save enough to visit Mother and help nurse her.

Miyoko had been making it on her own by blending in all these years, but pretending took a toll. She couldn't laugh with the other nurse aides as her true self or even speak Korean to a Korean patient for fear of being outed. With nursing, she found she could connect with people, but only from a safe distance. Loneliness occupied the space next to her when she went to bed at night.

Her isolation felt especially harsh when she received another letter from Taeyoung.

> February 1935
>
> Dear Miyoung,
> Your mother's health has not improved. She says thank you for the money you've been providing but wants you to save your money to go back to school. She doesn't want you to worry about sending money for her care anymore. She misses you but wants you to continue to get an education any way you can. That's more important than anything. Our father is helping your mother the best he can, even though he has my mother and siblings to provide for as well.
>
> I'm graduating soon. I've received an offer to work at the Korean central bank in Pyongyang! I start next year. It would be so good to see you someday soon.

You're always welcome to stay with me if you visit Korea again.
Taeyoung

Was her mother's condition getting worse? Is that why she was telling her not to send money home? Miyoko wouldn't take no for an answer. She would help provide for her, no matter what. Mother had no sons, so Miyoko would play that role.

Miyoko pulled out her old mulberry-paper journal. Writing always helped her understand what she was feeling. A haiku poem flowed onto the page.

Youth does not return
I am wearing white clothing
I will live humbly.

She stared at the words to decipher their meaning. Her youthful dream of becoming a teacher had not materialized, and she was wearing a white uniform as a nurse aide now. She would help people in some other way—by being a nurse. She would not be rich in material goods, but she would be enriched by giving to others. She was humbled by her new role, absorbing new vocabulary about diseases and treatments for patients, and expanding her mind. Taeyoung had achieved his goal of a good job, and maybe she could still do something worthwhile too.

A spark of purpose flamed again for her future.

CHAPTER FIFTEEN

March 1935

Miyoung feverishly wrote to Mother about her nursing work.

> Dear Mother,
> I received your letter asking me not to send money home anymore but to save for school. I have a job as a nurse aide now and am learning how to care for people. I enjoy wearing my white uniform and bustling around the hospital to help the doctors and nurses treat patients. I plan to continue to work in nursing and send you money, despite your protests. I will use some of my salary to buy books for correspondence school and try to earn my high school diploma.
>
> Taeyoung has offered me a place to stay when I get a chance to visit. I hope I will see you soon. As you probably know, he is graduating and will work at a bank in Pyongyang. I am so proud of him!
>
> Take good care,
> Miyoung

Miyoko hastened to the post office to drop the letter off. She had another goal that day too: to go back to church. It was a long overdue visit, as she'd had little time to herself over the past two years because of her live-in job at the baron's house and her busy schedule at the hospital. She had prayed and read the Bible on her own but missed the connection with others, especially since she kept to herself at work. She had been assigned to Sunday shifts but was recently given a change in schedule. She wanted to pray for her mother to get better and for Taeyoung to do well at his new job. She wanted to feel less lonely and isolated.

Excitement swirled as she approached the familiar street. The scent of jasmine floated along the Kamo River, and swallows called, promising that another spring would arrive. She pulled her sweater tighter to ward off the morning chill and walked into the wooden building that hid its name, Grace Church, inside.

After taking her shoes off in the entryway, Miyoko entered the bare hall with a low ceiling and simple altar. It was as she remembered, but the lights were dimmed and the tone quiet. People hushed their voices when they saw her. But after looking her over, they continued their conversations. She was surprised that it was so subdued, as the church had been so lively before.

She scanned the room and noticed her old friend Woosun talking to some people she didn't recognize. She hoped he would welcome her after her long absence.

Woosun looked up and smiled. "Hello again," he said with a sparkle in his eye.

"Oppa!" Miyoko said.

"We've missed you. You're all grown up!"

Miyoko blushed. Woosun made her feel like a little girl again, even though she was now eighteen. She babbled away like no time had passed. "I wanted to come, but I had to work. I read the Bible while I was a maid at the baron's house and thought of you."

"That's great! I'm so glad you came. I hope you'll stay for the Korean expatriate meeting now. Services start after that," Woosun said.

She had heard about these expatriate groups from Bohbeh, whose friends attended similar gatherings. The purpose was to discuss how to improve living conditions in the Korean community, but the groups also secretly supported resistance activities for an independent Korea. Ever since she had learned more about Japan's occupation of Korea, she had come to yearn for her country's freedom too.

Woosun whispered under his breath. "Be careful what you say here. The Japanese government is watching all independent Korean groups, including churches."

Miyoko had read in the headlines that the Japanese were quashing missionary work in Korea and closing down churches for fear of opposition to the military government. It was rumored that the Japanese considered Christianity a threat to their domination everywhere, so it seemed only a matter of time before government control over Christian activities gained momentum in Japan. She would need to be more careful coming to and going from church, her Christianity yet another thing she'd now have to hide. The fear of Mother's lashings for attending church in Korea seemed almost trivial now.

Miyoko moved to the back of the church as people assembled for the meeting. About twenty young men and a few women took their seats. A few wore round, wire-rimmed glasses and carried canvas backpacks like those of the college students she'd seen walking here and there in the city. Most seemed to know each other, chatting away and laughing. It felt comforting to hear so many people speaking Korean in one room. One man walked to the front to speak.

"Welcome," he said in Korean. "My name is Kwon Hojoon." He had a deep, soothing voice that sounded older than he looked. A brown wool blazer hung loosely over his body, as if it belonged to someone else. His high chin gave him an air of importance, yet there was a tenderness to his large brown eyes.

"As you may know, I'm studying law at Ritsumeikan University in Kyoto." Hojoon didn't sound boastful, although passing the entrance exam to study law was extremely difficult, especially at a Japanese university. "We must band together to help our Korean neighbors. There are over four hundred thousand Korean people living in Japan now, and many of them live in hovels right here in Kyoto. Some don't have clean water. Children aren't going to school and are becoming thieves in the streets. The Japanese view us as crude and offer little or no government assistance, even though we work those unskilled jobs that Japanese labor shun. We have many problems in our community that we must address." Hojoon's voice broke as he described the dire conditions.

"The Bible tells us to share with the Lord's people who are in need. And do not withhold good from those to whom it is due when you have the power to act. Our Korean neighbors need our help. Please find me after the meeting if there's anything you can do," Hojoon said.

Miyoko shifted in her seat. She thought of the skinny, ragged boys digging around in the trash near Bohbeh's house and wanted to do something for them. But she didn't know how she could help. This man opened her eyes to the needs of others in broader ways.

After the talk, Miyoko asked Woosun about Hojoon.

"Does he always speak so passionately at these meetings?"

"He's studying law so he can help the Korean community when he graduates. His parents can't afford to send him to college, so he works during the day as a journalist for the Korean-language newspaper and goes to school at night."

Hojoon's sacrifices for his education drew Miyoko to him. "What does he write about for the newspaper?"

They must have been talking too loudly, because Hojoon looked over at them. His gaze lingered on Miyoko's face before he turned away. Warmth crept across her cheeks.

"Mostly editorials," Woosun whispered. "He's one of the most promising leaders of a Korean resistance group. In fact, I think he's going to meet them after this." Woosun's voice was almost inaudible. Miyoko was barely listening anyway. She watched Hojoon grab his backpack and leave.

Miyoko decided to arrive early for the expatriate meeting the following week so that she could hear Hojoon speak. After the last meeting, she found herself forgetting her own troubles at work and being more attentive to patients' complaints. She scanned the newspapers more carefully for word about what was happening in Japan, especially as it related to possible Korean resistance efforts.

This time, Hojoon used a more solemn tone. "As you may have heard, a fire burned down many buildings in our community a few days ago. This is a tragedy for all of us. I can't help but remember stories of the Great Kanto Earthquake of 1923, when thousands of people lost their homes due to the fires."

Hojoon glanced around before saying the next part and spoke in a hushed voice. "As you know, Koreans were massacred by the Japanese when rumors spread that they had set off bombs, poisoned wells, and started even more fires. We can't afford to lose any more Korean lives. We're seeking volunteers to help rebuild the charred homes. It's time we looked to not only our own interests but those of others."

Miyoko had heard about the recent fires on the other side of the Korean ghetto. She also knew about the atrocities carried out against Koreans in the aftermath of the Great Kanto Earthquake more than ten years before. An urge rose in her to help the victims right in her own community. She remembered that after a blaze in her village, Mother had invited a woman widowed by the fire to stay at their boardinghouse. Miyoko recalled the injustice she had felt at Baron Ota's house upon seeing how the Japanese lived so well while Koreans suffered.

An idea surfaced that she shared with Woosun, who was sitting next to her. "I don't know how to build houses. But maybe I could help with basic medical needs."

"That would be wonderful."

After the meeting, Woosun made the introduction.

"Kwon-shi," Woosun said, adding the *shi* to address an adult with respect. "Thank you for your leadership. This is Suhr Miyoung. She goes by Haramoto Miyoko in Japanese."

"Annyeonghaseyo," Miyoko said in Korean, and bowed shyly. Her cheeks flushed with anxiety over using her Japanese name. It suddenly seemed to matter what this earnest stranger thought of her. "I'm a nurse aide. Maybe I can help."

Hojoon's mouth curved into a broad smile, showing his large, straight teeth. His eyes gleamed. "I go by Ando Hiroshi in Japanese. I would be honored to have your help. Could you come to Kujo Train Station next Sunday?"

"Yes," Miyoko said quickly, surprising herself by how fast she agreed. Her neck grew hot as he spoke to her. Something familiar, like the woodsy aroma of mountain pine, wafted in the air and seeped into her skin. His presence seemed to tap into a place deep inside, reminding her of her childhood, a sense of home she was sure she had left behind in her mulberry tree.

"Let's eat," Woosun said, ending her awkwardness. "Our American friends made some Western food for us and set up some tables and chairs over there. There's an American Presbyterian church close by—"

"Before we do, I have one more thing," Hojoon interrupted. He whispered to Woosun, but loud enough for Miyoko to hear. She looked down shyly as they spoke.

"You heard about the grandfather who owns the shoe shop being dragged from his home? They jailed him. For anti-government activities," Hojoon said. "His family says he's been beaten and starved."

"How terrible."

"Let's get some members together and bring food to the family. They don't know when he'll be released."

"I will," Woosun said.

Miyoko had heard stories of Koreans being arrested for resisting Japanese rule but had never met anyone directly affected. Anger churned in her. She didn't like sitting idly by, doing nothing.

Woosun gestured toward the food again. "Please, why don't you start first?" he said.

A tray of meatloaf and steamed vegetables sat atop a table next to some plates. Metal forks and knives stood in a caddy instead of chopsticks. Hojoon eyed the spread with suspicion. Confusion lined his face.

"They look hard to use, don't they?" Miyoko said, smiling as she recalled the first time she set a table at the baron's house.

"Yes," Hojoon said, holding up a fork and turning it over.

"I used to work as a maid, and I've seen Western people eat with these utensils. I can show you if you'd like."

They sat down, and Miyoko showed Hojoon how to cut the meat by holding the fork in her left hand and the knife in her right. Hojoon imitated her, slicing the meatloaf back and forth. When the knife slipped out of his fingers, they both laughed. Looking across at him, Miyoko felt the tension she had been holding in her shoulders for so long loosen a bit.

"Maybe I can find some chopsticks somewhere." Hojoon chuckled, glancing around for help.

"Don't worry, you can do it. It just takes practice." With each bite, she became more relaxed. She was daring to laugh with a man she hardly knew, and although she'd told herself not to get attached, Miyoko was pleased to share this moment—and to know something this man didn't.

Hojoon finished his lunch using a fork and knife, chomping the meatloaf slowly with a grimace on his face.

"You don't like it?" Miyoko asked.

"It tastes kind of like . . . wood." Hojoon laughed. "I appreciate the American congregation making us this food, but I guess I'm not used to it. I've never eaten Western food before."

"It does take time to get used to. I ate leftovers in the baron's kitchen and didn't like it at first. The cheese smelled awful. But eventually I grew to like some things. My favorite was turkey with gravy." Miyoko enjoyed the easy conversation. She couldn't remember the last time she had felt so unguarded. He seemed accepting of all the different sides of herself.

After they cleared lunch, Hojoon grabbed his backpack. "Unfortunately, I have to go. Thanks for saving me," he said, looking over at the fork and knife. "I hope I'll see you next Sunday?"

His eyes probed hers. Miyoko gazed up at him through her lashes and nodded. As she watched him leave, blood rushed through her veins at the thought of seeing Hojoon again and helping people in her community. But an uneasiness settled too. Something about this man made her self-conscious. She had been doing fine keeping to herself. But she had already told Hojoon so many personal things and laughed so freely.

Ever since Nakano's rejection, she had believed that she needed to hide her Korean identity to avoid being exposed. The pain had scabbed over, but the hurt could be picked open at any moment. Hojoon's presence was baring her wounds: her choice to pass as Japanese, and to forgo love. He was making her care about being Korean again. He was making her care about him when she had promised herself not to open up to anyone because it hurt too much.

She would be more careful the next time she saw him.

CHAPTER SIXTEEN

June 1935

Miyoko had not been able to meet Hojoon at Kujo Train Station the following Sunday. A runny nose and a fever had kept her in bed all day and from work that entire week. She'd found herself thinking about him, though, as she drank hot tea and rested in bed. She'd brushed off her feelings and told herself that she just wanted to get back to church to see how she could help others in her community.

When Miyoko recovered from her cold, she snuck into the church through the secret entrance. She was disappointed to find Hojoon absent, even though she didn't think she cared. She heard from Woosun that Hojoon and many others were working day and night to rebuild the homes in the Korean enclave that had burned down in a suspicious fire. If Hojoon was still going to school at night, he must be very tired.

Miyoko finally saw Hojoon a month later at church. He had hollows under his eyes, and his chin stuck out more than she remembered. There was a large scrape on the side of his head that had scabbed over. Miyoko's chest ached. She wished she could have helped with her nursing skills. Hojoon seemed so selfless toward others, and she longed to care for him.

Hojoon sat at the front of the room and didn't notice her until he turned around to talk to someone. He brightened when he saw her, offering a tired, feeble smile. His mouth opened like he wanted to say something, but he faced the pastor again when the service started. Miyoko barely heard the sermon, unable to focus on anything but Hojoon's frail appearance and how sorry she felt for him.

A strange yearning drew her toward him, to something she hadn't known she'd lost. She tried to tell herself that he was just another man and nothing more. But seeing him again, she felt alive. Her skin tingled, and her heart rattled in her chest, begging to be released. She wanted to tell him everything about her true feelings and thoughts—her real self, not her false one.

At the end of the service, he came over to talk to her. Miyoko's veins pulsed.

"I heard you were sick," Hojoon said.

"I'm fine now." Miyoko warmed at his thoughtfulness. "And how about you?"

"I'm all right. Much better off than those poor families who lost their homes." Hojoon gazed into Miyoko's eyes, but his mind seemed elsewhere.

"What happened to your face?" Miyoko leaned in to take a closer look at the wound.

"We had to sort through all the rubble after the fire. Walls came crashing down, and a piece of metal hit me . . ." Hojoon turned his head the other way.

She held her right hand down with her left, stopping the sudden urge to touch him. She wanted to tell him everything would be okay. These feelings surprised her. She didn't know where they were coming from.

"I'd be glad to put a bandage on that scrape," Miyoko said, immediately regretting her brazenness to touch him. She had become timid while living in Japan, no longer the bold girl who climbed trees and beat boys at the abacus for fun. She was careful with everything she did now.

A wide grin stretched across Hojoon's face. "You're good at a lot of things," he said playfully. "First it was how to use Western utensils, and now it's how to dress a wound!"

Miyoko laughed and unclenched her hands.

"I believe I don't know the first thing about you!" Hojoon said.

"Well, there's not much to know." Miyoko didn't want to tell him about the simple village she came from and her inability to finish school. She was embarrassed that she had given up her dream and feared Hojoon might judge her as a failure.

"I'm not sure about that . . . ," Hojoon said. "Let me start by saying I'm delighted to see you again. I'm from the Kwon family of Andong." He had introduced himself by his birthplace, as was typical. "That's why my Japanese last name is Ando. And you?"

Miyoko's mouth pressed together, like it was glued shut. Andong was in the southern part of Korea, and the Kwon clan were yangban, part of the traditional ruling elite. His family was in a far different class than hers.

When she didn't respond, Hojoon continued. "My father was a land surveyor in Korea and is doing similar work here."

Miyoko nodded for him to go on.

"He invested his money in the Japanese stock market in Korea, but when the value of his shares fell, he lost all his money and his house. He had nowhere to go, so he brought me, my mother, and my two brothers here over five years ago, in the late 1920s."

Miyoko willed herself to remain silent. She didn't want to tell him about her poor background and have him think less of her.

"Sorry if I get too close. I was sick as a kid and can't hear very well out of one ear," Hojoon said. He seemed to know how to pull her in, like the ocean tides.

"I'm from a little village north of Pyongyang called Maengjungri and live in Kyoto with my sister and her husband now," Miyoko said in a small voice. *There, I did it.* It wasn't as painful as she had imagined.

"Aha, you're from the north. That explains it. Northern women!" A mischievous grin crossed his lips.

"What's that supposed to mean?" Miyoko stomped her feet silently.

"Northern women are strongheaded. You appear small and delicate, but you're strong willed and smart!" Hojoon seemed half-serious this time.

"No, I'm not! Well, I mean, yes, I am," Miyoko bumbled. "I wasn't afraid to speak up when I first arrived, because I have no family here, except my sister, to bring shame on. But I've changed to fit into Japanese society."

"Why are you and your sister here?"

Without stopping, the words spilled out, like Hojoon had opened the dam to her lonely heart. Miyoko told him about the uniformed stranger, Bohbeh's arranged marriage, and how she narrowly escaped her own but wasn't able to fulfill her ambition to be a teacher. In hurried breaths, she explained that she was relieved her father hadn't pursued marrying her off but now worried greatly about her mother's illness. She disclosed that she used her Japanese name to get jobs and was angry at how Koreans were treated in Japan. It felt freeing, like running through her old barley fields again.

Hojoon listened quietly. Looking around, Miyoko noticed that the crowd had thinned out and they were practically the only two left in the church.

"I really like hearing all these things about you," Hojoon said, standing close. A loud horn blared outside, and Hojoon jumped back. "I could talk to you all day, but I have to go. I lost track of time. I need to ask the Japanese administrative office for more money to rebuild. Maybe we can meet somewhere other than church?"

Miyoko's breath seized, remembering Nakano's rebuff. She recalled, too, Bohbeh's disappointment that Miyoko had trusted him, so she wouldn't tell her sister about Hojoon.

"How about at Kamo River next Saturday at noon, on the east side of Kojin Bridge?" Hojoon's eyes pierced hers, and her knees weakened.

The mere possibility of meeting him alone filled her with excitement and apprehension. She had never met a man like this. But she needed to stay focused on her work—on saving money for her mother's care. She couldn't afford to lose another job, or any more friends.

Words tripped on her tongue as she tried to respond. She bowed gracefully instead, pushing away his offer.

"I'll bring some crackers to feed the ducks. Won't you please join me?" Hojoon persisted, bouncing on his toes.

Two wooden ducks were given to couples as a symbol of marriage, and suddenly she didn't want to say yes to Hojoon's invitation. Her parents' arrangement, Bohbeh's marriage, Nakano's rejection—all relationships seemed doomed.

But Hojoon made her feel less lonely and more herself. He seemed to see her spiritedness and drive, which had dimmed over time. He saw beauty in her Korean side, which she had quelled to fit in. She wanted those things again, so she couldn't say no. He was a man of conviction and faith who was encouraging her to help the Korean community.

"Yes, I'll meet you then," Miyoko said before she could stop herself.

He grinned so wide that dimples dented his cheeks. An earthy scent of pine coiled up Miyoko's nose as Hojoon turned around and left. She could barely contain her giddiness. She didn't know what was happening, but she felt happy.

CHAPTER SEVENTEEN

Summer 1935

Hojoon stood staring into the water as Miyoko approached him at the bottom of Kojin Bridge on the Kamo River. The noon sun hung directly overhead, heating her shoulders as she walked. Hojoon held a bag of crackers in one hand as a gaggle of ducks bobbed in front of him. When he noticed Miyoko coming, he stretched out his free hand to welcome her.

"Hello," he said shyly. "I'm glad you came."

Hearing his voice lightened Miyoko's heart. They strolled along the river's edge, and she was pleased at how natural it felt.

"Do you know that ducks mate for life?" Hojoon said as he tossed broken crackers to the quacking birds.

"Is that so?" Miyoko said. Her face warmed at talking so openly about relationships like this.

"My parents still have the wooden ducks they received as a gift when they got married." He chuckled. "It's on their armoire."

"Hmm." Miyoko found herself wondering for the first time in years if she would ever get married. She shifted in silence.

"How was work this week?" Hojoon asked, somehow sensing her discomfort and changing the subject.

"Well, it was bad today," Miyoko blurted, grateful for the distraction. Hojoon halted to give her his full attention. "One patient wouldn't turn over when I needed to give her a shot on the bottom, so one of the male doctors had to hold her down while I poked her, and she screamed!"

Miyoko flushed speaking about a woman's body so casually. But she felt emboldened to talk to him. No one had ever taken the slightest interest in her job, not even Bohbeh.

"It must be hard to stab a needle into someone." Hojoon grimaced like he was being given the shot himself.

"It's not pleasant, but it's part of the job. It's the only way they're going to get better. How was your week?" Miyoko, not used to the attention, tried to change the topic away from herself.

"I tutored students all day, then went to school at night," Hojoon said, rubbing his eyes. "I stayed up until two in the morning studying for an administrative law test. Sorry if I seem a little sleepy today." He yawned and stretched his arms.

"That's all right. You're lucky to be studying. I learn on the job at the hospital. But I wish I were still in school with other students, taking notes in my notebook, listening to the teacher tapping chalk on the chalkboard. I miss it."

"Hmm. Hopefully, you'll have a chance to go back soon."

"I attended correspondence school for a while and studied on my own, but work got busier, so I had to quit. I still try to learn as much as I can to be a good nurse aide by watching the senior nurses. And I still write poetry sometimes, though in my spare time."

The longer they walked, the more the words gushed. Hojoon made her feel relaxed and accepted for who she was. He actually cared about her education, unlike Father and many other men.

"What did you eat today?" Miyoko noticed his thin frame under the same wool blazer he always wore.

"Oh, a little dried squid with some gochujang sauce," he said, licking his lips.

Her mouth watered too, conjuring fiery red pepper tastes on her tongue. Her stomach knotted thinking of the red peppers drying along the village road at home. It was true—she missed eating the spicy condiment at the hospital, where they only served bland Japanese food, like soft tofu with watered-down soy sauce or rice with bonito flakes and a side of salty pickled tsukemono. She wanted to share a good Korean meal with someone other than Bohbeh.

"I guess I haven't eaten much, so I'm getting hungry," Hojoon said. "Let's get some pajeon and bibimguksu at the outdoor market."

"Yes," she said as her stomach rumbled at the thought of hot scallion pancakes and spicy mixed noodles. The sun went behind the clouds, and a gust of cold wind rippled across the river. The sky darkened, chilling the air. Miyoko crossed her arms over her sweater, noticing that the yarn was pilling at the sleeves and not in any better shape than Hojoon's frayed jacket. The green sweater was the only one she owned, and she had knit it herself.

An image flickered of Mother teaching her how to knit and purl yarn by candlelight back home. Taeyoung's letters this past year had confirmed that her condition was still stable, but it could change at any moment. As she thought about Mother, Hojoon placed his jacket over her shoulders and rested his hands there. The blazer hugged her small form and comforted her like a hot bowl of oxtail soup. She found herself wondering what Mother would think of Hojoon. Maybe she would like him? After all, he was from a good family yet also chose to help others. She imagined Hojoon becoming a lawyer and helping women like Mother fight back against those who would take advantage of them.

When Miyoko got home that night, she decided to knit Hojoon a sweater to keep him warm while he studied. Her needles clicked away each evening after work, creating a steady, soothing rhythm. She forgot about her worries and allowed herself to dream again—about Hojoon but also about continuing her own education. She imagined them grown up, he a lawyer and she a nurse, with their own pair of wooden ducks on the armoire. The brown balls of yarn disappeared into a sleeve, the back, and finally the front, which she then pieced together.

When Bohbeh asked her who the sweater was for, Miyoko said it was for a parishioner at church who had just arrived from Korea. It wasn't the right time to tell her sister about Hojoon. Bohbeh and Haramoto still fought a lot, and Miyoko didn't want to make her sister feel bad by announcing her growing relationship with Hojoon. Besides, she was supposed to be working, not going out with men and making things for them.

The next time the two met at the river a couple of weeks later, Miyoko brought the finished sweater wrapped in a pretty furoshiki fabric. It was similar to the bojagi cloth she had seen her mother use for enclosing sweet rice cakes in Korea.

"What have you got there?" Hojoon asked. "A blanket?"

The gift was big and bulky so not easy to hide.

"Are we going to sit on that and have a picnic?" A playfulness chimed in his voice.

"Well, we actually could." She stroked her arm over her bag, feeling the other surprise she had for him. A bento lunch box filled with salmon, umeboshi, and a little rice she had scavenged from Bohbeh's hiding place. She loved the tart taste of the pickled plum and hoped Hojoon liked it too.

Miyoko smiled, eager for him to see the sweater she had made first. "This, it's for you," Miyoko said, offering the present with both hands.

"For me?"

"Yes. Let's sit over there." Miyoko pointed to a stone bench under a tree.

"Why me? I haven't done anything to deserve a gift."

"Go ahead, open it." Her insides roiled nervously.

Hojoon creased his brows as he fumbled to unlace the bow of the wrapping cloth. She had made the furoshiki herself by painting stripes of orange and blue on a piece of square cotton fabric and leaving it in the sun to dry. When he was done unwrapping it, he stared at the neatly folded sweater and then at Miyoko.

Her cheeks warmed as she waited for his reaction.

Hojoon held the brown sweater up in the air and admired it. "Did you knit this yourself?"

"Yes," she piped quietly. "Do you like it?"

"I'm speechless." Hojoon rubbed the sweater against his cheek and gave Miyoko a big sideways grin. "I love it. I've never had anyone make anything for me before. Especially a beautiful young woman like you . . ."

Miyoko's face heated, turning tepid to hot like her skin in the ofuro bath. "Go ahead, try it on."

He took off his glasses and set them on the bench. He removed his tired blazer and pulled the new sweater over his head. It fit perfectly.

"Thank you," Hojoon said, his eyes softening. He turned to look out at the river and placed his hand lightly on Miyoko's. Shock rippled through her body, and she didn't retreat. They sat together like that for a long time. His stomach rumbled after a little while.

"I have another surprise for you," Miyoko said, remembering the bento box.

"Another present?"

"We're going to have a picnic!"

They shook the furoshiki cloth that the sweater had been wrapped in and laid it flat on the grass in front of the bench. It was just big enough for them to sit sidesaddle facing each other. She opened the lunch box between them.

"Wow," he said. "A gorgeous meal! You are full of surprises!"

They leaned their heads together, the air between them shrinking. After they finished eating, Hojoon gazed at a couple of passing ducks. His sweater hung loosely on his thin body, the neck part draping down. Feeling lighthearted and carefree, Miyoko pulled up a clump of grass and threw it against his neck, causing the earthy mess to slide down his back.

"Hey, that tickles!" he said, laughing.

At that, Miyoko jumped up and ran around to the other side of the tree behind them, daring Hojoon to catch her. He did, easily, and they stood there looking into each other's eyes, panting.

Her spontaneity and joy surprised her. It reminded her of playing hide-and-seek with the boys in her village, when she would throw a pebble into the distance to distract them, then run to another place to hide before they found her. A surge of contentment filled her soul like never before.

CHAPTER EIGHTEEN

Fall and Winter 1935

Summer turned to fall in the nearby Arashiyama mountains. Trees burst into red, gold, and orange hues, like the brightness of her heart. Over the next few months, she and Hojoon met frequently at the river. They strolled along the bank chatting, arms brushing casually.

One day during a sudden rainstorm, they found shelter at the Daimaru Department Store and made an adventure out of it. They rode the escalator up to the fifth floor and ate a hot bowl of curry rice in the cafeteria. They sat across from each other and enjoyed a glass of soda, smiling at the children eating ice cream at a nearby table. Hojoon bought her an umbrella at the bargain section in the basement, and they huddled together, arms linked, while walking home. Hojoon grabbed Miyoko's hand, and they ran through the downpour laughing. She missed him when they were apart and looked forward to their good times together.

In December, there was another reason for her happiness. She received a letter from Taeyoung.

> Dear Miyoung,
> Your mother is doing better. Father is still looking out for her daily needs. Your mother said she is proud of you for being a nurse aide and helping people like her.

> She said to use your money for your studies and buy something nice for yourself.
>
> I am living in a guesthouse in Pyongyang. I'm wearing a Western suit every day and going to work at the bank. I'm learning a lot. Please come visit at your first opportunity.
>
> Taeyoung

Hope coursed through Miyoko after learning the good news about Mother. She imagined her mother sitting up and knitting again. She smiled thinking of Taeyoung wearing a suit and tie and going to his prestigious job at the bank. She shared this letter with Hojoon, and all of a sudden, she felt more possibilities open up for her future. Maybe she could go back to school someday and not worry about Mother. Maybe she could even study nursing now that teaching seemed beyond reach. Maybe she could pursue this relationship with Hojoon.

Hojoon brought her to his two-story home not far from where she lived. He asked her to come in, but she declined, her cheeks burning at his family's possible disapproval of her lack of kin or money. She was a poor girl with no parents here, after all. Hojoon pointed to the wooden house and explained that there were three rooms around a small central courtyard downstairs and three more rooms upstairs. His large family included his father, his mother, and his two brothers and their wives. They all lived together under one roof.

Seeing Hojoon's house made Miyoko think of Father's big family in Korea. She hadn't heard directly from him since she had left. She thought about what a family of her own might look like. But she couldn't think too long about Father and his family without seeing Mother's stooped body and her flashing eyes as she told the story of the man stealing her family's land. Hojoon seemed so different from the men in her mother's life, but marriage still seemed too risky. Miyoko couldn't afford to indulge in fantasies—she only had the present and focused on enjoying each day with Hojoon as it came.

Miyoko brought Hojoon to her house too. The two were often alone in the mornings, since Bohbeh and Haramoto were at work and Miyoko's shift started in the early afternoon. They talked, laughed, and sipped tea. While it would have been forbidden for Miyoko to meet a man alone indoors without an escort if they had been in Korea, it wasn't so now. Miyoko didn't have parents or older villagers telling her what she could and couldn't do. The circumstances of living abroad freed her from some of those strict social rules. The price she had to pay for this freedom was great, though, because she had to deny who she was to work.

Miyoko treasured these visits, and the far-reaching conversations she had with Hojoon. He made her feel like her thoughts mattered. They would sit on the worn tatami floor, and he would ask her questions that even her beloved teachers hadn't broached with her.

"Can I read some of your poetry?" Hojoon asked one day at her house.

"It's nothing, really." Miyoko's ears heated up.

"Please," Hojoon pleaded, opening his eyes wide.

She reached behind her and pulled the drawer of the wooden chest open. She found her mulberry journal, which held the haiku she had written a year ago when she began working as a nurse aide. She hesitated to show it to him, nervous he would think it wasn't very good.

Hojoon read the words out loud.

Youth does not return
I am wearing white clothing
I will live humbly

Hojoon became quiet. Miyoko fidgeted as she waited for him to say something.

"This is beautiful." The glow from the morning light rested dimly on his face. "What does it mean?"

Hojoon's praise encouraged her to speak up. "I was just thinking how I used to wear my white hanbok when I was little, like all the village girls did. But now I'm in Japan wearing a different kind of white uniform as a nurse aide. My life has changed a lot. But some things stay constant."

"You're a lovely, strong woman now," he said gently.

Shivers crept up Miyoko's neck. When she had written it, she had not yet met Hojoon. She was humbled by the love she felt for him now.

"I love the poem. Would you mind if I keep it?"

"It's nothing special . . . but yes." Miyoko tore the page out of her journal to give to him.

Hojoon coughed and placed his beige handkerchief over his mouth. Blue stitching bordered the edges. "Thank you." He cleared his throat.

"Are you coming down with a cold? Here, drink some water." Miyoko handed him a metal drinking cup with both hands. While he took a long sip, she picked up her thick needles and continued to knit a blanket that she had been working on. Hojoon opened his law books to study.

They sat next to each other in comfortable silence. She wondered if this was what it would be like to be married to Hojoon. If so, maybe marriage wasn't as bad as she'd invented in her mind. Except what would happen to her job and education? If she had a husband and in-laws, wouldn't she be expected to serve her husband's family? Hojoon was the third son, so maybe his burden to care for his parents would be less, but then again, she might be expected to do more because she had less seniority among the daughters-in-law. It was a lot to think about and premature, so she tried to concentrate on her knitting.

As she worked, Miyoko peered over Hojoon's shoulders to see what he was reading. His law books were thick and filled with Japanese legal words she didn't know. It was her turn to ask him questions.

"Why are you so interested in law?"

"Because I want to help people. I want people to be treated fairly and equally, and make sure their rights are protected."

"What kinds of rights?" Miyoko thought about Mother being cheated out of her farm again. Mother would appreciate Hojoon's passion.

"Like Koreans living in Japan. We have a right to decent jobs and housing, but we don't get them because the laws aren't written fairly or applied equally. I want to change that." Hojoon's eyes flared with purpose.

Miyoko rested her knitting needles on her lap to listen. His voice resonated, like soothing currents in a stream.

"For example, having identification cards. Why do only foreigners have to register for them? The Japanese are monitoring us, that's why. I prefer to use my Korean name because I want to be seen as myself. Why should I have to use a Japanese name? Shouldn't we be treated as human beings too?" Hojoon's voice boomed.

Miyoko's stomach pitched at the thought of pretending to be Japanese while having one of those very same identification cards. She was straddling two worlds at once, and Hojoon seemed to be pulling her in one clear direction. He was true to himself, and she longed to be like him.

"You're right," Miyoko said. "We didn't do anything wrong. I'm tired of living this double life and fitting in the way the Japanese want me to. I'm so lucky I found you."

Hojoon inched a little closer. Slowly, he turned her toward him and leaned in. She lowered her eyes but didn't pull back. His fingers felt alive on her skin. He lifted her chin tenderly with his rough, calloused fingers, causing her resolve to soften and her heart to yield. She let him kiss her softly on the lips. Their first kiss. Desire throbbed her tongue.

Knocking his books over on the low table, Hojoon caressed her face with his palms and pressed his mouth on her neck. Shuddering, she closed her eyes, breathing in the deep, musky odor of his hair. His hands grazed the soft curve of her shoulders, sliding her cardigan off in one gentle swoop. His touch tingled like fresh spring air, heating the space between her legs. Deft fingers moved down her arm and lingered on her hip. When he unzipped the back of her nurse's uniform, desire unleashed. She surged toward him as he pulled her camisole over her head and unhooked her bra. Her back arched as he smoothed his fingers along her breasts.

A sudden shock rippled through her body, and she pulled in closer. He traced the edges of her full, eager mouth and pulled her toward him, kissing her hard. When he finally made love to her, their bodies naturally melded into one. Right or wrong, the physical joy of being with Hojoon was unlike anything she had ever experienced.

That morning, Miyoko first tasted real love. Head on Hojoon's bare chest, she listened to his heartbeat and heard her own. She learned the contours of his body and the heights of her pleasures. Something in her ripped open, and the tension she had been carrying vanished. She'd gotten it wrong about relationships after all; not only *could* she find love, but she *should* love.

When it was time to go to work, Hojoon walked her all the way to the hospital, but every few steps, he teased her and begged her to turn around.

"Don't go." Hojoon tugged at her arm. "I can't bear to be apart from you." He put his other arm over his mouth to suppress another cough.

"Are you all right?" A nagging feeling rose. She had heard coughing like this in the hospital, and it was sometimes a sign of something more serious.

"I'm fine," Hojoon said, brushing off her concern with a reassuring smile.

"Take care of yourself, then, and rest. See you tomorrow."

A contentment pressed against Miyoko's heart. Maybe this was what Bohbeh had been talking about so long ago in Korea, when she predicted that love was out there but you had to be open to it. Miyoko hadn't understood Bohbeh or believed it then, but she was beginning to now. She was not the same girl who feared relationships; she didn't know who she was anymore.

CHAPTER NINETEEN

March 1936

Miyoko's first year with Hojoon was more joyous than she had ever imagined. Hojoon's love fueled her and enabled her to see things she had never really noticed before. When they took walks, he would point to the cotton-ball clouds floating against a bright blue sky and say they were ocean bubbles pulling at their toes. Then he would tickle her under her arms, which would put a smile on her face for the rest of the day. She wanted to linger in these moments forever.

She wrote about it in her journal.

> *Hojoon has awakened me. I yearn to scramble up the mountains of my hometown with Hojoon by my side, slurp icy-cold naengmyeon noodles together, and be called by my Korean name. The memories of my childhood are so vivid, luminous, and real. Hojoon is showing me how I could be myself again.*

One day during this heady time, Miyoko was at work, taking a tray of sutures to the surgical recovery room, when she heard Korean voices. She froze. Kyoto Daini Hospital served mostly Japanese patients, and she rarely heard her mother tongue spoken there. A middle-aged woman with a large bandage across her eye was talking to another woman, holding her hand. Bruises darkened half of the injured woman's face.

"Eomeona! How did this happen?" the visitor said in Korean.

"My husband hit me. I needed stitches to close the cuts. I didn't want to come to the hospital because we can't afford it, but I was bleeding too much."

Miyoko's heart pounded as she eavesdropped on the conversation.

"Why? Why would he do such a thing?"

"He was mad at me for wearing my hanbok," she said.

"Aigo! That's awful. But he's Korean too."

"You know how ashamed he is. He doesn't want to be found out. He would rather kill himself, or me, than have his secret divulged."

The words curdled Miyoko's stomach. She fingered the top of her nurse aide's uniform, where she wore an identification badge that showed her Japanese name. She was hiding her identity while this woman was being beaten for proudly wearing traditional Korean clothing. She wished she had the courage to do that.

Miyoko recalled her sister's soft whimpers after Haramoto's drinking. She should have comforted her sister then, just as she should have told the patient that she was a Korean nurse and consoled her. But Miyoko was too afraid. She needed this job, and if the Japanese nurses knew . . . But how long could she keep this up?

Miyoko talked to Hojoon about it the next day before work, deciding this was the time to ask him the question that had been nagging her. Did he care that she was passing as Japanese? He chose not to use his Japanese name, after all. He was studying to be a lawyer so that he could change things. What could she possibly do?

"Something happened yesterday at the hospital."

Hojoon turned toward her, concern lighting his face. "What was it?"

The fullness of her heart allowed her to talk candidly. "A Korean husband beat up his Korean wife because she wore a hanbok."

"It's so hard to see so much suffering in our community," he said.

"I didn't do anything about it. What would you have done if you were me?"

"Working with sick people must be difficult. This one was personal."

"It's just . . . I can't fix everything. I can't do anything about how the Japanese treat us."

"I understand."

"That's why I took on a Japanese name when I first arrived here. To get along."

"The Japanese don't make it easy, do they?" Hojoon said.

"I've been very good at concealing who I am. Except when I met you, my feelings started to change. You inspired me to embrace my whole self. I don't want to disappoint you by being someone I'm not."

Hojoon's eyes softened. "I don't blame you. I think it's unfair that we're given such little choice to express who we really are. I'm fine with whoever you want to be."

Miyoko exhaled at hearing Hojoon's response.

"You should do what you feel is right. Maybe next time you'll act differently," Hojoon said.

"I can't give myself away now and risk losing my job. But maybe I could help more people like this Korean woman. She said she hadn't wanted to go to a hospital but had no choice. Maybe I could make house calls for those who might want to keep these matters private. I can take their vitals, clean and bandage wounds, even bathe patients . . . You must know people who need help."

"That's a wonderful idea!" Hojoon beamed. He seemed happy to see her so excited about this, and she was happy to feel this new energy surging through her. She wasn't helpless.

"If you give me a list of people, I'll go to them," Miyoko said breathlessly. She knew how to help her community cope with their pain and suffering now. This was what her nursing skills were meant for.

"I'll do that first thing. Here's the fiery woman I first met!" Hojoon chuckled, a gleam in his eye.

Miyoko leaned over and kissed him. His lips were warm and slightly parted. She closed her eyes and glided her hand over his face, pulling herself toward him. He tipped back and let the draping fold of her nursing cape envelop him.

The following day, Miyoko waited for Hojoon to show up at her house in the morning with a list of community members who might need her help. But he didn't show up. Maybe he was busy studying or writing an article? Could he be sick? She went to work as usual, thinking he would tell her what happened later.

The second day, Hojoon didn't come either. This sparked worry that something might be wrong. Miyoko wanted to go to his house, but she couldn't just show up. Hojoon's parents still didn't know about their relationship. Miyoko had asked Hojoon not to say anything yet, as she was afraid of what their response might be. And, for the same reason, she hadn't told Bohbeh either: Hojoon was from a yangban family. She also didn't want to hurt Bohbeh, since her relationship with Haramoto was so hard. If Hojoon's family didn't approve, would he still be interested in her?

She needed to go to Hojoon's house and find out what was happening. If she went, maybe he would see her outside the window and come out. If someone asked her why she was there, she could say she needed to talk to Hojoon about an article he was writing. She would find some excuse. She had to do something.

Before work on the third day, Miyoko hustled to Hojoon's neighborhood, then slowed down. She slunk by the front of his house under the umbrella he had bought her from Daimaru, hoping he would recognize her or the umbrella. He didn't come out, and nothing seemed out of the ordinary. The house was quiet, except for the barking of a neighbor's dog. Her concern that something more serious had happened to Hojoon intensified. Was he very sick, or was some other family member ill? Could he have been detained by the Japanese authorities for his activities involving the Korean community?

A few more days went by without a word, and Miyoko's panic spiked. Had she done something wrong? She went to the river and sat on the furoshiki cloth they had used for their picnic. She remembered the time she had showered him with clumps of grass in a gesture of affection, and her imagination spiraled.

Perhaps she had chased Hojoon away. She must have said or done something he didn't like. Maybe he thought she had been too forward with him. Maybe he had found a prettier woman. She wanted to talk to Bohbeh about Hojoon, but her sister would probably be disappointed in her loose behavior. Her face grew hot as she imagined admitting to Bohbeh that he might have spurned her, so she kept everything to herself. As one day turned into the next, however, her fear shifted to anger. She had allowed herself to fall for him, and he had stolen her heart.

The next Sunday, Miyoko scanned the church, looking for Hojoon. When she didn't find him, she asked Woosun.

"Have you seen Hojoon?" Miyoko said.

"No. As a matter of fact, he didn't show up at the community meeting last night. Maybe he's busy with his studies."

Miyoko's brows knit together as she pictured him absorbed in his books and forgetting about her. She snuck back to church week after week, but there was still no news. Hojoon had rejected her. There seemed to be no other explanation. But how could this have happened? They had been so happy together. She lost her appetite and slept fitfully. The strong antiseptic smells of the hospital sickened her. She felt numb and hurt.

A few weeks later, Woosun sought Miyoko out after the church service. "Hojoon's sick," he said. "He's been home in bed this whole time. I ran into his brother."

Miyoko cupped her hands over her mouth. Hojoon was ill. Anxiety pumped through her veins, and she wanted to go to him. She should have been more vigilant about his coughing and weight loss, but she had been too blinded by her happiness to see it. Through her worry, she felt a hint of relief: She hadn't chased him away after all. He might still care about her.

"It must have happened suddenly," Miyoko said. "I had just seen him the week before he disappeared."

"Yes. It seems he was so busy helping others that he forgot to take care of himself," Woosun said.

The creases between her brows deepened. "I'll go over and help him."

"That might not be a good idea right now. His family is taking care of him."

"What's wrong with him?"

"They're not sure, but it might be tuberculosis."

Her body tensed. Shock rippled through her muscles. No, not Hojoon. More people were coming into the hospital with high fevers, shortness of breath, and coughing. Tuberculosis attacked the lungs, causing a weakening of the immune system. The epidemic was growing, and there was no cure. Sometimes the patient's condition would improve on its own or with treatment, but other times it resulted in death.

Every ounce of Miyoko's being wanted to leap up and run to Hojoon. She could wrap him in a blanket and let him rest outside in the fresh air, like she had seen patients do at the hospital. They could watch the ducks, and she could feed him warm broth and help him sip water.

"I want to see him," Miyoko said.

"I know. I tried to visit him, but the family wouldn't let me in," Woosun said. "They say he might be contagious."

It was true. She knew from the hospital that tuberculosis was highly contagious, even when all precautions were taken to prevent the disease from spreading. It wasn't clear how it got transmitted to one person but not another. Miyoko didn't have any symptoms, but she could develop them at any time, since she and Hojoon had been intimate. She might never get it, or she might get it and pass it on to Bohbeh, Haramoto . . .

Miyoko was aware of the danger, but she cared for Hojoon, and nursing was her calling. She wanted to help him, if only she knew how. What could she do?

CHAPTER TWENTY

April 1936

Miyoko became obsessed with learning about tuberculosis. Tuberculosis patients at the hospital were segregated and given the rest cure, where they were made to sit out in the open air for hours and taken for daily walks in wheelchairs. Miyoko and the nursing staff usually tucked patients under heaps of blankets and wrapped their heads in scarves for the outdoors. When Miyoko brought them food, she always wore a surgical mask, washed her hands, and scrubbed the surfaces nearby with bleach.

One day, Miyoko spoon-fed a grandmother some miso soup after lung surgery. She was thin and frail and having a hard time breathing. She was scheduled to be sent to a sanatorium that had been built outside the city for the most severe cases. But she started showing signs of recovery, so Miyoko became hopeful. Unfortunately, the grandmother passed away, unable to recover from the tuberculosis that had ravaged her lungs.

Fear sliced Miyoko like a knife. Hojoon might not make it either, and with every day that passed, she became more distraught. She barely ate or slept, meandered aimlessly on walks, and found herself back in front of Hojoon's house. She hoped that he could somehow sense her energy and that it would strengthen him. She felt helpless otherwise.

Despite the growing danger to Christian groups, Miyoko continued to go to church and huddled in prayer for Hojoon's recovery. She read the Bible alone in her room at night, reciting scripture aloud. She had done this fervently when Mother was sick, and news had arrived that she was better. She prayed for a similar result for Hojoon.

A month later, Woosun gave her a letter after the Sunday service.

"It's from Hojoon. His brother asked me to give it to you," Woosun said.

Miyoko stared down at the bulky envelope, and her breath caught in her throat. She hoped Hojoon was writing to tell her that he was better and wanted to see her. She craved good news. Woosun backed up and turned away, as if knowing she needed privacy.

Miyoko's feet carried her to the river, their river. When she opened the unsealed flap, she recognized the items immediately.

One was her poem. On the back, there was something written in Hojoon's shaky handwriting.

> Dangshin, my dear,
> I'm sorry I disappeared so suddenly and for all the worry I must have caused you. I've thought about you every day but didn't have the strength to write. I dreamed of the mating ducks in the river and imagined that was us, bobbing together in the water. I wanted you beside me, and the possibility you loved me too sustained me during my illness. But when I found out I had tuberculosis, I felt selfish asking you to wait. I don't know what's going to happen to me, so please don't wait any longer. I can't bear the thought of you being unhappy. Live your life fully . . .

The last word trailed off the page, as if he couldn't finish the sentence. Her ears throbbed while she held the mulberry paper in her hands. He was telling her that he loved her, but he was also saying to move on, that the illness was unpredictable and might get worse. Miyoko was heartbroken. The hope she had held for their future seemed to vanish with his words.

There was something else in the envelope too: Hojoon's beige linen handkerchief with the blue trim. She held it to her cheek, a soapy smell rising, like it had just been washed. She remembered Hojoon taking it out of his jacket's breast pocket to dab his forehead. Tracing the stitching with her fingers, she imagined the soft curve of his face. Wetness glossed her eyes. *Maybe this is his final gift to me.*

Miyoko resisted the urge to run over to his house and help him. She had learned how to care for tuberculosis patients and knew the risks. Hojoon was likely going to die. She shouldn't hold out hope that he would get better and their relationship would be restored.

Even if Hojoon did get better, he might feel differently about her. People changed after a long illness. The uncertainty of his disease defeated her. Love meant loss, after all. Seeing his handkerchief was too painful a reminder of what could be taken away. Reading his letter proved that their relationship was over.

Miyoko had been foolish to open herself up to love. There was nothing left for her to do if she wanted to protect herself from the pain of losing him. She shoved the items back into the envelope and walked home with gloom trailing behind her.

That evening after dinner, Miyoko sat under cover of the kotatsu table, watching Bohbeh do her embroidery, lost in thought. Haramoto had gone out to get more sake.

"You didn't touch your food tonight. Are you all right?" Bohbeh said, looping the thread through the canvas. The beginnings of a beautiful pink rose emerged.

The needle moving in and out of the fabric felt like Hojoon's words stabbing her over and over.

"You've been acting very strange lately," Bohbeh said.

It was hard to keep this in any longer. Miyoko hadn't told her sister anything at first, because she didn't know if the relationship would last.

Then there was the shame over the possibility that Hojoon had rejected her. Now that Miyoko knew Hojoon was ill, she could tell Bohbeh everything. The fear that he might die was too great to endure alone.

"You remember the man I was telling you about from church—Kwon Hojoon, who was in charge of rebuilding after the big fire?"

Bohbeh nodded while continuing her smooth strokes.

"He's gravely ill. He has tuberculosis." Doom soaked her words. It sounded even more ominous saying it out loud.

"Really?" Bohbeh said. "My father died of that too." A mist covered her eyes.

"Yes, I remember now. I'm sorry." Sorrow welled for Bohbeh, herself, and Hojoon.

"That's all right. This Kwon, he does a lot of good things around here, right?"

Miyoko's resolve to stay strong collapsed. The tears that were threatening to escape finally burst free, and she covered her face with her hands.

Bohbeh's fingers stopped moving, and she looked up with troubled eyes. "What's wrong?" She dropped the wooden circle holding the embroidery in place.

"I think . . . I'm in love with him." Miyoko barely got the words out between big, heaving sobs.

Bohbeh's face softened, and she rested her hand on Miyoko's back.

Miyoko lifted her head, a sheet of wetness covering her face. "You once said that true love might exist, and I opened my heart to him. Now he might die!"

"Aigo!" Bohbeh said. "I was young and didn't know what I was talking about. Look at my marriage!"

Miyoko lowered her eyes, regretting her outburst. Her heart ached for her sister.

"You've heard us arguing . . ."

Miyoko's face softened.

"At least you experienced real love," Bohbeh said. "I have to live with a man I have never loved and never will. This is my fate, but it doesn't have to be yours."

"No," Miyoko said firmly. "I don't think I can take this. I shouldn't be involved in relationships anymore. I was lured into thinking there might be a future between me and Hojoon. Now he's sick and might die. I took care of tuberculosis patients so that I could be ready to help him. I want to be there for him, but he doesn't seem to want me."

"Why?" Bohbeh said.

"I don't know. Hojoon sent me a note telling me to move on. Maybe he doesn't love me anymore. If I wait around and he rejects me, I couldn't handle it . . ." Miyoko's voice trailed off, her throat parched. She felt selfish thinking of herself when Hojoon was ill.

"Well, this might be a good time to bring this up." Bohbeh straightened her back. "Haramoto-san is getting transferred to Osaka, an hour away by train. We'll have to move in about three months."

The walls seemed to be closing in and the floors splitting open at the same time. Miyoko's world was crumbling all around her. She couldn't live without Bohbeh.

"What?" Miyoko burst.

"You can come with us. I've already talked to Haramoto-san about it. Funny thing is, he likes you. He says I should be more like you, more Japanese."

"Thank you, eonni." Miyoko was relieved by this new development. Moving away was one option to deal with her mixed feelings for Hojoon. Maybe she would stop thinking about him if it was impossible to see him.

Even though she felt like a burden on her sister and Haramoto, she had to try to move on as Hojoon had urged her to do.

Hojoon's rejection hadn't changed her desire to go back to school and become a nurse. Caring for tuberculosis patients had helped her realize that there was so much more she could do with her nursing skills. She could crawl back into her shell again and work and save money for her education. If Hojoon got better, he could move on with his life too, if that's what he wanted. This transfer might be a blessing in disguise after all.

"I'll have to find a new job in Osaka," Miyoko said. Her palms dampened at the prospect of having to interview again.

"Yes, but I'm sure you'll find something. You're such a good nurse aide. There are lots of hospitals in Osaka too," Bohbeh said with big-sister certainty. Miyoko was grateful that if there had to be more twists and turns in her life, at least they kept pushing her toward Bohbeh.

Miyoko tried to imagine her life going forward. A blurry image of a woman walking alone slowly came into focus.

Relationships were fragile, and the pain of losing Hojoon seemed like more than she could endure. Was it ever worth it? She might have been better off if she'd never met him. There would be no more walks along any river where she would feel so close to another person. She would never throw grass down someone's shirt again, even if it was just for fun. The lines on her palms predicted a different kind of future, one that didn't involve romance or men. She would make sure of it.

PART THREE

Kyoto, Japan

1936

CHAPTER TWENTY-ONE

June 1936

As the warmer days drew Miyoko closer to her move to Osaka, she tried to concentrate on her work at the hospital and her plan to leave Hojoon and her life in Kyoto behind. But her mind kept roaming elsewhere, like it had when she was leaving Korea for Japan. What if he recovered completely and still cared for her? What if he died and she never saw him again? Her heart was torn into pieces, like the patchwork squares of a bojagi cloth.

On her last shift, Miyoko took the soiled linens to the staff kitchen instead of the laundry room. When she packed her belongings, she crumpled her kimonos and shoved them into her bag instead of folding them neatly. She hadn't heard from Hojoon in three months, and she was miserable. No matter how hard she tried, she couldn't dismiss her worries and feelings for him.

Clouds darkened overhead as Miyoko walked to church to say a final goodbye to everyone. She was taking off her shoes at the entrance of Grace Church when she saw a Japanese policeman talking to Woosun. Nerves crept up her neck, and she snuck to a corner of the room behind some apple crates.

"Where are your identification cards?" the policeman with a thick mustache shouted.

"Here is mine, sir," Woosun said, a slight tremor in his voice.

The police looked down at his card. "What are you meeting here for?"

"We are just a group of worshippers. We meet on Sundays to pray and help the Korean community."

"Well, this is your last meeting. The neighborhood association needs this space to prepare care packages for our troops in China. This will be a hub for military send-offs too."

Miyoko's stomach writhed. She had read about the attempted coup earlier in the year and about the conservative military faction gaining control. Haramoto had said this meant that Japan's encroachment in China would increase, and that there would be a crackdown on foreigners living in Japan who might oppose the war.

"I see," Woosun said solemnly to the policeman. "We will be out today."

Miyoko backed farther into the shadows as the officer left the building. It was clear that it was becoming more dangerous for Koreans to assemble. Just when her life was turning upside down, her sanctuary was being attacked too.

The Japanese government now required Koreans in Japan to carry identification cards at all times, not just register for them. The newspapers reported that the reason was to facilitate employment and welfare services for all, but Koreans knew the cards were used as surveillance tools to suppress independent Korean groups. Miyoko had heard of other labor organizations, and churches, being disbanded. Now that the Japanese government seemed to be more repressive than ever, she was glad that Hojoon was not able to engage in resistance activities.

A tap on her shoulder startled her. It was Woosun.

"I saw you coming in. You heard all that?" he said.

"Yes, I did," she said, exiting her hiding spot. "How scary."

"The Japanese government will not leave Koreans alone anymore. We can't meet here again."

Anxiety pounded her chest. Koreans were being watched more closely. Churches were being targeted. She would have to be better at concealing her Christianity and more careful where she went to church in Osaka. Her faith would be yet another thing she'd have to disguise. And if churches everywhere were in danger of being shut down, where would she find fellowship and a place to worship?

"We will meet at the Korean elementary school on Nijo-jo on Sundays from now on. You know that one, right? In the cafeteria at 10:00 a.m. starting next Sunday."

"I'll be able to attend for a couple more weeks, but then I'll be moving to Osaka."

"You're moving?" Woosun said, sorrow filling his eyes. "We'll miss you. You've been such an important member of this congregation."

"I'll miss you too. This church has been so good to me all these years." She would never forget how the church community had embraced her when she first came to Japan. She would have to pray alone again until she found a safe place to worship in Osaka. She would be without Hojoon and a church. Moving to a new city, Miyoko needed people more than ever, especially since she was still heartbroken over Hojoon. She feared she would be isolated again.

"By the way, I was hoping to see you today," Woosun said. "There's something I want to tell you. I saw Hojoon."

She stiffened.

"He's weak but better. He wants to see you."

Miyoko blinked rapidly.

"Can you meet him at your usual spot at Kamo River next Saturday at noon? He told me to tell you he's not contagious anymore."

Her heart banged against her ribs. Did he want to get back together? What would this mean for her and their relationship? "Of course. I'm glad he's better. Please tell him if you see him that I'll meet him. And thank you for telling me about Hojoon."

"I thought you might want to know," Woosun said, kindness coating his voice.

The rest of the week crawled by, and finally it was time to see Hojoon again. Nerves racked her body. The prospect of reuniting with him made her question her decision to let him go. What if she still felt the same way about him? What about her move to Osaka? She was supposed to be pursuing a nursing job and more education. She couldn't open herself up again and possibly lose him.

It was June, but the air felt warm and muggy, as if monsoon season had already arrived. The gentle silhouette of the distant mountains peeked from the thick clouds as she stood waiting for Hojoon by their spot at the bench. Miyoko remembered the day she had given Hojoon the sweater she had knit, and the surprise on his face. That seemed like a lifetime ago, before his illness, before he had told her to move on. She had tried to go on with her life without regret, but it was hard. Now that Miyoko was about to see him, she was excited and scared.

Hojoon arrived late. A man Miyoko barely recognized came limping toward her with a cane. Despite the heat, Hojoon was wearing the very same sweater she had knit. She steadied her arms to quell the sudden urge to comfort him. Inching forward, she tried to take in the changed man that he was. His pants bagged, and he was hunched over. Dark stubble marked his thin, pale face. He stopped and waited for her.

When Miyoko was within reach, Hojoon's eyes filled with color. He lifted his hand to touch her cheek but changed his mind and rested it on her shoulder instead.

"Dangshin," Hojoon said. The tender "my dear" lapped in her ear like waves.

A thousand pins pricked her skin. His letter had addressed her this way. She had yearned for this moment without knowing it. She wanted to know he still cared. The musky hint of oil from his hair lingered, reminding her of his vibrant nature, their deep connection. She still had feelings for him too.

"You've changed a lot," Miyoko said, her voice cracking as she took in his gaunt, sallow face and the puffiness under his eyes. She wanted to run her fingers along his skin to erase his suffering. Hojoon looked like a shell of his former strong self.

"The doctor says I'm better now. I can try to live a normal life again."

Her heart skipped. "That's great news." She had been so afraid of losing him, and now that worry was gone. But what did this mean for their relationship? It couldn't continue as if nothing had happened, could it? He had told her to move on, and she had already made plans to leave for Osaka.

"I'm so much better now. Of course, I can't go back to law school or do any community work for a while," Hojoon said wistfully.

"That's understandable." It felt natural to talk to him like this, like old times. Now that he was standing in front of her, she realized she still loved him.

"In the meantime, I guess I'll just have to bother you." Hojoon tried to laugh but coughed instead.

Miyoko softened at Hojoon's effort to make light of his situation. Seeing him like this choked her, and she realized how disappointed he must be about his changed life. *Their* changed lives. Could they possibly move forward together anyway? A small ember of hope rekindled.

"Why don't we sit down?" Miyoko said, concerned about the strain on his legs, and about what their feelings for each other could mean now.

She offered her arm for support, and they walked a few steps to the bench, shaded by a large maple tree. Hojoon sat down with a thud and laid his cane flat on the patch of overgrown grass.

"Does anything hurt?" Miyoko's words rang with worry.

"I'd rather talk about you. How have you been?" Hojoon asked, tilting closer to compensate for his bad ear. He looked haggard and tired.

"I've been all right," she lied, lowering her head to avoid his gaze. "Just working." Her plan to tell him about her impending move stalled.

She was feeling conflicted, like maybe she should stay instead of going to Osaka with Bohbeh. A vision of leaving Mother behind at the train station hovered, and she didn't want to make the same mistake again.

"I want to hear all about it. I want to hear your voice," Hojoon said, his energy surging. She could see glimpses of his old self again.

Miyoko answered slowly and deliberately, giving herself more time to sort out her feelings. Even though she thought she loved Hojoon, she didn't think she could take the pain if he got sick again.

"I had to stitch up a child's knee this week. He cried the whole time, since the family couldn't afford the anesthesia." The words flowed easily, as before. She hadn't thought she would miss talking to Hojoon like this, but she had.

Hojoon stared at her moving lips, his own curling into a smile as he listened. His quiet face absorbed her like someone taking a long drink after a hot day.

With each passing minute, another layer of icy reserve melted away. Miyoko paused, noticing that she was doing all the talking. "Will you please tell me about how you're feeling?"

He inhaled deeply before speaking. "I was so sick that I could only send you my handkerchief and the note on your poem."

Miyoko visualized the shakily written note in her armoire drawer, hidden away like her heart.

"I came by to see you."

"You did?"

"Yes, but it was quiet at your house, and I didn't want to make any trouble by knocking."

"It touches me to know you stopped by anyway."

"Then our friend Woosun said your family was not allowing visitors."

"I wanted to see you too. But I was very sick and didn't want to make you ill. I didn't want anyone to see me that way, especially you. I care so deeply about you." Hojoon's voice cracked.

Miyoko waited for the adrenaline rush to subside. It was more than his health that she had been concerned about—it was his genuine affection. Seeing him and listening to him talk, she still cared deeply for him. But hadn't she made plans to move on with her life? Her hand grazed her creased forehead.

"I told you to live fully because I thought I was going to die. But the more I thought of you, the better I started to feel. I realized I had made a terrible error by sending you my note to go on without me. That's why I asked you to meet me here as soon as I could. I need you."

All the air left her lungs. A crack of possibility opened again. Memories flickered of their love-filled mornings and their walks on the river, when they dreamed of a future together. She closed her eyes to savor those happy days.

Hojoon took her hands in his. "I have something I want to ask you."

Her eyes flicked open, the glint in Hojoon's eyes shining into her own.

"Will you marry me?"

Shock swallowed Miyoko whole. She yanked her hands back, and her mouth fell open, but no sounds escaped. She wanted to say yes with every ounce of her being, yet a heaviness pressed against her throat.

Hojoon reached for her shoulders, as if his touch would change everything. "I couldn't stop thinking of you the whole time I was sick. I wanted to be with you so much that I fought harder to get better. I told myself that if I made it, I would ask you to marry me. I'm not worthy of you, but it would bring me such happiness. Please marry me."

Miyoko let the proposal float in space this time, his sweet breath caressing her face. She allowed herself to hear his words, and they brought more joy than she had ever imagined. Hadn't she been secretly wishing for this moment? Marrying Hojoon and promising to commit to each other for life?

"Marry you?" Miyoko was unable to answer his question.

Hojoon smiled broadly. "I've been in love with you since I first met you. You're beautiful, smart, and different from any woman I've ever met."

Miyoko blushed at the image of herself a year ago, when she still seemed like a child and told him whatever came to her mind. He appeared to admire her opinions and even encouraged them. He acted like he was proud of her single-minded focus to go back to school. He supported everything she had set her mind to—her education, her work. She believed that he would still encourage her in all these things, even after marriage. Yet she was stiff, her tongue paralyzed.

"This is a big surprise," Miyoko finally said. "When you wrote me that note, I thought it was over. I made plans to move on with my life, like you said."

She had locked away her heart while Hojoon was sick, and she didn't think she was ready to open it again. She wasn't planning to marry now, whether it was arranged or not. Love hurt.

Hojoon blinked hard and continued. "That was wrong. I always loved you." His eyes perked up more. "If you're worried about how I'm going to support you, I can earn money by tutoring and writing articles for the newspaper. And I will become a lawyer soon. Of course, if you wanted to continue working, I would support that too. Please. More than anything in the world, I want to share my life with you, even if it might be short lived."

"Short lived . . . ?"

Hojoon's chest heaved. "The doctor said the tuberculosis might come back. But it's not certain. Being married to you will give me hope. You're all the medicine I need to stay healthy."

Miyoko's head spun. A picture flashed of the grandmother who had died of tuberculosis after returning to the hospital a second time. A parishioner had recently passed from the same ugly disease and left a grieving family behind. The pastor said, "What God giveth, God taketh away."

"Sorry, am I asking too much? I've always been honest with you," Hojoon said, his voice quieting.

A passing cloud dimmed the sky. She didn't want to hurt Hojoon's feelings, but tuberculosis meant death. Her mind replayed the agony of thinking Hojoon might not make it, and the terror that had caused. She couldn't bear it if she were to marry him and then had to watch him die. No, she couldn't do it.

A chill slid down her body. She couldn't stomach the thought of losing someone again.

Hojoon sensed Miyoko's reservation and stilled.

Miyoko stepped back. "I . . . can't . . . ," she said.

"It's because I might get sick again, isn't it?" Hojoon's voice rose, like he was angry with himself.

"No, it isn't." She stopped before saying the words *I love you*, though they were on the very edge of her tongue. Those words weren't usually spoken out loud, although Hojoon had said them to her. "I care for you deeply."

"Then what? Please tell me."

Miyoko looked left, then right, searching for an answer, but her mouth was frozen. If she did say something, she was afraid he might try to talk her out of it.

"What if I live a hundred years?" Hojoon said. "Won't you take that chance?"

A crazy idea crossed her mind. Maybe if she loved him enough and took care of him, he wouldn't get sick again. And even if he did, she was a nurse aide and had the skills to cure sick people. Maybe she could keep him safe. It was a long shot, and she shook her head at the sheer folly of it. She couldn't save Hojoon.

"I'm sorry. I can't." She could manage on her own without being married. She had learned how to shore up her heart.

Hojoon's shoulders slumped. His eyes brimmed with sorrow. Neither of them seemed to know what to say to each other anymore.

Hojoon finally reached for his cane, planted the stick on the ground, and pushed himself up with both hands.

"I love you, and all I want to do is marry you."

Miyoko couldn't look at him, in case she changed her mind. She heard Hojoon turn around and slowly limp away. When she lifted her head, he was dragging his cane in the dirt, as if marking a trail of hurt behind him.

A memory of her mother's curled body and her failure to help Mother gave her pause. She reached her hand out to call him back, but a searing pain in her side stopped her in her tracks. This could be the biggest mistake of her life, yet she couldn't move.

She had to protect herself at all costs.

CHAPTER TWENTY-TWO

June 1936

Back at Bohbeh's house, a dizziness gripped Miyoko so hard that she stumbled to her storage closet and collapsed onto the futon. No one was home except the scurrying mice. Miyoko couldn't move; a groggy feeling overcame her, like when she was on the ferry from Korea. Pressing her back against the cool wall, she waited for the nausea to go away.

When Bohbeh came home a few hours later, she called out for Miyoko. Hearing no response, Bohbeh banged on her door.

"Are you all right?" Bohbeh said, her urgent voice slicing through the thin screen.

When Miyoko didn't respond, Bohbeh slid the door open. Miyoko was balled up in the corner. The sunlight hurt her eyes.

"What's wrong?"

"Nothing. I just want to be left alone."

"You've been out of sorts lately. Did something happen?"

Miyoko blurted the truth. "I saw Hojoon."

"I see." Bohbeh's voice relaxed. "Is he feeling better?"

"Yes, but . . ." Miyoko could barely get the next words out. "He asked me to marry him."

Bohbeh's brows arched in surprise. "Oh my!" She started to say more but seemed to decide against it.

"I feel terrible for Hojoon, after all that he's been through," Miyoko said. "He looked so weak." Miyoko tucked her knees tightly against her chest.

"What did you say?"

"I think I love him, but I'm afraid to say yes. I want to help him get better, but what if I fail? What if I can't save him? What if he dies?" Miyoko shook her head. "I said no."

Bohbeh's mouth gaped open. "What? You said no?"

Miyoko startled at Bohbeh's response. She had thought her sister would be more sympathetic.

"I'm going with you and Haramoto-san to Osaka, where I will find another hospital job. I don't want a man in my life, or marriage."

With that last sentence, Miyoko felt her breakfast coming up. She scrambled to the kitchen to find the metal bowl used for washing dishes and threw up. The sour bile lingered in her mouth.

Bohbeh went to the kitchen and ladled fresh water into a cup. "Here, drink this," she said, offering it to Miyoko.

Miyoko pushed the cup away. "I can't."

Bohbeh felt Miyoko's head. "You don't have a fever."

"What's wrong with me?" Miyoko groaned, going through her symptoms and comparing them with those of the sick patients at the hospital.

"How long have you been sick?"

"I've been tired this whole week and feel dizzy all the time, especially in the mornings."

Bohbeh's eyes gradually registered something. "I'm not a doctor, but I think you might be pregnant."

"What?!" Miyoko's eyes blinked in slow motion, like she was coming out of a dream. "I haven't seen Hojoon in almost three months."

"You work at the hospital. You should know that it takes a few months for the baby to develop. Your symptoms sound just like those of my friend Kyungja, who had a baby last year. In the beginning, she would vomit anything she ate."

Miyoko squatted on the floor, stunned. *This can't be happening.* But what Bohbeh said made sense. She had seen plenty of women at the hospital with morning sickness similar to hers.

"The timing is right," Bohbeh said. "You told me you last saw Hojoon about three months ago, before he became ill."

Miyoko's cheeks burned. That explained why she hadn't gotten her period recently. She had thought it was odd but had been so preoccupied with Hojoon's absence that she'd ignored it.

Bohbeh knelt next to her, face pushed close. "Aigo! You should have been more careful. If we were in Korea, this would bring shame to our family. But we are here now, and it is what it is."

"What about Haramoto-san?" Miyoko said, imagining the look on his face when he saw her growing stomach.

"He's not going to like it, being the traditional man that he is. But you should see Midwife Yoo tomorrow to confirm."

Miyoko started counting backward to when she and Hojoon had made love, trying to determine how much time had passed between then and when she started feeling nauseous, which was about a week ago. She swallowed, gathering that Bohbeh was right. If it was true, at least her mother and relatives weren't here to see it. And Haramoto wouldn't have to know for a while. Miyoko smoothed her hands over her stomach, but she wasn't showing yet. *Please let this be a coincidence.*

"If the answer is yes, you might want to reconsider Hojoon's proposal."

Queasiness swirled again. "But I already said no." Miyoko didn't want Hojoon to think she had changed her mind because she was having a baby. She was supposed to be in Japan for an education, not babies. Her schooling had to be put on hold but not dismissed altogether. "I don't want to get married now, or maybe ever."

She straightened her body and sat up tall to think.

Bohbeh patted her sister's knee. "This is shocking. But remember what I said. Maybe there's true love. This man loves you enough to ask you to marry him. Your relationship might be very different from my marriage, and lots of others too."

Miyoko remembered how alive and real she had felt when she was with Hojoon. He had accepted her for who she was and had made her feel special with the gift of his handkerchief. Hojoon did love her, and she loved him back. Bohbeh was right. She might not feel this way ever again.

"Maybe having a baby is a sign that you should marry him," Bohbeh said.

"A sign?" Miyoko remembered Hojoon's prayer: that if he got better, he would ask her to marry him. Maybe Hojoon had prayed for a baby too but hadn't told her.

"I don't think you should have a baby without a father," Bohbeh continued. "You know that my father died when I was a baby. Your father has another wife and didn't raise you either. It's better for a child to have a father growing up."

Miyoko thought back to all the children who had gone home to fathers, when she had grown up with only a single mother. She had been jealous of the children who helped their fathers till the fields and were carried on their fathers' shoulders. But what if Hojoon got sick again? The child might lose a father and feel abandoned, just like she had felt. Given the lack of contact she'd had with her own father since she'd come to Japan, she knew how lonely that could feel. She didn't know if she wanted a baby at all.

"What am I going to do?" Miyoko pleaded.

"First things first," Bohbeh said. "Go and see the midwife. If the answer is no, you can come with us. If the answer is yes, you know my opinion on the matter. You need Hojoon. The child needs a father."

A child. She had been so foolish to think that this couldn't happen to her. She stumbled to the metal bowl and threw up for the second time that day.

CHAPTER TWENTY-THREE

June 1936

Miyoko visited the Korean midwife on her way home from the hospital the next afternoon. Thin clouds folded in layers against a blue sky as she made her way to a rickety building between a tofu shop and a stationery store. Midwife Yoo, who had plump cheeks and broad shoulders, ordered her to lie down on a bamboo mat in a makeshift examination room. A support rope dangled from the ceiling next to her. The midwife massaged Miyoko's abdomen with her eyes closed, almost like she was meditating. Digging her thick fingers inside, she poked and prodded. Miyoko stared at the wooden beams above, trying not to squirm.

"How long have you been feeling morning sickness?" Midwife Yoo asked.

"A few weeks," Miyoko said, bracing herself against the floor with her hands as the midwife's fingers pressed harder against her.

"Hmm," she said.

Miyoko's lungs filled with dread as she waited for the midwife's answer.

"It looks like you're pregnant. About twelve weeks."

Miyoko clamped her eyes shut to stop the ceiling from falling. "Are you sure?" she said, lifting her eyelids slowly.

Midwife Yoo scowled as she slapped a bar of soap around the basin to wash her hands. "I've been a midwife for ten years. I'm never wrong."

Miyoko shuddered as she changed back into her white nurse aide uniform. A baby changed everything. She knew deep inside that Bohbeh was right—this child should have a father. Hojoon would be a wonderful father, but for how long?

None of the nurse aides at the hospital were married or had children. Having a baby now was not what she had imagined for herself. Maybe she couldn't stick to her old way of thinking anymore. Maybe she had to open her heart to Hojoon and believe in love. Bohbeh had said she was blessed to have found Hojoon, and she was. She loved him, and maybe she shouldn't fear losing him.

Holding a small envelope in both hands, Miyoko handed the midwife a modest sum for her services and mumbled a solemn thank-you.

"Come back and I'll give you some herbs to help the baby grow." Midwife Yoo tucked the cash inside the elastic waistband pocket of her linen pants.

"Yes, I will," Miyoko said as her fresh worry about a baby churned. She feared creating this new life and growing attached to it. What if something bad happened to the baby? Her mother's pale face flashed, and now she understood Mother's despair and insistence that all her daughters leave. Miyoko didn't want that for herself.

The other day, a pregnant woman had come into the hospital unconscious and dehydrated. According to her friend, she had taken herbs to try to terminate her pregnancy. Miyoko knew that this woman was lucky because she hadn't tried to end her pregnancy with cruder methods, but she had still put her life in grave danger. Miyoko shuddered. Maybe a part of her unwished this baby, but she knew she couldn't risk her own life or the baby's by making it so. She had seen too many complications and deaths in the hospital.

Bohbeh was home when Miyoko returned.

"Well?" she said. One look at Miyoko's slouched shoulders and Bohbeh could easily guess. "It's true, right?"

Miyoko plopped down with her head slumped. "Now what?"

"You need to tell him about the baby."

"I know. I prayed for what to do. I didn't want to marry Hojoon, but at every turn he has shown up for me. I'm beginning to believe that Hojoon came into my life so that I could see the beauty of love, take a chance on marriage, and have this baby."

"If he still loves you, he'll take you back," Bohbeh said.

"Will he?" Miyoko folded her hands together, wondering if she would be so forgiving if someone pushed her away as she had Hojoon. She recalled how his eyes had clouded over when she refused his proposal. Miyoko bit her lip, picturing herself asking him to reconsider and having him shake his head.

Was she wrong for not having accepted Hojoon's marriage proposal? Should she have said yes for the very reason that she feared losing him? Maybe to have love, she had to be prepared to pay with her heart.

"I forgot. This came in the mail today. It's a letter from Taeyoung. I wanted to read it together, but with all this happening, it slipped my mind," Bohbeh said.

Miyoko opened the letter, and the first thing she noticed was the date. It was already four months old. And words were crossed out everywhere, like it had been censored.

February 1936

Dear Miyoung,

I'm writing this without your mother's knowledge. The last time I wrote to you, she was doing well. But her condition has taken a turn for the worse. I went home to visit Father while I had some time off from the bank. I stopped by to pay respects to your mother and bring her some money from Father, but she was lying in bed unable to move. A neighbor was tending to her and explained what happened.

> Your mother was at home at her cousin's house, and Japanese police officers . . .

The next paragraph had so many redactions, it barely made sense; but Miyoung gathered that the police had searched her mother's home. Someone in the village had told them that Miyoung was some sort of sympathizer. The censor hadn't bothered to cross out the news that the police had closed the church as well. Maybe her mother had been targeted because of Miyoung's involvement; after all, even owning a Bible was seen as a crime. The police had taken something from the house—that part was crossed out, too, though Miyoung thought she could make out the word for *rice*. Apparently, her mother had been saving it for her and Bohbeh's return. Miyoung's face burned as she imagined her sick mother finding her home ransacked and her few precious belongings gone. The last bit of Taeyoung's letter was intact:

> She collapsed, and the neighbor found her unconscious.
>
> She's frail now. She could use any extra money you have to spare. I will come back soon and send her what I can in the meantime. I'm sorry for the bad news.
>
> Taeyoung

Miyoko's knees buckled.

Bohbeh's eyes swelled with shock. "I hope Mother is all right. She must have been so scared when the policemen questioned her."

"The police came around the church here and asked Woosun for his identification card not long ago. They're closing my church here too."

"Things are bad everywhere. And why are all the words crossed out in the letter?" Bohbeh asked.

"The Japanese are censoring everything. Remember how the newspapers struck out Sohn's name?"

"The Korean Olympic hopeful?"

"That's right. The Korean marathon runner predicted to win medals for Japan at the Berlin Olympics around the corner. *Chosun Ilbo* tried to run an article using his Korean name, Sohn Kee-chung, and it was censored. The *Mainichi Shimbun* replaced it and used his Japanese one, Son Kitei, instead."

"It's so wrong," Bohbeh said.

Anger rose for the injustice done to Mother, to Sohn, to all Koreans wanting to assert their heritage. Uncertainty struck again about her decision to pretend to be Japanese. She wanted to stand up for what was right, to fight for Korean self-determination. She wanted her child to be proud of his or her culture too. By exposing her Korean side, though, she could be questioned and risk her future with Hojoon and her baby. Her Christian affiliation also made her a target. She felt torn in half.

"What are we going to do about Mother? What are you going to do about Hojoon?" Bohbeh said.

Miyoko's heart strained. She was pregnant. She shouldn't be traveling, even though she wanted to see her mother. She was going to be a mother herself and needed to take care of the baby. Her mother wouldn't want her to be a single parent like she had been, would she? She would probably want Miyoung to stay and take care of her own child. Mother's tears at the train station so long ago now made sense. Her mother hadn't wanted to let her go.

"I will send all the money I've saved to her. I will continue to work for as long as possible. I will say yes to Hojoon and hope he takes me back."

The next time she saw Hojoon was the following Sunday at the new makeshift church inside the Korean elementary school. It had been only a week since his proposal, but with the news that a baby was growing inside her, it seemed like she had stepped into the geta of someone else's life.

The congregation met quietly in the corner of the cafeteria. Miyoko eyed Hojoon's proud face, and her body pinched with nerves. She approached him, but he bowed curtly and turned away. He wouldn't look her in the eye, a sadness shrouding him. Miyoko's stomach tensed at his rebuff, but she tried to stay calm as she rested her hand on the faintest bump of her belly. Hojoon left immediately after the service, still limping but not using his cane anymore. Miyoko followed him out of the school. He stopped at a busy intersection next to a horse and carriage. A streetcar screeched somewhere.

"Please, I need to talk to you," she said as she touched the back of his shoulder.

Hojoon tensed and pulled away.

"I'm sorry about the other day. I know I hurt your feelings. I wanted to apologize, and . . ." Miyoko's voice faded away. Hojoon turned around slowly. His gentle eyes looked hurt but concerned.

"Let's move over there where it's quieter," he said, pointing to the front of a closed flower shop. The awning promised shade from the mid-day sun and much-needed privacy. They drifted over together, huddled closer than they had been in months.

"Are you all right?" Hojoon said, catching his breath. Miyoko could tell from the downward tilt of his eyes that he still cared about her. She blurted her news before she could change her mind.

"I'm pregnant."

Hojoon's hand flew to his chest, and his mouth dropped open. For a long time, they stood there staring at each other in silence. Miyoko hoped Hojoon thought it was good news, but she wasn't sure. Shock lined his face.

Little by little, Hojoon's gaze softened, and his face relaxed.

Heat rose in Miyoko's cheeks, and she whispered, "Saranghae, I love you." The words sounded foreign coming from her mouth, but she believed them with every cell in her body. "If you will still have me, I want to marry you." Her bold words quickened her pulse, like she was a schoolgirl with a crush. "You might not believe me, but I said no because I love you so much, because I feared losing you. Now with the baby, I know for sure we were meant to be . . ." Her lips quivered; she was nervous about whether he would take her back.

Hojoon's mouth broadened into a wide smile. He stepped back a bit, so he could see all of her.

"This is a dream come true—for you to be my wife." Hojoon's outstretched hands hovered over her stomach. "Now this. A child too. I'm so happy." He clasped Miyoko's hands, just like when he had first proposed.

This time, she massaged them back and let out a breath of relief. He was an honorable man and would be a good husband and father, even if neither knew what the future would bring. Her fear of losing him was quelled by a newfound optimism. If she could give Hojoon a family now, they could be happy. If she loved him and took care of him, he could get better. He might live longer if he had a reason to live—for his child.

"I had a chance to think hard about the future . . . now our future," Hojoon said, his tone turning solemn. "I want to help the Korean community here when I feel better. But eventually I want to go home. Let's go back to Korea when the occupation ends. Japan can't rule Korea forever. Promise me we'll all go back together."

The plan brightened Miyoko's heart. Mother's letter popped to mind. This would align perfectly with her desire to care for Mother and revive her connection to her roots.

"Yes, I would like that. I received a letter from my mother the other day, and she's not doing well again. I want to go back and try to help her. I want my baby to know his or her heritage. Let's go back to Korea as soon as possible." Miyoko guided Hojoon's hands to her stomach and let out a sigh of hope.

CHAPTER TWENTY-FOUR

June 1936

That night, Miyoko wrote to her mother and Taeyoung about the wedding and the baby, hoping it would raise her mother's spirits. In case of censorship, Miyoko was careful not to say anything about the Japanese charging into her mother's home. She didn't tell her that Hojoon had been ill either, because she didn't want to worry her.

> Mother,
> I hope you are doing better. Taeyoung has given me updates on your health, and I heard about your most recent difficulty. It's been a while since I've written, and I wanted to share some wonderful news. I'm getting married, and I'm pregnant. You're going to have a grandchild! I love my husband-to-be so much, and I'm very happy. I thought I would never find love and get married, but I can't imagine my life any other way now.
>
> My husband's name is Kwon Hojoon, and he's from Andong. He is the youngest of three boys. He is studying to be a lawyer and wants to fight for justice.

I'm getting bigger by the day, and the baby is due at the end of the year. I'm excited to be a mother. I wish you could be here for the birth, but I know your health is frail.

We will be living at Hojoon's parents' house along with his brothers and their wives. It will be hard to be the newest daughter-in-law, but I will learn. I wish you were here to teach me how to be a good wife to my husband and a good daughter to my in-laws, as I know you would want me to be. I want to continue my hospital job after the baby arrives too, if I can get help with childcare.

Bohbeh will be moving to Osaka, an hour's train ride away, and I won't be able to see her that much anymore. It's not going to be easy without her.

I miss you. It's been six years since I've seen you. Hojoon says we should return to Korea as soon as possible, and I hope that day will come before too long. Please take good care of yourself until then. I look forward to hearing how you're doing again soon.

Your loving daughter,
Miyoung

Nostalgia surged as she signed her Korean name. She missed her family and longed to share the joy of her upcoming marriage. Miyoko addressed the envelope to Taeyoung, including a separate note to him.

Dear Taeyoung,
Thank you for sharing my letter with Mother. You have all my news there, but I want to tell you a little more.

I am in love with my new husband more than words can describe. I admit, though, I am nervous

> about getting married and entering a new household with all its rules. I assume Hojoon will still support my dream of continuing my education, as you have all these years. And I want to work after having the baby. I know it's not what women typically do, but I am good at my job, and it gives me purpose.
>
> I didn't tell Mother this, but Hojoon was seriously ill with tuberculosis. He is better now, and I pray he will stay that way. I hope the marriage and the baby will give him renewed strength to be well.
>
> I'm sure Father will be happy since I'm finally getting married and he doesn't have to worry about me anymore. Please give him my best when you see him. I'll write again soon.
>
> Miyoung

Hojoon introduced Miyoko to his own mother a few days later. He had already told his parents about the marriage and the baby, and Hojoon said they were surprised but happy with the couple's decision to marry. She wondered if his parents judged her for being pregnant out of wedlock. She would soon find out.

This was Miyoko's first meeting with her future mother-in-law. Miyoko would greet her future father-in-law another day, because he was not at home. Miyoko hoped her new mother-in-law, whom everyone called Halmeoni, or Grandmother, would like her.

"Annyeonghasibnikka," Miyoko said, using the most honorific hello possible and bending deeply at the waist. Head cast down, Miyoung fixated on Halmeoni's tiny, padded white socks.

When Miyoko straightened up again, Halmeoni's gaze latched on to her belly. Miyoko shifted uncomfortably.

Halmeoni's stern face harbored suspicion in its wrinkled depths. The tight pull of her hair bun created a permanent frown, making it impossible for her to smile. Her future mother-in-law's stare seemed to squeeze shame out of Miyoko's very pores. Halmeoni's eyes said: *How dare you sleep with my son before marriage.* And worse: *You got pregnant on purpose to trap Hojoon into getting married, didn't you?* Korean mothers-in-law were critical of their sons' wives, and Halmeoni's eyes flashed with outright indignation.

"I trust you'll bring me a grandson?" Halmeoni finally said, one brow forming a perfect arc.

Miyoko's face flushed. She didn't care if the baby was a girl, so long as she was healthy. But the importance of having a son was deep rooted. Confucian tradition revered sons, as they were expected to take care of their aging parents, while daughters became members of their husbands' families. Miyoko knew the preference for boys existed, but she had grown up with sisters. She had tasted independence and made her own decisions, so this reception felt old fashioned. She hoped the rest of the household was more welcoming.

Halmeoni's attitude toward her became clear as the wedding approached. Miyoko might as well have been invisible, because Halmeoni rarely spoke to her when she visited. She only perked up when Hojoon was nearby, holding his arm for support and ignoring her other sons. He was her third and youngest son but clearly her favorite. Youngest sons had the least amount of responsibility to take care of their parents, but Hojoon seemed to get the most attention from his mother. Halmeoni usually only acknowledged Miyoko when she ordered her to fetch tea or arrange Halmeoni's gomushin in the entryway.

If this was what living in the Kwon household was going to be like, she didn't think she would fit in. When the baby was old enough, she would find a way to return to work. She wanted to make a home of their own for Hojoon and their baby.

Hojoon's father, meanwhile, was a compassionate and generous man who treated her kindly whether his son was present or not. Harabeoji, or Grandfather, had a broad face and a high forehead, giving him a dignified look that reminded her of her future husband. If she had a son, she hoped he would be just like Harabeoji.

"Please bring me my tea," Harabeoji, smoking a thin pipe, politely asked Miyoko after they first met. When she did so, he acknowledged her with a flick of his eyes and his wrist, causing the ashes to drift into the metal container. She noticed his large hands and remembered the saying that the size of a man's hands corresponded with the importance of his work. He was a surveyor for the Kyoto prefectural government and well regarded for his calligraphy on important city structures, like a bridge in the city. He also helped organize temporary housing for new expatriates, taught them Japanese, and assisted them in locating new jobs.

Once, when she had stopped by Hojoon's home, a neighbor had come over holding an envelope addressed to her future father-in-law. "We've collected a small amount of money for your son's wedding," Miyoko had overheard the man say. Harabeoji was obviously a respected leader in the Korean community. Come to think of it, Hojoon's hands were flat and wide too, and Miyoko recognized why Hojoon was so appreciated.

The July wedding was a modest ceremony at Hojoon's house. Only immediate family attended, including Hojoon's parents and his two brothers and their wives. Bohbeh and Haramoto came, just in time, as they were set to move to Osaka the following week. Miyoko wished Bohbeh could stay and be a part of her new life with her baby, but she was glad that her sister could at least be with her on this special day.

Bohbeh was dressed in a soft-pink hanbok and brought over mochi rice cakes to celebrate. When Miyoko had spent her last night at Bohbeh's the day before, Bohbeh had mentioned for the first time that she might want to have children too. She had said that maybe she and Haramoto would grow closer that way, and he had even agreed. Miyoko's happiness for her sister belied a sadness that they wouldn't live close by and share the joys of motherhood together.

Bohbeh set her umbrella in the entryway, sliding the door closed just as lightning cracked. It sounded like anger that Bohbeh was moving and that Mother and the rest of Miyoko's family couldn't be there. The menacing monsoon clouds that had been hovering all morning finally erupted, casting sheets of rain against the window of the temporary dressing room. Steam hissed from the clash of cold rain on hot roofs, sidewalks, and bicycles. Miyoko remembered the common Korean myth that rain on a wedding day was a bad omen, and she shook the thought away.

Miyoko concentrated on Bohbeh tying the sash of her borrowed Korean wedding jeogori in a one-sided bow, letting the fabric drape sideways across the chima. A knee-length red silk overcoat flared out at the arms, covering Miyoko's hands past her fingertips. The relaxed outfit hid her pregnancy nicely. Bohbeh rubbed a little bit of lipstick on Miyoko's cheeks to finish off the traditional bridal makeup. A scent of sweat mixed with floral soap drifted from Bohbeh's upper lip. She was ensuring that the red circles on her cheeks were even, and Miyoko was grateful for her care and attention.

"There," she said. "Perfect."

"I'm so glad you're here." Miyoko's eyes moistened.

"I am too. I never got to have a wedding ceremony. You look beautiful."

Sympathy tugged for all the things Bohbeh had missed.

"You'll always be my dongsaeng, even if you're now a wife and soon a mother too." Bohbeh's voice rang with pride.

"I wish Mother could be here," Miyoko said.

"Let's fix this," Bohbeh said as she adjusted Mother's jade hairpin. Miyoko had fastened it to her bun that morning, holding back tears.

"Yes, Mother would be beaming," Bohbeh said, "especially seeing you in this. Here you go." Bohbeh crowned Miyoko with an ornate, traditional jeweled headpiece strung with dangling beads that they had borrowed from Hojoon's neighbor, who had recently married. The shimmery baubles danced before her eyes.

The sisters walked into the main room together. Bohbeh guided her with both hands, as Miyoko had difficulty seeing where she was going. Her face was completely hidden behind her raised arms, an embroidered white cloth draped over them like a long muff. When Miyoko saw her future husband from the corner of her eye, her skin tingled with anticipation over sharing her life with this handsome, decent man. She was marrying the man she loved. She had never thought this would be possible for her.

Hojoon wore a traditional groom's outfit: a white shirt with wide, extra-long sleeves and an embroidered royal-blue robe cascading over black boots. He donned a black high-top hat with curved wings on the sides that extended well beyond his ears. He walked stiffly, like he was uncomfortable and nervous too.

The couple stood before Hojoon's parents. They both bowed deeply to pay their respects. They did the same with Bohbeh and Haramoto, who stood in for Miyoko's mother and father. Miyoko believed that her mother would be glad in knowing that she and the baby would be cared for by a man devoted to his family.

Then Miyoko sat down on her knees, with her hanbok flared all around. Hojoon's parents threw the customary pine nuts onto the extended skirt to promote fertility, even though everyone knew they didn't need it. After a few words from Harabeoji thanking everyone for coming, all the guests shared rice cakes, and the newlyweds received small gifts of cash tucked into envelopes.

Miyoko took a nibble of a sticky rice cake, soaking in the joy of her wedding day. She chewed to the beat of the rain pelting against the house, the chatter of the family buzzing in the background. Marrying the man she loved was more satisfying than words could ever say. She was truly happy. Seeing Hojoon smiling too, she went to him.

CHAPTER TWENTY-FIVE

July 1936

Miyoko nestled into Hojoon's arms as they shared their marital bed for the first time that evening. The summer rain had subsided, leaving the air thick and sticky.

"Yeobo," Hojoon said. Warmth crept up Miyoko's back upon hearing Hojoon call her his wife. "Everything went well today, don't you think?"

"Yes." She stroked his bare chest and traced her fingers along his lean rib cage. "You looked so handsome."

He shifted sideways so that their heads touched. She noticed a small mole on his collarbone that she had never seen before. *This will be the first of many things I will discover about my new husband.* The pleasure and possibility of marriage shimmered.

"And you looked lovely, as usual."

"I was hot in all my layers," Miyoko said, "but it was wonderful."

"I couldn't wait to take everything off; I was so sweaty!" Hojoon chuckled. He leaned in closer. "I couldn't wait to be alone so I could take everything off you . . ."

"Yeobo!" she said, giggling. "Wait. I want to talk some more . . ."

"All right," Hojoon said, listening.

"Bohbeh told me she regrets not having a ceremony. I realized how lucky I am. I just wish Mother had been here to see it."

"We'll go back to Korea soon. In the meantime, we're going to have a beautiful future here," he said. He inched closer and pulled her toward him.

Comforted by his tender words, she closed her eyes and allowed herself to float. His lips grazed her neck, arousing her. Her legs interlaced with his, and their bodies moved to the same rhythm, his hips pressing down on hers. She felt herself letting go, releasing all her fears about his health and their future together. She loved these intimate moments with Hojoon and wanted them to last forever.

The months after the wedding were the happiest of Miyoko's life. Her doubts about marriage washed away like deadwood in the monsoon rains. The frequent downpours fanned their heated faces with cool breezes as they took walks and ran errands shoulder to shoulder. The buzzing of cicadas muffled their lovemaking and lulled them into sleep so deep that they both struggled to wake up the next morning. Hojoon rubbed Miyoko's rounded belly for signs of baby kicks and listened for gurgling noises with his ear pressed against her stretched skin. A magical contentment filled Miyoko like never before. Her heart bloomed, awakening all her senses.

Miyoko's mother sent a lovely letter too.

> September 1936
>
> Dear Miyoung,
> Congratulations on your wedding. And you're having a baby too! I wish I could be there to meet your new husband and help you when the baby comes.
>
> My health is about the same. Not better. Not worse. It's time to stop worrying about me and focus on your own pregnancy. Go to the midwife often, and

take whatever herbs she says you need for you and your baby to be well.

Taeyoung visits me once in a while and brings me my favorite soondae. He is a good brother to you by coming in your stead. I often think he's my own son, even though he is not my blood. He knows I have nothing here but memories of my daughters.

Write me when you can. I'll be thinking of you and my first grandchild.

Mother

(written by Mrs. Lee)

Reading her mother's words calmed Miyoko's worries for the time being. She would allow herself to enjoy their marriage. Hojoon took her to see her first movie at a theater that had just opened in downtown Kyoto. Inside a wooden building adorned with signs and posters for upcoming films, people packed into a large auditorium with seats bolted to the ground. Red velvet curtains hung on either side of a big screen, and a projector shone out of a glass window from the floor above.

Hojoon held Miyoko's hand, and she rested the other one on the bump of her belly, which was growing fuller each day, like her heart. They watched a black-and-white talkie called *The Only Son*, which was about a widowed mother who visits her only son in Tokyo and discovers his lack of outward success. Miyoko only half watched the movie, her stomach rumbling with pleasure to be spending this kind of time with her husband. Afterward, they strolled in the park eating yakitori.

"What did you think of the movie?" Hojoon asked.

Miyoko tilted her head to slide the savory chicken off the skewer with her teeth. "I liked it," she said, chewing. "Although the mom was disappointed that her son didn't live a better life, even after going to university, I think she was still proud of him." She felt a pang for her own mother and thought of how disappointed she must be that Miyoko hadn't been able to finish her studies. Miyoko regretted it too, despite her happiness with Hojoon.

"I want to continue my education when the baby is old enough," Miyoko said, emboldened to tell Hojoon all her feelings. "I stopped working and taking correspondence classes because of the baby and our marriage, but I want to go back to it. Even if I don't get a high school diploma, I'd like to study nursing and work at a hospital. I feel drawn to it, like a calling."

"Of course. I would support anything you want to do. Is there an exam for a nursing license, like there is for law?"

"Yes," Miyoko said. "I've heard the nurses talk about it at the hospital. I'd probably want to get more work experience first, but it's something to strive for."

"I would be very proud of you. Your happiness is more important than anything," Hojoon added, his voice gravelly even as he cleared his throat.

"Are you all right?" Miyoko asked, worry stirring.

"I'm fine," he said, squeezing her hand tight.

They walked in the direction of home hand in hand. All her concerns dissipated in her joy.

They arrived home just in time for Miyoko to do her daily chores. She'd had to quit her job at the hospital because there was a strict policy that nurses could not be pregnant and treat patients at the same time. She also wanted to protect her baby from disease during her pregnancy. But she missed the hustle of the hospital and her sense of purpose when helping others. She had reverted to being a maid for Hojoon's family, like she had been at the baron's house, and loneliness flickered again. Hojoon rested in their room, drained from the day's activities.

Miyoko learned the dynamics of the new household quickly. Hojoon's oldest brother and his wife, Inja, a delicate but strong-tempered woman, did the least amount of work around the house. They occupied the lower bedroom along with their three-month-old baby girl.

"Heat the fire and boil the water first thing tomorrow morning," Inja had ordered Miyoko the day after the wedding. "After everyone eats, then you can eat."

Miyoko did as she was told, and by the time it was her turn to eat the breakfast leftovers, she was ravenous. Soon after breakfast, Miyoko had to turn right around and prepare the family's next meal. Meanwhile, Inja spent most of her day nursing her baby girl and embroidering beautiful flowers on handkerchiefs, blankets, and screens that the family later sold at the market. Miyoko watched Inja nurse and looked forward to the day she could do that with her own child. When she could go back to hospital work, she would financially contribute to the household too. Meanwhile, Miyoko felt inadequate as a daughter-in-law.

Hojoon's second brother and his wife, Yoonhee, shared a room on the second floor next to Miyoko and Hojoon. Yoonhee had a round face and sturdy body and was pleasant and friendly. She chatted with Miyoko as they scrubbed the laundry on the rippled wood board in the courtyard. They often talked while hanging the wash to dry on the clothesline outside their windows, which faced the street.

"Don't mind Inja. She did that to me too, when I first arrived. She gets to do whatever she wants because she brings money to the family from her embroidery, even though it's not much," Yoonhee said. "Remember, just a pinch of salt in our mother-in-law's favorite seaweed soup. And our father-in-law likes his tea lukewarm."

"Thank you," Miyoko said, taking note of Yoonhee's advice. Miyoko was grateful for her company and friendship.

"You eat after the men and women have all eaten too. The Kwon family was originally yangban, but they have very little money now. You have to be frugal and eat just the leftovers."

Miyoko loved her new husband, but she hadn't expected to be a servant in the house. Her hope that her in-laws might support her when she was ready to work and continue her studies seemed foolish now.

Bohbeh's move to Osaka prevented her from still having a sister to talk to. Miyoko felt like an outsider again.

Despite his own concerns, Hojoon picked up on Miyoko's sorrow. "Things aren't easy here being the new daughter-in-law, are they?" Hojoon said one night. He gently massaged her belly in their room. Miyoko could barely keep her eyes open, having woken up at dawn to start the day's cleaning and washing.

"No, it isn't pleasant," she said yawning. "But I'm happy being here with you."

Miyoko rolled her large stomach over to the other side, and Hojoon curled up behind her, nuzzling the nape of her neck.

"I was thinking, though," Miyoko said. "I'd like to return to work when the time is right with the baby."

"I understand. I want to go back to work too," Hojoon said. His last article for the Korean-language newspaper had been about how Japanese policies affected housing and government services for Korean residents. Because of his physical weakness, he now wrote essays in lieu of attending community-building activities. Miyoko felt sorry for Hojoon, as it would be a long time before his energy returned enough for him to go back to law school.

"If I went to work, maybe we could have a place of our own someday. You could write articles from home." She felt a spark of hope about changing their situation.

"That would be ideal. I want to get better first so I can help you."

"How are you feeling?" she asked, his uneven breaths making her uneasy.

"I'm fine, don't worry," she heard Hojoon say before he drifted off to sleep.

The next day, Miyoko woke to find that her hands and feet were swollen like dumplings. She had to lie down in the middle of the day and prop her legs up on some cushions to relieve the pressure. Over the next months, her cramps got so bad that she had to grip counters, doorframes, and anything stable to prevent herself from falling over in pain. Although she wanted to devour food, she refrained so that her parents-in-law and weak husband could eat more. Once, Harabeoji did not come home for dinner, so she secretly scraped every morsel of millet into her mouth with chopsticks and licked the inside of the bowl. Millet was a staple because rice was being rationed to support Japan's growing military expansion in China. Most of the time, there was so little food to eat that Miyoko went to bed hungry. Still, the baby grew.

On the other hand, Hojoon's condition worsened. Miyoko would hear him gasp for air one minute only to find him sleeping peacefully the next. She cooled his head with a cold washcloth, but his temperature still spiked. Neighbors and friends offered expensive remedies, such as deerhorn broth and snake soup, yet he lost more weight. The shine in his eyes dimmed.

Despair seized Miyoko. All that she had feared seemed to be coming true. She suffered from headaches, body aches, and diarrhea. But she wouldn't give up. She was a nurse aide. She took care of Hojoon the best she could. She threw all her love and energy into Hojoon's care, despite her pregnancy. She wanted to make sure he got better.

Halmeoni led the charge, though. She said Hojoon was cold and ordered Miyoko to bring him a blanket. Then she said he was hot, or thirsty, or hungry. When Hojoon became too weak to use the stairs, the couple switched to the living room downstairs. Miyoko was relieved that she didn't have to climb the steps anymore, but now her mother-in-law demanded things all day long as Miyoko tended to Hojoon. Halmeoni suffered from bad knees, so she couldn't do much to help, nor did she try. Miyoko's sisters-in-law were busy caring for their own husbands. She went to bed exhausted and hungry.

"I'm sorry I'm such a burden on you," Hojoon said one day when his mother was out of the room. His cheeks were sallow, and he had lost more weight. He was supposed to go back to the hospital and get another tuberculosis test soon.

"You're not a burden. You're my husband." Miyoko blew on the muddy concoction that the herbalist had said was supposed to help

Hojoon get stronger. "Here you go. Please get better for the baby." The powdered remedy required hours of boiling and stirring, creating a leathery smell that made Miyoko want to throw up. But she stirred it with all the love she could muster. After he drank his medicine, she bathed him with a wet cloth, wringing it in a washbasin and doing it over again the next day.

Miyoko's fatigue grew alongside Hojoon's. When the baby squirmed inside and the skin on her stomach tightened, her entire body clenched into a single question. What would happen if her husband died? She curled up next to Hojoon at night, shielding herself from the answer. She prayed that her baby would be healthy. She prayed that she would wake up the next morning to find Hojoon better. She wanted them to be happy again.

CHAPTER TWENTY-SIX

November 1936

On a brisk November morning, contractions clenched Miyoko's stomach. It was a month before her due date, so she wasn't expecting the baby to come yet. Sharpness seared like a tiger's teeth, and she let out a scream. Yoonhee, who was crouched next to Miyoko in the courtyard washing laundry, flung the wet clothes from her hands and gripped her sister-in-law steadily.

"Hurry!" Miyoko panted. "I think the baby is coming. Get the midwife."

Yoonhee helped guide Miyoko to the living room, where Hojoon was resting. Miyoko heard Yoonhee run out of the house to get help, but not before Miyoko screamed from another stabbing contraction.

"Yeobo, hold my hand," Hojoon said. Miyoko clutched him so hard that he flinched.

When Midwife Yoo arrived, the family helped Hojoon out of the room and waited outside. Miyoko then felt an expert's calm hand prodding her stomach. "Push," the midwife said.

As she gritted her teeth and pushed, the hands around her enormous belly pressed the baby downward. When Miyoko yelled out again, the midwife shoved a washcloth into her mouth, muffling her shouts.

Perspiration slid down Miyoko's face, forming a pool of sweat around her head. After several hours of pushing, she finally gave birth to a tiny baby boy. He was a month early, and his small, wiry body was purplish and limp.

"It's a boy!" Midwife Yoo bellowed as she slapped his bottom to test his lungs. The baby's shrill cries reverberated through the house.

Miyoko twisted her head to see the baby, her body heavy with exhaustion. The midwife snipped the baby's umbilical cord and wiped the white paste off his body with a wet cloth. Something slimy slid between Miyoko's legs, and she was barely conscious of the afterbirth being tossed into a chamber pot. The midwife placed the baby on Miyoko's chest and went out to where Hojoon was waiting.

Miyoko looked into her baby's face for the first time, and her breath caught. His big ears, thin cheeks, and square jaw were perfect, just like his father's. His button eyes stared back with such trust that her heart flowed over, like rice water bubbling in a ttukbaegi pot. The scent of warm earth perfumed the air around him. She inhaled deeply, her sweet baby's smell reaching her very core and filling her with boundless love. Being a mother was beyond words. All her other worries lifted away, replaced by unspeakable joy.

"How is she? Is she all right?" Miyoko overheard Hojoon say, his voice soaked with concern. Hojoon came into the room, and his eyes searched hers. She tried to smile, and his brows uncreased. His face seemed to relax with relief.

The midwife lifted the baby into Hojoon's arms, and Hojoon's mouth dropped in awe. He stroked the baby's cheek and bounced up and down to soothe him. He clucked his tongue softly, as if to say hello. When Hojoon gave him back to the midwife, the baby glanced up at his father with his tiny eyes. Hojoon beamed with pleasure, and Miyoko's heart throbbed with tenderness at seeing her newborn and husband together.

"You should go. He needs to eat, and she needs to rest," the midwife said.

"I'll go," Hojoon said. "I just want you to know that Harabeoji has named the baby already."

Miyoko's ears perked up. Naming a baby was an important rite of passage reserved for the elder in the family.

"If it's a boy, Harabeoji said his name will be Soonho. Soon is the generational name that my ancestors from Andong had previously chosen."

"Soonho," Miyoko mouthed, trying out her son's Korean name.

"He will be called Joonko in Japanese," Hojoon said.

"Joonko," Miyoko said.

"Ko-chan," Hojoon said, "for short."

Children in Japan were usually given a nickname by adding the word *chan*. Ko-chan's cousins in the house were called by their Japanese nicknames, even by Halmeoni, so Ko-chan would probably also be called by his.

"Ko-chan," Miyoko said softly.

Ko-chan cried as she repeated his name, his small mouth wanting. His eyes were now glued tight with tears. She put her pinkie into his mouth, and he sucked instantly, stopping his crying. Miyoko had had so little to eat during her pregnancy that she had no breast milk to offer Ko-chan. She stroked his cheeks, trying to soothe him. His plaintive cries caused Halmeoni to take matters into her own hands.

"Give Ko-chan your breast," Halmeoni barked to Inja.

Inja had given birth to her daughter, Emi-chan, about six months earlier, and her breasts were overflowing with milk. Miyoko had watched Inja nurse Emi-chan during that time and longed to feel that connection when she had her own baby. Now that it was Miyoko's turn and she couldn't nurse, her heart broke.

Inja followed Halmeoni's orders and untied her jeogori top with one swift pull. The aroma of sticky-sweet milk struck Miyoko so hard that it caused her own empty breasts to tingle. Inja brought Ko-chan to her nipple to latch on to her full breast. Then she switched him to the other side and did the same thing. Ko-chan stroked Inja's veiny blue skin, making loud sucking noises with closed eyes.

Seeing another woman nurse her newborn made Miyoko feel a deep emptiness inside. She was afraid she wouldn't bond with her son or be a good mother to him.

Fortunately, Hojoon's health improved after Ko-chan's birth. He had more energy than he'd had in months and spent more time with her and Ko-chan. Miyoko was grateful that Hojoon seemed to have found a new will to live for their son, as she had hoped.

During the first weeks of Ko-chan's life, the small family of three spent evenings in their bedroom together. It was Miyoko's favorite time of day. Hojoon traced his finger over Ko-chan's face and watched Ko-chan grab it with his little hand. Miyoko blew bubbles on Ko-chan's stomach and made him smile.

Even though Ko-chan couldn't understand a word, Miyoko liked to tell him stories.

"Can you recite the Dangun legend to Ko-chan again?" Hojoon said.

Ko-chan reached up for his father's chin as he heard Hojoon's voice. Ko-chan's eyes rounded, like he was tucking his father's voice away into the folds of his big ears.

"Once there was a hero named Dangun who founded Korea . . . ," Miyoko began. Ko-chan turned his face to her and opened his mouth as she talked. She delighted at his attention.

"Go on. Tell him how Korea has a history, even though the Japanese say we don't," Hojoon whispered, stroking Ko-chan's head. They were huddled together with Ko-chan between them, and she felt safe and content.

"There was a tiger and a bear who lived in a cave. They prayed to God to become human, but their wish would only be granted if they could eat mugwort and garlic for one hundred days. The tiger gave up, but the bear didn't, and turned into a woman. She gave birth to Dangun."

Hojoon's body slackened, and his breathing became more regular. Ko-chan sucked his thumb, and his lids soon closed too. The moonlight crept across the room, casting a warm glow over Miyoko's heart. Ko-chan was healthy, and Hojoon was feeling better. She was happy to be a mother and slept peacefully with her small family around her.

Miyoko soon understood the complicated family dynamics she would have to face regarding Ko-chan's care.

One day, Miyoko overheard Inja complaining loudly to Yoonhee while Miyoko had Ko-chan strapped to her back. "I'm tired of having to nurse her baby every day. She's lucky I have milk, or he'd starve! His poop is black too, when Halmeoni tells me to wipe him. She's obviously lacking as a mother."

Miyoko's hands grazed across her flat breasts, and her brows furrowed at her lack of milk. Inja confirmed what she was already feeling. Her vision of a son she could nurse, a husband she could cure, and a home of their own that she could create collapsed heavily on her chest. She crumpled up a burping towel and threw it onto the floor.

Although Hojoon's health improved after Ko-chan's birth, Miyoko's mother-in-law was still more focused on her son's well-being than on her newborn grandson. Yoonhee was the one who had to hang peppers on the door to show the neighbors that a son had been born in the house. Halmeoni didn't seem to hear Ko-chan's cries while she crocheted yet another blanket for her own son. When she wasn't busy making something with her hands for Hojoon, Halmeoni paced the courtyard in front of their bedroom, lost in thought.

Miyoko wanted to climb out of this miserable life with her in-laws. She wondered what her life would have been like in Osaka, what kind of nursing job she would have had there. She yearned for the bustle of the hospital and the satisfaction of helping others. Although she was caring for Ko-chan and Hojoon here, she was alone and doing housework that no one appreciated.

Could they possibly move to Osaka and be close to Bohbeh? Maybe she could still do something outside the home when Hojoon got stronger. Miyoko wanted to talk to Hojoon about it, but she didn't want him to worry about anything. She would wait to talk to him later, when he was more stable.

Bohbeh's visit from her new home in Osaka to bring a present of cash for the baby lifted Miyoko's spirit. Sunshine brushed her shoulder as they took a walk with Ko-chan on her back.

"Congratulations again!" Bohbeh said, squeezing Ko-chan's cheeks. "What did you decide to name him?"

"Joonko. Or Ko-chan for short."

"Ko-chan," Bohbeh cooed. She patted Ko-chan's bottom. "Are you doing all right?"

"I love Ko-chan so much. I never knew I could love another human being this way."

"He's adorable."

"I'm also tired, and a little sad," Miyoko said.

"Sad?" Bohbeh stopped to listen carefully. "Is Hojoon all right? Are your sisters-in-law helping?"

"Hojoon is actually doing better. He plays with Ko-chan a lot, and we try to spend as much time together as possible, the three of us."

"That's great! What about the rest of the family?"

"Halmeoni ordered Inja to nurse the baby because I have no milk. I feel terrible that I can't feed him."

"Don't worry. Ko-chan doesn't know the difference."

Miyoko's shoulders slumped. Bohbeh wasn't a mother yet, so she probably didn't understand how sensitive babies could be. Nevertheless, Bohbeh's presence was a comfort—a family member who wasn't critical of her and took her side.

Bohbeh kissed the top of Ko-chan's head. "Seeing Ko-chan, I think having a child will be good for my marriage."

"Wonderful! Ko-chan could have cousins on my side!" Miyoko hoped Haramoto's drinking had stopped.

"I'm excited! Settling into Osaka has been busy too. It's much bigger than Kyoto, so it takes time to get from one place to another. I'll try to come around and see you more when I can."

"Now that you mention it," Miyoko said, "I haven't had a chance to talk to Hojoon yet, but I would like to move our little family to Osaka when he gets better to be closer to you. I want to start working again too, when Ko-chan gets older."

"That sounds terrific!"

Bohbeh wrapped her arm around Miyoko, and they giggled like old times, when they'd planned for a future in which they lived near each other. Hope sparked again.

One night, when Ko-chan was about five months old, Miyoko dabbed her husband's hot forehead with a washcloth. In the last few weeks, he had become feverish again, and his condition was rapidly deteriorating every day.

"Yeobo," he called to Miyoko, his raspy voice barely audible.

Miyoko pressed her ear to his mouth, like he had done listening to her pregnant belly. In that instant, the happy memories from that time flashed before her. But they just as quickly dimmed, and she was swallowed up by a growing darkness. Everything she had hoped for seemed to be unraveling with Hojoon's worsening state.

"Saranghae," he said. "I love you."

"Dangshin, my love. Rest," she said, stroking his thinning hair.

He pulled something out from under the blanket. "Here, keep this for me," he said.

It was his dojang, his personal name seal: a square wooden stamp with the Korean characters of his name carved on the bottom, used as his official signature. *Kwon Hojoon*, it read, the residual red ink smeared against the script carving.

"But . . . ," Miyoko protested. A dojang was someone's identity, their life. Was he giving it to her for safekeeping? Or did this mean he was giving up? Terror sliced through her. Death would mean her biggest fear coming true. The possibility of loss was always there, but she had denied it. She couldn't imagine what she would do if it actually happened. She would have to make a life of her own with her son. Without Hojoon. Alone.

"No. Please," he said firmly, pressing it into her palm, "promise me you'll go back to Korea with Ko-chan and take this, as soon as you can. As soon as it's safe." Hojoon sucked in big gulps of air. "I know it's not easy living here with my family."

"Shhh. We can talk about it tomorrow."

"We're supposed to return to our homeland together, but I'm not sure I'm going to make it."

"Don't say that. Don't give up!" Miyoko's pleas rang with desperation. She roiled with uncertainty about Hojoon's future, and theirs.

Ko-chan stirred between them. Miyoko kissed her son's forehead. She closed her eyes and prayed silently for Hojoon to get better.

CHAPTER TWENTY-SEVEN

March 1937

Miyoko woke the next morning to Ko-chan's wails. Hojoon lay next to him, unmoving. She shook Hojoon awake, but his body fell limp. Panic rushed through her as she pressed her ear against his mouth and felt no air. She screamed, her shrieks slashing through the house.

Hojoon's older brother ran into their bedroom, shot a look at Hojoon, and took his pulse. He too listened for Hojoon's breathing. Miyoko hardened, fearing the worst. Hojoon's brother gazed across at Miyoko and shook his head. "I'm sorry."

Miyoko coiled into a ball, and sobs left her lungs. She felt raw, like her skin had been ripped off and she'd been left to die too. All that she had hoped for with Hojoon was gone. The life she had dreamed of, with her husband and Ko-chan and a home back in Korea, vanished instantly. All was lost.

Hojoon's mother rushed in frantically, throwing her body over her son's and pounding his still chest. Others said things in hushed voices, and the howls of Miyoko's infant son pierced her ears again. Someone took Ko-chan away, and his cries receded. At just twenty, she was now a widow and a single mother. Hojoon had been only twenty-two, and their nine-month marriage had been so short that Miyoko thought it could have been a dream. Ko-chan had known his father for only five months.

Miyoko pulled at her husband's limp arm as his brother lifted him and took him away. "No!" she shouted, crawling after them before she slumped over on the floor in defeat. On top of the crumpled bedding, she spotted the smooth dojang that Hojoon had given her last night. She picked it up and rubbed it between her fingers. Tears welled under her lids, as she knew it was his last gift to her. She caressed the small stamp in her hand and lifted it to her cheek before she hid it in the folds of her pajama bottoms. She pulled Hojoon's blue-stitched handkerchief from the drawer of their armoire and used it to soak up the tears streaking down her face. She wanted her mother beside her, but she knew that was impossible, and despair thrummed as she imagined how something might happen to her mother too.

She opened her journal and scribbled the first words that came from her heart.

> *You wrote me once that we were like two ducks bobbing in a river.*
>
> *Ducks mate for life, and now you are gone. How will I go on without you?*
>
> *I loved you with a love I never thought possible.*
>
> *You brought joy and tears when I believed love didn't exist for me.*
>
> *You folded me in your arms and changed everything I imagined for myself.*
>
> *You adored Ko-chan and made him squeal with your tickles.*
>
> *You walked with me, even when you were going through your own pain.*
>
> *You laughed with me and made my loneliness disappear.*

How lucky I was to have loved you, even for this short time.

I will protect Ko-chan like you protected us.

I hope you find peace where you are and wait for me.

I will find no other love greater than yours.

Saranghae, my darling. I love you.

Miyoko dropped her journal and wiped her wet eyes with Hojoon's handkerchief. She looked around for Ko-chan and jumped up to find him. She wanted to hold him tight and whisper, *Everything will be okay.* She wanted to say that they would be all right. Inja had taken him to her room to nurse, but when she got there, Miyoko stopped. With emptiness and longing searing her chest, she watched Inja nurse her baby. She wanted to have Hojoon back. She missed him with an ache beyond words. She wanted Ko-chan too, but she didn't want her sadness to rub off on her baby. She needed to feel stronger for her son.

That day, everyone left her alone with her grief. The same thing happened the next day, and the next. Miyoko dreamed of her mother making her favorite doenjang jjigae and telling her to be strong. She cried for Bohbeh, but she was sure no one had fetched her, because her sister didn't come. She retreated to her room and tried to will her despair away so that she could be a good mother to Ko-chan.

But the days blurred as Miyoko lost interest in food and even shunned her baby.

"Here's Ko-chan," Yoonhee said, delivering the baby to her. He bawled.

"No, I don't want him to see me. Not like this," Miyoko said, shooing them away.

"Well, at least eat this," Yoonhee said, leaving her a small bowl of radish broth.

Miyoko's eyes grazed over the thin salty soup without interest, and her attention rested instead on the window. Images of her mulberry tree and her childhood home in the village appeared so vividly that she thought she was there. She found her mother's jade hairpin tucked under her green sweater and pinned it in her hair. She closed her eyes and prayed that her mother's condition would improve. Now that Hojoon was gone, maybe it really was time to go home. Her mother wouldn't get to meet Hojoon, but it wasn't too late for her to have a relationship with her grandson. Waves of sadness over the loss of Hojoon again pounded Miyoko, each one harder than the last. She felt helpless and lost.

Miyoko's grief soon turned into guilt. A pang stabbed her chest—she hadn't been able to save Hojoon, and now she couldn't even take care of her own baby. Her body and soul were shattered, and she didn't know how to fix either one.

Halmeoni charged the sisters-in-law with taking care of Miyoko and Ko-chan.

In her half-conscious, half-awake state, Miyoko overheard Yoonhee talking to Inja.

"She's not getting better," Yoonhee said. "Mother-in-law says to watch her carefully and take away all the medicine around the house. She might want to end her life. Remember Neighbor Song's daughter, who lost her husband last year? He left her with three children. She hanged herself in the kitchen. Awful."

"We'd better keep an eye on her," Inja said.

It was true. Miyoko had fallen into a deep depression. She missed Hojoon more than she had ever thought possible. She sat for hours with her knees bent in front of the altar that Hojoon's family had prepared for his funeral. In the center was a photo of him taken in his black law school uniform that had big brass buttons down the front and a small *J* on the collar showing that he had studied law. He looked so distinguished, only twenty-two, ready to fight injustice, if only he'd had a chance.

Miyoko missed her conversations with Hojoon and watching him play with Ko-chan. She longed to feel his warm touch, see his bright eyes, and be sheltered by his generous heart. She had tried to prepare herself to be strong, knowing that he was very ill and might not survive. She prayed and reminded herself that Hojoon would be at peace if he died, relieved of all his physical pain. But she wasn't ready for this.

She had become a single mother, a widow, and an unwanted daughter-in-law overnight. Although humble, the nursing job she had given up for her family had been her own. Now she had neither a marriage nor a job. All she wanted for herself had slipped away. Her dreams seemed so far off, out of her reach.

Except she was Ko-chan's mother now, and she loved him. She would try to be a better mother to him. She would take charge of his care, play with him, and sleep with him. She would resume the life that Hojoon would have wanted for them.

Later that night, she took Ko-chan from Inja's room, where he had been sleeping, and brought him into bed with her. She watched her son yawn and settle into slumber. Miyoko's heart pumped with love and a newfound resolve to take care of him as best she could. She lit a candle and read the Bible. The words consoled her, especially as she read Psalms. "God is our refuge and strength, an ever-present help in times of trouble." An image of Teacher Kim flashed, and Miyoko remembered to pray for courage to live life and have hope again. She curled up next to her son and let the fuzz of his baby skin brush her cheeks.

CHAPTER TWENTY-EIGHT

April 1937

Hojoon's funeral was held at their home ten days later. Even though Hojoon was Christian, funeral rites were still traditionally Buddhist. A bald monk cloaked in a brown habit struck a match and burned a photo of Hojoon inside a rusty barrel in the courtyard, marking his death on earth and the release of his spirit.

The family moved to the altar in the sitting room, where his cremated ashes rested in a silver urn. The photo of Hojoon in his college uniform sat framed in the center, surrounded by offerings of candles, incense, fruit, and flowers donated by the church. After the mourning period, Miyoko wanted to go back to the makeshift church again. Following Buddhism, she would have to wait forty-nine days, because Hojoon's spirit wandered the world between the living and the dead for that time before moving on to the afterlife.

The monk clicked a wooden stick against the gourd in his hand and chanted. The family, all dressed in white hanboks, knelt in a line before the altar with their hands on their thighs and their eyes closed. Halmeoni was hunched over with her forehead touching the ground, as if unable to hold herself up. At the end of the monk's prayers, everyone walked by the altar with their heads bowed to pay their last respects.

When Miyoko looked back, Halmeoni was still in the same rounded position, pounding the ground with one arm.

Bohbeh and Haramoto, who had come from Osaka for the funeral, stood next to Miyoko, who had Ko-chan strapped to her back. Bohbeh came bearing big hugs and comfort, which Miyoko gratefully accepted. Sorrow plunged into her heart when she thought of how her mother would never know her husband.

Miyoko and Bohbeh stepped outside the house to talk. Ko-chan squirmed but eventually fell asleep on her back.

"I'm so sorry about Hojoon," Bohbeh said.

Miyoko sniffled. "I miss all the goodness that he was. He was everything to me." All that had been bottled up inside now burst forth. "There was a darkness for a while. My in-laws thought I might want to hurt myself."

"I'm sorry for all you've been through." Bohbeh held Miyoko's hands and rubbed them softly. "Your son needs you now."

Miyoko bounced Ko-chan, feeling her baby's warmth against her. "I feel guilty that I haven't been able to nurse and care for him. He used to cry when I tried to hold him, so I only carry him like this when he's sleeping. It's getting better, though. I've been playing with him more, and we've been laughing together. I'll try to be a better mother for him."

"I'm sure you will be," Bohbeh said. "I'll help as much as I can."

"I've been thinking. Do you think Ko-chan and I could come live with you? I know I said we could live close by when Hojoon was here, but now I won't be able to afford it. I could work and pay you for living expenses. Maybe you could help me with childcare until I get settled."

Miyoko's anticipation grew the more she talked. She had been worried about how she was going to support herself and her son going forward, and had planned to talk to Bohbeh about it. Although her in-laws probably wouldn't kick her out because of Ko-chan, she didn't think she could stay much longer. She would resume being a servant in the house again. If she continued to live there, she would lose her independence and the opportunity to live life the way she saw fit.

"I'm not sure Haramoto would like anyone in the house right now. We want to have a baby ourselves. Since our last talk, we've been trying but haven't had any success. Haramoto has been a better husband, and I don't think I want to complicate things right now."

Miyoko squeezed her sister's hand. She was thrilled for Bohbeh, despite being disappointed for herself. "I understand." She didn't want to disrupt Bohbeh's marriage and their chance at having a baby. Was there anywhere else she could go? Miyoko remembered how Hojoon had urged her to go back to Korea as soon as possible. "Then I think I'm going to write to Mother to see if Ko-chan and I can live with her in Korea. Hojoon would have wanted that. He knew how difficult his mother could be too."

Bohbeh's eyes softened. "It must be hard here. At least I don't have in-laws to deal with." Her tone turned more cheerful. "Let me know how Mother is and what she says. I'll miss you terribly if you go back."

Miyoko's heart stung when she thought of leaving her sister behind, but her world in Japan now seemed untenable.

Although Miyoko had written to her mother a while ago about the wedding, she hadn't heard back. Because of the censors, Miyoko had been careful not to say anything critical in her letter. She decided to try again and, cautious with her words, wrote another letter to Mother care of Taeyoung.

> Mother,
> I hope you received my last letter. I had a baby boy! You would be proud—the first boy in our family in a long time. His name is Soonho, or Joonko in Japanese, and we call him Ko-chan for short. He is precious.
>
> Sadly, Hojoon died last week on March 31. He never recovered completely from tuberculosis. I loved him, and my heart is broken. Bohbeh has been a great comfort.

I miss you so much. And I miss Korea too. May I come home with the baby and live with you? I know you don't have the boardinghouse anymore, but maybe we can live together somewhere, just the three of us. I will work and help take care of you. We could be together, like in old times.

Your daughter,
Miyoung

Miyoko considered writing her father to ask for help but remembered that he was probably Mother's primary support and had enough financial responsibility for his own family and business. Visions of going back to Korea and seeing Mother again brought some glimmer of hope that Miyoko could change her circumstances. She wanted to provide for Ko-chan. That's what Hojoon would have wanted, and she wanted that too.

She wrote a separate letter to Taeyoung.

Dear Taeyoung,
You will read in my letter to Mother that Hojoon died last month. I am devastated and find it hard to still live here with my in-laws. I would like to take you up on your offer to help me find a nurse aide job. I want to help Mother, see you, and start a new life.

I will wait for you to write back before I start to make plans.

Your sister,
Miyoung

She took the envelope to the post office and was surprised by the clamor in the streets. She had been absorbed by Hojoon's death and hadn't been outside in a while. Miyoko passed by neighbors clanging teapots and hibachi sets, assembling them into piles to donate to metal collection drives. From inside a store, a radio station blared that metal was needed for Japan's military incursion into China. She overheard an older Korean man whispering something in Korean to another man.

"Japan is saying war is inevitable because China has resources Japan needs. Pretty soon, Japan will take over all of China the way it did Korea."

Miyoko's temples pounded, warning her that war was near. She wanted to take Ko-chan and go home to protect Mother. She didn't want to support a Japanese war against another country. Maybe she could use her nursing skills in Korea to help her own people. She hoped her letters to Taeyoung and Mother would make it to them quickly.

After the funeral, her mother-in-law took a turn for the worse. Every morning, Halmeoni knelt at the altar in front of Hojoon's photo, then threw her arms above her head and down again, over and over. Her gestures fanned the incense smoke and caused the flames of the candles to shudder. "Aigo, Aigo," Halmeoni moaned plaintively, like a sad Korean ballad.

Halmeoni took out her anger over her son's death on her five-month-old grandson. One time, Ko-chan cried especially hard, and Halmeoni shook him before Miyoko could stop her. Miyoko ran over and grabbed Ko-chan from Halmeoni's arms, terrified that she might hurt him. Ko-chan cried against Miyoko's shoulder as she rubbed his back, comforting him.

"You're the one who should have died, not my son!" Halmeoni shouted over Ko-chan's cries.

Miyoko knew that Halmeoni was still in shock, and she didn't think her mother-in-law would ever hurt her grandson, but she kept a close watch over her son, even when he was napping. She swaddled him on her back when she did the chores, trying not to draw attention from her mother-in-law. She waited for word from her mother or Taeyoung.

Miyoko devised games to play with Ko-chan to bring them closer. There was one that he seemed to like best. She wiggled his nose and taught him how to do the same to her. Then she lowered her forehead to touch his. He giggled. Then they did it again—wiggle, wiggle, bump—and he laughed harder.

She sang him "Swanee River," a Western song that she had learned at the baron's house. "Hmm . . . hmm . . . Su-wa-nee Lee-ber," she hummed, trying to pronounce the two English words she remembered. She sang it while she worked with Ko-chan strapped to her back. It seemed to soothe him.

Miyoko showed Ko-chan his father's dojang and Hojoon's old beige handkerchief with blue trim. When Ko-chan tried to put the seal in his mouth, she took it away. She would give it to him someday when he was older. Ko-chan sucked on the edge of the handkerchief, and a soft contentedness stroked Miyoko's heart. Ko-chan was her sole source of comfort now, and they were bonding.

At night before bed, she would read the Bible aloud while Ko-chan lay next to her. He must have been listening attentively, because when she stopped speaking, he grunted. When she continued, he quieted. She would continue reading aloud until she heard the gentle purring of his breathing. Then she would close the book and fall asleep too.

Once the forty-nine-day grieving period was over, Halmeoni underwent a complete transformation. She transferred her fervent love for her dead son to her tiny seven-month-old grandson, now her only living memory of Hojoon. She doted on Ko-chan day and night, never letting him out of her sight. She sang "Cha chang, cha chang" over and over, lulling him to sleep. She even supervised Inja's nursing of Ko-chan. Shock gripped Miyoko over her mother-in-law's behavior.

"Give him your larger breast first!" Halmeoni ordered Inja. Having no choice, Inja complied while ignoring her own baby's needs. Ko-chan became so precious to Halmeoni that she wouldn't let anyone else near him, not even Miyoko. While Miyoko empathized with her mother-in-law's grief, it became increasingly difficult to bear. Just as she was feeling closer to Ko-chan, she was being separated from him. She hoped this wouldn't continue much longer.

To top it off, the fear of war with China came true when Japanese forces invaded the mainland in July 1937. Government-run newspapers made it sound like the battles of Shanghai, Beijing, and then Nanjing were inevitable, and that Japan was fulfilling some divine order of the emperor. Like residents everywhere, Hojoon's family members and their neighbors were forced to give more to metal drives and to witness more send-offs of soldiers to China.

Meanwhile, Halmeoni continued to center the household around Ko-chan's needs. When Miyoko tried to spend time with her son, Halmeoni kept Miyoko so busy with chores that she was left with only evenings for Ko-chan.

One cold day in early November, after Ko-chan's morning feeding, Harabeoji called the family out to the street.

"We have to bow toward the Imperial Palace of Tokyo at 9:00 a.m., for one minute," he said, a dark scowl crossing his face. "Order of the emperor."

Miyoko strapped Ko-chan onto her back and marched outside with the whole family. Their neighbors gathered too, and everyone turned to face north along the street. Miyoko bowed stiffly, as did everyone else. A cloud of fear seemed to overshadow all of the country.

Japan was becoming ever more nationalistic, and Miyoko feared that Japan's aggressions in China could lead to war with other countries. She wondered what Korea thought of Japan's increased militarism. She wanted to be with Mother in case the Japanese extracted even more from Koreans—they were probably donating metal, rubber, and other items to Japan's war efforts too. Her desire to return home grew stronger.

Ignoring what was happening outside, Halmeoni wanted to throw Ko-chan a big traditional dol, or first birthday party, later that month.

"Since we couldn't celebrate Ko-chan's special one hundredth day because of Hojoon's illness, let's make this big. Every Korean baby who reaches this milestone deserves to live a full life!"

Miyoko agreed. They could all celebrate something happy for a change.

Halmeoni demanded that the household prepare a feast even bigger than the one for Miyoko and Hojoon's wedding. Oranges were stacked into pyramids. Apples, cakes, noodles, pens, and money were placed on a table in front of Ko-chan; what he picked was supposed to represent his future—prosperity, scholarship, longevity, or commercial success. Ko-chan wore a bright-red jacket with balloon pants cinched at the ankles and pointy white socks. His hat was cone shaped and bordered in colorful stripes.

Even though it was only one special day filled with food and treats, Miyoko's plan to take Ko-chan away from this comfortable place and back to Korea tugged at her heart. She hadn't received any news since her letters six months back. Raising Ko-chan in an occupied Korea would deprive him of the attention of his grandparents and their financial support. Doubt surfaced about her decision to leave. Miyoko's financial situation was precarious too. She might have to borrow money from Bohbeh for travel expenses.

Clapping their hands together, Ko-chan's grandparents urged him to pick something from the table. Ko-chan's eyes darted around the room at all the attentive faces. He scanned the selection and reached for a long writing brush, all the while whimpering in confusion.

Halmeoni immediately hailed it as the appropriate choice. "Eomeona! Oh my! Just like his father, he's going to be a lawyer!" Ko-chan wailed in response, no doubt scared by all the excitement and attention.

The birthday celebration further fueled Halmeoni's obsession with her grandson. Nothing Miyoko did could distract Halmeoni from her singular focus. Even when Miyoko cut up the apples from the table, assembled some ddeok rice cakes, and arranged them all on a plate for Halmeoni to eat, she shoved Miyoko away. Before the apples turned brown, Miyoko bit into a sour one and puckered her face, the tartness tasting like her life under her mother-in-law.

Miyoko yearned for her own mother and Taeyoung to respond. Maybe Taeyoung would meet them at Pyongyang Station and they could go out to see Mother together. She could find a nurse aide job near Mother and enroll Ko-chan in school. She could seek meaningful work again and start over.

Meanwhile, Halmeoni was becoming even more protective of Ko-chan, insisting that he now sleep with her too. Miyoung couldn't do much to protest, as this was Halmeoni's home, not hers. To fill the emptiness of her evenings, Miyoko knit tiny socks for Ko-chan. She stole moments with her son, reading and singing to him, as she used to do. Joy brimmed at seeing Ko-chan's feet snuggled in her handmade socks. Her heart ached for Hojoon, and she wished he were still with them.

CHAPTER TWENTY-NINE

December 1937

Miyoko finally received a letter from home, over a year since the last one. It was from Taeyoung. Chills slid down her arms to her fingertips as she opened it.

> Dear Miyoung,
>
> I'm sorry to tell you this, but your mother passed away a week ago. She was more ill than she wanted anyone to know. She had long suffered from a debilitating illness. She never really recovered movement on one side of her body. Her heart finally gave out. Father is taking care of arrangements.
>
> I did read her your letters about your marriage, the baby, and Hojoon's passing. She seemed happy and sad too.
>
> If you can come back to Korea, I would welcome you and Ko-chan. You could stay at my house in Pyongyang. The bank has promoted me, so I have a

larger place where you both could stay, and I can help you find a job as a nurse.

Take care of yourself,

Taeyoung

Miyoko's legs bowed, and she fell to her knees. First Hojoon, now Mother. Two more loved ones, gone. Her hopes of a future with Mother in Korea withered away. She reached inside her dresser to retrieve Mother's hairpin. She fingered the round curve and slid it through her own bun. Now this delicate token was all she had left. Tears streamed down her cheeks.

Miyoko rushed to a neighbor who had a job in Osaka and could relay a message to Bohbeh to come as soon as she could, as Miyoko had news about their mother. Telegrams were too expensive, and a telephone was impossible to access, since so few people had one. Besides, Miyoko wanted to tell Bohbeh in person. A few days later, Bohbeh came, and they went into Miyoko's bedroom.

"Mother—she passed away," Miyoko said. She threw herself into Bohbeh's arms. "I never even had a chance to say a final goodbye."

"Poor Mother!" Bohbeh's chin trembled. "She must have suffered so much alone. It makes sense now—her hurry to marry me off and send you to school." Bohbeh pounded her chest with a fisted hand.

"She was sick for a long time," Miyoko said, her eyes puffy with regret. "Remember the back pains she used to have and how she dragged her legs? She pretended it was nothing so that we wouldn't worry about her. I wouldn't have left if I had known she was so ill. I would have taken care of her and helped with the boardinghouse."

"I wouldn't have come either. But she wanted better for us," Bohbeh said.

"Yes. She wanted you to have a good marriage and me to be educated and make something of myself. Neither of these things actually . . . happened." Miyoko felt disappointed that she had let Mother down and wanted to make it up somehow.

"Her spirit is finally at rest, though," Bohbeh said. "Since Mother has no child nearby, I'm sure your father will give her the proper Buddhist burial she deserves."

"I hope so." Miyoko leaned her head on Bohbeh's shoulder. "When I go back to Korea, I will pay respects to her. I was afraid I would never see her again, and I was right."

Miyoko wanted to forget that moment of looking back at Mother from the moving train and watching her fade away, disappearing from Miyoko's touch. The finality of that moment struck her now that her mother was gone. "Now she will never meet Hojoon or know her grandchild."

From outside her bedroom, Miyoko heard Ko-chan crying and Halmeoni calling for Inja to feed him. Poor Ko-chan. He was without a father and now a grandmother. Panic tightened her chest. Could she lose him, like she had Hojoon, her mother, and her oldest sister?

"I can't let it happen again," Miyoko said. "Ko-chan needs me, and I need him."

"Being a mother is a big responsibility," Bohbeh said. "But you can do it. You were so young when you came here. I was worried about you, all alone in a new country without Mother nearby. But you survived on your own."

Miyoko was heartened by her sister's words. She would find work and figure out how to support Ko-chan by herself. Though nursing seemed like the logical choice, going back to Korea without a job seemed too risky until she had more experience. And, sadly, the urgency to see her mother was no longer there. It made sense to stay in Japan a bit longer and save money. When Ko-chan was older, they would go to Pyongyang and live with Taeyoung.

In the meantime, her living situation, though not ideal, would have its benefits. If she moved out, she would have no one to take care of Ko-chan while she worked. For now, they would stay put.

She wrote to Taeyoung to thank him and tell him about her plan. At home, Miyoko tried harder to take care of her one-year-old son. She carried him on her back, but he squirmed to be let down. She played peekaboo; he cried. He now preferred Halmeoni, who tickled his feet until he gurgled. And the loneliness still haunted her as she watched her sister-in-law breastfeed Ko-chan.

A week later, while dusting the shelves, Miyoko noticed the white porcelain vase that had held Hojoon's funeral flowers. Woosun had brought them as a gift from the church. His kind voice called to her, inviting her back to a place where she had found belonging when she first arrived in Kyoto. Woosun was also Hojoon's friend, and he would understand her grief.

Woosun was at church the Sunday Miyoko finally went back. Services were still being held in secret at the Korean elementary school. The church members were being more careful than ever when congregating; they'd been under terrible scrutiny since the war with China had begun in the summer.

"Miyoko!" Woosun said. His hair had grown longer and covered one of his eyes. His round glasses sat crookedly on his nose. His schoolboy looks reminded her of Hojoon so much that her breath hitched.

"It's good to see you, oppa," she said, still calling him "big brother."

"It's wonderful to see you too," Woosun said. "We've all been praying for your family."

Miyoko looked around at the smiling faces and warmed at the expressions of condolence. This community of expatriates, the solidarity of fellow brothers and sisters, was what she had been missing.

"Thank you for the flowers and the donation for Hojoon's funeral. If there's anything I can do for the church, please let me know," Miyoko said.

"We're just happy to see you back. How are you?"

"It hasn't been easy." Miyoko choked up. "I just found out I lost my mother too."

Woosun's face fell. "I'm so sorry to hear that."

"It was hard." Miyoko stroked the jade pin in her hair. She had worn a hanbok today in her mother's honor. She felt at home in it, even though she hadn't worn a traditional Korean dress since Hojoon's funeral. She was still careful to walk the backstreets to the church so that she wouldn't be seen.

"I'm glad you decided to come here. You're not alone."

"Thank you." Gratitude rose in her chest.

"I know this might be too soon," Woosun said, "but some of us thought that being of service might actually help you in your grief."

"What kind of service?" Miyoko said, thinking about Hojoon's selflessness.

"We could use some of your nursing skills to help our parishioners."

"I'm not a licensed nurse yet, but . . ." Miyoko wasn't sure she was good enough to work alone without a supervising nurse. But it would be good practice.

"A title doesn't matter. Some of our church members don't feel well but can't afford to go to the hospital. Maybe you could provide some basic medical advice, since you used to work there." Woosun's voice grew more animated. "We know you took care of Hojoon too, so we think you're more than qualified."

"I . . ." Maybe this would give her purpose again. "I can give it a try."

At the church, Woosun set up a small makeshift consulting corner with a screen for privacy, and Miyoko treated patients after the Sunday service. She applied what she had learned from her job as a nurse aide and her time caring for Hojoon. She cobbled together a few medical supplies and carried them in a bag to church every week, always careful to look around before entering and leaving. If she was suspected of doing something the Japanese police disapproved of, she might be questioned and detained, further removing her from Ko-chan's life.

"A little antiseptic there would help that scrape," she said to an elderly man who had fallen on the street. She squeezed the stopper and dabbed the wound with the antiseptic. "Let's put some gauze on it so it stays clean." Miyoko ran out of these basic first aid items quickly, so the church paid for more. The church leaders also slipped her a small bag of white rice as a thank-you for her services. She couldn't wait to share it with Bohbeh the next time she saw her.

"When you get home, lie down, and raise your feet to take the pressure off your back," she advised a pregnant woman.

By the second Sunday, word had spread, and even people who hadn't come to church started attending just to talk to Miyoko. Her confidence grew, and she began feeling better about herself. She was able to mourn the deaths of Hojoon and her mother by helping others. A sense of self-worth emerged again. She was building a future for Ko-chan and herself.

This activity was something she kept secret, away from the judgment of her in-laws. They might think she was doing too much outside the home instead of in it and try to stop her. She asked Halmeoni to take care of Ko-chan while she was welcoming new congregants at church, and Halmeoni never questioned her.

Miyoko's mother-in-law tried to keep her apart from Ko-chan even when she was at home. She ordered her to do extra chores around the house and sent her on long errands. Once in a while, Miyoko would play with her son, and they would enact the old game of wiggling each other's noses and bumping heads. She loved spending this time with Ko-chan but resented the wall that Halmeoni was building between mother and son. She needed to do something, or she might lose her son too.

Miyoko was in the kitchen one night making seaweed soup for dinner when she heard the women talking. The sitting area was next to the kitchen, so Miyoko positioned herself at the doorway, where she could see them from the side. She pretended to be reaching up for some dishes on the shelf while listening in on their conversation.

"Inja, that's a beautiful screen you're working on," Halmeoni said proudly. "How much do you think it will make at the market?" Halmeoni, seated cross-legged on the floor, fanned one-year-old Ko-chan, who was crawling about and babbling.

"I hope it will sell at a good price. Enough to buy new blankets for the family this winter," Inja said. A smugness laced her voice as she embroidered. Her baby daughter lay on her stomach, watching the needle move in and out of the canvas.

It was now a bitter February, almost a year after Hojoon's death. The cold northern winds whipped across Kyoto, whistling in through the gaps between the slats of their old wooden home. The warm blankets would come in handy. Halmeoni turned to Yoonhee, who was washing the earthenware kimchi urns in the courtyard.

"How's the kimchi selling going?" Halmeoni asked. Miyoko had helped Yoonhee with kimjang, or kimchi making, this past December. It was Yoonhee's specialty, a collective activity carried out over two days to preserve the kimchi for winter consumption. One day consisted of washing the long napa cabbage, sprinkling sea salt directly between leaves, and cutting the leaves into wedges lengthwise. The next day, a yangnyeom sauce was made by mixing fermented shrimp paste, sugar, and gochugaru, a red pepper powder.

Miyoko had been charged with cutting items for the yangnyeom mix, consisting of radish, garlic, ginger, scallions, and pears. She helped insert the yangnyeom stuffing into the cabbage and then folded the preparation into the large urn to ferment in the yard to be eaten during the winter and spring. Despite Miyoko's contribution, Yoonhee received the praise from Halmeoni because she sold the kimchi at the market.

"I sold ten jars this week," Yoonhee said to Halmeoni, chest puffing.

Halmeoni's small head bobbed up and down with satisfaction.

Miyoko went back to stirring the boiling seaweed soup. She tested the thick, slippery soup, which contained the ideal mix of protein and vitamins for breast milk, and singed her tongue. Inja, who was still nursing Ko-chan and her own baby girl, would eat this nutritious soup almost every day, like most new Korean mothers. Miyoko was making food that nourished her son through someone else's breasts.

Miyoko brought the hot soup in on a tray. Halmeoni turned in Miyoko's direction. "We could use some extra money in the house for Ko-chan now that Hojoon is gone."

Miyoko knelt and ladled the soup into individual bowls. She had an idea. If Inja and Yoonhee could gain her mother-in-law's respect by earning money through their skills, she could too. Her time giving medical advice at church had inspired her. She could try to go back to the employment agency and get a job as a nurse aide—she could earn her in-laws' approval while obtaining the experience she needed to return to Korea with strong prospects.

A crescendo of momentum seized her. The family doubted her abilities, and she wanted to prove them wrong. This would mean spending more time apart from Ko-chan at first, but it seemed to be the only way. Miyoko decided she would broach the idea with her mother-in-law.

A few days later, while Ko-chan was napping, Miyoko brought Halmeoni some tea. She was knitting a sweater for her grandson. Miyoko felt a pang as she remembered the sweater that she had knit for Hojoon. She missed him.

Miyoko cleared her throat. "I was thinking of working again to help pay for expenses at home."

The knitting needles clicked louder.

"I might be able to get a job as a nurse aide. But I would need someone to watch Ko-chan."

Halmeoni's eyes widened. "That sounds like a fine plan. Don't worry about Ko-chan. I'll take care of him, like always."

Halmeoni's tone didn't sit well with Miyoko. But she would try to be a better mother by providing for her son, just like her mother had done by running the boardinghouse. Ko-chan would be safe with her in-laws until she could take him back to Korea. Halmeoni didn't have to know the real reason for her plan right now.

CHAPTER THIRTY

1938

The employment agency was still there on Kawaramachi Street, not far from the Kamo River, where she and Hojoon used to walk. The sharp winter air chilled Miyoko's bones as her eyes spotted the familiar trees and paths. The image of sunlit days with lovers laughing and holding hands faded, vanishing like their love.

The glass on the sliding door rattled as she walked into the old wooden building. A gentleman in a gray suit and red tie stood next to a filing cabinet, shuffling papers. Unlike the last gentleman who had taken her application, this man was short, with hair so slick it looked like he had soaked his head in oil. He motioned her over to a chair in front of his desk.

"Dozo, please come sit down," he said stiffly.

"I'd like to apply for a job as a nurse aide. My name is Ando Miyoko. I was assigned to a position at Kyoto Daini Hospital before through your office . . ." Japanese rolled off her tongue. Using her Japanese name this time, though, made her body twinge. She had gradually reembraced her Korean heritage with Hojoon. She wanted Ko-chan to be proud of his culture too. Miyoko didn't mention her son. She couldn't risk not getting hired because she had a child, and Halmeoni had already agreed to take care of him.

His eyes traveled up and down Miyoko's blue striped kimono, the same one she had worn when she interviewed for her previous job.

He riffled through some papers and found her file. "You need to be studying for the nursing license test in order to get a job as a nurse aide now."

"Is that right? I had that job just a few years ago." She knew that getting a nursing license was difficult, and she didn't know if she would pass.

"The position is in high demand these days, and the country needs nurses."

"Are there any requirements, like a high school diploma?" Miyoko hoped he wouldn't ask for that.

"No."

"When is the next exam?"

"October. Do you want the job?"

"Yes. Thank you. I'll take it," Miyoko said quickly, not wanting to lose this chance.

Worry twisted inside her because she didn't know what the exam would entail or how much it would cost. But she would figure it out. The problem was that studying would mean spending even more time apart from Ko-chan. He might grow more distant from her than he already was.

That night, Miyoko decided to ask her mother-in-law to watch Ko-chan again, this time so that she could study for the nursing exam. After toweling off the last of the dinner dishes, Miyoko knelt in the sitting room next to Halmeoni. Ko-chan and his cousin Emi-chan were playing with rattle drums. Halmeoni seemed relaxed.

"I need to get a nursing license to do any kind of nurse-related work now. It would require me to study for the nursing exam too."

"Is that so?" Halmeoni said. "Do you have to pay money for that?" One eyebrow rose higher than the other.

"I'll probably need to get some books. But I'll be able to do some part-time nurse aide work to help with Ko-chan's expenses in the meantime."

"As long as we don't have to pay for anything." Halmeoni's lips tightened.

"I have enough saved for books," Miyoko said. Hojoon had given her his earnings from his articles, and she had saved up some money to return to Korea. "But I would still need your help to take care of Ko-chan a little more." Miyoko reached over to touch her son's rosy cheek. She was already missing him.

"Of course. I'll take care of my grandson." Halmeoni swooped Ko-chan over her shoulder and patted him on the back. He let out a big burp.

Halmeoni seemed content spending more time with Ko-chan. She showed love through intense affection and togetherness. That wasn't how Miyoko's own mother had demonstrated love. She had provided for Miyoko and her sisters financially by running the farm and later the boardinghouse. Even though Miyoko wanted to connect more with her son, the way she was taught how was through service and work.

Miyoko threw herself into her books for her and her son's future. Memories of Hojoon studying for his law exams and the dream that had never materialized pushed her to continue. However, she soon discovered that it was impossible to study at her crowded in-laws' house after work. The babies cried, the sisters-in-law gossiped loudly, and Halmeoni still called for Miyoko to fetch things that she could get on her own. Miyoko found herself falling behind.

Every day, she would hop onto a crowded streetcar in the morning for her job at the hospital and return exhausted that afternoon. Then she would have to cram for her nursing exam at night. It was so stressful that Miyoko dozed off while she studied and missed her periods again. But she couldn't afford not to pass.

Miyoko needed her own space to study. She used some of her earnings to rent a small room at a boardinghouse across the street from the hospital. She hated the thought of being separated from Ko-chan and dipping into the money she was saving for Korea, but she needed to make this sacrifice for their future. She obtained Halmeoni's approval without a fight. In fact, Halmeoni seemed happy to see her go.

Her temporary place was a tiny, four-tatami-mat room with just enough space for a table and a futon. In one corner sat a brazier for boiling hot water and heating soup. She missed seeing Ko-chan every day, but he didn't seem to notice her absence. Her son had latched on to his grandmother as his playmate and his aunt as his nursemaid.

When Miyoko visited on the weekends, Ko-chan ignored her when she shook the toy drum to draw his attention. Usually, she was left as a bystander, merely observing him playing with his cousin or his grandmother. Miyoko returned to her boardinghouse with an empty heart. She craved her son's hugs and time alone with him, and she hoped these things would happen after she passed her exams.

After another six months of little sleep, she took the nursing exam. She sat in a small room at the hospital, answering question after question on anatomy, physiology, biology, and more. When the results were posted on the door, Miyoko held her breath while she scanned the list for her exam number: 2122. Oh, the joy when she saw those digits! She let out a big sigh of relief and felt a weight lift off her shoulders.

Her mother-in-law was lukewarm about her accomplishment.

"So this means you'll get a well-paying job now, right?" Halmeoni said.

"I plan to go back to the agency next week to apply," Miyoko replied, masking her disappointment. There was no praise for her hard work or her success in getting her nursing license.

Members of her church, however, reacted differently. Miyoko had missed services to study, but when she snuck back and told Woosun, he yelped. "Miyoko passed the Japanese nursing exam! Do you know how rare this is for a Korean? Manseh! Hooray!"

Miyoko reddened and lowered her head at the attention. The crowd of thirty or so members clapped their hands in unison to celebrate her success, filled with joy that one of their members had managed to pass this difficult test. Despite the danger and the risk of a shutdown, the congregation was still meeting, showing how much the community of fellowship meant to them, and her.

"Now the gift of a small bag of rice won't be enough," Woosun teased, winking. "We'll definitely have to pay you something for your services now that you're an official nurse."

"Oh no, that won't be necessary. It's my pleasure." Miyoko lifted her head with pride. It was heartwarming that the church celebrated her accomplishment in such a public way.

Miyoko again slid open the wooden door of the employment agency, this time with her nursing license in hand. A different man, older and wearing glasses, was sitting with his head buried in the newspaper.

"Can I help you?" he asked.

"I'd like to find a nursing job, please," Miyoko said, handing over her certificate. "Here are my credentials."

"Hmm," he said as he read it over, absently flicking his ashes into a large glass tray brimming with cigarette butts. "Suhr Miyoung." As an official document, her nursing certificate bore her Korean name.

Heat rose behind Miyoko's eyes upon hearing her name pronounced incorrectly. She had hoped that having the credential would be enough, but she feared that potential employers might not want to hire a Korean nurse. Miyoko tightened her fists.

"You're Chōsenjin," he snarled.

"Yes," Miyoko said. It had been a while since she'd been in the workplace and heard those stinging words. Her nationality was a scar she would carry forever. It would be the same for Ko-chan too, if he stayed in Japan.

"Well, there's a nursing post in Osaka available for a . . ." He cleared his throat. "But not here." He looked down, averting his eyes.

"I . . . I was hoping to find something closer to my family."

"Sorry, that's all there is. Do you want to interview with the head nurse there or not?" he said abruptly.

Miyoko's palms dampened. "Yes. If that's all you have."

He stamped her application and told her where to go for the interview.

The next day, Miyoko gazed out the train window at the foliage of burned oranges, browns, and reds as she left Kyoto Station. She tapped her legs nervously in anticipation of her possible new job. That morning, Ko-chan hadn't wanted to come to her when she left. Anguish pelted her heart. She folded the corner of the application over and over as the train pulled her farther away from Ko-chan. On the approach to Osaka, she saw plumes of smoke spewing from tall concrete buildings. Miyoko's only ray of hope was seeing Bohbeh, whom she hadn't been able to meet with often while she was studying for her exam.

"Konnichiwa," Miyoko said when she arrived in the waiting room of Osaka Imperial University Clinic, a cold, gray building across from a park. A nurse with a wide face and bright eyes glanced up and smiled.

"Hai, dozo," she said, welcoming Miyoko in.

"I'm looking for Nurse Sato," Miyoko said, looking at the piece of paper the agency man had provided.

"That's me," she said in a friendly tone.

"The employment agency in Kyoto sent me for the nurse position." Miyoko handed her paperwork over with shaky hands. Nurse Sato read Miyoko's certificate out loud.

"Passed nursing test for Shiga Prefecture on October 21, 1938 . . . Suhr Miyoung."

Miyoko shifted her legs as the nurse read over her Korean name. Nurse Sato pronounced it perfectly.

"Wonderful! I see you were born in December 1916, so you're twenty-one. You'll fit right in with the other single women in the nursing dormitory. Welcome," Nurse Sato said with a broad grin. "I'll be your supervisor."

"Arigatou." Miyoko bowed, surprised that everything was moving so quickly. Nurse Sato had assumed that she was unmarried and childless, like most nurses.

"We require all of our nurses to live on the premises."

Dread throbbed in the hollow of Miyoko's throat. She'd thought she would be commuting by train to Osaka every day, not living away from Ko-chan again. But she couldn't afford to tell Nurse Sato about Ko-chan and possibly lose this job.

"Can you start next week?" Nurse Sato asked, scraping her chair as she moved closer.

"Next week?" Miyoko's voice quavered.

"Here are the keys to the dormitory room. You can start on Monday." Nurse Sato's voice was cheery, like she was eager to have her.

Miyoko hesitated, knowing this meant that she would have to wait even longer to make a home for herself and her son. The unexpected delay and separation struck her like a needle in a vein. She wanted them to be together sooner. But Hojoon's patient face appeared, and the anxiety dissipated.

"Thank you." She decided to take a chance. "Can I ask you a question? You know from my certificate that I'm Korean . . ." Miyoko clutched the dormitory keys in her hand.

"Yes?"

"I would like to be called Ando Miyoko here." She cast her eyes down as a pang of sadness washed over her.

Nurse Sato nodded. "There was another Korean nurse here just before you. She asked me the same thing. She was a great nurse, and I was sad to see her leave. She just recently moved to Tokyo. She was also a certified midwife, and because of her additional training, she was offered a post at a hospital in Tokyo. I don't mind at all."

No wonder Nurse Sato seemed so friendly and open—she had worked with other Korean nurses. And that nurse was a midwife too. Miyoko remembered Mrs. Yoo and her rudimentary midwife techniques. She wondered if she could become a certified midwife. She could keep it a secret from her in-laws and save more money faster. She could have additional skills to bring to Korea. If she had to be away from Ko-chan, she would use the time to study for the midwife test. She would be around babies and feel close to them, which might make up for the time lost with her son.

"Thank you." Miyoko bowed low with gratitude. She'd done it. She'd gotten the job.

Miyoko stopped at Bohbeh's house in the Korean section of Osaka to tell her the news. Bohbeh was happy that they would live close by, but understood Miyoko's disappointment at being an hour's train ride away from Ko-chan. She would only be able to visit him when she got time off, and the distance would pull them even further apart.

Later, when she arrived home and told Halmeoni about her new job, her mother-in-law's lips curved at the edges. "How much more money will you make for the household?"

"A little more than my nurse aide job, but not much," Miyoko lied. "I would have to live in the dormitory and visit when I can. Would you take care of Ko-chan full-time?"

"Why, of course I will," Halmeoni said, a glimmer in her eye.

Miyoko got ready for bed that night and made a space for Ko-chan in the room she had shared with Hojoon. Halmeoni had finally moved Hojoon's altar there, and she felt his loving presence. She had bought Ko-chan a top to play with, and they sat on the floor laughing while watching it spin. As soon as Ko-chan heard Halmeoni retire to her bedroom, though, he scurried over to her. Miyoko called out to him, but he didn't return. She heard laughter where Ko-chan now slept with his grandmother. Halmeoni seemed glad to continue this living arrangement and push Miyoko out of her son's life even more.

Miyoko's eyes misted as she thought of the long separation from her son that loomed ahead. She had missed so much of his first two years already. Was this the same sacrifice her mother had made when she sent them away for a better life? She would work even harder for Ko-chan now. That was what she was good at.

CHAPTER THIRTY-ONE

1939–1941

Miyoko wore the name badge ANDO MIYOKO in her new post at Osaka Clinic. She pulled her hair back tight into a white cap and donned a crisp white uniform like all the other Japanese nurses. She did her work quietly, visited Ko-chan one Sunday a month, and doubled down on her studies. She thought it might take a year or two to get her midwife certificate and some experience.

Miyoko kept to herself at the hospital. She sat alone in the staff dining room and didn't socialize with the other nurses. When she came back to her dormitory at night, she crammed for the midwife test. She shadowed a Japanese midwife and learned how to treat and soothe pregnant women. To fill her empty time as she waited to visit Ko-chan, she read all sorts of books, from nursing textbooks to popular novels to the Bible. When she closed her eyes to sleep, she made a mental list of things to bring him: pastries, toys, books, a new pair of socks, an envelope of cash for his care. She imagined her son playing hide-and-seek in her old yard in Korea and climbing her mulberry tree. Miyoko turned to these thoughts to keep her going until her next reunion with Ko-chan.

She took her midwife exam the following October, in 1939. On the eve of her twenty-third birthday, she became a midwife. Miyoko began assisting doctors with deliveries and was recognized for her skills. Nurse Sato, her supervisor, added a stripe on her cap for excellent service. Miyoko told her in-laws about her midwife certificate but avoided telling them that she had gotten a raise. She only received small bonuses and kept this to herself.

On the Sundays when she wasn't visiting Ko-chan, she worshipped with the congregants of a temporary Korean church behind the walls of a community hall. Fellow worshippers helped her celebrate becoming an official midwife, the way her church in Kyoto had. Miyoko always looked forward to going to church at the end of her workweek, despite the ever-present danger of the Japanese police questioning them or closing them down. No one from the hospital knew she was attending a Korean church, because she was still hiding her identity at work. And no one from the hospital or the church knew she had a son. She was always concealing a part of herself, no matter where she was. Her isolation grew.

Miyoko did some extra nursing work for the Korean community too, making house calls to Koreans who couldn't afford medical care or didn't want to visit the hospital. The church gave her a list of congregants, and she went to them to serve their needs. It was classic nursing duty: washing and dressing patients, changing beds, helping people to the toilet, observing them, feeding them, and listening to their stories. She was fulfilling the promise she had made to Hojoon and carrying on his spirit and his work.

Miyoko served as a midwife at her patients' homes and at the hospital. She enjoyed reassuring mothers during the long months of pregnancy and the birthing process. Helping bring new life into the world filled her with joy and satisfaction. Most of her cases were successful, but occasionally there were complications. Miyoko once cared for a healthy Korean woman who had a full-term pregnancy, but in the end, her child was stillborn. At the hospital, she also looked after a premature baby who didn't survive. These cases frightened Miyoko to her core and reinforced her desire to reunite with Ko-chan as soon as possible.

Bohbeh was Miyoko's sole companion in Osaka. She was so proud of Miyoko's nursing career, and Miyoko visited her as much as she could. They would eat a good Korean meal together and catch up on each other's lives. And not long after Miyoko had earned her midwife certificate, Bohbeh shared some news.

"I think I'm pregnant!" Bohbeh said happily. "Remember how you used to throw up in the mornings? Well, that happened to me all week. My breasts feel fuller too."

"Hmm. When was your last period?"

"Two months ago, I think. I didn't want to hope, because I had missed my periods before, but then they started up again. This time my body feels different."

Miyoko visited Bohbeh regularly in the following months and confirmed Bohbeh's pregnancy. She checked Bohbeh's blood pressure and fundal height, as well as the baby's position and fetal heartbeat. Miyoko was thrilled at how well Bohbeh's pregnancy was progressing and at the prospect of becoming an aunt. Watching Bohbeh's joy over her new baby was bittersweet, though. Miyoko's heart pined for Ko-chan, and she suffered from a dull headache almost every day. The divide between her and Ko-chan had widened over time, and the loneliness was now a physical presence by her side.

Haramoto seemed happy with Bohbeh's pregnancy. He was more helpful around the house and even hummed tunes when he came home from work. He said he was lucky that he still had his meter-reading job and that he was too old to be conscripted into war. Miyoung was glad he was being nicer to Bohbeh, but she knew better than to assume he was a changed man. Would this new attitude stay after the baby was born?

One day, he interrupted Miyoko at the hospital. "Bohbeh's water burst!" he shouted. Miyoko asked Nurse Sato for the afternoon off and rushed to Bohbeh's house. Her sister was fully dilated, and after only a few pushes, Bohbeh delivered a healthy baby boy. Haramoto held his firstborn son with a tremendous grin on his face. They named him Tomiyo.

Miyoko helped Tomiyo latch on to his mother's breast, and he sucked happily. Memories of her days trying to nurse Ko-chan flooded Miyoko's mind, and her chest tightened. Seeing her sister bonding with Tomiyo, and caring for sick and dying babies as a midwife, motivated her to work harder so that she could be with Ko-chan in Korea. It saddened her, though, that Bohbeh was starting a family here when she was planning to leave. She spent as much time helping Bohbeh as possible, knowing how much work a newborn took, with feeding, changing diapers, and getting the child to sleep. Sharing in new motherhood made her feel even closer to her sister.

Although Miyoko had thought she and Ko-chan would be separated for only a year or so, time slipped by quickly. The sky seeped blue one spring morning in 1940 as Miyoko prepared to see him on her monthly visit. Her son was already three and filled with curiosity. As usual, she stuffed her overnight bag with a few items of clothing and her journal. She had bought Ko-chan a book about animals and was looking forward to reading it to him. She went to the train station early to purchase her ticket.

The government had begun to ration fuel, which it needed for the war with China, so train departures were limited. There was only one daily train from Osaka to Kyoto. Miyoko had to catch the 8:00 a.m. train or risk not seeing Ko-chan at all. The Japanese government's austerity campaign included milk and sugar too. Patients who needed certain sugary foods suffered. Babies whose mothers couldn't nurse suffered from a lack of baby formula. Miyoko wanted to get out of Japan before things got worse, but she had lingering worries about leaving Bohbeh and her growing family here.

When she arrived to see Ko-chan, she slid open the front door of her in-laws' house and smelled the scent of gardenia coming from a pot in the courtyard.

"I'm home," Miyoko said to Halmeoni, taking a deep bow. She fingered the space between her obi and kimono to make sure that she had the envelope of cash for Ko-chan's expenses. She would present it to her mother-in-law later.

Halmeoni was in the sitting room watching her grandchildren. Ko-chan was playing jacks with small rocks, like Miyoko and her brother used to play when she was a little girl. He smiled when he saw her holding the familiar white paper bag in her hands.

Ko-chan stood to greet her, and she admired how tall he'd grown. He was blossoming from a thin toddler into a chubby child. His female cousin, Emi-chan, whose mother's breast milk he had shared, was also three but much more petite. She pretended to be drinking tea with her grandmother. His male cousin, also three, eyed the pastries and licked his lips. His aunt and uncles had had several more children while Ko-chan was living with them. The other two cousins were playing outside.

Miyoko always stopped at the corner bakery on her way to her in-laws' house. The sweet smell of bread lured her in the right direction and sparked joy over the chance to see her son. She would perform the same ritual to mark the end of a long period away: bringing Ko-chan something delicious to eat. The red bean paste doughnuts were his favorite. She was lucky that the bakery had some today and hadn't run out due to sugar rationing. Miyoko would buy these doughnuts even when she had to go to the more expensive store to do it. The doughnuts cost more than she wanted to pay, but seeing Ko-chan's face light up was worth it. She didn't want to disappoint him or her in-laws. If treats were available, she always bought extra for the extended family.

Ko-chan ran toward her and swallowed hard, as if imagining the sweet fried dough already in his mouth. This moment was one of the rare connections she and Ko-chan shared. To prolong it, Miyoko tried the game they used to play. She squeezed the tip of his nose and wiggled it. To Miyoko's delight, he lifted his finger and pinched her nose back. But when she tried to lean her forehead against his, he squirmed away. Longing pushed her toward him, but only empty space stood in between. Miyoko tilted her head in his grandmother's direction.

"Take this to Halmeoni first, please."

He snatched the bag and skipped to the sitting room. He knew he wasn't supposed to eat before his elders, but he shoved his hand into the bag and stuffed a doughnut into his mouth anyway. He handed the remainder over to his grandmother with a wide grin. Halmeoni accepted his delayed gift with a chuckle. Without a scolding of any sort, she took a sweet bun for herself and gave one to each of the other grandchildren. Two more grandchildren emerged out of nowhere and she handed them the rest. Ko-chan was becoming spoiled, and no one was doing anything about it. Miyoko had tried correcting him before with a spanking, but Halmeoni wouldn't have it. Disappointment as a mother swelled.

"Please help get dinner ready," Halmeoni ordered Miyoko while the rest of the group sat chewing the sweets together. She dipped into the kitchen, even though she longed to linger with Ko-chan. She resisted the urge to smash the dishes against the wall and take her son away with her, but she was dependent on Halmeoni for now.

For the rest of the afternoon, Miyoko assisted Inja and Yoonhee in cooking maeuntang, a spicy fish stew, and mung bean pancakes while observing Ko-chan from afar. She followed Inja's orders to fry the pancakes crisp and fetch the kimchi from the earthenware pot. During dinner, Ko-chan quickly ate the biggest portion of food while sitting happily next to his grandmother.

Miyoko studied her son from across the table. She desperately wanted to connect with him in some small way. She placed a small piece of white fish on top of his bowl, a little offering from her heart. Halmeoni, seeing this, put a larger piece of fish right next to it.

Ko-chan stared into his bowl at the small and large pieces of fish. Miyoko avoided Halmeoni's gaze and picked at her kimchi with her chopsticks. From the corner of her eye, Miyoko saw Ko-chan hesitate before picking up the smaller piece of fish first, then the bigger one. Hope pushed against her heart, and she felt comforted that Ko-chan might still have a shred of affection for her.

"Mother-in-law favors Ko-chan," Inja said to Yoonhee in the doorway of the kitchen while Miyoko washed the dishes. She said it loud enough for Miyoko to hear.

"He can do anything he wants. My son never receives favors from Mother-in-law." Even Yoonhee, who had been so sweet in the past, agreed. Miyoko's spirit deflated at losing her single female ally in the family.

"Did you see what she's wearing?" Inja said.

Miyoko had become used to this kind of criticism, but it still stung. She wore knee-high socks, an A-line skirt, and a striped blouse with a pointed collar. She preferred Western clothing these days, whereas her sisters-in-law still wore hanboks.

While living on her own in Osaka, Miyoko had begun noticing the modern ways people dressed and lived. She wore collared blouses buttoned to the neck and pleated skirts to run errands. When she needed a new pair of shoes, she bought herself a pair of black dress shoes with thick heels. A sense of style and unexpected confidence developed as she made these choices on her own. She even daydreamed of someday driving a car—a crazy idea for a woman—but she liked to fantasize about going wherever she wanted at any time, like picking up Ko-chan and driving away with him on an adventure.

Miyoko yearned to see Ko-chan's face so much during their separation that she wanted to get a photograph of them together. Many Japanese people took family photographs, and studios were popping up around town. Even though it was outside her tight budget, Miyoko set aside a few yen each week and was able to save just enough money to have a photo of her and Ko-chan taken at the cheapest studio she could find.

During one of her next visits to Kyoto, she coaxed Ko-chan into taking the photograph by dangling the promise of more sweets. Halmeoni initially opposed the idea, saying that photos were unnecessary and expensive, but she eventually consented. Miyoko urged Ko-chan to take a bath beforehand at the sento, the public bathhouse down the street. Even though children his age usually accompanied their mothers, he refused to go with her, preferring instead to go with his grandfather, as he had done before.

Miyoko went to the women's side and washed off before soaking in a large in-ground tub of hot water. Sitting on a low wooden stool, she scrubbed her body, adjusting the temperature of the water coming out of the wall faucets. She imagined Ko-chan and his grandfather splashing together while she sat alone among the chatter of mothers and children. Her loneliness and despair hung like the moisture on the frosted-glass doors.

For the studio shoot, Miyoko wore a white blazer with puffed short sleeves and pulled her hair back into a bun. Ko-chan donned a sailor's outfit with a flap collar and matching shorts she had bought him, topped with a white sailor's hat that curled at the brim. Miyoko smiled into the camera to preserve this rare mother-son moment.

That afternoon, Miyoko took Ko-chan on the bus to the Kyoto City Zoo so that they could actually see the animals from the book she had bought him. Away from Halmeoni, Ko-chan seemed like a different child. Now four and attending a free preschool, he was curious about animals and asked lots of questions: *How much do elephants weigh? How do hippos sleep? Are tigers related to the cats roaming the streets? How many babies can monkeys have?* Miyoko enjoyed listening to all his questions, though she couldn't help but think that she had missed out on so much of his development. He was changing every day, and she wanted to keep up with his ever-expanding mind.

"I'll read you the animal book I bought you when we get home," Miyoko said. She always enjoyed the times when she could read to him. "I loved books when I was your age." She felt that she could really talk to him now about things that mattered. He was growing up.

"Yes!" Ko-chan said. "I like reading too." He walked next to her, brushing her side. She took his little hand, and a flicker of electricity inched up her fingers, warming her whole body.

As they moved to the lion area, Miyoko noticed Ko-chan studying a mother and her son, who was nearly Ko-chan's age. They were sitting at a table, laughing and sipping a soda through two straws. "Can we have a soda too?"

"Of course," Miyoko said, remembering the afternoon she and Hojoon had shared a soda at the department store's cafeteria. It was like Hojoon was there somewhere, bringing her and Ko-chan together.

After finishing their drink, they went to the petting zoo. Ko-chan gently held out his palm and offered peanuts to the goats. He even asked Miyoko if she wanted a bite of the candy that she had bought him. He wasn't the sullen, selfish child he was with his grandmother. She saw a different, more thoughtful side of Ko-chan. He was delightful.

Strolling to the exit, Miyoko saw a large group of kids on the zoo's playground. "How's preschool?"

"It's okay," Ko-chan said, his face cast down.

"Have you made friends?"

"No."

"How come?"

Ko-chan rubbed his finger around his earlobe, something he did when he was nervous.

"They don't like me. A Japanese kid knocked me over and called me Chōsenjin."

Sadness plunged into Miyoko's heart. Memories flooded through her. She thought of her early school days in Japan and of how terrible she had felt when the other students called her that hurtful word. She wanted to protect Ko-chan from that pain and help him grow to appreciate his full self.

"Why do Japanese say those mean things?"

Words tripped on her tongue. Her mother had told her to accept this treatment because life was better in Japan than in Korea. Mother had said she had no choice. But something else came out of Miyoko's mouth.

"It's not right. They shouldn't say that."

Ko-chan's face brightened. He looked so much like his father right then. It gave her courage to speak frankly.

"But they do tease me," Ko-chan said. "I keep to myself now." Disappointment tinged his words.

Miyoko's heart sank. She had to stop the loneliness from striking Ko-chan too.

"I'm sorry," Miyoko said. "It's easy to fall into the habit of being alone, and I've done it too. But we all need each other. I need you. I'll never let you go." She touched his cheek and rested her head on his. He let her hold it there.

At that moment, the late-afternoon sky shifted from pink to purple, creating a brilliant haze. She vowed to work harder to get them out of Japan. She didn't want Ko-chan to grow up as she had, feeling like an outsider in her own home.

After the mother-and-son photo was developed and framed, Miyoko placed it on her dormitory table. The photo stood next to Hojoon's—a copy of the one on the altar at her in-laws' house—along with Hojoon's dojang and handkerchief. After her day at the zoo with Ko-chan, she felt their connection. Her spirits had been flagging over their separation, but the photo gave her the spark she needed to keep going.

CHAPTER THIRTY-TWO

December 1941

December 8 was a clear, bracing winter day, and Miyoko had just finished eating breakfast in her dormitory room. She was cold and sipping warm tea at the low table surrounded by stark white walls when a short radio announcement as spare as her room crackled on the radio: Japanese forces had attacked and destroyed American warships at Pearl Harbor.

Miyoko's chest heaved with fear. She threw on her nurse's uniform, bolted out the door, and rushed to the hospital. When she arrived, everyone was abuzz with conversation. Soon Miyoko heard people shouting "Banzai! Banzai!" outside. From the windows, waves of rising-sun flags fluttered, and people marched toward the nearby Shinto shrine to celebrate victory. The world as Miyoko knew it had erupted. A nervous energy filled the air. What did this mean for her plan to return to Korea with Ko-chan? War would change everything.

Public enthusiasm for the wider war grew, even more than for Japan's invasion of China in 1937. But Miyoko remained skeptical of Japan's military abilities. Uncertainty remained about Japan going to war against stronger Western countries. Miyoko had experienced the arrogance of these Western powers while a maid at the baron's home.

Doubts rose as she heard the news of Japan's victories in Malaysia, Singapore, Hong Kong, and the Philippines; she wasn't sure they were even true at all.

Still, she participated in mass rituals like everyone else because she had to. In the months following Pearl Harbor, she observed a moment of silence at 11:59 a.m. on the eighth of every month. The flag was raised at the hospital and elsewhere precisely at that time, and restaurants and cafés closed. Colonial citizens were also required to perform the same ceremony of Shinto worship, and she assumed that Taeyoung and her remaining family in Korea were forced to do it too. Japan's subjects were expected to support the war wherever they were. Miyoko heard that Korean and Taiwanese soldiers were being sent off to fight for the Japanese. Her skin crawled. Taeyoung was too old to be a soldier, wasn't he?

To Miyoko's great despair, she had to delay her plan to return to Korea. It was too dangerous to take Ko-chan during wartime. The goal she had worked so hard for, and sacrificed so much for, was now just an impossible dream. She was in Osaka without her son in the midst of war, and there was no way out. She prayed for the war to be over quickly.

Her trips to the makeshift church came to an abrupt halt too. Shock hit when she hurried there the Sunday after the attacks and discovered that the church had been shut down. Instead, a neighborhood association had gathered to make comfort kits, stuffing boxes with dried fish, blankets, and manga for Japan's soldiers.

Now she was living firsthand what she had read about in the newspapers: After Pearl Harbor, the Japanese government was shutting down all Christian churches because of their association with Americans. She had lost yet another thing that she cared about.

Miyoko ran to her dormitory and scrambled around for her journal, which was now almost full. She had taken painstaking steps to write small so she could use it longer. She scribbled a few words before taking a breath.

My world is in chaos. Japan is at war. My church has been shuttered, my dreams shattered.

I can't be with my son. He doesn't know who I am. He's five years old and doesn't know that I am his mother. He thinks his grandmother is his mother . . .

She looked up to stop a tear from sliding down and smudging the page.

Ko-chan's grandfather and uncles were collectively his father. Ko-chan didn't remember his father, who had passed away when he was five months old. He only knew that his father had died when he was a baby, and now his uncles, aunts, grandparents, and cousins were his family.

Sadness and then a bubble of anger surfaced.

All the love that was intended for his father now flows down to him, especially from his grandmother. Ko-chan can do no wrong. When he talks, everyone stops what they're doing to listen, as if his dead father were speaking. But he is a child—his own person, not his father. He has his whole life ahead of him. He deserves to be himself, and I deserve to be his mother.

Tears fell on the fibrous paper, blurring her words. She needed to be there for Ko-chan. Hojoon would have wanted that. Right now, she had no control over her own life, let alone Ko-chan's future. The only thing she knew was this: she loved Ko-chan, and he had feelings for her too.

PART FOUR

Osaka

1943

CHAPTER THIRTY-THREE

April 12, 1943
Monday

"Ando Miyoko-san!" Nurse Sato called.

Miyoko shifted her gaze from the red azaleas outside the window to the sound of her supervisor's voice across the hospital ward. She had been thinking about her next visit with Ko-chan while taking a patient's temperature. Another year of send-offs, rations, and shrine observations had passed as Japan ramped up its war efforts across the Pacific. Miyoko's relationship with Ko-chan remained the same, although she was hopeful that things would change when the war ended.

"Please come to the reception area. A soldier has a letter for you," Nurse Sato said, waving for her to come before turning her attention to a patient.

Shock rattled Miyoko's chest. A soldier? What could he want? Soldiers were everywhere these days, but not in hospitals unless they were sick. Curious eyes stared back from the large, silent room lined with white cots. The aroma of bleach hung in the air.

Holding a blank face, Miyoko retrieved the mercury stick wedged under the patient's armpit and read the temperature line, which showed a normal reading. She shook the thermometer clear and set it back on the metal tray next to the bed. She lowered her head as she walked toward the reception area. Heat flushed her cheeks as patients' gazes followed her out of the room. She didn't like to stand out.

When she reached the waiting room, a young, khaki-wearing Japanese soldier clutching a thin envelope stood by the front desk. Miyoko stiffened when she spotted him from the other side of the room. The receptionist hunched over her paperwork while everyone else looked up at Miyoko expectantly.

Dread pounded Miyoko's ears as she smoothed her hair and straightened her white nurse's cap. The soldier triggered uneasy memories of another uniformed stranger who had burst into her life when she was a girl in Korea. He had tricked Bohbeh into coming to Japan, and now Miyoko was here too. She was still pretending to be a Japanese nurse, a practical stranger to herself. She was worried the soldier's arrival meant that something was about to change in her life again.

Miyoko took a deep breath and walked between the line of patients sitting on either side of the room, avoiding their probing stares. She had taken pains not to be noticed at this job by blending in, just like she had at her other posts. Could this soldier know that she was Korean and have her fired for taking a Japanese nurse's job? If she couldn't work, what would happen to Ko-chan?

When she reached the receptionist's desk, the soldier handed her the letter, tipped the brim of his cap, and clomped away in his thick boots. Sweat beaded against her brow as she eyed the beige envelope in her hands. Her arms seemed to be glued tight against her rib cage, unable to move. This couldn't be good news. The envelope was addressed using both her Japanese and Korean names.

A cackle of voices behind her caught Miyoko's attention. There in the doorway where she had just been standing were two of Miyoko's colleagues, both notorious for gossiping and spreading rumors. Nurse Iida would surely chatter about this with the other nurses, as she often did while Miyoko sat alone in the lunchroom.

"Ne, this young, handsome soldier came by today and gave Ando-san a letter! I wonder what it said. I didn't dare ask . . . because you know how private she is. Do you think she has a brother or someone serving in the military, and something has happened to him? Or maybe she has a boyfriend?"

Miyoko couldn't wait until after her shift to read the letter. She shoved it into her pocket and slipped out the front door of the hospital. She dashed to the park across the street, which was lined with cherry blossoms. The buds burst open with honeyed fragrance, and the wispy petals floated gently in the breeze. But Miyoko was oblivious to the beauty as she sat down on a wooden bench. She hastily pulled the letter out of her pocket and tore open the envelope bearing the official seal of the Imperial Japanese Army.

> "You are ordered . . . report for service in a week . . . to headquarters in Osaka . . . serve as a nurse in Saipan."

The letter fell from her hands, landing on a sea of pink flowers. It was a draft order. Saipan was a war zone. The news had said that Japan was trying to defend its expansion by fortifying other parts of Asia. This small island in the Pacific was being used as a military base.

She would be forced to serve, with no guarantee of return. Her heart thumped wildly and banged against her chest.

How could she go and leave Ko-chan behind?

CHAPTER THIRTY-FOUR

April 13, 1943
Tuesday

The drumming of rain against the dormitory window woke Miyoko from a restless sleep. She tossed and turned on her small futon, trying to clear the fog in her mind. Reeling from the order she had received yesterday, her body refused to sleep as she wrestled with what to do. The clock ticked as doom swirled.

When Miyoko's eyes adjusted to the thin morning light, she noticed her journal and the Bible that she usually hid under a blanket on the low table where she had left them the night before. Her journal was open next to the nub of a spent candle. In the wee hours, Miyoko had feverishly penned her fears.

Leaving Ko-chan and never coming back would make him a motherless orphan. Miyoko had felt this way when she left Korea to live in Japan. She had cried herself to sleep, longing for her mother, a sea between them, separated as she would be from Ko-chan if she went to Saipan. And even if Miyoko managed to survive the war, Ko-chan might be grown by the time she returned.

What would Hojoon say? She fingered his dojang, which still sat next to the photo she had taken with Ko-chan. She stamped his name on her notebook, and traces of the red ink smudged on the page. *Don't go,* Hojoon would say. *He has already lost a father. Stay with Ko-chan.* But the Japanese authorities would find her and force her to go anyway.

Could I take Ko-chan with me? she wondered. How ridiculous! That would be impossible and dangerous. He loved his grandparents and had a comfortable life in Kyoto.

Miyoko picked up the Bible, holding it against her thumping chest. *Please, God, help me find a way. The road to my future with Ko-chan seems impassable.*

A train whistled in the distance. Miyoko remembered her goodbye to her mother on the train platform and the vow she had made to herself afterward: if she were ever a mother, she would never let her child leave too soon and experience the loss she had. Leaving Ko-chan motherless terrified her. She had adapted to a life without one, but at the cost of distancing herself from others. She didn't want the same thing for her son. He needed her, even though he might not know it yet. And by the way she longed for him at every moment, she knew she needed him too. She stared at the photo of the two of them, hoping for inspiration.

Trembling in her cotton yukata, Miyoko lit the single-burner gas stove with a match and boiled a kettle of water for tea. She poured the scalding liquid into a porcelain cup, stirred the green matcha powder with a wooden whisk, and watched it foam. She blew on it and drank slowly, trying to settle her nerves. She would go see Bohbeh and ask her what she should do.

By the time she left for work, Miyoko had a throbbing headache. She walked toward the hospital through a garden fragrant with roses, hidden from a conversation happening on the other side of the bushes.

"Did you hear that Nomura-san at our sister hospital got an order the other day to serve in Guam?"

"Really? That's awful."

"I heard from Nurse Iida that a soldier came by looking for Nurse Ando yesterday. I wonder if that was an order."

Miyoko's knees buckled. The nursing credential she had studied so hard to obtain was the reason why she was being required to serve on the battlefields. And now she knew there were other nurses being drafted too.

Nurse Sato appeared around the corner, and the nurses' voices stopped. Miyoko saw them walking in the opposite direction toward the administrative building.

"Good morning," Nurse Sato said cheerfully, seeing Miyoko. Her eyebrows drew together. "Are you all right? You look tired."

Miyoko responded with a barely audible yes.

"I hate to pry, but I was worried about you yesterday. What did the soldier's letter say?"

A lump formed in Miyoko's throat. Although Nurse Sato still didn't know about Ko-chan, she had been kind to her and accepting of her Korean identity all along. "I've been ordered to go to Saipan as an army nurse."

Her supervisor's eyes flashed alarm. "I'm sorry about that. Some nurses in other hospitals have been recruited to serve as well." Nurse Sato reached out and touched her arm.

"I've heard rumors too, but nothing certain until now." Miyoko was moved by Nurse Sato's sympathy, though her jaw tightened at the same time for her uncertain future.

"Since the National Mobilization Law passed in '38, civilians have been drafted. Female nurses are being enlisted too," Nurse Sato said. "It's dangerous. A trusted friend told me that a nurse was killed in a bombing in China. You have to take care of yourself."

"Do you know anyone who's come back?" Miyoko asked.

"No, not yet. The only nurse I know personally who received an order is Nurse Fuji from our sister hospital. She was supposed to go to Burma." Nurse Sato shook her head. "The thing is, she never went. No one could find her. She might have run away or hidden somewhere so that she wouldn't have to go."

Miyoko's lips parted. *Run away?* That thought hadn't even crossed her mind. How could someone do that?

"Does anyone know where she is now?" What could happen to someone who evaded orders?

"No, it's still a mystery. I heard that the army was knocking on her neighbors' doors, but they gave up. Come to think of it, her supervisor told me she was Korean too, but using her Japanese name."

Miyoko's mind buzzed. Could it be a coincidence that the nurses being conscripted were Korean? Father's and Hojoon's voices hovered in the air. *Of course Koreans would be drafted first. This is what happens when you're a poor colony.* Her nursing certificate bore her Korean name. She carried a Korean identification card. She had completed a census saying that she was Korean. Nurse Nomura, who had been drafted to Guam, was probably Korean as well. Anger and fear twisted inside her.

"When do you have to report for duty?" The corners of Nurse Sato's mouth fell, like she was sad to see her go.

"In a week." Miyoko's voice cracked as she thought of having to say goodbye to Ko-chan. No one here, not even Nurse Sato, knew about him. They had no idea how lonely and isolated she'd been all these years just to protect her job. Opening up would require trust, and that was still difficult for her.

"Let me know if you need anything," Nurse Sato said, like she meant it.

Nurse Sato's kindness prompted her to act. She needed time to figure out a plan.

"Actually, I'd like to take a week off."

"Of course. You've had perfect attendance, so it won't be a problem."

The two nurses walked shoulder to shoulder across the grass to the hospital. Near the entrance to the concrete building, the Japanese flag flapped in the breeze. It was a cold spring morning, and the red circle against the stark white background caught Miyoko's attention. She would be fighting another country's war.

A sharp pain pierced Miyoko's chest. How could she possibly die for Japan? It was not her country, and she had never felt fully welcome here, even though she had lived here for more than half her life. She was of the Korean race—a low-status citizen. So was Ko-chan. What would happen when Ko-chan was old enough to be drafted? Would he be conscripted too?

Going to war for Japan would be against everything she and Hojoon had believed in. He had dedicated his life to opposing the unjust treatment of Koreans in Japan. He'd want her and their son to live as Koreans again, no matter what the conditions in Korea were like. She wanted to fulfill their dream of returning home. And she yearned to be Ko-chan's mother.

When Miyoko opened the hospital door to go inside, the wind picked up and slammed it shut again, startling her. Did she have a choice in the matter?

CHAPTER THIRTY-FIVE

April 14, 1943
Wednesday

The next day, Miyoko rushed to Bohbeh's house to tell her about the order and ask for her advice. She couldn't possibly tell her in-laws yet, and she thought she knew what they would say to her. They would tell her to go, to leave Ko-chan with them. She had done that for too long.

Exiting near a newsstand at Bohbeh's station, Miyoko stopped to read the headlines. One of them hit her cold: Man's Family Questioned for Dodging Military Draft. A Korean man who had been conscripted to serve in the Japanese army had disappeared. His wife and child had been detained at the police station until further notice. Miyoko's hands trembled.

"Hey, move out of the way!" a big soldier barked, bumping into Miyoko. The hairs on her arms stood as he and another serviceman clomped past her in their heavy boots. Shaking, she reached into her coin purse for some change and shoved the paper into her bag. She would show it to Bohbeh.

Miyoko hurried to her sister's house in Ikuno-ku and calmed when she smelled the familiar aroma of fermented soybeans, garlic, and gochujang paste as she entered the Korean neighborhood. She heard

Korean being spoken behind the thin walls of the shabby, dilapidated homes.

Since she'd started working as a nurse in Osaka five years back, Miyoko had visited Bohbeh when she had time off. After Bohbeh had given birth to Tomiyo four years ago, Miyoko had helped her deliver a girl named Nobuko a year later. Bohbeh and Haramoto had moved to a larger place when the babies came, but it was still not big enough for their growing family. Pain had racked Miyoko's heart to watch Bohbeh breastfeed and take care of her babies when Miyoko couldn't do so, but Miyoko was truly happy for her.

She knocked on the main door to Bohbeh's house, a typical cluster of wooden buildings housing multiple families. It opened to a dirt hallway with a few units on either side. She hoped Haramoto and the children weren't home so that she could talk to Bohbeh in private.

After a few minutes, Bohbeh appeared and greeted her with a warm smile. Miyoko was comforted by seeing her sister's welcoming face. She could trust Bohbeh with her secret.

"What are you doing here? Shouldn't you be at work?" Bohbeh asked.

"I need to speak to you." Miyoko's voice crackled with desperation.

"Is everything all right? Come in." Offering a reassuring hand, Bohbeh led Miyoko toward the back unit that she shared with her family. "Haramoto-san took the children to the school playground. He'll be back soon."

Bohbeh was in her warm, padded happi coat, probably enjoying a few minutes alone without her family.

Miyoko whispered to her, like they used to under the covers at their mother's house in Korea. "I've been drafted to Saipan as an army nurse."

Bohbeh's mouth dropped open.

"A soldier came to the hospital yesterday to serve the order."

"Aigo!" Bohbeh said, her eyes stretched with fear.

"I'm scared. I think they're sending Korean nurses to the battlefields first."

“That’s awful! You can’t go! You could be killed!” Bohbeh pulled a handkerchief from the outside pocket of her coat and wiped the sweat forming on her upper lip.

The truth of that statement speared Miyoko in the heart. She recalled Nurse Sato’s story. *A nurse was killed in a bombing in China.*

“I don’t want to go either, but I have no choice!”

Bohbeh’s lips tightened as she confronted her sister’s dilemma. “I can’t help but think about Bohkee, who never came home from Manchuria. That can’t happen to you! We’ve got to figure out a way to stop you from going!”

Miyoko thought of her missing sister, never seen again. Now war was everywhere, and nurses were being killed or going missing. She wanted to be with her son, and this order pressed her to answer the question of whether she needed to take him with her now or possibly never see him again. Was she a bad mother for wanting to keep him when he was deeply loved and given everything he needed by his grandparents? But how could she leave Ko-chan when she knew she might never return?

“I don’t think there’s anything I can do.” Miyoko cast her eyes down, shaking her head.

She remembered something else Nurse Sato had said. Miyoko repeated it out loud. “There *was* a nurse who was ordered to go to Burma, and she didn’t show up for duty.” Her heart banged against her chest. *Would she . . . Could she . . . ?* It seemed dangerous but not impossible. She opened and closed her mouth several times before testing the possibility.

“I can pass as Japanese. I could try to escape.” A burst of energy pushed through Miyoko’s veins.

“That would be dangerous! Where would you go?” Bohbeh’s eyes flickered with fear.

Children’s laughter floated from the entrance.

“They’re back,” Bohbeh said, getting up. “Let’s go take a walk.”

The innocent voices reminded Miyoko of Bohbeh's visit to their village in Korea to escort Miyoko to Japan all those years ago. The village children had chanted with glee at Bohbeh's return, touching her sister's arms with their skinny hands and squealing with delight. Miyoko had always longed for a similar homecoming for herself.

"I could go back to Korea now and take Ko-chan with me." Miyoko held her breath, buoyed by this prospect.

Before Bohbeh could answer, her children bounded into the room, chattering away. Seeing their aunt Miyoko, they quieted and bowed.

"Ohayo gozaimasu," little Nobuko-chan chirped, saying good morning. Tomiyo hung back shyly.

"Ohayo," Miyoko said, hugging both her nephew and her niece tight. She felt attached to them because she had helped deliver them and watched them grow. She acknowledged Haramoto with a nod. He mumbled hello and went to the other room to smoke a cigarette.

"Auntie and I are going for a walk. I'll bring back some pastries."

The children grinned and went back outside to play. A sharp yearning for Ko-chan, already six, seized her chest. She wanted to be close to him like Bohbeh was with her children. She could change that now. She could take Ko-chan with her, and they could finally be together again.

The sisters left the house, and Bohbeh briskly led Miyoko through a maze of busy Osaka streets laden with Korean stores. Miyoko huffed as she tried to keep up with Bohbeh. As the two walked, Miyoko shared her plan.

"I'll get Ko-chan right away and leave for Korea. We can stay with Taeyoung in Pyongyang. He said we would always be welcome."

Bohbeh stared straight ahead without responding. Miyoko wondered if she was concerned about their well-being once they got to Korea. "Taeyoung is still working at the Korean central bank there and said he would help me find a job in the city."

Bohbeh stopped abruptly in front of a dressmaker's shop. "You shouldn't take Ko-chan with you."

Streetcars clanged nearby. She shouldn't take him with her? She couldn't leave Ko-chan behind if she escaped. Taking him with her was her only option.

"If you go, it's going to be hard enough making it out safely by yourself. Why would you bring a child?"

The truth of Bohbeh's words stabbed her heart. She was right that Ko-chan would be in danger if she fled with him. She could get arrested, and what would happen to him?

"You could send for him later," Bohbeh said.

"But . . . I can't do that. I can't leave Ko-chan behind." Miyoko's courage wavered.

"Wouldn't Ko-chan be safer with his grandparents and his aunts and uncles and cousins back in Kyoto?"

Miyoko furrowed her brows. She felt torn between her dream of a life with Ko-chan in Korea and his safety with his grandparents in Japan.

"But I'm his mother. No one will love him as much as I do." The words rang true. Of course his grandparents loved him, but they were not his mother, and who knows what would happen to Japan if they lost the war? Shouldn't Ko-chan's future be in Korea, as his father had wanted?

"No one is going to want to marry you in Korea if you have a young son."

Miyoko took a large step back, surprised at Bohbeh's concern for her marriage prospects rather than her future with Ko-chan. A bicyclist swerved to avoid her, and Bohbeh pulled her in. They continued walking, slower this time.

"But I don't want to marry. That's the last thing on my mind. I can work as a nurse and a midwife in Korea to support us. I don't need a husband." While she thought it might be good for Ko-chan to have a father in the future, she had made it this far without a husband.

Bohbeh's voice turned solemn. "It'll be hard for you to work as a nurse with Ko-chan in the picture. What are you going to do with him while you're on the job? Taeyoung's not going to stay at home and take care of him."

Miyoko slumped. She hadn't thought through all these details. Maybe she was kidding herself that she could bring Ko-chan with her, that they could start their lives over again. Bohbeh was probably right. Even if they stayed with Taeyoung, there would be no childcare. And if they couldn't stay with Taeyoung for some reason, who would hire her and allow her to stay in a nursing dormitory with a child? They wouldn't even do that here.

Her sister's words continued to chip away at her confidence. "Wouldn't Ko-chan prefer to stay home and grow up with the only family he knows? Don't you remember when you first came to Japan as a child? How lonely you were? I don't think you'd want that for him."

Miyoko was flooded with memories of missing her mother and crying herself to sleep. Bohbeh had expressed what she thought was best for Ko-chan, but Miyoko believed that being with his mother, with her, was best. *He would have me.* "I'm his mother. I don't want Ko-chan to go through what I did without a mother."

A new boldness gripped Miyoko. She had pulled away from Ko-chan for too long. His grandparents' indulgence had made it easy for her. They had allowed her to escape the sorrow of losing Hojoon through her work and freed her from the daily tasks of caring for a child. She had detached herself in part so that she wouldn't feel the pain of her separation from Ko-chan, and perhaps his rejection of her as his mother. The risk of losing someone else she loved—her own child—had been too great. But she didn't want to be apart from her son anymore. She had missed so much of Ko-chan's life already and wanted to be his mother. She wanted to embrace love and her son again. Ko-chan needed her too. But was this even possible? Was it too late?

Bohbeh halted. They had reached the pastry store. She stepped in to buy the sweets she had promised her children. Miyoko leaned against the glass storefront and took a deep breath. She closed her eyes and prayed to do what was necessary for her and Ko-chan to stay together. *God, please help me.*

Opening them again, Miyoko noticed a newsstand across the street. She remembered the article from earlier and fumbled around in her bag for it. A photo of the boy and his mother being questioned about the father's evasion of the order stared back at her.

When Bohbeh came out with a white bag of fried dough for the children, Miyoko's chest heaved.

"I have to tell you this story." Miyoko pointed to the article as she summarized it to her sister. "Imagine if Ko-chan were questioned because I eluded the draft! How scary! And what would they do with him? Put him in an orphanage because he's motherless?"

As Miyoko said this out loud, her face burned. She became more convinced that the threat to Ko-chan's safety would be greater if he stayed than if they left. All of Bohbeh's concerns about Miyoko finding a husband and someone to take care of Ko-chan while she worked were no longer as important as keeping her son from the authorities.

"I have to take Ko-chan with me."

Bohbeh considered this new information. "Maybe it's a chance for you to go back to Korea again, where you can be yourself, and be Ko-chan's mother for a change," she said, her eyes brimming with sympathy. "Now that I'm a mother myself, I know."

"I would miss you and your children," Miyoko said, anticipating the pain of another separation. "I was so sad when you left Korea and am grateful for all you have done for me here. You've been everything to me. It'll be hard to leave you again."

"Yes, and I'll miss seeing Ko-chan grow up. Maybe if this occupation ever ends, I can convince Haramoto to go back. He's been more open to his Korean heritage since having kids too. I'll explain your decision to him when the time is right. He'll be out of town starting tomorrow, so come here when you get Ko-chan. You can stay with us until you're ready to go."

Miyoko embraced her generous sister. Bohbeh was giving her permission to leave, because she knew how hard this would be. Bohbeh's support gave Miyoko the courage to do what she had to do.

"I'm going to Korea with Ko-chan. I would write to Taeyoung to tell him we're coming, but I don't want to risk the letter getting confiscated. I told him in my last letter that we were still planning to make it over, so hopefully he won't be too surprised when we arrive."

Was she really going to defy the order to report to the Japanese army? She had never done anything like this before. The deadline to appear for service was less than a week away. She had no time to lose.

CHAPTER THIRTY-SIX

April 15, 1943
Thursday

Miyoko tugged open a chest drawer in her dormitory to get dressed. Her fingers trembled with nerves. Today was the day that she would put her escape plan into action. Last night, after she had returned from Bohbeh's, she had pulled out her journal and outlined what she needed to do. First, she would need to get train tickets to Shimonoseki, the port by which she had entered Japan thirteen years before. Then she would need to pick up Ko-chan and convince him and his grandparents that she was taking him to visit Bohbeh. Finally, they would need to travel west by train across the country to get to the port and catch a ferry to Korea.

Could she do all this? Was she ready? She would be giving up the life she had made in Japan, the only life she had known since she was a child. Ko-chan's life would be disrupted, and he would be separated from his grandparents. But images of her and her son together kept getting clearer and sharper. If she made it back to Korea, she would work as a midwife from home and take care of Ko-chan. She wanted to be his mother, and this was her chance to become the mother she knew she could be.

Stacked next to her white nurse's uniform were a few neatly folded kimonos. She pulled out the blue striped one she'd had for more than a decade, since she was sixteen. She was good at hiding who she was then and even better now. Wearing it had helped her get jobs, so she hoped for similar luck today. She needed both a shot of courage and a stroke of good fortune to get train tickets to the port of Shimonoseki. From there, she and Ko-chan could board a ferry to their goal destination: Korea.

Escaping by train was her only option, since the bus would take too long, but getting long-distance train tickets now was more difficult than ever, as many were being used for the war effort. These trains were different from the commuter ones she rode back and forth to see Ko-chan. Japan's recent military losses in the Pacific meant that it needed more fast-moving trains like this to transport war supplies from one part of Japan to another. Women didn't normally purchase train tickets for long-distance trips, because they didn't travel alone. She would attract suspicion, so she would need a man to help her buy them. But who? Who could she trust?

Miyoko tightened her obi, and her resolve to get the tickets. She brushed her short bob and rounded it at the bottom in the popular Western style. As she slipped on her tabi socks, she recited the story that she and Bohbeh had invented: *I am the wife of a Japanese military officer in Korea. I need to go visit my husband with my son because he was injured and is gravely ill. This might be the only chance we have to see him alive.*

The last thing Miyoko donned was a short cream jacket that fit neatly over the wide arms of her kimono. After sliding into her wooden geta slippers, she walked down the cold, narrow hallway of the nurse's dormitory and out into the street. Fortunately, it was early, and no one was outside. Relief stirred, as later there would be more people who might question where she was going.

She walked briskly through the empty streets toward Osaka's train station. The morning dew clung to the rhododendrons, their white blooms still wilted from sleep. She reached inside the draped sleeve of her kimono, making sure that she hadn't forgotten her envelope of cash. It was more than she needed to purchase two train tickets to Shimonoseki, but she wanted to have enough tip money to entice someone to help her.

Dread and anxiety weighed her down like anchors while she pushed her way forward, hurrying a few steps, then pausing, going and stopping. When she arrived at the station, she saw policemen at the far end and slunk behind a large pole to avoid scrutiny. Would they see her fear and question her? Miyoko would have to lie deftly in order to succeed.

Miyoko craned her neck and noticed the policemen speaking to a group of soldiers. Closer to her, she spotted a man in a blue railroader's uniform standing next to some passengers. Maybe someone who worked at the station would be more successful than a random stranger at getting her a ticket. She shuffled across the platform, trying not to make any clacking noises with her geta. When she got alongside the uniformed man, she peered at him through her lashes, hoping for kindness. He was an old gentleman, and deep lines crossed his face, marking hard times. He seemed like someone who might be receptive to her. She squared her shoulders and spoke up.

"Sumimasen," Miyoko said. "My husband is a Japanese officer serving in Korea, and he's been injured. Please, sir, I need to bring our son to see him because my husband is gravely ill."

She delivered her message flawlessly, saying exactly what she had rehearsed. She didn't have a Korean accent at all. Even the mispronunciation of one sound in Japanese would give Koreans away.

Only silence echoed back. Did she sound persuasive? Maybe he was thinking of turning her in. Instead, he looked at her expectantly.

She took this as a cue to continue. Miyoko's voice broke as she beseeched the station worker. "We need to reach my husband before he dies. Please help me and my son. I have some extra money here for you if you can get me two tickets to Shimonoseki. I beg you."

She bent her head low, displaying her neck above her kimono, and rested her hands on her lap. After a brief moment, she looked up to gauge his reaction.

The man blushed, looking embarrassed at her attention. "If your husband has served our country and needs you, I'll try to help. Let me see if I can get the tickets."

Miyoko bowed over and over again. "Domo," she said as she handed him the envelope of cash with both hands.

She paced to relieve the anxiety of waiting as she watched the uniformed man amble to the ticket office. He talked to the clerk and exchanged some cash for the tickets. Maybe her plan had worked!

The trainman returned and handed her the tickets and the change. "Here you go. The only time available was three days from now, Sunday morning. Good luck on your journey to your husband."

Miyoko stared at the tickets, then at the gentleman. She felt relief wash over her as she realized her plan was working. She now had the means to escape in her hands. "Please take the change for your trouble. I can't begin to thank you enough."

"You're welcome," the man said. "Be careful." His eyes signaled a warning. "There's a lot of checkpoints out there."

Before she could say more, a commotion across the way grabbed his attention. He turned and blew his whistle to warn someone to back away from the tracks, leaving Miyoko to grapple with a new fear. Although she now had the tickets to Shimonoseki, there were checkpoints, and possible imprisonment awaited her if she were discovered trying to leave Japan. Images of trains being stopped and passengers interrogated flashed through her mind. The government didn't want to let people like her escape the army, and what would they do if they found out she was headed to Korea? The Japanese police dealt very harshly with Koreans. Miyoko's knees quaked at the thought.

The tickets fluttered in her shaking hands, reminding her that she could do this. She had succeeded in lying. It was terrifying, but she had survived. She was stronger than she had thought. But today was Thursday, and she still had to go get her son from his grandparents in Kyoto and bring him back to Osaka in time to catch the Sunday train.

The deadline to report to the army was Monday, only four days away.

CHAPTER THIRTY-SEVEN

April 16, 1943
Friday

Miyoko caught the early commuter train to Kyoto the next morning to fetch Ko-chan. As she and Bohbeh had discussed, she would bring him to Bohbeh's house to start their escape, since Haramoto was out of town reading electric meters. She mouthed what she and Bohbeh had practiced: "Ko-chan, this is going to be a fun trip to Osaka with lots of adventures and delicious food . . ." She imagined her son's excitement when she told him that he would be taking his first train ride. Surely his eyes would grow wide at the idea. Guilt wedged itself deep inside her heart: she would have to lie to Ko-chan and his grandparents for her plan to succeed.

Sitting upright in her train seat, Miyoko played back the events of the last few days and envisioned what was still to come. She double-checked her kimono sleeve to make sure that the train tickets were still tucked inside. Sweat dampened her forehead as she visualized the train's wheels screeching to a stop at checkpoints along the way and the dark waters of the sea churning underneath them on the ferry to Korea. Doubts clouded her mind when she considered the many obstacles in her path.

She beckoned the strength to push forward and said a little prayer. She had faith that God would provide for her and help her.

Miyoko walked to her in-laws' house from the station the same as always, toward the sweet smell of the corner bakery. The sugary buns reminded her of her happy visits, but also of how much she had missed, and propelled her forward. The store bell clanged as she entered for Ko-chan's favorite red bean paste doughnuts, even more expensive now with continued sugar rations. This would put him in a good mood, so maybe he would agree to go with her to Osaka.

The aroma of spring daffodils perfumed her path as she left the store with the doughnuts in hand. Birds chirped and flitted across the trees. Dotted with outdoor space and smaller in scale than Osaka, Kyoto awakened Miyoko's senses and lit her hopes. Arriving at the family home, Miyoko slid the large wooden door open and stepped into the dirt courtyard. Ko-chan was kicking around a ball made of old socks, and her heart warmed.

Ko-chan's face lit up with surprise when he saw her holding the familiar white bag. Her last visit had only been a week ago, so she wasn't expected for almost another month. His broad smile revealed one eye bigger than the other, just like his father. His head was shaven, like all kindergartners, and accentuated his round face. He gulped at seeing what was in her hand.

"Ko-chan, I got some time off work," Miyoko said in a cheerful voice. She extended her arm straight. "I have doughnuts here for you."

He bounded toward her outstretched hand. Looking around, he snatched the bag away. The paper crinkled as he tore it open to pop one of the treats into his mouth. Miyoko wanted to scold him, but she let him be.

She bent forward to meet Ko-chan's eyes. "How would you like to go to Osaka with me on a train?" She held her breath expectantly, waiting for his response.

"What?" he mumbled, his mouth full. "A train?"

Miyoko's chest tightened as she thought of the lies she was about to tell her son.

"When will we leave?" Ko-chan asked, standing up tall.

Miyoko relaxed a little. "As early as possible—tomorrow morning—because I don't have a lot of vacation time." She listed off what she had practiced with Bohbeh earlier. "I also want to take you to Aunt Bohbeh's. She would love to see how big you've grown!"

Miyoko hoped his face would brighten at the mention of Bohbeh. They had shared a fun day together at the street fair in Kyoto a few years ago, when Bohbeh had come to visit. But Ko-chan's smile faded, as did Miyoko's expectations. She tried to jog his memory again.

"Remember how you rode the Ferris wheel together and ate that delicious popcorn?"

"Yes, but . . . ," Ko-chan said, tilting his head in question.

"She's looking forward to taking you to another fair in Osaka!" Her voice climbed, trying to sound upbeat.

Ko-chan shot her a quizzical look.

Could he be worried about how long the trip might be? "It'll only be a few days."

"Hmm," Ko-chan said. "Are Halmeoni and Harabeoji going too?"

Miyoko sighed, understanding that he was anxious, since he'd never been away from his grandparents. "I know how close you are to them. But they're too old to travel far."

Ko-chan scowled. "I don't want to go, then!" He sprang up and darted out of the courtyard.

Miyoko was crushed. Was it too late? Would he always refuse her? Would he remember their good times, even though they had been few? Doubts crept back—maybe he was better off with his grandparents.

"What's happening?" Halmeoni slurred as she slid open one of the shoji screen doors, her white hair disheveled from a nap.

"I'm sorry to startle you. I came home because I got some time off work." Nerves pulsing, she changed the topic. "Would you like some tea?"

Miyoko prepared her mother-in-law's favorite barley tea as she gathered up her courage. "I want to take Ko-chan to Osaka with me to visit Bohbeh. She's sick, and the doctors don't know what it is. She wants to see Ko-chan, in case things get worse."

Uneasiness shifted inside her. She hated to lie to Halmeoni, who had cared for Ko-chan every day while Miyoko worked at the hospital. There had been enough sickness and death in this house that she didn't want to invent another tragedy, but it was necessary to create urgency. Her mother-in-law would appreciate what it meant to tend to a sick relative, having seen Hojoon suffer. The last time Miyoko had suggested traveling alone with Ko-chan to see Bohbeh, her mother-in-law had refused, and that's why Bohbeh had come to Kyoto to see him then. This time, Miyoko hoped Halmeoni would be more flexible now that Ko-chan was six and his aunt reportedly ill.

Halmeoni pressed her lips together. She was a strong woman, but she was still broken over the loss of her son, and her grandson was all she had left of him. Halmeoni still chanted at the altar for Hojoon, whose photo remained on display in their old bedroom. She would be shattered if she couldn't see her grandson anymore.

But Hojoon's last words called to her: *Promise me you'll go back to Korea with Ko-chan.* It was now or never.

With fresh resolve, Miyoko spoke directly to her mother-in-law. "I'm planning to leave in the morning for Osaka with Ko-chan. Since tomorrow is Saturday, I'll bring him back Sunday evening so that he can go back to school on Monday." Her throat thickened at telling this bald-faced lie.

Halmeoni stared back, shaking her head. "This doesn't feel right. I still think Ko-chan's too young to be gone from home." She looked away with wet eyes. Miyoko had seen her mother-in-law like this before and presumed she was thinking about Hojoon. His death had caused her to grip her grandson even tighter. She simply didn't want to let Ko-chan out of her sight, even if it was just for a weekend.

Miyoko chose her next few words carefully. If she convinced Halmeoni, she was certain Ko-chan would go too.

"I know it's hard to let Ko-chan go, but he's growing up fast. I know you've lost your son, but I'm a mother too. I'm Ko-chan's mother. I need him to be with me so that I can have memories with him, just like you had with Hojoon. I don't get a chance to do that, being away for work. I have this vacation now. Bohbeh wants to see him. Ko-chan will enjoy himself. Please." Miyoko twinged with discomfort.

Is this how Miyoko's mother had felt when she convinced Father to let Miyoko and her sisters leave Korea for a better future? Miyoko finally understood why she had done it. Her mother had had to make difficult choices, trusting her maternal judgment to do so, just as Miyoko was doing here. It was a mother's responsibility to make decisions that she felt were best, even if they were complicated. Miyoko was beginning to make peace with her mother letting her go all those years ago, despite the pain it had caused. Miyoko hoped Ko-chan, too, would forgive her someday.

Halmeoni's dewy eyes wilted. Her skin sagged, and Miyoko noticed how much older she seemed. Her brashness and steely demeanor had weakened after Hojoon's death. She would not be able to take care of Ko-chan forever, even if she wanted to. Maybe she would finally recognize that Ko-chan needed his mother.

In a monotone voice, Halmeoni relented. "Hojoon is gone. Ko-chan is still here. I can't stop you. You're his mother, and your sister is ill. If Ko-chan wants to go, then I can't object."

Miyoko's head fell back in relief. At this moment, she felt a deeper connection to her mother-in-law than ever before. She understood Halmeoni and the pain of having a child taken away. She knew that from her own experience, as well as from her mother's.

"Thank you. Ko-chan ran off a little while ago. When he comes back, I'll tell him that you said it was all right." Miyoko hoped that if she conveyed to Ko-chan that his grandmother approved of the trip, he would go willingly. If he didn't, Miyoko didn't know what she would do.

Ko-chan didn't return from his hiding spot for hours. Darkness set in as Miyoko prepared dinner of pollack stew and barley for the extended family. She waited anxiously for Ko-chan so that she could tell him about his grandmother's consent.

The front door creaked as Ko-chan opened it slowly, peeking his head around to see who was home. Miyoko was sweeping a corner of the courtyard, where he couldn't see her. When his aunts Inja and Yoonhee entered the courtyard, Ko-chan darted behind some large urns filled with water like he was playing hide-and-seek.

"Did you hear that Halmeoni is letting Ko-chan go on a trip to Osaka with his mother?"

"Yeah. I hope they stay there together."

Miyoko's breath caught.

"He's so spoiled. If it weren't for his grandparents, he wouldn't have anyone to take care of him. His father's dead, and his mother is too busy working."

"Yet he doesn't even have to do chores like his cousins. How long will it be before his cousins get upset that he's treated differently?"

"Once his grandparents are ill or too old to protect him, he will have to face the truth that he doesn't belong here."

Miyoko clenched her fists. She hoped that Ko-chan had not heard those hurtful words.

"Eoseowa," Halmeoni interrupted, opening her door. "Come in."

The aunts scurried to the kitchen without looking back. Ko-chan dashed out of his hiding place and into his grandmother's arms. Miyoko followed behind.

"I heard all about your trip to Osaka," her mother-in-law said to Ko-chan. "How exciting! I'm sure you're looking forward to getting on that big train!"

Miyoko blinked rapidly with surprise at Halmeoni's generosity. Maybe she thought that Ko-chan would enjoy the train ride and the sights of Osaka. Maybe she finally realized that Ko-chan should spend more time with his mother. Regardless, Miyoko was grateful that Halmeoni had kept her promise.

She couldn't read Ko-chan's face, however. If he was hurt by what his aunts had said, he wasn't showing it.

"We're going tomorrow," Ko-chan said. His voice sounded more subdued, but his change of heart was clear. He had always looked to his grandmother for approval. When she called for her knitting needles, Ko-chan was the first to jump up and get them. Had what his aunts just said changed his mind too? She was sure it was shocking to overhear his aunts' conversation.

"I'm going to go tell my cousins now," he said.

Ko-chan hurried off to spread the news. He was competitive and liked to score more goals than his cousins and neighbors in their games of street soccer. This would be a victory for him. Miyoko paused in her sweeping and bowed to her mother-in-law. "Thank you. You have made this possible. He wouldn't go without your blessing."

Halmeoni's next words would haunt Miyoko later. "Ko-chan means everything to me as my grandson and the only living memory of my son. Take care of him. Don't let him out of your sight. He could wander off and get easily lost. His safety is the most important thing."

"Yes, I promise I'll take care of him." Miyoko's stomach churned. She knew she was telling a terrible lie. Her son would be leaving the only family he knew. She would be taking him from his grandparents who had cared for him to honor the memory of his father. Her path was uncertain, and Ko-chan might end up worse off.

But she couldn't waver now. She had the tickets to Shimonoseki, and her son was willing to go with her. She had to continue, although Ko-chan didn't yet know how far she planned to go. She would have to calm Halmeoni's fears and leave Kyoto with Ko-chan the next morning. Lying was the only way.

CHAPTER THIRTY-EIGHT

April 17, 1943
Saturday

Under hazy gray skies, the family gathered in the morning to say goodbye to Ko-chan. A long line of relatives stood outside the front door and patted Ko-chan's head one by one—his grandparents, two uncles, two aunts, and four cousins all living together with Ko-chan. The young cousins rarely left the neighborhood, and this was the first time that one of them would be gone for even a short period.

"Itte ki nasai," squealed one of Ko-chan's cousins, telling him to be sure to come back safely. Although the adults spoke in Korean, the children spoke in Japanese, the language they had learned in school.

"Jal danyeowa," Halmeoni said in Korean, bidding her grandson a safe return.

Wearing his black school uniform, Ko-chan slouched with his brimmed cap tilted on his head and his hands crossed in front of him, his large backpack slung over his shoulder like a sack of potatoes. His pointy ears reddened, and Miyoko wondered if it was from the attention or something else. He had seemed unusually quiet that morning, moving the barley around his bowl with his chopsticks and not eating much.

"Let's go," Miyoko said gently. "We'll miss the train." She was dressed in the same blue striped kimono that she'd worn when she purchased the tickets to Shimonoseki. The inside of her draped sleeve made a crinkling sound as the fabric brushed against the small envelope of cash tucked there. She had withdrawn everything from her savings account at the post office. This was all she had saved from her earnings over the years, and it would probably support them for only a few weeks before she would have to find a job in Korea. She pushed the hair out of her face to confront her uncertain future with Ko-chan. She couldn't stop now.

Miyoko and Ko-chan bowed goodbye to everyone. Wrapping one arm over Ko-chan's shoulder, she spun him away from the group toward the train station. After they had walked about fifty paces down the dirt path, Ko-chan halted and sprinted back. His hat fell off as he charged into his grandmother's arms and squeezed her tight. Miyoko's hopes dashed at that moment, and she wondered if he had changed his mind once more.

"I'll miss you, Halmeoni!" Ko-chan shouted.

Halmeoni stooped over him and rested her hand on his bare head. She was hardly a foot taller than Ko-chan and looked childlike from a distance. The only thing giving her away was her now silvery hair fastened tight into a low bun, the long wooden binyeo like a chopstick sticking through it. She wiped her eyes with the backs of her hands and shooed him away. "Get going. You'll miss the train. See you tomorrow night!"

Miyoko's eyes blurred as she saw herself as a little girl hugging her own mother at the village station. Nostalgia weakened her resolve. This might be the last time Ko-chan would hug his grandmother. And she was risking her son's future for the unknown. Black clouds seemed to shroud the farewell party.

Miyoko walked back to the family, scooping up Ko-chan's cap on the way. This time, she clutched Ko-chan's limp hand and hustled back toward the station while he lagged a step behind. A dull pain throbbed in her head as she tried to justify what she was doing.

She hurried to the station with Ko-chan before he could change his mind, or before she could. Breathless, they boarded the commuter train. It took most of the hour from Kyoto to Osaka for her heart to steady. They were on their way, but they had a long journey ahead.

Ko-chan pressed his face against the window to see the green rice paddies spanning the two cities. He splayed his whole hand against the glass when he saw oxen pulling carts in the fields next to the railroad tracks. He wasn't used to rural life, since Kyoto was jammed with shrines, temples, and old castles. He seemed excited.

"Ichi, ni, san . . . ," Ko-chan said, counting one, two, three with his fingers when each train whizzed by in the opposite direction. Miyoko was happy to see his bright eyes and quick mind take in each new sight. Maybe she had made the right decision after all.

The train's wheels screeched into Osaka Station. The conductor blared the horn, announcing their arrival. Tall, stark buildings stood shoulder to shoulder against equally gloomy skies. Ko-chan stared out the window wide eyed at the commotion of people sprinting to catch their train or leave the station. Miyoko waited until the crowds had thinned to finally venture out. Osaka was much bigger than Kyoto, and Ko-chan could easily get lost.

Clasping his hand tight, Miyoko led Ko-chan into the busy streets, heeding her mother-in-law's warning to keep him safe. Ko-chan's well-being was now solely in her hands. When Ko-chan was younger, Halmeoni had tied a cloth leash around his waist to take walks in the neighborhood. He was too old for that now, but Miyoko made sure he stuck close by.

After walking about thirty minutes from the train station, they arrived at Bohbeh's house. Ko-chan hid behind his mother's kimono. Tenderness welled for her son, who wanted her protection.

"We're here at Auntie's house," Miyoko said. She huffed after the long walk. The sun shone brighter at midday, and a line of sweat dotted Ko-chan's face.

"I don't remember her," Ko-chan said in a wobbly voice, even though it had only been a couple of years since he last saw her.

"Remember how she came to the street fair with us in Kyoto a few years ago? She's a little-older version of me and really nice." Miyoko tried to sound upbeat. "She has two children who are also your cousins. The boy, Tomiyo, is a little younger than you. I'm sure you'll get along, like with your Kyoto cousins."

Bohbeh had promised she would help convince Ko-chan to go with Miyoko to Korea if they made it this far. It would be easier if Ko-chan liked Bohbeh. But now that the time had come to meet his aunt again, he seemed shy.

The boardinghouse door opened, and Bohbeh held a pinwheel to her face. "Guess who!" she said. Joy flashed in Ko-chan's eyes at the colorful plastic toy. Bohbeh blew on the pinwheel before offering it to him.

"This is for you!" she said, beaming. "You've grown up so much!"

Ko-chan grinned widely at his aunt's gift and affection. "I remember you!"

Bohbeh got down on her knees so that their eyes met. "How about we take a bus to the fairgrounds, where you can ride a Ferris wheel, like we did in Kyoto last time? Or would you rather go to the fish market and see the fresh fish?"

Ko-chan's eyes sparkled. "Both!"

"Okay! Let's go, then!" Bohbeh said playfully. She winked at Miyoko with a knowing eye.

Ko-chan clapped his hands together. "Let's go now!"

Tomiyo and Nobuko joined the commotion and squealed. This part of her plan was working out more smoothly than Miyoko had thought it would. At the same time, guilt throbbed over the reality that she was taking him away from his grandparents and his aunts, uncles, and cousins. She might be subjecting Ko-chan to a life as lonely as hers had been. She hoped she was doing the right thing, but she couldn't be sure.

Later that afternoon at the fish market, Ko-chan crinkled his nose at the salty, pungent smell of fresh-caught fish while his cousins wandered around wide eyed. They gawked at a vendor slicing a huge tuna in perfect rectangular fillets. The shrill sounds of men and women yelling out specials had them pressing their hands over their ears.

Ko-chan caught his foot around one of the hoses and tripped, cutting his finger against the edge of a sharp plastic box. Miyoko always carried a few first aid supplies in her bag, and she pulled out some Mercurochrome and gauze.

"There—sit over there on that bench, Ko-chan. I'll fix it for you," she said.

Ko-chan studied her as she dabbed the red liquid on his cut to sterilize the wound. She blew on it and taped some gauze around his finger.

"Is this what you do all day at the hospital?"

"Yes, it's part of what I do," she said. The moment reminded her of when Hojoon used to ask about her nursing duties.

"And it didn't hurt!" Ko-chan faced his Osaka cousins to announce the good news, his small chest stretching. Miyoko heard a hint of pride in her son's voice. There was a connection between her and her son after all.

Bohbeh came back with some red bean paste doughnuts from one of the food stalls. Ko-chan seemed to momentarily forget about his cut while he chewed. His lips glistened like he had kissed a plate of sugar. He smiled at her, and a dimple dotted his face—a smile that reminded her of Hojoon.

In the last hour of daylight, the three children rode a Ferris wheel at the nearby fairgrounds. When they reached the apex, Ko-chan pointed to the sun, which was casting its final orange rays over the horizon.

Miyoko looked up at them from the ground and her heart lifted too—for her and Ko-chan's future.

When they returned home, Bohbeh's house was quiet. Haramoto was still away on his trip.

"Why don't you go in the other room and let Auntie rest for a minute," Miyoko said to Ko-chan and his cousins.

"I liked spending this day with you!" Ko-chan said to her, without prompting. "Thank you for fixing my cut." The words tingled Miyoko's face like a gentle breeze. Ko-chan seemed to be opening up, giving her more courage to move ahead with her plan.

The children hopped into the bedroom to look at the comic books they had bought at the fair. The rooms were small and separated by thin shoji doors, so the sisters whispered.

"Ko-chan had a good day today," Bohbeh said, plopping down on the floor cushion and rubbing her feet.

"Yes, he did. Thank you for making him feel so welcome."

"We had fun together, and we'll miss you both. I think Ko-chan will go with you, but you're still not safe." Bohbeh's expression turned serious.

"I know. I'll make us some tea," Miyoko said. She wanted to settle her nerves.

"There's some mulberry leaves in the drawer in the chest over there," Bohbeh said, pointing to the only piece of furniture in the room besides the low table.

Miyoko lit the brazier with a match and boiled some water in a metal pot. She opened the drawer, and the fruity scent of mulberry glided up her nose, reminding her of the tender white berries in her village tree. She poured the hot water into an empty teapot and watched the burned leaves float to the top. After the tea had steeped, she held the lid with one finger and poured them each a steaming cup. Inhaling something familiar and earthy, Miyoko felt the need to tell Ko-chan the truth.

"I think I need to tell Ko-chan about going to Korea and staying with Taeyoung," Miyoko said.

Memories of climbing rocks with her brother flooded back. He must be a smart, important man now, at twenty-nine. Her breath hitched to see him again.

"How am I going to convince Ko-chan to go to Korea? Can you help me?" Desperation hung in Miyoko's voice. She had been mulling over the options and was torn between complete honesty and continued deception. "I could say that I got a new job in Korea. That another uncle lives there and has invited us to stay with him. I'll remind Ko-chan that he's the one who used to send us the chocolates with the sweet, squishy middle. There'll be plenty more of that there."

Bohbeh shrugged like that wasn't going to work.

Miyoko offered another possibility. "Or I could start by saying we will take another train ride and get on a big ship. We will even sleep on the ship overnight."

"I think that's better," Bohbeh said. "Another adventure, a ship, a visit to a nice uncle. Then you can tell him what'll happen once he gets there. Maybe you can say that he'll continue to use his Japanese at a Japanese school once he arrives. That he'll make new friends."

Miyoko hadn't thought through all these details. She felt a wave of nausea overtake her as she considered the immensity of what lay ahead for Ko-chan. He would be separated from his extended family and would have to adapt to an entirely new life. He would have to go to a new school and learn Korean too, if he was going to live there. This was what she'd had to do when she first came to Japan. Her throat dried with doubt.

"What if he decides he doesn't like the idea of going to Korea and wants to go back to his grandparents?" Miyoko said. The room swayed, and she sipped her tea to steady herself. Going to another country, even his parents' homeland, would be demanding for a six-year-old who considered another place his home.

"You'll have to be extra mindful of his feelings," Bohbeh said.

"I could say that his grandmother is getting old and would probably be happy he could see the world in her place."

Miyoko searched Bohbeh's eyes, as if Bohbeh must know how uncertain this felt for Miyoko. "I like the idea of you telling Ko-chan about Taeyoung. He will help take care of Ko-chan. He could be a father figure to him. It's all going to be fine. I'll back you up when you tell him. He'll want to go with you."

Miyoko was grateful for Bohbeh's reassurance. But she was repeating to Ko-chan the same types of lies that her mother had told her when she went to Japan. Mother had known she was very sick and had lied to Miyoko and Bohbeh about her illness so that they would be willing to leave her.

Could lying be an act of love? She was sure that her son needed her the same way she had needed her mother as a child. Miyoko needed him too. She loved Ko-chan more than she could have fathomed. She had felt this way with Hojoon. And just like with her husband, Miyoko would do anything to provide for him and protect him.

Laughter pealed as the children skimmed their comic books in the next room. Miyoko and Bohbeh stared into their cups in silence. Their conversation about how to persuade Ko-chan to leave Japan had cooled Miyoko's drink, as well as her drive. It was already evening, and the day was slipping by.

"I'm going to the dormitory to pick up my things." Miyoko hoped the fresh air would bring clarity to what she needed to say to Ko-chan.

Bohbeh sat alert, ready to help. "I'll watch the kids. You go."

"Let me tell Ko-chan that I'll be right back." Miyoko worried he might get nervous if he found her gone.

She opened the sliding door to the next room and saw the children propped up on their elbows reading. "I'm going back to the hospital for a little bit, but Auntie is here. Let her know if you need anything, okay?"

Ko-chan's head bobbed without looking up.

Miyoko put her shoes on to leave. "Thank you for watching Ko-chan. I'll talk to him when I get back. I also want to double-check the 6:00 a.m. train departure time."

Bohbeh was already clanging pots, getting ready for dinner. "Go ahead. Be safe."

Miyoko went to the train station first. When she arrived, throngs of people were pushing their way to the ticket booth. More soldiers and policemen patrolled the area than two days before, when she had come to purchase the tickets to Shimonoseki. Stiff men wearing khaki and black uniforms assailed passengers in jagged tones. Miyoko wondered what was happening as she strode past one of them snapping at a young couple. Maybe it wouldn't be enough to just have tickets; maybe she wouldn't even be able to get on the train. She slowed to listen.

"Where are you going?" the policeman in black said sharply to a man of about thirty.

"I'm traveling to Nagasaki with my wife to visit a relative," he said, shaking.

"Where are your papers?" the policeman barked at the young wife. Panic drained the wife's face as she riffled through her bag and produced a Japanese passport. He scanned the document and looked them both up and down. He waved his hand, motioning them away. The couple rushed off into the crowd.

The police were questioning passengers! Sweat beaded on Miyoko's forehead. What would this mean for her and Ko-chan? Maybe this was what the earlier newspaper article was referring to. The police were looking for people who might be dodging military service, including Koreans like her. A chill shot through her body.

Keeping her eyes down at her feet, Miyoko hurried to the ticket office at the other end of the tracks to scan the big board for tomorrow's train departures. To her dismay, her train time had been postponed. It was now scheduled to leave at 8:00 a.m. on Monday, the day after she was supposed to be back in Kyoto with Ko-chan. Halmeoni would be worried, but she had to move forward. Miyoko would write to her when they arrived in Korea to say that they were safe. Monday was also the deadline to report for service, but since the train was leaving in the morning, she hoped they would be long gone.

Thinking about the passengers being interrogated, Miyoko felt her throat tighten. She would be a prime target for questioning: a woman traveling alone with a child. *Where's your husband?* they would ask. And she would need to tell them a credible story, like the one she had told the train station employee. *I'm a military wife, and this is my son. We're visiting my sick husband, who's an officer in Korea.* Just when she was satisfied that might work, she saw the police talking to a child. The girl didn't look much older than Ko-chan. What would Ko-chan say if he were asked where he was going? What if he unmasked her lie because he didn't know the truth?

She would have to tell Ko-chan everything. He needed to appreciate the obstacles they would face. She didn't have the luxury of explaining things as she went along. There would be soldiers on the train and possibly on the ship. She couldn't afford to have him be surprised. He might protest and blow their cover. She had to tell him they were traveling to Korea, and why.

Miyoko scampered to her dormitory, picked up a few things, and dashed out without being seen. She raced back to Bohbeh's house in the cool dusk air, which helped release her taut nerves but not her fears. She imagined Ko-chan not wanting to go with her when he heard the real story, and the thrum of her heartbeat sounded like officers shouting in her ears.

As Miyoko entered the house, Bohbeh shushed her with a finger to the lips, tilting her head with her eyes closed to show that Ko-chan was sleeping in the other room. Her sister's two children were sleeping soundly before them.

Miyoko spilled what she had seen into Bohbeh's ear.

"Our train schedule has been changed. We aren't leaving until the day after tomorrow. And there are police questioning passengers about their travel plans. They're even asking children! I have to tell Ko-chan what's happening so we have the story straight. It's dangerous. We may get caught." Miyoko rubbed her pounding temples.

Bohbeh responded without hesitation. "You're right. You have to tell him about the whole trip and hope he'll agree. And you might have to tell him that his grandparents approve. It might be the only way. I'll help you."

Miyoko hugged Bohbeh tight. Her big sister was always there for her, and Miyoko was going to miss her. Tears clung to her lashes, but she had no time now for regrets.

CHAPTER THIRTY-NINE

April 18, 1943
Sunday

The next morning, the children played outside and enjoyed their last day together. When it was time to come in for lunch, Miyoko mustered the courage to tell Ko-chan the truth. She beseeched Bohbeh, "Help me if you hear me struggling."

Bohbeh dipped her head and took her children into the other room.

Miyoko offered Ko-chan a cracker and watched him eat. The front tooth he had lost last year was growing back but hadn't quite reached the other. At six, he was only half-grown in every way, still just a little boy. She pinched his nose like old times. He laughed, as though he remembered. Now she was about to change his life forever.

Miyoko cleared her throat and spoke softly to Ko-chan. "Do you remember your uncle Taeyoung I told you about who lives in Korea, the one who sends us those chocolates at New Year's?"

Ko-chan sat up and circled his mouth with his tongue. "Yeah. You said he was your favorite brother because he played hide-and-seek with you. And those chocolates were yummy!"

Buoyed by Ko-chan's response, Miyoko continued. "Yes! He's been asking me to visit him in Korea for a while, and he told me there's a hospital in Pyongyang that needs more nurses. He'll help me get a good job there."

Ko-chan's brows crinkled. "Why are you leaving?"

"That's a good question," Miyoko said, stalling. "You see, the Japanese army wants to send me to the war in a faraway place, where I may never see you again."

Ko-chan shook his head. "I don't understand."

"The only way for us to stay together is to go away for a while, just the two of us." Miyoko reached out her hands for his, holding her breath for his answer.

Ko-chan looked down instead and folded the edges of his comic book.

Sensing his uncertainty, Miyoko tried another tactic. "We would have to take a ship."

"A ship?" Ko-chan said. "I've never been on a ship."

Miyoko talked faster. "I've only been on a ship once. Remember how I told you I came to Japan on one when I was thirteen. It was so exciting!" Miyoko's voice cracked as she continued to stretch the truth. "They even had food on the ship. And rooms with beds and curtains. I even saw children going to the captain's deck to watch him steer the ship."

"Really?" Ko-chan chirped.

"Uncle Taeyoung said we could stay with him in Korea. We would ride on a ship and then take a train to see him. He'll be thrilled to meet you!"

Ko-chan's eyes grew two sizes. "I want to ride on a train again!"

Miyoko grasped Ko-chan's arms with both hands. "Then let's go! We could go away together, just you and me! It'll be a grand adventure. We can sip Coca-Cola." Miyoko believed with her whole heart that even if it weren't a perfect life, it would still be better than military service and never seeing each other again. It would still be better than possibly one day seeing Ko-chan conscripted to fight for a country that persecuted Koreans.

A shadow descended over Ko-chan's face. "For how long?"

Miyoko kept talking, not wanting Ko-chan to change his mind. "It'll take several days, maybe even up to a week to get all the way to Pyongyang."

"But . . . what about Halmeoni and Harabeoji?" Ko-chan's eyes sought hers.

Miyoko blinked hard for an answer. "The trip is really for you and me. They would want you to travel in their place because they're too old to go so far."

"I don't want to leave them that long, or my cousins!"

Miyoko understood how much Ko-chan would miss his family in Kyoto. His cousins were his playmates, and his grandparents had been his surrogate parents. "I know how much they mean to you."

Ko-chan's lips quivered, like he was about to cry.

"Gomen ne. I'm sorry I surprised you with this news." Was she being selfish in wanting him for herself? Wouldn't he have a better life with his extended family than with a single mother running away from military service?

Agony ripped her heart at this choice, but she could not bear to leave him now. And if she didn't leave Japan immediately, her only other option would be to go to war in Saipan and risk never seeing Ko-chan again.

"I know I haven't been around much. And your grandparents have taken such good care of you. But I love you too, and I want to spend more time with you. Your father would have wanted us to be together. It was his dream for all of us to go back to Korea."

Ko-chan's small lips pursed tight, and his nose flared. He turned his head away as she reached her hand out to touch him.

"Halmeoni and Harabeoji would probably say it was all right for you to go." Miyoko's cheeks burned. She was enlisting her son's trust through more lies. She feared losing it when he learned the truth, but she resolved to gain it back later—when they were safe in Korea. "They would want you to go and have a good time. They would be excited for you!" Miyoko gritted her teeth.

Ko-chan's mood seemed to change. "Is that what Auntie meant when she said that they would be too old to take care of me? That I wouldn't be wanted at their house?"

So he had overheard that dreadful conversation after all. "Sorry you heard all that."

"The aunties aren't nice to me. They offer their kids more food when Halmeoni's not looking."

Miyoko's heart broke for her son. "Mothers want to protect their own first, if they can," she heard herself say. "I would do the same." She spoke like she knew what she was talking about, like she was an experienced mother. It was refreshing how sure she felt.

"Is that why Halmeoni looks at Father's picture all the time?" Ko-chan asked. "Halmeoni always pats my head and lets me sit next to her, but sometimes I feel she's far away. Like she's thinking about Father and not me."

Ko-chan was unveiling a lot of his feelings to her. He was trusting her. Miyoko's head pounded for lying. She hoped he would forgive her later.

"It's human nature," Miyoko said. "That's why I want you with me, Ko-chan. You're perfect the way you are. I am your mother. I will always love you, no matter what."

"What's Korea like?" Ko-chan said, his voice lighter.

"It's beautiful. You'll love my hometown. There's a mulberry tree you can climb. There's a whole world waiting for you and me in Korea. Remember how you said the kids were making fun of you for being Korean? Well, you won't have to worry about that when you go back. Your friends will like you for who you are. And I'll support you, whoever you want to be."

Ko-chan's face brightened, and he nodded.

"I overheard that you might be going to Korea. How lucky you are!" Bohbeh said in a cheery tone as she entered the room. "Your uncle Taeyoung is very nice, and I heard he likes to play games. Hide-and-seek, Go . . ."

Ko-chan burst into a smile. Bohbeh eyed Miyoko, saying everything would be all right. Miyoko felt herself relax just a little as her sister came to her aid.

Ko-chan scooched closer to listen to his aunt. "You'll take a train to the south of Japan and then ride a big ship to Korea. From there you'll get on another train and travel all the way up to Pyongyang. You'll be very happy there."

Miyoko allowed herself to think so too. It would be wonderful if Ko-chan and Taeyoung could get along, and if Ko-chan could be happy being with her. On the other hand, he might be miserable. Miyoko's stomach churned with uncertainty.

"I don't know . . . ," Ko-chan said, pulling at his ear.

A hush filled the room, but a clock ticked in Miyoko's mind. She swallowed hard and told her son the lie she had been trying not to tell, believing that she needed to do so now to save them both.

"I know you'll miss your family here, Ko-chan. If at any point you want to return, we can do that." It was the same white lie that her own mother had told her about returning from Japan if she wasn't happy. Of course Mother had not kept her promise when Miyoko had begged to go home. Now she was doing the same thing to her own son. But she couldn't lose him; she had to fight. She had to protect Ko-chan and give him the opportunity to grow up where he could be proud of who he was, instead of living in the shadows like she had.

Bohbeh patted her knees to bring Ko-chan's attention to her. She glanced at Miyoko with a reassuring nod. "Yes, Ko-chan. Go, and if you get homesick, you can come back. I'll come meet you if you need me to." Miyoko wondered if Mother had told the same lie to Bohbeh when she went to Japan to marry Haramoto.

Pain seared her chest as she pondered what she would do if Ko-chan refused to continue on their trip. She would have to insist, but how could she make him go against his will?

Ko-chan squirmed. "All right, I'll go. But you promise I can come back?"

"I promise," Miyoko said weakly, the weight of the lie pulling her down.

Ko-chan's shoulders relaxed.

"Just one more thing," Miyoko said. She had to make sure that Ko-chan knew what to do if they were questioned. "It's dangerous for Koreans to travel now because of the war. You might see soldiers and policemen, and they may even ask you questions. If anyone talks to you on the trip, don't say you're going to see your uncle in Korea. We have to pretend we're Japanese and say we're going to see your sick father there."

Ko-chan scrunched up his face, as if puzzled over why his mother was asking him to lie to the police.

"I know it's hard for you to understand all this, but please listen to me. It's the safest way. Follow what I say."

Bohbeh offered the right words to shift the mood. "Do you know where Pyongyang is? I'll show you a map of Korea. And let's have a snack too!"

They moved to the other room to wake up Ko-chan's cousins, leaving Miyoko alone with her thoughts. Worry brewed over the officers she had seen talking to the little girl at the station about her travel plans. Would Ko-chan be questioned too, and would he be able to easily deceive a policeman or stumble over his false answer? One hurdle overcome, another tomorrow.

CHAPTER FORTY

April 19, 1943
Monday

Miyoko's eyes shot open to a pitch-black morning. Sleep had eluded her the night before as she thought about the dangers ahead. Ko-chan, though, was snoring softly next to her in the living room, and Bohbeh and her children were asleep in the bedroom. Blood coursed through Miyoko's body, rushing like the high-speed train she was about to take with Ko-chan. It would be a six-hour trip, with stops in Kobe, Okayama, Hiroshima, and finally Shimonoseki—plenty of time for something to go wrong. The pain of leaving her sister, nephew, and niece would grow too, the farther they traveled away from them.

Miyoko's breathing deepened, and she closed her eyes, conjuring Hojoon's spirit. *I want to keep my promise to you. I'm bringing Ko-chan home. I hope I have the courage to do whatever is needed to get there.*

A sense of calm glided over her. She reached over to pick up her Bible and pack it. She would be careful to keep it hidden, as she was exposing them to the double danger of being Korean and Christian. It opened to a verse in Hebrews that she had earmarked: *But to do good and to communicate forget not: for with such sacrifices God is well pleased.* She tucked it away in her head for her journey.

Bohbeh entered the main living area where Miyoko and Ko-chan slept. "Good morning," Bohbeh whispered. She closed the door behind her to let her children sleep.

"Good morning," Miyoko chimed back quietly. "Thank you for seeing us off at the station."

Bohbeh boiled some water and dunked a sheet of dried bonito into the pot to make a soup base for breakfast. "I made these last night," she said, pointing to two bento boxes stuffed with food. "There's rice, dried salmon, and some pickled radish. I made lots of onigiri rice balls too, to last the whole day."

"Thank you," Miyoko said, her mouth watering. Rice was still rationed, so it was even more expensive and hard to find. It touched her heart that Bohbeh had spent so much time and money preparing all this treasured food, and how welcome it would be on their long journey. The pleasure of the gift, however, would never fill the void of losing Bohbeh.

"Why don't you get Ko-chan up now so he can eat something. You need energy too." Bohbeh dropped seaweed into the boiling soup and dished out cold millet to eat with it.

Miyoko shook Ko-chan. "Wake up."

Ko-chan rubbed his sleepy eyes and yawned loudly.

"Come eat breakfast. It's the big day!" Miyoko said.

After Ko-chan slurped some soup, his gaze rested on the suitcase in the entryway. Bohbeh had given it to Miyoko for the trip, and gratitude surged again for her sister's thoughtfulness. Miyoko took this opportunity to remind Ko-chan about what was happening today.

"You may see some policemen and soldiers on the train," Miyoko said.

Ko-chan's eyes popped wide. "Will they have guns?"

"Probably," Miyoko said, recalling Ko-chan and his cousins pretending to shoot each other with their fingers. "Remember what I told you last night? No matter who it is, we have to pretend we're Japanese and visiting your sick father in Korea. We have to say he's serving in the Japanese army so that they'll let us through."

Fear flickered momentarily in Ko-chan's eyes. But then he smiled again and stuck out his thumb and forefinger like he was holding a gun. Miyoko hoped his boyish interest in weapons would make the journey less frightening.

The clock said it was already after 7:00 a.m., and they had to go. The white wall calendar—the kind where you tear off each day as it passes—still showed yesterday's date in large black print. Miyoko ripped it to bare today's date: Monday, April 19. It was time.

Bohbeh asked a neighbor to watch over her sleeping children, and the three of them bustled to Osaka Station. Bohbeh had arranged this childcare the day before, saying that she had to drop her sister and nephew off at the station to visit a relative in Okayama, the second stop on the early train. The morning light brightened the spring sky. Weaving in and out of the tight alleys, Miyoko strained her neck, looking for any signs of danger. Ko-chan's little feet pattered fast, then slow, like he was as excited and nervous as she was.

When they arrived at the station, only a few passengers lingered near the tracks. No officials were in sight. Miyoko exhaled deeply. The departure board said they needed to be on track two. Miyoko wanted to have a few minutes to say goodbye to Bohbeh before getting on the train. She didn't know when she would see her sister or her niece and nephew again. She choked back tears.

"I'm so grateful for all you've done for us." Miyoko bent over at her waist in deep appreciation.

Ko-chan stretched his arms, his body still heavy with sleep. Miyoko nudged him, and he bowed to Bohbeh with his eyes still half-closed.

Bohbeh gave Ko-chan a bear hug and nearly knocked over his black school hat. His shaved schoolboy haircut emphasized his childlike innocence. "I'm so glad you came to visit. I had the best time these last few days. I know you'll have a wonderful trip."

Ko-chan thanked her in his familiar Kyoto dialect. "Okini, Auntie."

Warmth moved into Miyoko's cheeks to see them so close. The two sisters pressed up next to each other. Tears stung Miyoko's eyes as she recalled saying goodbye to her mother, not knowing it would be the last time. She prayed it would not be the last time she would see her sister.

"Good luck," Bohbeh said, clenching Miyoko's hands in hers. "Please write and let me know you and Ko-chan are all right."

"I will," Miyoko said. "Okini. I'll miss you. I promise to write all the time. I'm not going to forget you."

Before more tears flowed, Miyoko directed Ko-chan to the train steps. They climbed in and sat by the window right above Bohbeh, who reached her arms up toward them. Miyoko leaned out, grabbing her sister's hands firmly.

"Go now. We'll be fine," Miyoko said, feigning courage.

She caught sight of men in khaki army uniforms marching over to their train. Bohbeh must have seen the terror in her eyes, because she quickly looked back over her shoulder, then squeezed Miyoko's hands tight before releasing them.

"Be calm," Bohbeh mouthed, and stepped back.

Chills crept up Miyoko's neck as she scrambled to recall her story. *Family of a Japanese army officer. Visiting him because he's ill . . .* If anyone asked for her papers, though, they would know she was Korean, and it would be over. Her whole cover-up would be discovered. They could be ordered off the train before their trip even started—or, worse, arrested for lying about their plans and evading military orders.

Ko-chan had been leaning out the open window and watching the people go by, but he pulled back as soon he saw the soldiers enter. Thumping boots caused all the passengers to look up as the soldiers found their seats. Miyoko wondered what Ko-chan was thinking, hoping it was his scripted lines. His eyes were riveted on the uniformed men.

The soldiers heaved their duffel bags up onto the shelves above their seats and sat down. They must be passengers, not on active duty, since they were traveling with their belongings. Miyoko had heard that more Japanese army personnel were being sent to Japan's colonies to bolster Japan's war efforts. It was natural that they would be traveling to Shimonoseki to take the ferry to Busan or other Asian ports. If the soldiers were just passengers, though, they probably wouldn't ask questions. They were talking loudly among themselves and didn't seem interested in anyone else. It would be best to avoid them anyway. She slumped down in her seat and cast her eyes at the floor.

The train whistled and started to chug along the track. Miyoko glanced at the station entrance and caught a flash of orange sweater that looked like Bohbeh's. No doubt Bohbeh had been as terrified as Miyoko. She would write to her as soon as they were safe in Korea.

Miyoko finally settled into her seat, and Ko-chan sat next to her by the window, looking at his comic book. The conductor came by to punch their tickets but didn't ask a single question. Miyoko reached into her draped kimono sleeve and pulled out a lollipop. She had brought several small treats for Ko-chan and kept them hidden in her sleeve, as she often did with loose items. Ko-chan laughed like this was a game, and she was glad to see him light up. Sucking the sweet candy, he seemed serene as he looked out at the miles of rice paddies and tiled-roof houses dotting the landscape. He turned to offer her a lick of his lollipop, warming her heart. She again tried the game they used to play. She pinched his nose. This time, he pinched back. And they leaned in so that their foreheads bumped. They both let out a laugh.

Miyoko rested her head on the back of her seat. Relief settled in her chest. Most of the Japanese soldiers were asleep. They were on their way.

After about an hour, the train slowed. Miyoko craned her head out the window and noticed Japanese policemen in the field next to the tracks. It looked like a checkpoint. Her hands dampened, and she sat upright.

"What's happening?" Ko-chan asked, stirring from a nap.

"I'm not sure," Miyoko said, panic rising in her throat. "There's policemen, and they might be coming onto the train to ask questions." Whispering, she said, "Remember that you're visiting your sick father in Korea."

Ko-chan nodded as he mouthed the words. Miyoko's eyes followed a policeman's movement as he entered their car. He was in a black uniform and greeted the seated army soldiers, giving Miyoko a chance to catch her breath.

The policeman abruptly started questioning the man sitting next to her. "Where are you going?" he asked.

"I'm going to see my brother in Hiroshima," the man said, his voice cracking.

Miyoko stared down at her trembling hands. The man's shaky response made her even more nervous.

"Are they with you?" he asked the gentleman, motioning his head in their direction. By this point, Miyoko's heart was beating so loudly that she was sure everyone could hear it. The man shook his head.

"Where are you going?" the policeman asked Miyoko gruffly.

She lowered her eyes and nodded to acknowledge the interrogator's question. As lightly as a bird, she answered in Japanese: "I'm visiting my sick husband in Korea. He's a Japanese officer stationed there. I received word that he's gravely ill, so I'm taking our son to see him." Miyoko purposely turned sideways to block Ko-chan, hoping he would be spared questions.

The policeman stared at Miyoko's lips, like he was looking for some mistake in her pronunciation. She had heard of Japanese policemen ordering people to say specific words to test whether they were really Japanese. Some Koreans had difficulty saying certain Japanese sounds, but she never had any problems.

He moved on to Ko-chan, who was looking down at his feet. "Where are you going, young man?" the policeman asked Ko-chan directly. Miyoko froze, knowing that his answer could change everything.

Ko-chan looked up calmly and repeated in Japanese, "My father is sick, so we're going to visit him." Ko-chan's Japanese was fluent, and he had no accent whatsoever. Miyoko exhaled in relief. Ko-chan had done what he'd been told to do. She hoped the policeman would stop questioning them now, but he continued.

"How old are you?" he asked.

Miyoko gripped her seat. A question they hadn't practiced.

"I'm six, sir," Ko-chan said seamlessly.

"What's your name?"

He needed to give his Japanese name. She bore her fingers deeper into her chair.

"Ando Joonko desu!" Ko-chan piped.

Miyoko's hands loosened.

The policeman tapped a wand on his palm.

Just when Miyoko thought he would ask for her papers, the policeman moved on to the other passengers.

An enormous weight lifted from Miyoko's shoulders. Ko-chan had given the right answers, and the policeman had let them go. She gave Ko-chan a quick flick of the head and rested her hand on his lap. He seemed pleased with himself and smiled back. One of his hands grazed hers and stayed there. Miyoko felt a gap close between them.

When the policeman left the train and they got underway again, Miyoko took out the bento boxes that Bohbeh had wrapped for them. She offered one to Ko-chan, who unwound the pretty floral furoshiki fabric to reveal a wooden box filled with delicious snacks. Ko-chan gobbled down his rice along with the cold salmon. He looked up, wanting more. Miyoko handed him one of Bohbeh's seaweed-wrapped rice balls.

"Do you want another one?" Bohbeh had packed six.

Ko-chan shook his head and patted his full stomach.

By this time, most of the army personnel were awake again. Perhaps it was the smell of the bento box, but a young soldier with pockmarks on his face peered over his seat to look at them. He had a small mole on his cheek and was swirling his tongue over his lip. Despite her fear of Japanese soldiers, Miyoko instinctively offered a rice ball to him. After all, he was just a hungry boy she might have cared for as a nurse.

The soldier took the onigiri gratefully with both hands and grinned so broadly that something dawned on her. It was the Bible verse that she had read that morning to share with others and good things will come.

Bohbeh had provided them with food for their journey, and now she was doing the same for the soldier.

If a small gesture like this could bring her and Ko-chan some goodwill for the rest of the trip, maybe she should give the other rice balls away. Kindness could go a long way and be a good lesson for Ko-chan. She offered another rice ball to the next soldier and the next until they were all gone. She hoped it would bring them luck.

Ko-chan had proved he could do what was required under pressure. His touch had shown her he had feelings for her too. Maybe the hard part was over.

CHAPTER FORTY-ONE

April 19, 1943
Monday

The train lurched to a stop at Shimonoseki Station, their last stop before the ferry home. Her homeland was now just one ride away, almost within reach. She remembered her last time here, when she was just a frightened girl of thirteen entering a strange new country. Now she was a mother bringing her son home. She couldn't wait to be back where she belonged. There was an empty space in her heart for her mother, but she finally let herself imagine being able to return to her old village to pay her respects. She hoped Ko-chan would feel at home in Korea too.

Exhaust fumes clogged her immediate view, and Miyoko saw only a blurry crowd of people zigzagging along the platform. The station looked busier and louder than Miyoko remembered it, half a lifetime ago. A stench of fish mixed with seaweed pointed her nose in the direction of the water. The golden sun hung low beyond the glimmering sea.

In the other direction, Miyoko spotted a red Shinto shrine. A stream of visitors entered, likely praying for a safe journey. She looked around for a church but knew she wouldn't find any, since they had been banned after Pearl Harbor. A multitude of shrines had replaced them to show Japan's national strength. When she had arrived in 1930,

Japan was not the major world power it was today, the aggressor in World War II.

Japan had transformed from a small island country into a military giant. She had gone from a little girl with dreams of becoming a teacher to a single mother, nurse, and midwife forging an unknown path. Everything had changed, including herself. She would charge forward and do the best she could to make a better life for herself and her son.

Shimonoseki was the beginning and the end. There would be no going back once she got on the ferry to Busan. She wanted more than anything to keep her promise to Hojoon and build a new start in Korea with Ko-chan. But she still had to purchase the ferry tickets, the final obstacle to leaving Japan. She was still a woman traveling alone without a man, and she could be questioned at any time.

Soldiers and policemen milled about the port, and the hairs on Miyoko's arms stood at attention. She squeezed Ko-chan's hand tight and dragged him along at a fast clip. Her other hand clasped the suitcase that Bohbeh had given her, sparking courage. It carried the whole of her life's belongings, including the precious photo of mother and son taken after her nursing exam. She didn't know exactly what time the overnight ferry to Busan was leaving, but it was already almost four in the afternoon, so she had to hurry.

The pier was a short walk from the train station. They bumped into passersby while dodging honking bicyclists and streetcars, taking in big whiffs of soot and grime. Ko-chan's eyes clicked like a camera capturing the large container ships and ferries directly ahead. His stiff backpack banged against him as he pushed toward the sea. He tugged Miyoko along instead of the other way around. The space between them had narrowed over the last few days, and Ko-chan was more relaxed around her than ever. Hope crammed her heart.

In the ticket line, Miyoko overheard people talking in shaky tones.

"Did you hear what happened yesterday?" one man said in Japanese.

"No," another one replied.

"An American submarine sank the ferry! All aboard were killed!"

"What? The ferry to Busan? The one we're getting on?"

"Yes! The one that left at the same time yesterday!"

Miyoko's breath lodged in her throat. Her first instinct was to run away. Boarding a ship today might be suicide. Maybe she and Ko-chan should seek refuge somewhere safe, if she only knew where.

The Japanese men continued talking loudly. "See the empty boat behind the ferry? It's being towed in case there's another attack and the ship sinks!"

"Oh no!" a man said.

Ko-chan tugged Miyoko's arm. His eyes darted with fear. He must have overheard the conversation as well.

"Look up there," Ko-chan said, pointing to the pinkish-red sky. Two large planes rumbled overhead. Some looked up, while others hunched their shoulders and pressed their hands over their heads to brace themselves for what might come next. Miyoko and Ko-chan crouched down together at the same time.

The men shouted over the roar of the engines. "They're Japanese military planes! They're looking for enemy submarines!"

Ko-chan flattened his hands over his ears to deflect the noise of the motors, or maybe to stop hearing more of the troubling conversation.

Warning voices swarmed in her head. *This changes everything. I can't take the chance that a submarine might sink our ferry! Should I go back? Ko-chan would be safer with his grandparents. I'm making a grave mistake.*

A voice from outside her head startled her back to reality.

"Ando Miyoko," called a large, stocky, square-faced man who stood a few feet away. He wore a black jacket stretched tight over his boxy chest and a red hunter's cap that covered one eye. His hands were balled into fists. She had never seen him before in her life.

"I need to talk to you. It's about Ko-chan," he said in Korean.

Miyoko was so shocked that she couldn't speak. Who was this man? How did he know her name? And Ko-chan's? Miyoko pulled Ko-chan closer. The stranger speaking Korean to them could give her and Ko-chan away. The man's thick brows and angled jaw menaced. He was in civilian clothes, except for what looked like combat boots.

Could he be a Korean soldier working undercover for the Japanese to catch draft dodgers? Many Koreans served Japan in the war and were complicit in keeping Koreans in line. She had heard they did side work for the Japanese too. But then why had he asked about Ko-chan? She scanned the area quickly. She couldn't run, and she had nowhere to hide.

Keeping Ko-chan glued next to her, she moved off to one side as people walked around them.

"My name is Choi," he mumbled in Korean. "Ko-chan's grandmother sent me."

His words stabbed Miyoko's gut like a knife.

Ko-chan squared his shoulders. "Halmeoni?"

The man flashed a photo of Miyoko and Ko-chan that had been taken last year when Ko-chan started kindergarten. Ko-chan was wearing the same black school uniform. "I've been looking all over for you," the man said, his eyes locking on Miyoko's son. "I've been hired to bring you back home."

Miyoko's hand flew to her mouth. When they hadn't returned home, Halmeoni must have panicked and paid Choi a good sum of money to find Ko-chan. Maybe he had confronted Bohbeh this morning and even threatened her to disclose where they were going. Or maybe Choi had shown their picture to the trainman who had bought her the tickets to Shimonoseki, and he had identified her. What was she going to do?

"Halmeoni is looking for me?" Ko-chan said wide eyed. "I thought she wanted me to go with you."

"Your halmeoni told me to bring you back. She never wanted you to go," Choi said.

Confusion struck Ko-chan's face.

"Your mother lied and tricked you into leaving. Your grandmother is waiting at home for you," Choi said.

Redness, like a slap, flamed Ko-chan's cheeks. Miyoko's heart burned at seeing her son's trust in her destroyed. She'd thought she would have time to explain later, but she had no choice but to do it now.

"Give us a minute," Miyoko commanded Choi. She was surprised at the sharpness of her tongue, the urge to shield Ko-chan from this man.

Choi narrowed his eyes. Then he moved backward a few steps and struck a match to light his cigarette.

Miyoko squatted down to Ko-chan's eye level and grasped his shoulders.

"Listen. I know Halmeoni would like you back. But I want you here with me too. I am your mother, and I know I can be a good mother to you." Miyoko crept closer, touching his bandaged finger. "I can take care of you if you're hurt. I can work as a nurse and buy you all the books you want to read. I will make sure you go to school and get a good education. You'll be my most important priority."

Ko-chan's face softened slightly. "I like you. I'm having a fun time."

Ko-chan's response surprised her. Could he be thinking that she was nicer than his aunts? Could he be wondering why Halmeoni thought about his father all the time? He was more mature than his mere six years. Miyoko sensed a crack, a sliver of opportunity to do something to cement their connection before it was too late. If this man was going to try to take Ko-chan, she had to make sure that her son would want to stay with her.

"I'm your mother," Miyoko said, touching his cheek. "I've been gone for too long. I want to be here for you now."

A space between Ko-chan's brows opened.

"I had to leave my mother behind when I was a little girl, and I missed her very much. I don't want that to happen to you. I couldn't risk you not coming with me. That's why I didn't tell you the truth." She was desperate to avoid losing his trust and love at this revelation.

Ko-chan's face hardened. He had to believe her this time. Miyoko pushed again to get through.

"The Japanese are sending me to war, Ko-chan. They want me to be a nurse on the front lines to care for dying soldiers. If I don't come back alive, I don't know what will happen to you. Your grandparents can't take care of you forever. So I took the risk to escape to Korea. I took the risk to bring you with me because I couldn't live without you." A tear traveled down her cheek.

Ko-chan's eyes followed the droplet, now clinging to her chin. His gaze shifted to the stranger in the red hat.

"Come with me. Come home to where you belong," Choi said, more gently this time. He crushed his cigarette butt with his foot and extended his hand.

Ko-chan shuddered and cast his head down. He looked up sideways at Choi, then at Miyoko. Miyoko's grasp tightened on Ko-chan's shoulders, and he raised his eyes to hers. Her nerves rattled, not knowing what he would do next.

"I want to go home," he said, looking at Choi, then her.

Miyoko's neck jerked sideways. No. She couldn't lose Ko-chan. She looked into Ko-chan's eyes and saw pain and fear. She could understand how torn he must feel, especially if he wasn't sure he could trust her.

"Wait," she said. Panic rushed. She couldn't think of any words. Her world was closing in, and she didn't know what to do. In that moment, time stopped. She pinched Ko-chan's nose and rested her forehead on his.

"Saranghae," she said tenderly. "I love you. I might not be able to give you everything your grandparents can, but I will try my best to be a good mother. To do that, I have to make difficult choices, even if you might not understand why right now. I had to accept my own mother doing that. I will always be on your side. I will always be your mother."

Their heads remained touching. And then she felt it. Ko-chan squeezed her nose. Her heart raced with hope.

Just then, a loud voice boomed over the megaphone. "Excuse me, ladies and gentlemen. This is the captain. Is there a doctor or nurse here? We have an emergency! Please come to the ferry office immediately!"

In the chaos, she heard Ko-chan's small voice. "Okaasan," he said, tugging at her kimono sleeve. "They're looking for a nurse!" He grabbed her hand with both of his and pulled.

He was leading her. She wasted no time.

They darted away from Choi and ran to the ferry office as quickly as they could. They wove through people in line. Breathless, Miyoko found herself banging on the ferry office's door.

"I'm a nurse. I can help!" she shouted in Japanese, panting. She looked over her shoulder and saw Choi's red hat hovering nearby.

Miyoko's body tightened. She was caught between running away from someone who could take Ko-chan back and exposing her true Korean identity as she responded to the medical call.

But she had to get away from Choi, who was the greater risk now. Her nursing skills might save them.

The office door squeaked open. The captain, wearing a white hat and uniform, stood with creased brows. The blinds were drawn in the dark, cramped room.

"I'm a nurse," Miyoko said in rapid Japanese. She glimpsed a woman on the floor, writhing in pain. Her stomach stuck out like a watermelon on end, and she was slapping a blanket against the floor. Miyoko recognized exactly what was happening.

"I'm also a midwife," Miyoko said to the captain. "Do you need help?"

"Yes!" the captain said, a big exhale escaping his mouth. "I'm Captain Mori. This is Mrs. Ota. She's the wife of a high-ranking Japanese officer in Korea."

"I'm Ando Miyoko. This is my son. He'll stay with me." She was desperate to protect him from Choi.

Ko-chan's eyes roved over the captain's crisp white uniform, its gold buttons and colorful ribbons shimmering.

"Your son will be safe here. I will have my sailors on watch outside," the captain said, as if reading that very worry on her face.

"Ko-chan, you sit over there," Miyoko ordered, pointing to the floor in the opposite corner. He would have to be in the same room, but she didn't want him to see what was about to happen.

"I'll need some clean towels and water," she said to the captain, taking charge this time. "And I left my trunk in the ticket line. It has a green ribbon tied to the handle. I need it. It has my midwife's bag inside."

The captain cleared his throat, tilted the brim of his cap, and left the room. A sailor stood guard outside. They were safe from Choi, at least for that moment.

"It's all right," Miyoko said calmly to the pregnant woman. "I've delivered a lot of babies. I'm an experienced midwife, and I'm here to help you."

The woman moaned louder. By the frightened look in her eyes, Miyoko guessed that this was probably her first baby.

"Breathe in," Miyoko said. "Now release."

They practiced this until Miyoko heard a light tapping on the door. A sailor showed up with her trunk, some towels, and a pail of water. He left in a hurry after hearing the woman's distressing wails.

Miyoko opened her trunk and removed her small midwife's bag, which contained a stethoscope, forceps, and scissors. One by one, she laid the implements out on a small towel, as she had done many times before. She undressed the woman below her waist and drew a deep breath through her nose.

Closing her eyes, Miyoko listened to the baby's heartbeat with her stethoscope. Feeling around the surface of the woman's stomach with her hands, she confirmed that the baby's head was in the correct position. She pressed the woman's stomach and ordered her to push. The woman's face puffed up like a balloon as she propped herself up on her elbows. Her forehead was drenched with sweat, and her hair clung to her face. Miyoko could see the crown of the baby's head, but it wouldn't budge. After several more attempts, the woman fell back in defeat.

Taking the forceps, Miyoko clamped the baby's head and eased it out. The mother's shrieks switched to a baby's howling cry.

"It's a boy!" Miyoko shouted.

The mother let out a long groan.

Miyoko cut the umbilical cord and rubbed the white vernix off the baby's skin. She placed him gently on his mother's chest to nurse. Looking around, she found another towel to discard the afterbirth. Even though Miyoko had delivered dozens of babies before, this birth was a miracle, like all the others. This tiny being had stayed alive in his mother's womb for nine months and fought his way out. Miyoko now shared motherhood with this woman, and she was proud that she had been able to deliver the woman's son. She was grateful that both mother and baby were safe. She hoped that she and Ko-chan would be too.

Resting on the floor with her back against the wall, Miyoko dabbed the sweat from her brow with her handkerchief. She peered over at Ko-chan, who was sitting cross-legged on the floor, facing the other direction. He was squirming, and clearly uncomfortable. Meanwhile, the baby cried in frustration as he tried to latch on to his mother's breast. The mother moved the baby to her other breast. Her difficulty triggered memories of Miyoko's own struggles to nurse Ko-chan. They'd had a tough beginning as mother and son. Would Ko-chan change his mind and want to go back? Choi could be waiting just outside, and danger still loomed.

"Relax," Miyoko said to the new mother, trying to settle her own anxiety too. "Tuck him in a little closer and move your nipple toward him, like this." She guided her gently. "There!" When the baby latched on and began to suck, his body relaxed. His mother closed her eyes, her face wet with exhaustion.

Watching the mother and her baby, Miyoko fought back waves of regret. Since she hadn't been able to breastfeed, it hadn't taken long for Ko-chan to think that his aunts and grandmother were his mothers. Miyoko had yearned for a greater connection with her son, and now they finally had a second chance.

A loud knock on the door jolted her. Was it Choi? He could still reveal that they were Korean and ruin everything. She didn't yet have the tickets, and there was the submarine strike and the threat to their safety.

"It's the captain. May I come in?"

"Yes," Miyoko said, her jaw unclenching.

The captain entered and closed the door behind him. Ko-chan finally turned around when he heard the captain's bellowing voice.

"Is everything okay? I heard a baby crying." The captain met Miyoko's eyes and followed them to the baby and mother curled on the floor.

"Thank you," the captain said, his tone laced with respect. "I'm sorry to delay you. Where are you going today?"

"My son and I were planning to go to Busan on the ferry. I'm not sure what time it is and whether we already missed it." Miyoko looked at Ko-chan. His eyes roamed the room to the door, like he might be wondering if Choi was still outside.

Ko-chan stood and took a step forward toward the captain. "My father is an army officer in Korea. We are going to visit him!" he said in a bold voice.

Relief flooded Miyoko's chest.

The captain smiled at Ko-chan. "I'm the captain of the ferry, so it can't leave without me. But the ferry departs very soon, so we should board right away. Mrs. Ota here is supposed to be on the ferry too."

The quick birth had been a blessing. Given how far along the mother was, she should not have been traveling. How fortunate Miyoko was here. If she and Ko-chan hadn't gotten to the ferry today, the mother would have had to give birth alone.

"Mrs. Ota wanted to get to her husband in Korea before her child was born. Her husband is waiting for her in Busan."

"I see," Miyoko said, her chest aching for Hojoon.

What the captain said next caught her completely by surprise.

"May I ask you to escort her there? It would be a tremendous help to me, since I don't know the first thing about babies. I would be happy to pay for your fare and your son's. You'll be in a first-class cabin next to hers."

Miyoko couldn't believe her ears. *Free passage to Korea.* And the captain hadn't asked for her papers. Ko-chan had convinced him they were Japanese. This was too good to be true.

She glanced at Ko-chan for his reaction. He beamed too, seemingly happy to hear the news. She hoped this meant that he would stay with her.

She gave the captain a grateful smile. Wasn't this the moment she had been waiting for? Freedom and safety at last? But could Choi take it all away?

"It's auspicious for a newborn baby to be on a ship," the captain said. "It would be an honor to have you as guests on this trip, a kind of good luck charm."

"That would be wonderful. Thank you for your kind offer," Miyoko said. "I'll get Mrs. Ota and her baby ready to board. They'll be in good hands during the crossing."

The captain touched the brim of his white cap. "I'll send someone over to fetch you shortly," he said, and left the room.

Ko-chan perked up and clapped his hands together. He seemed to have forgotten about Choi and was looking forward to boarding the ship. Most important, he had chosen to stay with her. She would be his mother. A contentment kindled deep inside.

Despite passing another hurdle, Miyoko knew that Choi's presence and the threat of a submarine or air attack remained. But they were now under the captain's protection. By luck, or by the grace of God, they were headed home. Would they make it?

CHAPTER FORTY-TWO

April 19, 1943
Monday

Two stocky young sailors jostled a stretcher into the ferry office to carry Mrs. Ota to the ship. An older sailor, the one who had delivered towels and water to Miyoko earlier, barked orders at them. Miyoko swaddled the newborn baby while the men strapped the tired mother and lifted her like a feather. When Mrs. Ota reached out her hands, Miyoko nestled the sleeping baby into her waiting arms.

"Please come with me," the older sailor said, picking up Miyoko's trunk and following the younger sailors out. Keeping Ko-chan by her side, Miyoko trailed the men closely. The line of passengers parted when people saw the woman on the stretcher.

"Move out of the way!" one of the young sailors shouted.

Scanning the crowd, Miyoko noticed Choi watching them, picking his teeth with a straw. Her chest pounded as she pulled Ko-chan closer. Ko-chan molded to her side and grabbed her waist. Choi stepped forward but recoiled when he realized that the sailors were right next to them. Miyoko pressed Ko-chan even tighter. Choi might stop at nothing to take her son away from her.

She saw Choi talking to another sailor. He seemed to be arguing with him, pointing at her and Ko-chan. What was he doing? Would he tell them she had kidnapped Ko-chan? Would he tell the captain that she was Korean and get the captain to take back his offer? Would Choi know she was fleeing the draft and have her detained? Panic rose that he would somehow prevent them from boarding. She was so close, but Choi might end it all. The ship's engines rumbled like it was ready to depart. They had to get on board fast.

Miyoko hustled to the gangplank, pulling Ko-chan along. After she and Ko-chan passed through the entrance, the older sailor hooked the rope behind him to prevent others from boarding. Miyoko felt as unsteady as the wooden boards of the walkway beneath her. Water sloshed below the slats, and her palms dampened. Reaching the ferry deck, Miyoko felt a cold breeze blast her face, but they were aboard. And when she looked back at the crowd, there was no sign of Choi's red hat. The tightness in her body gave way, and she let out a relieved sigh. They had lost him, for now.

The older sailor summoned a young porter, who directed Miyoko and Ko-chan to their cabin next to Mrs. Ota and the baby. The luxurious first-class cabin was furnished with velvet couches, mahogany tables, and rich wood paneling. The musty scent of cigar smoke clung to the dark-purple curtains framing the round window. Their mouths fell at the same time as they swiveled around in awe.

"Please make yourselves comfortable," the porter said. "I'll send along some refreshments."

"Thank you," Miyoko said as Ko-chan dropped his backpack with a thud and dashed over to the window.

"Wow! This ship is huge! I wish I could tell my cousins about it!"

Miyoko's heart ached for Ko-chan, knowing he might not see his cousins for a while. She wondered if he was talking about his Kyoto cousins or his Osaka ones. He had formed a bond with Bohbeh's kids during the last few days, and Miyoko was sad that he would miss growing up with them too. She hoped she was making the right decision by taking him away from the only family he knew.

Ko-chan grazed his fingers over the fine wood and tugged on the tassels of the drapes. He flopped down on an overstuffed chair, lifting his arms over his head and stretching his legs. "Okaasan, look at this!" he said, hopping over to the large Western bed and bouncing up and down on his bottom.

Miyoko's heart warmed at hearing him call her "mother" for the second time. The word rang pure and true in her ears. A piece of her that had been missing seemed to snap back into place. She thought about Hojoon and how happy he would be if he were here with them. She savored these moments watching their son.

A sudden knock startled her.

"Come in," she said, her pulse racing. Choi wasn't chasing them all the way to Korea, was he? She hadn't seen him board the ship, but that didn't mean he couldn't have gotten on.

Another porter appeared in the doorway with two red bento boxes stacked one on top of the other in his hands. Delicious smells tickled her nose.

"Dozo. From the captain," he said as he placed the food on the table and left.

Ko-chan tilted the top lid open to uncover the most exquisite Japanese delicacies. The box was divided into small sections of fried fish, grilled salmon, lotus roots, skewered chicken with a sweet brown glaze, and cold scrambled eggs shaped into blocks. Assorted pickled vegetables and steamed rice filled the rest. It was the cuisine of the Japanese nobility, and they were eating it for the first and probably last time. Miyoko had never tasted anything like this before, although she had seen it served at the baron's house. The simple bento boxes Bohbeh had made for their trip paled in comparison. Miyoko wished her sister could see this bounty and eat it with them.

"Sugoi!" Ko-chan said, licking his lips at the delightful assortment of food.

Another knock startled Miyoko again.

"Yes . . . ?"

It was the captain. "I just want to make sure you're settled."

"Thank you," Miyoko said, relieved. "The room, this food—it's more than we deserve."

Ko-chan stood at attention facing the captain, saluting as he had seen the sailors do. The captain laughed and saluted back.

"You did a great service today, helping deliver the baby. I don't know what I would have done without you," the captain said.

"It was my duty," Miyoko said. She was pleased to have provided midwife support to a woman in need. Her skills gave her a sense of worth and pride.

She studied the captain more closely. He was a middle-aged man with wide shoulders and a broad nose. He was unshaven, and his eyes were bloodshot, as though he hadn't slept for days. His haggard appearance seemed consistent with the rigors of his job, which now included protecting a newborn.

"Well, I must return to my post," the captain said. "I have other matters I have to attend to."

The captain must have been talking about possible submarine attacks and air strikes. It was an overnight ferry ride, so they would be under threat for many more hours. Miyoko's nerves jumped at the knowledge that they weren't out of danger yet.

The mouthwatering aroma from the bento boxes drew Ko-chan to the table, and he settled into a chair, eager to eat. Miyoko signaled that he should wait until she said it was all right to start. She gently took Ko-chan's hands and folded his palms together.

"Now close your eyes," Miyoko said. Ko-chan followed her direction but not before glancing at the food and swallowing.

"Thank you, dear Lord, for bringing us safely on board and for all this good food. I pray for the health of the mother and her new baby, and for safe passage on our journey." Miyoko exhaled and said, "Amen."

She nodded for Ko-chan to begin eating. He pinched each piece of food with his chopsticks. He turned the lotus roots around, inspecting every hole and chewing slowly to savor the crisp, sweet taste. He ate everything in his box. After eating her fill, Miyoko gave the rest of her box to Ko-chan. Just watching him eat made her satisfied and content, even with the uncertainties still ahead.

A baby's cry floated from next door.

"Let's check on Mrs. Ota and her baby," Miyoko said.

They headed toward the direction of the cries, and Ko-chan rapped on Mrs. Ota's door.

"Come in, please," a woman's voice said wearily.

Mrs. Ota was sitting up on the bed, rocking the baby. Her eyes sought Miyoko's for help.

"Let me take him for a while," Miyoko said. "Why don't you try to get some sleep?" She took the crying baby and cradled him in her arms. His sweet, milky smell reminded her of holding Ko-chan for the first time and sharing the wonder of his birth with Hojoon. She remembered their first days with Ko-chan, and all the plans they had made together for their future as a family.

Relief flickered in the mother's eyes. "I am Ota Kazue. What's your name?"

"Ando Miyoko," she said, noting that they had barely exchanged words during the frenzied birth.

"And your son?" Mrs. Ota asked.

"Ando Joonko desu!" Ko-chan chimed.

"Arigatou gozaimashita," Mrs. Ota said, thanking Miyoko as her back fell against the pillow in exhaustion. "You brought my son into the world."

"Doitashimashite. You're welcome. I'm sure your son will bring you much happiness, just as Ko-chan has brought me."

A tired smile formed on Mrs. Ota's face. "My husband's going to be so surprised and happy to see his son." She curled her body sideways into a sleeping position.

"Please rest," Miyoko said. "I'll be right next door with the baby."

"Hmm," Mrs. Ota said, her eyes already closed.

Back in their cabin, Miyoko rested the baby between two pillows on the bed and finally lay down next to him. Ko-chan rushed toward the window again when the large anchor creaked and groaned, lifting for departure. Choi hadn't appeared yet, so maybe he hadn't made it on board. If they could just leave the port, they might be safe.

The engines rumbled louder, and soon they were pulling away from the docks. Past Ko-chan's head, Miyoko could make out the posts holding up the roof of the pier like soldiers standing at attention. Once they were out to sea, Ko-chan fell fast asleep on the other side of the baby. When the baby shifted and whimpered, Miyoko returned him to his mother to nurse.

On the way back, she passed an open door to the deck and stepped outside to admire the sky, sparkling with a million stars. Those stars were probably the same ones she had seen from her tree as a little girl, and now she was almost there. A hush fell over the ship as people settled down for the night. She heard only a few male voices.

"Did you hear that the US mistook the ferry yesterday for a Japanese naval ship?"

Miyoko's blood pumped. She envisioned US submarines accidentally blowing up this ship. It could happen again. Many of those who had perished in that attack might have been Koreans returning home, like them, escaping from war.

Miyoko went to bed in her kimono and wooden geta slippers in case she and Ko-chan needed to flee. She held her son close and listened to his soft breaths while he slept. She couldn't rest until they were finally safe on Korean soil.

CHAPTER FORTY-THREE

April 20, 1943
Tuesday

Miyoko awoke to the squawking steel anchor hitting water. Ko-chan rubbed his eyes and gazed out the window at the sun inching up the horizon in Busan. His face broadened upon seeing the line of passing ships and the buildings hanging on the very edge of the hillside. They were in Korea, and Miyoko absorbed her first glimpses of her homeland after thirteen years. She was finally home and overcome with joy.

Miyoko had made it safely with Ko-chan, as she and Hojoon had dreamed. Hojoon was not here, but he was with them in spirit and would be happy for them. Miyoko now had a chance at a brand-new start with Ko-chan, even though their future was still uncertain. Taeyoung was here, although they would be without their family in Japan. She would try to reconnect with her father and her half siblings too, and she hoped they would welcome her and Ko-chan.

The horn blew, announcing it was time to disembark. Nostalgia mingled with anticipation as Miyoko readied her belongings for this next step on her journey. She carried her trunk, and Ko-chan strapped on his backpack. She checked on Mrs. Ota and her baby in the next cabin and helped them gather their bags. A porter escorted the new mother and her dozing baby on a stretcher again. The mothers exchanged earnest goodbyes.

Miyoko envied Mrs. Ota, who would be reunited with her husband. She wondered if she would ever find real love again, and if she would have more children. Maybe there was someone out there who could be a father to Ko-chan and love him like a son. And maybe Ko-chan would have siblings one day who looked up to him as their older brother.

As she reflected on these thoughts, Miyoko realized that she had changed during her time in Japan. She craved a family of her own now, as much as an education and a career. For so long, she had believed that she had to forgo love and a family to achieve financial independence. But Hojoon had shown her that she could have love too, and that she needed it to be complete. Ko-chan needed her love now, and she needed his. It was love that made her whole. Her heart filled with a deep yearning for a different kind of future than before.

Korea had changed too, while she'd been gone. As they disembarked from the ferry, a gasp of disbelief left Miyoko's lips. Busan was nothing like she remembered. A thick fog of pollution blackened the skies over the port. The stench of trash wafted toward them. Grime slid down buildings, and paint flecked off walls. Military vehicles lined the streets. Stores that had once flaunted Korean souvenirs now sold Japanese wares and trinkets. All the signs flashed Japanese words. Busan was being used as a major base for all of Japan's colonies in Asia. It seemed as if the soul of Korea had been ripped away and only the shell remained.

Uncertainty dangled in the cool morning air. Had she made this escape for nothing? Had she made a mistake by tearing her son from the rest of his family? Would Taeyoung be glad to see them?

Miyoko's ears perked at hearing a familiar Korean accent.

"Yeogi! Buy fresh kimchi here!" a Korean ajumma yelled as Miyoko passed the market. The pungent, salty aroma of kimchi penetrated the air. Memories drifted back: she saw great big urns of buried fermented cabbage being unearthed after a bitter, cold winter. The scent of red pepper flakes transported Miyoko to her old village and filled her with a sense of connection and belonging, despite the changes she now saw.

Ko-chan was eager to explore his new surroundings. He walked ahead, and she had to call after him to keep him in sight as they pushed their way through bustling crowds. Civilians in kimonos and hanboks walked among Japanese soldiers carrying bayonets and machine guns. People fired Japanese words everywhere, the official language of all of Japan's occupied territories. By law, Koreans had to change their names to Japanese ones. It was ironic that Miyoko had done this by choice, and now she couldn't use her Korean name even if she wanted to. This was a stumbling block she hadn't been expecting. Their journey wasn't quite over yet.

Japan had occupied Korea for almost thirty-three years now, longer than she had been alive. Miyoko wondered if she might be considered a Japanese collaborator, since she had lived in Japan for so long. She had met Koreans in Japan who had gone back to Korea and returned, only to report that they were treated poorly because of their association with Japan. Even though she was no longer evading laws in Japan, danger continued to lurk, since they were still surrounded by the Japanese military and could be questioned at any time. To get back to Taeyoung and Miyoko's village, they still had a long road ahead.

But she was home, where she and Ko-chan fit in. She believed that the occupation would end soon, and Ko-chan would grow up with his Korean culture, language, and identity restored. It was just a matter of time before he could walk proudly in his hanbok and speak the Korean language again without shame. Even though she couldn't use her Korean name yet, she would now think of herself as Miyoung, no matter what. Someday, people would call her by her real name, and she would feel complete.

Miyoko, now Miyoung again, reached for Ko-chan's hand as they walked. Feeling his small, warm fingers in hers, she felt at ease. He gazed up at her with trusting eyes, and memories of his newborn days flooded back; she remembered the bliss she had felt when she became a mother.

She would take care of her son the best she could, with all her heart. She would make sure he was safe and loved so that he could grow up to be all he could be.

When they reached Busan Train Station, Miyoung pulled out the mulberry-paper notebook tucked into her obi and made sure she had Taeyoung's address. The woodsy smell of her mulberry tree perfumed her nose as she flipped through the pages, recalling how Teacher Kim had gifted her the journal when she was just a girl of thirteen. She had a sudden urge to see her teacher's kind face again. Pyongyang was not far from her old village. Images glided by: Mother picking melons and cooking over a boiling stew. She wished Mother could have met Ko-chan. She would have been proud of him, and of her. Miyoung would make sure they paid their respects at her tomb. Excitement swelled over seeing Taeyoung, Father, and their side of the family again after all these years.

Her brother's gentle face danced before her eyes. Like Miyoung, Taeyoung had a narrow nose and a wide forehead, and she wondered if he still looked the same now. He had taught her many things growing up. "You play jacks like this," he had said patiently, showing Miyoung the right way. "You throw a pebble in the air, sweep the right number of pebbles on the ground with the palm of your hand, and catch the falling one before it lands." They had spent hours playing that game, and she smiled at the thought that he would now teach Ko-chan similar ones.

Taeyoung would help her navigate a new Korea too, just like he had when she was a little girl. He had encouraged her to go to middle school and to continue her studies all those years ago, and here she was now. She had the skills to make it on her own because he had believed in her. No one could take Bohbeh's place, but she was lucky to have her brother's support as she made a new life in Korea.

Miyoung's heart brimmed with hope for Ko-chan and their future together. She was no longer an unsure girl struggling to define herself and her place in the world. As a Korean woman, single mother, nurse, midwife, and spiritual believer, Miyoung had discovered the "brave" part of her Korean name. Not only could she want all these things; she could have them too. She had fulfilled that old Korean proverb that carried her mother's hope: *At the end of hardship, happiness had come.*

The strangers who bumped against them probably saw nothing remarkable about Miyoung and Ko-chan, just an ordinary mother and son. As the street widened to a bright spring morning, they clasped hands and walked toward the train bound north for home.

AUTHOR'S NOTE

Miyoung's story is inspired by the true tale of my Korean grandmother, or Halmeoni. I hungered to understand how Halmeoni ended up as a nurse and midwife in Japan during the nation's harsh occupation of Korea—a single mother raising a son alone in an unwelcoming country and being forced to make the impossible choice of saving herself or leaving her child. I wanted to share Halmeoni's journey with my children.

Halmeoni was reluctant to talk about her past. When I asked her about the old, faded Japanese nursing and midwife certificates I found at my father's house, her lips tightened. She was in her early eighties at the time and living in a senior apartment in LA's Koreatown—thousands of miles from the barley fields of northern Korea, where she was born. But she slowly started to open up. After listening to her searing tale, I knew I had to capture her legacy, and *White Mulberry* was born.

I recorded Halmeoni's story a number of times and understood the arc of her life, but the part that tugged at me the most was her years coming into womanhood—the stranger who came into her life and tricked her sister into marriage, leaving Korea to go to Japan for an education, becoming a new mother, and finding faith to deal with her husband's death and her demanding in-laws, and of course, her brave decision to come home to Korea in the middle of a world war.

My father—Ko-chan in the novel—helped me translate and understand the historical context. My Korean is limited, as I immigrated to LA with my family from Korea when I was seven. Growing up, my father told me he was born in Japan and spoke Japanese, but I never really understood how he got there and why he left. I studied Japanese in college, spent a couple of years in Japan, where I met some of my Korean relatives, who have lived there for generations, and became more curious about my family's history. When I shared with Halmeoni that I wanted to write her memoir, her face crinkled with hesitation. Even at the end, she was reluctant to reveal her past.

In February 2012, Halmeoni passed away. We buried her at a memorial park in Los Angeles, and I began to assemble my notes and recordings of our conversations. My first thought was to write Halmeoni's story as nonfiction, capturing the facts and chronology of her life. But as I wrote, I realized I couldn't explore the depths and nuances of her character as much as I wanted. It was then I decided to share Halmeoni's story through fiction.

Writing a novel allowed me the freedom to tell Halmeoni's tale through Miyoung's eyes and to fill out gaps in her story. I could more richly imagine how her life might have been, what her goals and conflicts were, and how she changed at the end to become the strong, independent woman she was. I altered a few details—names and sequences of events—but the essence of Halmeoni's journey remains the same. I researched the history of the period and the few autobiographies of Koreans living in occupied Korea at the time. I read the heart-wrenching stories written by Koreans living in Japan about the internal turmoil and discrimination they faced, and still face, as Korean ethnic minorities. I incorporated these specifics into the world I envisioned Halmeoni must have navigated and endured.

I also took numerous trips to Japan, where I had the chance to speak with my extended Korean family. I realized their struggles were similar to what I experienced growing up as a Korean immigrant in the US. I was moved by their challenges to be themselves in Japanese society, even as third-generation Koreans. Some still kept their Korean names, others passed as Japanese and intermarried with Japanese, and many continued to live as outsiders in the only country they knew and the land they called home. Hearing my relatives' stories, and reflecting on my own, raised questions: What happens to the self when you leave someplace, and what self do you meet in the new? What self do you sacrifice?

Halmeoni triumphed over poverty and a patriarchal, racist society designed to break her. I wanted to lift up her story of resilience and shine a light on this little-known period of Korean and Japanese history. While there have been narratives of light-skinned women of color in the US and elsewhere "passing" as white, Halmeoni's story explores "passing" in Asian society at a particularly harsh and oppressive time. Halmeoni's courage to save her family from racial injustice despite grave danger is timely and inspiring, given that our gender, race, and identity are still being challenged today.

I yearned for stories of strong heroines like Halmeoni but couldn't find many growing up, or even as an adult. My favorite book was *A Tree Grows in Brooklyn*, about a poor, spirited Irish girl coming of age in New York in the first part of the twentieth century, the same period in which Halmeoni grew up in Korea and Japan. This is one of the reasons I decided to name my book *White Mulberry*. The mulberry tree was Halmeoni's best friend, as that book was mine. I needed a story like Halmeoni's to realize there are others like me. If Halmeoni had the courage to be herself, I could too. We all can.

The other reason I was drawn to the title *White Mulberry* is because white is an important color in Korean history and symbolizes humility—a trait I saw in Halmeoni and the word she actually used in her haiku at the beginning of this book. Of course, Halmeoni wore white too, because she was a nurse. White means truth and goodness in Christianity, and Halmeoni embraced Christianity throughout her life for solace and hope. Many Koreans turned to Christianity during Japanese colonization because it signified Korean nationalism, and it is still the dominant religion in Korea today.

Moreover, the mulberry tree produces many beautiful and useful products. The inner bark is used to make delicate hanji paper, and its leaves provide nutritional and medicinal benefits. The image of silkworms eating mulberry leaves and then being transformed into beautiful silk is also representative of Halmeoni's life. And the mulberry tree being a hearty tree, withstanding the severe North Korean winters and blooming over and over again in the spring, is a metaphor for Halmeoni herself.

In the last ten or so years that I have worked on this novel, I finally discovered what I was searching for: a version of myself I could accept, which I saw in Halmeoni. I have a deeper understanding of the circumstances and forces that have shaped me: a little girl coming to a new country without knowing the culture or the language, being neither Korean nor American, learning to trust myself and who I am, and to claim my unique place in the world. I wanted Halmeoni's story, and mine, to be seen.

Halmeoni didn't want her secrets exposed. After all, keeping her secrets had kept her alive. I wonder how many stories, especially those of the older Asian generation who suffered the traumas of war, occupation, racism, and displacement, have been hidden like Halmeoni's. If this book inspires even one person to open up about difficult events, and feel valued and seen, I will be gratified. Sharing vulnerable stories can help release the stigma associated with trauma and allow people to heal.

I believe that Halmeoni would forgive me and understand that her secrets are actually gifts to her children, grandchildren, and future generations. Her double life as a Japanese nurse and midwife, as well as Korean mother, wife, sister, and daughter-in-law, affirms the power of an individual's decision, no matter who they are. Concealing her Korean identity and passing as Japanese to protect herself and her family from racial persecution was an act of sheer determination and a testament to the human spirit of survival. Her courage to make her own decisions and define her future benefited her loved ones and all the lives she cared for and touched, including mine.

By amplifying Halmeoni's story, I hope to empower all of us to explore, share, and celebrate our authentic selves. I hope we will see ourselves and others differently and, in some small way, change the way we think.

Author's grandmother and father, circa 1943.
Courtesy of the author's family.

ACKNOWLEDGMENTS

I am deeply grateful to everyone who helped me write this book and bring it out into the world. Thank you to my wonderful agent, Joelle Delbourgo, for believing in Miyoung's story from the beginning and championing me throughout the publishing process. I don't know how the stars aligned for me to find you, but I am so lucky I did! I can't thank my acquisition editor, Melissa Valentine, enough for taking a chance on an unknown debut author and buying not just my first book but the next one, which I had not yet written. You made my publishing dreams come true! Carissa Bluestone, Tiffany Yates Martin, and all the editors and staff at Lake Union and the Amazon team—your expertise helped make my manuscript shine and be the best it could be. My heartfelt thanks.

To my writing community: you have been there for me for decades, and I appreciate all of you. Thank you, Jennie Nash, for jump-starting my creative life with your writing class. Thanks also to my book coach, Kemlo Aki, and instructors Susan Aminoff, Dan Blank, Lisa Cron, and Marlene Wagner for helping me learn about writing and publishing early on. I owe a debt of gratitude to many writing programs, especially Anaphora, Sackett Street, StoryStudio Chicago, VONA, and Writer's Digest. StoryCenter.org published one of my first stories and CRAFT Literary my most recent: thank you. To Lindsay Kavet and the *Expressing Motherhood* show: I never thought I would perform a motherhood story onstage, and you helped me face my fears. Thank you for making my writing better and allowing me to share it widely.

To my writing mentors, author friends, and endorsers whom I have the privilege of knowing: thank you for your camaraderie and encouragement. Teri Case, Kristy Woodson Harvey, Eugenia Kim, Min Jin Lee, Lisa Manterfield, and Nami Mun—you taught me the importance of writers supporting writers. Eugenia, you read the first fifty pages of my novel, then later the entire manuscript, and urged me to keep going. To the authors I admire who took the time to read my novel and provide an endorsement, thank you for your immense generosity: Mathieu Cailler, Leland Cheuk, Jimin Han, Lindsay Hunter, Alka Joshi, A.H. Kim, Juhea Kim, Margaret Juhae Lee, Marie Myung-Ok Lee, Lisa See, and Annabelle Tometich.

To my lovely Write Circle group—Rieko Mendez, Jennifer Townsend, and Holly Vanderdonck—I was able to finish my novel during the pandemic thanks to your weekly feedback. To my many other writing group members: thank you for being in the trenches with me, Paige Asawa, Julie Brown, Cathleen Daniels, Mary Jo Hazard, Jessica Patay, Agnes Regeczkey, and Lorrie Tom. Hugs to Nancy Fagan, Shella Pacarey, Hyeseung Song, my Ragdale gang, and my Lake Union Debut 2024 Slack group—dear writing friends I can reach out to any time of the day. To my Fourth Kingdom writers—you inspired me to think I could write a story about Korea and Japan that people would read. No one should write alone.

Thank you to my book club friends who have kept me reading and been huge supporters: Cornerstone School Book Club (Jeri Berlin, Amy D'Ambra, Siri Fiske, Stacy Upton), Smith College Book Club of the South Bay (Donna Day, Mary Kenney, Pam Learned, Judy Milestone, Janice Mottinger, Rachel Nyback, Diane Silva, Noriko Ward, Liz Zuckerman), and my Asian Author Book Club (all fifty-plus of you!). Thank you, Susan Kim, for suggesting I start my own book club, and Lydia Ho, Sharon Oda, and Jennifer Zeller for being part of my book-launch committee. Walking Group Buddies, thanks for making me laugh and exercise while I wrote. Your friendships are precious.

My gratitude goes out to all librarians and library staff, but especially those at the Palos Verdes Library District for loaning me the books I needed and making my work as a trustee meaningful and engaging. A special shout-out to librarian and friend Monique Sugimoto for being a beta reader and meeting with me regularly to research my novel. To the authors and scholars whose books and articles informed my novel and are too many to name here: thank you for your passion, knowledge, and insights.

To booksellers, book promoters, book publicists, and all those who help support authors and bring authors and readers together, thank you. My appreciation goes out to owner and friend Linda Figel of Pages: A Bookstore, for lifting up local and debut authors like myself. Susan McBeth, your creativity and dedication to connecting authors and book clubs through Adventures by the Book is inspirational. And Kaye Publicity, kudos for helping me identify what makes me unique as an author and getting the word about my book out there to readers.

Pamela Boboc, thanks for setting up my website back in the day and for your ongoing support, and Karin Fuire for those decade-old author photos and new ones! Bennette Turpanjian, I'll never forget your generosity in reading early chapters of my book. To my late best friend, Ruth Haring, who always said I could do it: I wish you were still with us so I could celebrate with you.

Thank you to my late paternal grandmother, Soongdoh Suhr, for allowing me to record your remarkable story and sharing your memories, even when it was painful to do so. To my dad, David Soonho Kwon, for helping me translate and recount Grandma's story and describing your own with such tenderness and clarity. To my mom, Jean Yoon Kwon, for feeding me so I could listen to Dad and speaking up when you remembered something differently. To my late maternal grandmother, Youngsub Uhm, who also has an amazing story: my heart is always with you.

Thank you to my aunt Soon Yetasook, for sharing anecdotes of Grandma that helped me bring Miyoung more alive on the page, and my cousin Amy Yetasook, for helping me brainstorm titles for my next two books. To my brother Kenneth Kwon and sister-in-law Deborah Min Kwon, for letting us coparent Maltipoo Joey so he could be my furry writing companion. To my cousin Ann Lee, for reading a very rough version of my book many years ago and providing helpful comments.

To my Korean family in Japan: thank you for hosting me back in 1984 during my junior year abroad in Kyoto, when I had my first inkling to write about the plight of Koreans living in Japan. You were so gracious then, and during my recent trip this past spring, answering questions about our family history and sharing your stories. To my remaining family in Korea, whom I have visited over the years: thank you for showing me the Korea I left behind and the new, transformed country it is today.

To my mother-in-law, Ruby Easton, and my late father-in-law, Cabot Easton: thank you for encouraging me to record my family's story and reading the previous memoir version of this novel. I appreciate my sisters-in-law Martha Easton and Margaret Watson for cheering me on along the way. I also want to remember esteemed educator Don Graves, who was related to my husband's side of the family and urged me to "touch" the story every day. Your early enthusiasm fueled me and steered me in the right direction.

To my children, Matthew and Claire: I wrote this book so you can remember your rich family legacy. Thank you for being the reason. And my husband, Mark: thank you for being there for me, always. You are my everything.

Last, but not least, thank you, readers. To my loyal Journey newsletter subscribers and social media followers: I am honored to connect with you. And to new readers who would like to get in touch: please find me at www.rosakwoneaston.com or on Instagram or Facebook @rosakwoneaston. I look forward to hearing from you.

READING GUIDE

1. The novel begins with Miyoung in a white mulberry tree, and she continues to remember the tree throughout her time living in Japan. What is the significance of the mulberry tree for Miyoung? What does it symbolize in the novel as a whole? What is the meaning of the color white in the novel?
2. *White Mulberry* is an immigration story set in Japan in the 1930s and '40s. How is one's identity formed and changed by the experience of living outside one's ancestral homeland? Is Miyoung's experience different from immigrants in other parts of the world? If you're an immigrant, how is your experience similar or different from Miyoung's?
3. Miyoung learns to keep others at arm's length to protect herself from the pain of separation and loss. How does her fear of losing people she loves play out in her relationship with Ko-chan? How would you characterize her love for her son? Does it change, and if so, how?
4. Hojoon's love for Miyoung is deep and heartfelt. Why does Miyoung love Hojoon? If Miyoung hadn't been pregnant, do you think she would have married him? What would you have done in Miyoung's situation?
5. The relationship between Miyoung and her sister Bohbeh is very close. How does Bohbeh's advice influence Miyoung

over the years? Why doesn't Miyoung tell Bohbeh about Hojoon initially? Why doesn't Miyoung talk to Bohbeh about Haramoto's abusive behavior? If you have a sister, do you hold things back from her? If so, why?

6. Ko-chan is only six years old when hc leaves Japan with his mother. If you had to describe Ko-chan, how would you characterize his personality, conflicts, and goals? How does his relationship with his mother evolve throughout the novel?
7. Even to this day, many Koreans who live in Japan assume Japanese names and live as Japanese. What does the novel show about the discrimination against Koreans in Japan? What do you think of Miyoung's decision to pass as Japanese? Would you have made the same choice?
8. Motherhood is an important theme in the novel. Miyoung's mother, Hojoon's mother, and Miyoung herself represent very different kinds of mothers. How are they different, and how are they the same? Does this depend on cultural factors? Are their sacrifices different from what is expected from mothers in other parts of the world?
9. Christianity plays a large role in Miyoung's life. Why is she attracted to Christianity? Does it seem plausible she would embrace it even against her mother's wishes? How were Westerners considered vis-à-vis the Japanese at this time?
10. Miyoung is faced with an impossible decision when she is ordered to serve in the Japanese Imperial Army. What do you think of her choice to escape? How about her decision to lie to her mother-in-law and son? What do you think Miyoung learns about herself at the end of the novel?
11. The novel takes place during a tumultuous time in Asian

history. The Japanese occupation of Korea displaced Koreans, broke up families, and forced great economic and political change on Korea. How do world events affect Miyoung's choices? Do you think she will return home to the northern part of Korea before the country is divided after World War II? Does this story change any assumptions you have of North Korea now?

12. Strangers are a recurring motif in the novel—beginning with the man in uniform who appears at Miyoung's farm and ending with Mr. Choi, the investigator who tries to bring Ko-chan back to his grandmother. What do these strangers portend? Have strangers appeared in your life at unexpected times?
13. In the beginning, Miyoung is a spirited child who identifies herself with the fiery dragon that represents her birth year on the Chinese zodiac. Later, she grapples with loneliness and isolation as a result of having to hide her Korean identity and her son to survive in Japan. What else does she suffer as a result of this duality? What does she gain?
14. Miyoung's nursing and midwife career set her apart from other mothers during her time. To what extent have women's roles changed since then? How have they remained the same? Does Miyoung use her nursing career as a form of personal resistance? If so, how? Against what?
15. Is this novel a work of tragedy, irony, or something else? Is it tragic that Miyoung takes her son away from the only home he's ever known, just like she was removed from her own? Is it ironic because the nursing credentials she worked so hard to obtain create the risk that she will be sent to war to support Japan, the occupier of her own country? Or is this a story of family, survival, or hope? Why?

ABOUT THE AUTHOR

Photo © 2024 Karin Fuire

Rosa Kwon Easton was born in Seoul, Korea, and grew up with her extended family in Los Angeles. Easton holds a bachelor's degree in government from Smith College, a master's in international and public affairs from Columbia University, and a JD from Boston College Law School. She is a lawyer and an elected trustee of the Palos Verdes Library District. She is an Anaphora Writing Residency Fellow, and her work has been published in CRAFT Literary, StoryCenter.org, *Writer's Digest*, and elsewhere. She has two adult children and lives with her husband and Maltipoo in sunny Southern California. For more information, visit www.rosakwoneaston.com.